DRIVING HEAT

RICHARD CASTLE

TITAN BOOKS

NIKKI HEAT: DRIVING HEAT
Print edition ISBN: 9781785650000
E-book edition ISBN: 9781783299997

Published by Titan Books
A division of Titan Publishing Group Ltd.
144 Southwark Street, London SE1 0UP

First edition May 2016

2 4 6 8 10 9 7 5 3 1

This edition published by arrangement with Kingswell, an imprint of Disney
Book Group.

A CIP catalogue record for this title is available from the British Library.

Printed and bound in Great Britain by CPI Group UK Ltd.

Did you enjoy this book? We love to hear from our readers. Please email
us at readerfeedback@titanemail.com or write to us at Reader Feedback at
the above address.

To receive advance information, news, competitions, and exclusive offers
online, please sign up for the Titan newsletter on our website:
WWW.TITANBOOKS.COM

Because of you.
Because of us.
Always.

ONE

The last thing Nikki Heat expected when she received her promotion to captain of the NYPD was how much the proud expression on Rook's face in the audience would make her want him. Throughout the ceremony she had been dignified, attentive, focused, and deeply moved. But toward the end, as she relaxed from the formal constraints and propriety required of her for the program, she clutched her new gold badge, surveyed the rows of family and friends in the auditorium, and found her fiancé.

In the cab on the way back to his place, when Nikki was telling Rook about how the *Heroes* video they played, narrated by James Earl Jones, had made her cry, she caught him staring, listening intently as she recounted her experience, and thought of taking him right there. Then he held her gaze in a way that told her he felt it, too.

The unspoken heat of their longing and the eagerness of anticipation on an elevator ride to his Tribeca loft was nothing new. All that and plenty more crackled between them on their slow rise, as they leaned against opposite corners of the rattling beast. But this time, in the industrial lift's sexually charged atmosphere, the eye games and the frank appraisals and the transparency of desire grew thick enough to take on life. Decorum vanished, giving way to animal impulse.

As if of one mind, they hurled themselves at each other. Nikki, with a bit of a head start, had enough power in her lust to meet Rook beyond halfway and walk him backward into the steel accordion gate of the elevator cage. His moan on impact sounded nothing like pain but a lot like aching. He folded his long arms around her. She pressed against him from below, shuddering and taking his earlobe in her teeth. One of his hands left her backside and fumbled for the control panel. The car jerked to a stop between floors, lurching them hard against each other.

They found each other's mouths. He brought his palm back to cup her bottom, pulling her to him. She resisted, but only in order to create enough space to fit her hands between their bodies and undo his belt. By the time she did, his fingers were already pulling at her zipper.

After a cosmic union drowned out by a series of impatient hollers up the shaft from a pizza delivery guy in the lobby, they sent the cage clanking downward and strolled the short hallway toward his loft, still adhering to one another magnetically. "I can't believe we never did that before," she said.

Rook smiled. "The key is to get the elevator all to ourselves. Trust me, you don't want to pull a stunt like we just did with Mr. Zeiss from 302 in there watching."

Nikki pictured the tiny neighbor with the thick glasses and laughed. Then an afterthought earned Rook a side-glance from her. "You've never done it in there before, have you?" she asked. "I mean, you were pretty deft with that switch."

"Let's just call this a day of firsts and leave it there." He turned at the door to face her and touched the new twin gold bars on her white uniform collar. "For instance, you were my first captain, Captain Heat."

Nikki startled at the sound of the title, just as she had when the police commissioner had uttered it at her swearing-in. Once again Heat felt the strangeness of her new rank and the daunting weight of her new responsibilities. Even though she had known for months that the promotion was coming, now that she had taken the oath, affixed her bars, and upgraded her shield, the good news no longer felt like talking about Christmas at a Labor Day picnic. The day had come, her captaincy was official, and with it came a twinge she nicknamed Happy-Scared.

Rook opened the door and let her go in ahead of him. From the threshold, he heard a muted whimper and joined Nikki inside, where she stood wiping a tear from one cheek. Sprawling before her stretched a loft transformed into a parade float of NYPD colors: blue tablecloths blanketed the countertop and the dining table in the great room beyond it; blue and white crepe streamers hung from the ceiling, interlaced with blue and white ribbons anchoring blue and white helium balloons; a half-dozen floral arrangements of white spray roses mixed with blue irises adorned the tables and shelves; a white sheet cake with a photo transfer of a captain's badge in blue and gold, complete with the laurel and crown insignia, sat on the coffee table beside a blue ice bucket with her favorite white, a Jean-Max Roger Sancerre.

"Wait for it," Rook said, and picked up a remote to start

"Blue Champagne" by Glenn Miller on his Spotify. After a few bars, Nikki closed her eyes and dropped her chin as if to hide her face. "Too tacky?" he asked.

Nikki raised her head and turned to face him—etching the memory of her friend, her lover, her fiancé so perfectly filling the Hugo Boss made-to-measure he had bought just for her ceremony. They kissed again, tenderly this time, and she hooked his elbow with hers, drawing him to the coffee table. She picked up the ice bucket and said, "Bring the wine glasses."

"What about the cake?"

"Dessert first, then cake," she said, then led him up the hall to the bedroom.

A single purr of her new department-issued BlackBerry on the nightstand woke Nikki two minutes before her five-thirty iPhone alarm. She rolled on one side to check it and found an email blast from One Police Plaza apprising her and the roster of seventy-six other precinct commanders of new protocols for filing CompStat numbers on the database. As she scrolled through the assault of seemingly endless text about complaint categories, warrants served, and arrest activity, the familiar Happy-Scared tightness wormed into her gut, with Scared leading the way. This marked Captain Heat's first official received email as the new commander of the Twentieth Precinct, after waiting over half a year for the job to be hers.

The past seven months had been an exercise in patience and diplomacy for Nikki, who had struggled to run her homicide squad under the bland leadership of the interim precinct commander who had taken over after the death of Captain Irons—with everyone, including the PC, aware of the open secret: that the gig was hers as soon as the machinery of department politics could spit out a date.

The captain's bars had come the day before. Today the cold truth hit home: assumption of command.

She had heard Rook get up a half hour earlier and found him sitting at the dining table in a tee and boxers, illuminated by the lunar glow of his laptop. He closed the lid and put it to sleep as soon as Nikki shuffled into the room. "You don't have to stop working because of me."

"No problem." He squared the edges of some notes and slid them inside a file, which he also closed, almost furtively, she thought. "Good a time as any for a break."

"What are you working on?"

"Now, do I ask you that?" He rose to meet her and enveloped her in a warm embrace, which they both held.

"All the time," she said into his chest. "But if you caved and you're ghostwriting another romance novel, like you swore you would never do again, I can understand why you're not eager to own up—*Victoria St. Clair.*"

"Thankfully, Disney has renewed the movie option on my dispatches from Chechnya, so I no longer have to rip any bodices under that nom de plume. Except yours, of course."

"Speaking of. You seemed very into that 'Leave your uniform shirt on' thing last night."

Rook frowned, feigning innocence. "I did?"

"You definitely did. And you asked me to say 'I'm the captain now.'"

"OK." He bobbed his head from side to side and grinned. "I'll admit there was a bit of an unexpected turn-on to the whole starchy white shirt with the captain's dealies on the collars."

"Seriously? Rook, my uniform turned you on?"

"I rarely see you in one. Certainly not in bed."

"This is sounding like role-play. Was I role-playing and didn't know it?"

"Not at all. Unless you liked it." He chuckled. "Nothing wrong with something to keep it all interesting and playful."

"We need that?"

"Need? Absolutely not. But it's good to keep it fresh, right?"

"It's not fresh?"

"I seem to have found myself digging a hole." He felt her appraising stare, which only made him keep digging, "It's very fresh. Although occasionally—only occasionally—you have to admit you have been a bit . . . preoccupied."

"Like in the elevator?"

"Definitely not preoccupied in the elevator. Or most of the time. This is coming out all wrong. All I'm saying is that I want to make sure that when we get married, that we . . ."

"Keep the spark?"

"Well said. Yes. The spark." He shifted gears as fast as he could. "Let's have breakfast. I made coffee."

"Great," she said, "I'll have it with my cake."

"Look at you, Captain Cake-for-Breakfast."

Nikki arched a brow. "Keeping it fresh."

He pretended to be wounded by her jab and moved off

to the kitchen for cups and plates.

As they finished, Rook ran a forefinger around his plate to collect rogue icing and said, "We should have this baker do our wedding cake."

That only made Nikki start to panic about how far behind they were in their wedding plans. Both had long before agreed on August, which was still four months away, but with all his work and all her work, so far they hadn't reserved a venue for the ceremony or the reception, or planned the honeymoon beyond discussing the what-ifs of Venice, Nice, and Portofino. For two high-functioning, big-career planners, this was sheer madness. "At the very least," she said, "we should settle on the weekend so we can send out some save-the-dates."

"I totally agree." He offered her his icing finger, which Nikki waved away like Sabathia rejecting a sign from Stewart. "Otherwise, some of the guests on my tentative list are going to get locked into commitments." He dragged the frosting across his tongue and began to enumerate a few of his invitees. "Sir Paul has got his Out There tour. Annie Leibovitz is constantly booked. Bono said to name the date, he'll drop what he's doing, but I don't want to press our luck, especially if it's one of his charitable things. Lena Dunham's writing her memoir—another? George Stephanopoulos is working every day of the week—he'd have to invent a new day, as it is . . ." Rook noticed that Nikki was staring pensively at a blue balloon that had sagged during the night. "Am I hogging the conversation? You have a guest list, too, I know."

"Well, let's see. There's my dad and his new girlfriend. And his sister, Aunt Jessie."

"Jessie. Have I met her?"

"Twice."

"Right. She's . . . You sure it's Jessie?" Heat's phone buzzed. "It's very inconvenient the way people always die when we're trying to have a conversation."

Reading Nikki's expression after she answered, he slid a pen and one of his spiral reporter's notebooks across the blue tablecloth toward her. This was one end of a case call he had witnessed many times: a series of *uh-huh, uh-huh*s, her nodding head with its angel's face tautened by earthbound realities.

"Detective Ochoa," she said after she hung up, although Rook already had identified the voice from the call spill.

Rook stood and grabbed their dessert plates and said, "I'll come with you." But by then Heat was already on her way to get dressed.

As they crossed West End Avenue at 72nd, Heat asked Rook to have his car drop them mid-block, before they got to Riverside. As a precinct commander, she would be issued her own undercover vehicle when she got to the station house, which already made her feel conspicuous enough. "My first day after the promotion, I don't want to arrive at a crime scene in a limo."

"Technically, it's a luxury SUV," Rook said, adding, "And it's not mine, it's a Hitch! I love using my Hitch! app to hitch a Hitch! And a true five-thumb ride, Vlad. Right here is fine." The driver's troubled eyes flicked to Heat's in the mirror, but she told him not to worry about the no-stopping zone, that this was official police business.

"As if he couldn't figure that out," said Rook once they were out on the curb. To make his point, he used his cuff to polish the captain's bars on her crisp uniform shirt. And when she didn't respond, he cocked his head. "You all right?"

Nikki nodded absently. She had already gone within herself, peering west to the far corner and the two patrolmen stationed in front of the caution tape at the entrance to Riverside Park. Behind it, she knew a life had ended. Heat stilled her mind, taking her ritual beat of silence for the victim and his family—assuming that he had one. Even though it only took her three seconds, the sign of respect never became merely perfunctory. Life mattered. Maybe more when your business was homicide.

As the pair of unis lifted the tape for them, she noted that both were in short sleeves, a sign that April might finally be getting serious about turning milder. Which only made Nikki stress for a flash about an August date racing ever closer with no plans yet made. From the statue of Eleanor Roosevelt, Heat and Rook walked along the downward-sloping footpath past the dog run, which was empty that morning because of police activity, then heard their footsteps echo inside the arched stone underpass beneath the Henry Hudson. On the other side of the tunnel, between the softball field and the river, the Greenway had been transformed into an impromptu parking lot of six cop cars, one idling ambulance, and a white van with a blue side stripe that read "Medical Examiner." Rook said, "All my experience as an investigative journalist tells me this is our murder scene."

Nikki didn't acknowledge him because she was immersed

in her walk-up scan, making her appraisal of the geography, the sounds, the smells—letting the feel of the area talk to her. Lazy detectives showed up and asked questions. Heat liked to have a few thoughts of her own before she spoke to anyone.

What she observed at 6:20 A.M. was a clear spring morning full of fresh promise. The ball field was empty, but an aluminum bat leaned against the backstop next to a white bucket full of softballs, with three of their companions lying like little white domes in the uncut grass out in right field. Joggers and cyclists were out, but they were being held back at the north and south ends of the blacktop trail, inconvenienced by a murder, and sent off to seek alternate routes. The sun had risen minutes before and had not yet crested the range of high-rise apartments on the West Side, so the strip of tree-lined parkland running along the Hudson remained in shade. A cooling breeze blew across the river from the New Jersey side, strong enough for the gulls to open their wings and coast in place and to mottle the water with shapeshifting patterns. On the idle cricket pitch adjacent to the softball diamond, Detective Rhymer talked with a red-faced man forty pounds too portly for Lycra standing beside his Cannondale Slice. Forty yards away, at the edge of the bike path, Detective Feller interviewed an ashen-faced young woman in batting gloves and a Barnard sweatshirt with sawed-off sleeves. To Nikki, it was all silent movie. Voices were lost in the white noise of morning rush hour on the highway behind her and the churn of a barge transporting a construction crane upriver, most likely part of the Tappan Zee upgrade. But she didn't need to hear any words to recognize two eyewitnesses who had seen something they would not soon, if ever, forget. Heat knew. She had been about the age of the Barnard coed when she found her mother's body.

Nikki's friend Lauren Parry hadn't seen her yet. The medical examiner's head was inside the back of the OCME van, prepping her kit for the job ahead. Detectives Raley and Ochoa, partners so inseparable that they had earned the single mash-up nickname Roach, made note of her, rose from where they were crouching at the riverbank, and approached in tandem. "How'd you manage a full-squad turnout here?" asked Rook while the pair came trudging up the grass slope of the Hudson. The other detectives, Rhymer and Feller, also spotted her and started to approach. "Is it a celebrity victim?" Rook continued. "I won't name names, but there's a handful whose passing wouldn't sadden me. Does that make me bad?"

"Very," replied Nikki. "But I don't know who we're working. The turnout is about something else."

"Do I get a hint?"

The four detectives were nearly within earshot, so Heat kept her reply to one word. "Ambition."

Rook's expression lit up as soon as she said it. "Ri-i-i-ight," he muttered as the synapses fired. Heat's promotion had created a void in her old position, homicide squad leader. Now four candidates, presenting faces ranging from eagerness to practiced aloofness, drew around the newly minted precinct commander.

"Congratulations, Captain Heat," said Randall Feller. "Hip-hip!"

Heat held up two palms toward him. "Do. Not."

The detective's brow knotted. "What? It's a big deal."

"It's a crime scene."

Feller was a born cop, but he frequently brought too much street to the job. Correctness was not Randy's forte, and he provided an example by pointing toward the river and saying, "It's not like he can hear me."

"I can," was all Heat needed to say, and he lowered his gaze to the ground. He would apologize back at the precinct, and she would let it go. The dance was the dance.

"Here's what we've got," said Ochoa. "The cyclist—"

"Who I interviewed," Detective Rhymer injected for no reason other than to be heard—a move quite out of character for the soft-spoken Virginia transplant. Feeling their eyes on him and losing his nerve, he pinked up and mumbled, "More later."

Miguel Ochoa continued, with an undisguised eye roll toward his partner. "The cyclist was riding north on the path at approx five-oh-five A.M., when he saw a kayak bobbing against a busted piling from the old pier that used to live out there."

"The near one," added Raley, indicating the closest of the three rotting posts jutting up out of the Hudson like the remnants of a giant prehistoric beast's ribcage.

"He saw it in the dark?" asked Rook.

"He caught the kayak in silhouette," said Rhymer, who now had cause to jump in and spoke with his usual relaxed authority. "The river picks up a lot of light from those buildings and the terminal at Jacob's Ferry. Plus you got the reflection from the George." They all pivoted north, where the sparkle from the George Washington Bridge's lights cast a silver sheen on the Hudson even in the early moments after sunrise.

Raley got back to the timeline. "He sees a guy who's immobile inside, and no paddle, so he makes his 911 call at five-oh-seven. He stops on the bank, calling out to the guy in the kayak—no answer—and keeps tabs on the boat until the EMT and radio cars get here."

"While he's waiting," added Detective Feller, "the wind and the current push the kayak off the piling. It starts drifting to shore. Bicycle boy hears my eyewit pinging softballs and calls her over to help him grab hold as it comes ashore. They're afraid to touch him, he's a goner. GSW to the head, unresponsive, and as pale as—" Lesson learned, Feller checked himself. "Pale."

Heat took two pairs of nitrile gloves from her pocket, handing one pair to Rook as the group deployed past the coroner's van and down the grassy incline toward the water. "Watch your step," said Ochoa. "Lance Armstrong lost his breakfast here . . . and here."

"Good morning, Captain Heat," said Lauren Parry, who was crouched over the victim with her back to her colleagues. "You'll pardon me if I don't salute."

"I'll live."

"Lots of people say that right before I see them," said the medical examiner. In spite of the lightness of their banter, Heat knew better than to be impatient with her friend and waited her turn to see the corpse while the ME performed her prelim on the body, which was still seated upright in the cockpit. The kayak wasn't going anywhere. First-on-scene had roped the carry handles and staked it, bow and stern, to the bank.

"Who's got the rundown on the vic?" asked Heat, eager for something to do other than pretend to be patient.

"*Moi*," said Ochoa. "Black male, forty-six. We had to open about six zippers in his life vest to find ID. Turns out he's kinda family."

"Cop?" asked Heat, wishing Lauren would hurry the hell up.

"Not in the strict sense. He's got PD credentials as a contractor."

"Consultant, actually." Rhymer held up a plastic evidence bag and read the laminated card zipped inside it. "Here it is, 'Consulting Psychologist to the NYPD.' "

The flutter in Nikki's chest accelerated so much that her heart skipped a beat as her head whipped toward the kayak. She wondered if anyone else had noticed her startle, but only Rook was watching, intrigued by her reaction. Protocol be damned, she stepped up beside Dr. Parry and stared at the corpse.

"His name," said Raley, "was—"

"Lon King," finished Heat. Beyond that she couldn't summon breath for more words. Nikki looked down at the corpse in the boat, wondering who the hell would put a bullet in the forehead of her shrink.

TWO

Heat felt more than saw all the heads of the homicide squad slowly rotate to face her. But with the vortex of disbelief swirling within Nikki all she could manage was to keep her eyes fixed on the body beneath her as she groped for an emotional handle. Still more disquieting, the psychologist's face looked not much different in death than it had in their sessions: neutral, dispassionate, amenable. How many times had she stared at the blank canvas he so studiously presented and seen him with his eyes relaxed and his mouth slightly open just as they were now, betraying no judgment or pleasure—or, in this case, no life itself.

Lauren Parry whispered a soft, "Nikki?" and slipped a gloved hand into hers. "Do you need to sit down?" Heat gave her a no-look head wag and made an instinctive, albeit pointless, visual survey of the area for the killer. An al-Qaeda sniper on the fishing pier to the left? It was unoccupied. A drug cartel's menacing cigarette boat speeding away? There was none. A PTSD cop scrambling upslope into the thicket above the Greenway? Nothing but robins on worm patrol in the grass.

At last her gaze came back to the squad, every one of them still attending her, patiently waiting for Heat to speak.

Then she sought Rook, who stood with the others but was staring down at the shrink's body with an expression of distress that appeared out of scale for someone who didn't know the victim. Could it be, she thought, that their relationship had reached some point of emotional fusion and that Rook had taken on her upset as his own? Under other circumstances that would have made Nikki feel very happy. But not these.

"Guess you've all figured out that I knew the victim," she said, trying to dig herself out of the moment she had created. Rook's eyes came up to meet hers, and she took a pause, rummaging in the uncomfortable instant for the version she dared to tell about the extent of her counseling with the shrink. Nikki, usually one for transparency, opted for the smallest truth she could tell, instinctively protecting herself from personal disclosure—to the detectives, to her fiancé. "You remember back a couple of years when Captain Irons tried to get me off a case by ordering an evaluation from a department psychologist?" She tilted her head toward the victim but didn't look at him, responding to some irrational expectation that Lon King might sit up and urge her not to withhold.

That much seemed just enough for the detectives. Rook still came off a little pinched to her, but Heat judged it better to get off the thin ice so she wouldn't fall through, and switched gears to logistics. "All right, this is complicated. Let's huddle up and see where to take this," she began.

But then Detective Raley chimed in ahead of everyone else. "First place we need to start is a time of death guesstimate," he said, taking it on himself to address the group, but speaking for the ears of Lauren Parry, too.

And did she ever hear him. The ME stood up from her crouch and regarded him with the same cool stare the others were giving him.

"Hoo-boy," said Rook. "I've seen that look. I've gotten that look. It's all yours, buddy."

"What? Well we do, don't we?" Rather than cowering, Raley was doubling down on taking point on the investigation himself. "We need a window so we know where to start, based on when." He scanned the squad, but they offered no encouragement and mostly looked away.

"Detective," said Dr. Parry quietly, evenly. "Are you suggesting I take direction from you on this case?"

Her measured response set Raley back on his heels. "No, I'm just . . . Taking some initiative, that's all."

"Dynamic, homes," said his partner, with some unmistakable stink on the remark.

Raley pushed back against Ochoa with a fake smile. " 'Tude's not helping."

If there had been any doubt in Heat's mind that the true jockeying for squad leader had begun, Roach's trading elbows like that erased it. "Glad we're all eager to jump in," she said. "So let's." She turned to Lauren Parry, very much wanting a TOD window, but loathe to ask after what had just occurred. "Doctor, do what you do, and we'll check in." Parry gave her a you-got-it nod and crouched again beside the kayak to run her tests. Nikki continued, "Since what we have here is a scene of discovery more than an actual crime scene, we need to gather information about where the murder could have taken place."

"And when," said Rook. He turned to the ME. "Can't help it, Doc. I see pigtails, I gotta pull 'em."

"Nikki?" said Parry.

"Lauren?"

"Prelim, twelve to fourteen hours based on temp and lividity. Rook?"

"Lauren?"

"Suck it."

Unfazed, he turned to the other detectives. "It's a small price to pay to get you boys critical information on a timely basis. Your unspoken thanks is all I need."

Nikki ran the math and peered across the wide expanse of waterway at the New Jersey bluffs. The windows of the high-rise apartments over in West New York and Union City were just starting to kick back glints of the sun's first rays that in turn reflected off the water. There, where a cool-headed aviator had once miraculously set down an airliner, Nikki tried to envision the situation just before sunset the night before and to trace the path of an adrift twelve-foot Perception Tribute.

"Getting a fix on his point of origin's going to be a bear," said Rhymer. "I did a lot of kayaking in Roanoke, growing up. A boat like this with a shallow draft, in windy conditions, nobody steering . . . Criminy, who knows?"

Heat continued her survey anyway, following potential courses from upriver near Harlem and the Bronx. Rook moved close beside her and said, "Mahicantuck. That's the name Manhattan's indigenous tribe gave the Hudson.

Translated, it means 'the river that flows two ways.' Which is to say it's an estuary. Which is to say he could have just as easily come from the opposite direction, up from the Battery. To calculate the drift pattern, you're going to have to check tide charts to find out the ebb and flood over two cycles." He saw the frustration this observation provoked and said, "Hey, facts are my business. You get in a relationship with a journalist, it's not always going to be good news."

With no other useful information likely to pop up at a secondary crime scene, Heat left Dr. Parry and her crew to finish the prelim on the body, assigned a foot patrol to keep an eye out for fishermen in case any of them had spotted unusual activity the night before, and set out for the Twentieth to convene the squad and get a Murder Board started.

Eager to get the investigation rolling, Heat blew right past her newly assigned precinct commander's office and, on her first day in charge, sat at her old desk in the homicide bull pen while the other detectives, plus Rook, found their way in with coffees and what passed for breakfast scrounged from the station house break room. While they gathered, Nikki opened her department email for a habitual spot check. She thought there must have been a server error. Her monitor filled, buffered, then filled again with a cascade of messages, more than she ever received in a week, let alone in one morning. A few were slugged "Congratulations" and "Well done" from commanders at other precincts. One marked "Urgent" came from the precinct's union rep, who said he needed to have a meeting with the new PC immediately on her arrival. A second email came from Personnel downtown, directing her not to meet with the Police Benevolent Association rep yet. Another, with the intriguing subject "Time Sensitive," included a petition from five of the precinct's administrative aides asking what the policy would be on e-cigarettes in the building. Heat closed her email and strode to the blank whiteboard to do some real police work. By the time she had block-printed Lon King's name atop the shiny blank surface, Raley, Ochoa, Feller, and Rhymer had rolled chairs in a semicircle around her. The squad's newest addition, Detective Inez Aguinaldo, whom Nikki had recruited a month before from the Southampton PD as a replacement, ended a phone call at her desk and unfolded a chair off to one side.

It never took much to bring this roomful of pros to order, but as Nikki turned to face them, something in their silent attention felt more like scrutiny—as if she were naked. But it was quite the opposite. Captain Heat stood before them today in a uniform of all-regulation white shirt, dark-blue trousers, and gleaming metal instead of the jeans and untucked oxford she had worn to work the last time the bull pen had convened. She made a mental note to check regs for loopholes and see how strict they were about the starch and brass. The things you never think about before you take a job . . .

"Lon King," she began. "Psychologist with a private practice but also under contract with the NYPD to provide counseling within the department." Without making a conscious color choice she used her blue dry erase to write

"NYPD SHRINK" on the board. "What else do we know?"

"Kayaker," said Detective Rhymer.

Feller shook his head. "Why, just 'cause he died in one? Last month we found some dude buried in wet cement near that restaurant they're building near Lincoln Center. That sure didn't make him a construction worker. Or a restauraunteur."

"Actually, it's restaur-*a-teur*," said Rook as he entered, ending a call and slipping his cell phone into his blazer pocket. "Common mistake. Like *laundrymat*. Or *libary*." He rolled a chair over from his borrowed, unofficial desk. One caster squeaked the whole way.

"Nonetheless." Heat paused, studying a tightness in Rook's face as he took a seat, then she turned and wrote "kayaker?" on the board. "Since the victim was discovered in a kayak, we can at least post that and make it part of our investigation to see if it was a one-time activity or a hobby."

Sean Raley called out, "Family," and Nikki made that a heading, too, then felt everyone's gaze again. This time, it wasn't about the uniform.

"If you're wondering if I know, I don't. Anybody here been to counseling? You don't learn too much about the shrink; they kinda make it all about you." Feeling herself moving into an uncomfortable neighborhood, she turned the page with another heading: "COD." "Cause of Death is prelim, but obvious."

"No-brainer," said Feller, who immediately held up surrender hands. "I fucking swear, I wasn't goofing on him. Come on."

Nikki gave him a pass and continued, "Single GSW to

the forehead. Small caliber, no exit wound. Ballistics will get a slug to analyze by this afternoon."

Ochoa scrawled that in his notebook. "Small bore kind of rules out sniper."

"So does this." Nikki held up a printout one of the administrative aides had come in with and placed on her podium. "Follow-up from ME Parry says there were trace metals and gunpowder residue surrounding the entrance wound." The significance of that hung in the room while the investigators pondered.

"Takes away a passing boat, too," observed Raley. "Unless it was mighty close."

Rhymer raised his hand. "Like another kayaker?"

"Or somebody on his dock. Or a boat that launched him," said his partner.

"Or suicide." Detective Feller tucked his boots under his chair and leaned toward Heat. "It's tough, but it's got to be in the mix. Shrinks off themselves, too. I'm just sayin'."

Nikki, who had always drilled it into her squad to approach every case with beginner's eyes—not to be complacent, not to work by rote—nodded in agreement. "Everything's on the table." She added "suicide" as a subheading along with the other options and, like the others on the list, put a question mark beside it. "When we left the Greenway, I saw Dr. Parry bagging the victim's hands. Detective Ochoa, as soon as we break here, I'd like you to put in a call to Lauren and let us know immediately if she found any residue on them."

"Done."

"Mind one from left field?" asked Rook.

Nikki, glad to see him finally engaging in the process, said, "Well, left field is sort of your area."

"That, and Area Fifty-one," added Feller, who was about as much a fan of Rook's passion for spitballing conspiracy theories as he was of having his pronunciation tweaked.

Undaunted, or perhaps merely oblivious to his fellow cop's disdain, Rook said, "What if he wasn't killed in the boat? The shooter murders King somewhere else, puts him in the kayak, and either gives it a push or a tow just to confuse us and keep us from knowing where the crime scene was." By the time he had finished, other brains were chewing that very real possibility—even Randall Feller's.

Detective Aguinaldo raised a tentative hand and spoke for the first time in the meeting. "Not sure whether this is too half-baked for group discussion . . ."

"No such thing," Rook said, chuckling. "Didn't you hear my theory? Let 'er rip."

"It's not so much a theory."

The new detective's transition had been a slow one. Heat, who had liaised with Aguinaldo in the Hamptons on a case around the time of Hurricane Sandy, knew her potential and constantly prodded her not to feel intimidated by the squad of veterans in a big-city department. "Inez, if you're holding, don't be shy, let's hear it."

"OK. Since I was on duty here this morning instead of down by the river, I called Forensics to touch base with whoever was assigned to this case."

"Benigno DeJesus," said Heat. "I pushed for him to catch

this one, because he's simply the best there is."

Aguinaldo nodded. "So I've heard. And we had a nice chat while you were en route here."

"You already talked to him?"

"Seemed like routine meeting prep to me."

That was one of many reasons Nikki liked Inez. She was always thinking, always anticipating.

"He said that, in addition to the wallet contents you guys bagged," Aguinaldo continued, "when they removed the body from the kayak, they were able to access a cargo pocket on his pants thigh with some loose cash in it. Mostly singles and a five. Also . . . one custom clay poker chip. Detective DeJesus texted me this photo of it." She stepped up to the front and showed Heat the shot on her iPhone. "You can see it has a molded rim of a repeated hourglass design. And it's purple."

"That means it's worth five hundred bucks," said Feller. "I worked vice. Purple is the traditional color casinos use for five yards."

"They haven't run it for prints yet, but the RTCC traced this unique design and pattern to a place called Fortuna's Wheel, per the Organized Crime Unit database."

"Got to love those monster computers downtown," said Heat.

"I know Fortuna's Wheel," said Rook.

Feller chimed in, "Me too. There's a big not-so-secret secret gambling den in the basement. Very mob."

"Run by my old friend and yours . . ." Rook slapped his knee and said to Nikki, "Fat Tommy."

"He's not my friend." Then, as Heat wrote Fat Tommy's

name on the Murder Board, she added, "But I am going to renew my acquaintance with Mr. Tomasso Nicolosi this morning." Then she turned to the group. "Time to make some assignments. Detective Aguinaldo: nice work following up on the chip. Since you did so well with the RTCC, contact them again. Lon King was an NYPD contractor, so have them run any threats against him. Then hit Personnel. Find out about family, next of kin, whomever. Pay his loved ones a visit and interview them about the usuals."

Aguinaldo nodded as she made notes, saying, "Last seen, state of mind, friends and enemies, financial worries, affairs, drugs, drinking, unusual behavior."

"Also ask about his kayaking. How often he did it, where he stored it, places he put in and liked to go."

"And did he belong to a club or float with a regular buddy?" suggested Rhymer.

"Good thought, Opie," said Nikki, using the clean-cut detective's squad nickname. "And since you know a little bit about the sport, call DeJesus in Forensics and find out all there is to know about the boat. Not just fingerprints, hairs, and damage or wear to the hull, but maybe there's a serial number that tells you where it was bought or perhaps a sticker from REI or Eastern Mountain Sports. If not, door-knock the local kayak retailers and outfitters. See if anyone knew King and if he hung out with anyone in that world. Visit the float and nature clubs, not just for members who knew him but for any habitual spots for a sunset excursion on a spring evening."

"I didn't see any paddle at the crime scene," said Detective

Rhymer. "Not sure what to do with that, but it's worth noting. Also no cell phone on him."

Taking her own advice that nothing is nothing, Heat posted that, too: "no paddle." "Detective Feller, contact the NYPD Harbor Unit and the Coast Guard. Chances are, if they had seen anything, they would have responded, even if it was just because he was adrift, but ask anyway to cover the base. What we really want is what they have on any known barge or shipping traffic yesterday in the TOD window and after. Contact the shipping companies and talk to the captains, pilots, and crew. Might as well work in the Circle Line and the other tour and booze cruises while you're at it. Somebody might have seen something they shrugged off but that would make sense now."

"Coast Guard would also have accurate tide tables and currents," Feller added. "I'll check that, too."

"How is my King of All Surveillance Media?" asked Nikki with a grin.

"Somehow, I knew this was coming," said Raley, who had earned his title by breaking numerous cases over the years thanks to his talent for—and sheer tenacity in—scanning video recordings from surveillance cams.

"Really? Then what else do you know is coming?"

"Well, my liege, if His Highness was to guess, it would be a request to locate any cams that pick up pieces of the Hudson or other waters the kayak could have been on yesterday."

"Uncanny," said Heat. "And when you find footage, also look for shipping. Get the names of the vessels and share them with Randall to cross-check. Sadly, I'm going to have to separate you from your partner."

Feller chuckled. "You'll need a garden hose."

"Detective Ochoa, I'd like you to visit Lon King's practice on the Upper East Side."

"On it," he said. "Interview his receptionist and colleagues. Basically, the same drill Inez is doing with family, only at his workplace."

"Right. We're going to want to ask if they know about any disgruntled clients. It's a sensitive area, since he dealt mostly with police officers past and present, but all possible motives need to be explored. Especially if any threats were made."

Rook shifted in his chair and exhaled loudly. When Nikki turned to him, he said, "Sorry. Missed breakfast. I need a muffin." He smiled thinly and looked away. She wondered what was up with him.

Ochoa said, "Captain?"

Which made Nikki glance to the back of the squad room, expecting to see the precinct commander watching in the doorway. But she quickly realized he was addressing her and chuckled. "Sorry. Not quite used to that," she said. "Changes."

"That's what I wanted to ask about," Miguel went on. "The squad wanted me to ask, actually. Now that your promotion has finally come down, have you made a decision about who will replace you as squad leader?"

Heat had anticipated this and took a moment to survey the five detectives surrounding her: one new addition, curious about who would be her new boss, and four veterans showing various degrees of eagerness to be the one chosen. "That's a fair question. But this is my fair answer: I'll make my appointment when I am ready." Nikki saw the tide of dissatisfaction rising in the room and added, "Obviously, I've had some time to think about this. And, yes, I do have some leanings. But I'm two hours into my first official day. I haven't even turned on the lights in my office yet. And now we have this case in which the victim is one of us. Or as close to being one of us as you can get. So I'm making a decision on the fly to keep one foot in this bull pen as we move the investigation forward. All while I juggle my new responsibilities. Which are considerable. So to backstop me, that is why I am naming—on a temporary basis—Miguel Ochoa and Sean Raley as interim squad co-leaders."

To characterize the ensuing applause as a smattering might be generous. It began with Detective Aguinaldo and Rook. Rhymer and Feller joined in a few beats too late to be considered gracious. Raley and Ochoa regarded each other with a bit of surprise but only a bit of pleasure.

"I'm going to ask you to coordinate all your moves with Team Roach who, in turn, will coordinate with me," Nikki concluded. "One more thing. This is the best homicide squad in the department. We are going to keep that good thing going. You have my word that, as soon as we wrap this case up, I will name your permanent squad leader to carry on the success of this group. Now. Let's go find a killer."

"Tell me about Lon King," said Rook as Heat steered into the rotary at Columbus Circle on their way to brace Fat Tommy.

"What's to tell? Like I said, he was the department shrink

Wally Irons forced me to see. You know about that."

"I do. I also know, down by the river this morning, you made it sound like you only went to your one assigned session."

"So I went a few other times. The squad didn't need to know my personal business. It's not relevant." Nikki cranked the wheel to turn onto Broadway, at the same time steering the conversation in a different direction. "Is that what's been up your butt?"

"Speaking as one who *ass*-iduously self-monitors, last check, I detected nothing foreign."

"If you say so. All I know is that I've been reading a vibe off you since we hit the crime scene."

"By staring at my butt?"

"Joke it off if you want to, Rook. I know what I see." At the stop light in front of the Ed Sullivan they sat in silence. Heat waited him out. Rook peered up at the Letterman marquee. "Is it the wedding plans? Am I pressing too hard?"

When the light changed, it became his turn to deflect. "Let's talk about Management 101."

"OK . . ."

"Just an observation from your loving spouse-to-be."

"I already don't like where this is going."

He rested a gentle hand on her thigh and smiled. "Relax, just something to put in your head. Your squad is not only ambitious. My take is they're also worried about loss of leadership."

"Which is why I appointed Roach to run the shop."

"Using the words *temporary* and *interim* in the same sentence, you anointed them. If they're your guys, why not just pull the trigger?"

"Because I'm not sure."

"So not like you," said Rook, and he was right. In the months when Nikki had been kept on a string, wondering when the nod would come for her own promotion, she had done all sorts of forecasting about long-range goals as well as nuts-and-bolts thinking about the short term. She had drawn up wish lists and org charts in her head, some of which made it to paper or to her Evernote app. All her plans became the subject of continual revision and second-guessing as her own appointment process became ever more protracted. Now, on her first official day on the job, she had what golfers call the yips. Instead of hitting the ground running, she had balked.

"My original plan was to have Sean and Miguel share the job."

"What happened?"

"I can't describe it. Overthinking. They have been in my squad the longest."

"And they are amazing. When you let them take point on the murder of that old stockbroker on West End, they kicked ass. They even tied his missing maid into your skyfall case."

"True."

"I'm hearing a *yeah, but* in your voice." He regarded her. "Are you holding a grudge because they also gave you a ration of shit along the way?"

Nikki shook her head no. "All about passion for the job. They never made it personal, and we all came out better on the other side. Maybe it's the partner idea. That made me reconsider. Then I started to choose, OK, which of the two? And then I saw nothing but a rift there. So then I started wondering whether they would be as good if I busted up the set. And that led me to wonder if a solo choice should put Feller in the running. And Rhymer."

"Food truck!" Rook pointed to a produce delivery van with its blinker signaling a parking spot about to open up in front of Keen's Chophouse. When Nikki had eased into the space and killed the engine, he said, "As your trusted advisor, may I make two observations?"

"Sure."

"First, careful consideration is one thing, but when you can't make a decision, something else is going on."

When he said it, the words made her feel exposed, affecting her in a way that resonated beyond the task at hand. "And second?"

"You're going to make 'em scatter like cockroaches when you walk in this club dressed like that." He chuckled and got out.

Fortuna's Wheel sat mid-block, a former restaurant fronting the sidewalk between a watch repair shop and a nail salon that advertised foot rubs. The club's original neon sign, dating from the 1940s, hung like a flag above a heavy wooden front door painted chocolate brown to match the faux-Tudor half-timbering inset in the tan stucco wall. At ground level the plaster was scalloped by ancient gingery piss stains of passing dogs and carefree drunks. The smell of CDC-strength disinfectant, already conspicuous from the street, prickled the backs of their throats as Heat and Rook entered the dim nightclub with an unwelcome blast of light.

As Rook had predicted, heads ducked low and back

doors slammed as half of the dozen morning rummies in the place caught sight of Nikki's captain's uniform and scrammed. "Help you?" said the bartender, a big woman with an eyepatch. She didn't sound like she meant it.

"I'm here to see Tomasso Nicolosi," said Heat.

Just to be a smartass, Rook jerked a thumb toward Nikki in her uniform and added, "NYPD."

After an exchange of whispered intercom chatter, a busboy opened a door for them hidden behind some heavy velvet curtains and they descended a winding oak staircase to the secret gaming parlor, which amounted to an unoccupied craps setup and seven poker tables, also not in use. The dusky lighting in the windowless basement put everything in shadow, but there was just enough to make out Fat Tommy sitting at a back booth in his signature circa-1979 tracksuit and oversized shades. The closer they got, though, it was apparent things had changed since they last saw him. "I've been sick," he explained without being asked, even before a hello. Fat Tommy had slimmed down years before at his wife's behest, but now he had gone beyond thin. Not only was Fat Tommy no longer fat, he'd become so emaciated he could hide behind a stack of poker chips. Instead of a mobster, he looked like ET in Jackie O's sunglasses.

They took seats facing him. "Sorry to hear," said Rook with genuine sadness. He had met Tommy years before while researching an article on the mid-level New York crime families, and the two had struck up an arms-length friendship. Subsequently, Rook had set Nikki up with confidential meetings to get information on cases from time to time, with nothing even close to a relationship developing between the detective and the hood.

"Yeah, well I'm gonna beat this." Tommy slapped the table and laughed. "The fuck I will. Look at me. Say your good-byes." In the awkward pause that followed, sounds of men and women laughing bled through a closed door behind him. "Friendly card game among friends. Nothing you need to worry about, right?"

Nikki took that as her opening. "We're not here to hassle your little enterprise, Mr. Nicolosi."

"Good. And *Tommy* would be nice."

"I want to know if you recognize this man." She held out her iPhone with the shrink's ID photo on it. Fat Tommy lifted his sunglasses to give the pic a once-over and leaned back. "His name is Lon King. I have reason to believe he may have had a connection here. Perhaps as a customer.

"See, here's the thing. This little enterprise, as you call it, is confidential. You know, discreet. Just like you." He chuckled. "What are you dressed up for, the St. Paddy's parade?"

When Heat gave him a stone face, Rook jumped in. "Tommy. The captain is here about a homicide."

"Uh-huh. And you want to know if I had him whacked? The answer is no."

Heat opened her notebook and uncapped her pen. "Then you did know him."

"Now that I'm getting the drift that he's dead, I'm not feeling the need to be so, um, circumspect." He turned to Rook. "How's that for vocab, writer boy?"

Nikki kept to her all-business tack. "And I can take that as your statement? You did indeed know him?"

Fat Tommy waved his hands in front of himself as if to warn off an oncoming car. "Let's just get to it, all right? Yes, I knew him. Yes, he was a regular. No, I did not have anything to do with his death. It's generally considered bad business to kill someone who owes you money."

"How much did he owe you?" She held her pen poised.

"Thirty-two thousand, one hundred. I staked him for his losses."

Rook said, "That's a mighty big stake."

The mobster shrugged. "Is it? Keeps them in the game's another way to see it."

"Do you recognize this?" Heat showed her cell phone shot of the custom poker chip that had led them there.

"It's a fiver. I use them as coasters for my Ensure."

"This one was found on Lon King's body."

"I gave it to him. Last week after he got cleaned out at Hold 'Em, I figured he shouldn't leave with nothing."

"It's not like he could spend it anywhere. Are you that generous?" asked Nikki.

"Just a reminder of his debt."

"Or intimidation?" she asked. Heat's phone vibrated.

"Either way, see? It worked. He kept it on him." He tapped her notepad with his forefinger. "Meanwhile, I'm out thirty-two large. Get that down."

The buzz was a text from Ochoa. She showed it to Rook and they both immediately stood to go. "You guys got a plane to catch or something?"

Nikki flipped her spiral notebook closed. "I may be back in touch, Mr. Nicolosi."

Fat Tommy mopped his mouth with a soiled handkerchief and called after them as they bounded up the creaking stairs. "Wouldn't wait too long."

The Crime Scene Unit hadn't even gone in yet. When Nikki and Rook stepped off the elevator onto the twelfth floor of the medical tower where Lon King kept his practice, the CSU team was just bootying up in the hallway. Snapping on blue nitrile for the second time that morning, Captain Heat self-consciously returned their salute with a gloved hand and went inside.

Detective Ochoa saw them enter and handed off the sobbing receptionist to the uniformed policewoman he'd requested from the Nineteenth. As he crossed over to her, the sight of the young woman smacked her with a sudden rush of dread. Heat had been there for an appointment just two weeks before. How awkward would it be if the receptionist, Josie, recognized her and said something? Nikki positioned herself with her back to the lobby desk and drew Ochoa and Rook into the adjoining room. She knew it was only a stall. Heat would somehow have to try to deflect the receptionist's familiarity, but later. Her immediate concern was what Ochoa could tell her about the burglary, in hopes it would give up a clue to finding Lon King's killer.

"So here's how it came down," began the detective. "I got here at ten of nine and waited in the hall for King's receptionist . . . Josie," he said after consulting his notes. "I ID'd myself, told her I needed a moment of her time, she unlocked the door, we came in, and, as you saw, the news hit her hard."

"The break-in wasn't apparent right away?" asked Heat.

"It was and it wasn't. The girl was distracted—obviously—by the ton of bricks I dropped on her. So it wasn't until a few minutes into my interview, after she started to recover, that she noticed some of the things in the place were out of whack. We did some room-to-room checking, and that's when we knew there'd been a B&E overnight."

Nikki surveyed the room they were standing in, the one King used for counseling sessions. She'd been in there fewer than ten times over the last three years, yet it appeared as tranquil and welcoming as ever. "Doesn't appear tossed to me." Then she added, "Going from memory."

"You'd have to know what to look for." Ochoa walked them past the psychologist's overstuffed chair to the small desk off to the side. "Josie said there was a laptop there that's gone."

"Any chance the doctor could have taken it with him or come back for it?" asked Rook.

"I wondered the same. She says no. The MacBook stayed there all the time. He didn't like lugging them and always used the cloud or thumb drives. To that point, the rest of the room is neat, no hacked-open pillows or tossed books off the shelves, right? But check it out . . ." Ochoa carefully slid open the single desk drawer by its edges instead of the handle, using the fingertips of his gloved hands. The slim drawer was a mess: spilled paperclips ripped from a box, a tangle of pencils and pens upended out of a teak tray, a torn deck of gold Kem playing cards, even a matchbox from The Dutch had been poked open and shaken empty.

Heat said, "A search for thumb drives?"

"A safe bet," said Ochoa. "Josie says he kept them in this drawer, but in one of those leather zip pouches from that froufrou stationery-geek catalog."

"Levenger?" said Rook, a little too quickly.

Ochoa shook his head and groaned, "Oh, man. So busted." Then the detective led the way out of the room. "Let's see if Josie's up for showing you the rest." Since the encounter would come sooner or later, Nikki followed behind to get it over with. She had a homicide investigation to conduct and couldn't do the job if she hid from witnesses for personal reasons. It might have been better, though, she thought, if only Rook hadn't been along today.

"Josie," said Detective Ochoa, "this is my precinct commander, Captain Heat."

Lon King's receptionist looked up from a deep-trauma stare at Nikki. The two women made eye contact and, in it, Heat saw clear recognition. But then came something unexpected. The young woman extended a hand to shake and said only, "Hello." While she watched Josie give Rook a similarly polite, neutral greeting, Heat wondered, was it training or common sense not to out the client of a psychologist? Whether it was due to professionalism or courtesy, Nikki was grateful for the discretion and embarked on the rest of the tour undistracted.

As with the counseling room, the other areas of the office

suite had been disturbed, not ransacked. Whoever did it wanted something specific. This was a surgical strike. "Josie, did Dr. King keep any drugs here? Prescription meds, I mean?" asked Nikki.

"No, he counseled only and didn't prescribe. Not even any samples."

The spilled playing cards in the desk made Heat think about the jumbo debt to Fat Tommy. "What about money? Did he keep any cash here, perhaps in a safe or locked drawer?"

"There's a metal box in the file room, but that's petty cash." When she took them into the back room and put on gloves to open the file drawer, the petty cash box indeed turned out to have been pried open, however the variety of small bills and receipts was still inside, albeit stirred. Then Josie's face lost color. "This is too creepy," she said. "This drawer was completely full of files. Patient files." Heat, Rook, and Ochoa drew around her as she pulled the drawer out. It hit the end of its runners with a hollow bonk. Empty.

After the four of them had pulled open every drawer of all the filing cabinets, they determined that exactly half the files were gone, encompassing patients with last names beginning A through M. The N-to-Z cabinets seemed full and undisturbed, at least at a glance. Heat's gaze came to rest on the yawning Hastings-to-Henderson drawer, the one where her file would have resided—and felt a gnaw.

Rook's eyes lifted to hers, and when they met, they both looked away.

Back out in reception, the lead CSU tech, an Australian

transplant named Murphy, gave Heat and the others his prelim. "All right, then, here's your quick-and-dirty, just to get us started, mind you. Your intruder, or intruders, were pro or semi-. Door lock shows no signs of forced entry. Inside, not much of a pillage, is it? More of an incursion, really. Here's the tally: A-to-M surname files stolen; laptop missing, as noted; the hard drives have been expertly removed from the two desktops; and lastly, the Dragon speech recognition app, probably used for postsession notes dictation, has been removed from both computers, as well. All up, I'd call this a fairly neat operation, with whoever pulled it off taking his sweet time after closing yesterday with loads extra to fill the shopping trolley before dimming the switch and fucking off."

"Do they have a security camera?" asked Ochoa.

"Sure enough, mate." Murphy pointed up to a lipstick cam. Its lens had been blacked over with spray paint.

"Maybe it caught something before they disabled it," said Heat. "Josie, did you guys record your video on-site or at a security company?"

"The building management handles that. I've never really needed to know where."

The building's super met them in the lobby, holding open an elevator at the south end of the banks. They got on without much conversation other than to hear his grim, "I hope you fry that bastard who killed the doc," on the one-floor descent to the basement. He led them through a labyrinth of stored office furniture and medical equipment, some of it swaddled in plastic, to a large shed that had been constructed in the corner. "We use this for storage," he explained as he ran through a chunky ring of keys at the end of a belt chain.

The super flipped on the lights once he had got the shed door open, revealing a space about as large as a two-car garage. He led them toward a closet door at the far end of the room, past aluminum racks whose shelves were filled with desk lamps, out-of-date telephone equipment, bulky old-tech TVs, stacks of medical-office-appropriate framed art, empty aquariums, and potted artificial plants.

"Hannibal Lecter hasn't sent anyone here looking for severed heads, has he?" said Rook.

The super laughed but stopped abruptly. "What the hell is this?"

The hasp on the closet door hung open. The padlock sat on the bench beside it.

Heat and Ochoa put their hands on their sidearms. Rook took a step back and brought the super with him out of the way. The two cops took positions near the closet. Nikki nodded to the detective and began her silent three-count. Then the lights went out and the door slammed behind them.

"The door, the door," called Ochoa. In the absolute blackness of the shed, they scrambled hopelessly, bumping into each other and the racks until the super lit the flashlight on his belt and they oriented themselves to the exit.

By the time they raced out into the basement, the elevator was purring toward the first floor. Rook asked where the stairs were, but by the time he got an answer, Nikki and Miguel were already taking them two at a time.

The passenger door was slamming on a waiting MKZ when the two cops pushed through the lobby congestion and bolted down the six granite steps to the sidewalk. They both yelled, "NYPD, freeze!" but the Lincoln burned rubber—in reverse—on York Avenue, backing up through its own tire smoke at high speed against traffic, barely missing a northbound ambulette.

Heat and Ochoa gave chase, and a block away, the car lurched to a stop, but only long enough for a gear shift followed by another piercing squeal as it right-turned onto the ramp to the FDR south and was long gone.

Since it fell within their precinct, detectives from the Nineteenth tagged in to continue the B&E investigation at Lon King's office. Heat, however, carved out one piece of turf for her team. They had lucked out and got to the digital recording closet just before the intruder could gain access, so the security video from the York Avenue medical tower would travel crosstown to the West Side with her.

With Roach taking co-lead, and Nikki feeling pressure to dive into the administrative tasks that were piling up in her absence, she rode back to the Two-Oh without Rook, who said he had plenty to keep him occupied anyway. As he waved from the back window of his cab, she hoped at least some of his attention would shift to wedding logistics.

Captain Heat went about her new duties with a spirit of enthusiasm, even though answering compliance emails from One PP, booking meetings with community leaders, and ignoring station-house nicotine enthusiasts pestering for an e-cig policy felt very little like policing. Nikki was glad that two of the four walls of her new office were all glass so she could at least peer out into her old familiar space, the homicide bull pen, and keep tabs on the case. From inside her goldfish bowl, she liked what she saw. Rook might have been right, that punting a key leadership appointment amounted to a stagger out of the starting gate, but watching Raley and Ochoa in action gave her confidence that her stumble might pay off.

"Knock-knock," said Roach in unison at her door.

"Did you guys rehearse that, or are you just that joined at the hip?"

"Totally ad-libbed," said Ochoa.

Raley shivered. "Kinda creeps you out, don't it?"

The pair didn't make a move when she gestured to her guest chairs. "Thanks, we're on the fly," Miguel said. "Just wanted you to sign off on something. The security video just arrived from Lon King's medical building and I wanted to pull Sean off screening river cams and put him on that."

"It's the hot lead," added Raley, selling Heat with another one of her own detective's edicts: In any investigation, always follow the hot lead.

"Go for it." Then, as they started off, she stopped them. "What do we hear about Lon King's family?"

"Detective Aguinaldo just got off the phone with his partner," said Ochoa. "He is a portrait artist who does official likenesses of governmental leaders. You know, those stiff oil paintings you see in state houses and courtrooms?

She tracked him down in Vermont, where he's doing Senator Leahy, and said he would be returning to the city on the next jetBlue. She's going to meet his plane at JFK."

"Keep me looped," Heat said. Then she added, "By the way. What's the freshness date on the recordings from the medical building?" Heat tried to sound nonchalant, asking a mundane procedural question to camouflage her concern that her own face might appear on Raley's monitor and spark some personal awkwardness.

"I talked to the private contractor who set up the building's system," said Raley. "It's not high-risk retail or a bank, so they went economy. There's only ten days' worth of room on the drive before it resets and records over itself. So it shouldn't take me too long to scrub through, if that answers your question."

"It does." The date of her last appointment fell outside the window. She relaxed. "Thanks, Rales."

But Nikki's sense of relief did not last. Later that afternoon, Detective Raley returned while she paced her office on a phone call, executing an order from the deputy commissioner to lend fifteen of her patrol officers to the Critical Response Unit, to monitor the protests that had broken out after the arrest of a Syrian college student engaged in counterfeiting. The detective hand-signaled that he'd come back, but she didn't like the tension she read on him and pointed to a chair. Sean sat and waited out her call.

When she at last put down the phone, two more lines rang. Nikki ignored them and gave Raley her attention. He rose and said, "I think you should see something."

Heat followed him to the former storage closet Raley had converted into his makeshift screening facility and closed the door. After he had taken a seat at his worktable, she stood behind him to surf the image frozen on his monitor. It was of an empty hallway; the date and time stamp in the lower left corner showed it to be from 9:14 A.M., six days prior. "What floor are we on?"

"Twelve. Lon King's hallway. Ready?" He didn't wait for an answer, but double-clicked the trackpad. The video unfroze. There was no sound, but time code started to roll, counting seconds and video frames. The elevator arrived and a man walked out, advancing with full face in clear view of the camera. He entered the psychologist's office without hesitation and closed the door.

"Roll it back," said Heat, unable to keep the rasp of sudden dryness out of her voice. The detective rewound four seconds and froze the image on the screen. Even with the graininess of the security video there was no doubt that Lon King's visitor was Jameson Rook.

THREE

J ameson Rook, reporting as ordered, Captain." He slid
into one of the guest chairs angled in front of her desk
and crossed a leg as he leaned back. "I have to tell you
that this driving up and down town all day is cutting
into my nuptials planning. Speaking of which: I told Jill
Krementz that the only way she can come is if she'll be our
wedding photographer. I'm teasing, of course. Unless she
says yes." He let out a self-satisfied laugh and flicked his
eyebrows. Then he saw Heat's expression, and his smirk
withered. "What?"

"Ever since you saw the body at the river this morning
you've been . . . off. Now I know why." Nikki woke up her
iPhone, which sat poised in the center of her empty blotter,
and swiveled it toward him. Rook leaned forward, elbows on
the edge of her desk. He watched himself on the security
video; Heat watched him grow a shade paler.

When the clip finished he sat back in his chair. A few
seconds passed with the background chatter of the precinct
as the only sound. At last he said, "You know, sometimes I
hate technology." Then, a little too quickly recovered from
his video smack to suit Nikki, he gave a minor shrug,
saying nothing.

"You're not going to tell me what this was about?" she asked.

"I think it's probably best we not get into it."

"Are you fucking serious?" Nikki, who rarely swore and always discouraged swearing among the squad, lost her filter. "Rook, we already are into it."

"All right, I can see that. But can we keep some sense of scale here?"

"Scale?" Heat spoke so loudly that heads turned in the homicide bull pen. She got up and closed the door, calming herself by the time she regained her seat behind the desk. "Let's enumerate, shall we? One: You had knowledge of a homicide victim you didn't disclose. Two: You—my fiancé— had a meeting with my shrink without telling me. Where do I put that on the goddamned scale?"

"If I'm hearing you, I'd guess way up there."

"Stop. Stop being glib. This is not a glib moment for me."

"I apologize. I'm sorry." He nodded in a belated attempt at conciliation. "But I'm not trying to be glib, I'm trying to play this down."

"You can't."

"Because," he pressed on, "you don't have anything to worry about. Yes, I had some meetings with Lon King. And that—"

"More than this one? Not feeling too assuaged here, Rook."

"If you let me finish, you will." He paused and cocked his brow toward her. She made a steeple of her fingertips in front of her lips, a listening pose. He continued. "My conversations with King had nothing to do with you." He sat back and crossed his leg again, as if what he had just said qualified him to drop the microphone.

"That's it?"

"Yup. All there is to it."

"Not to me."

"But it's the truth. You were never mentioned. The psychological community has strict protocols when it comes to being discreet. You saw that yourself today when Josie never acknowledged you as a client in front of me or Ochoa." He couldn't help himself and added, "Even though, much like me, you didn't disclose your relationship with the victim to your own squad."

"OK," she said. "This is going nowhere good."

"Which is why I said, maybe we shouldn't walk this path."

"And you won't tell me why you were seeing him?" When he didn't reply, she gave him a frown and said, "He counseled cops. You weren't in therapy with him, were you?"

"That, I'll answer. No. The reason I was seeing him has to remain confidential. It's my right as a journalist not to disclose."

"You saw him about a story you're working on? What?"

"Nikki, I'd love to tell you, but there's too much else going on with this. My ability to do my job depends on my sources' knowing that I will honor confidentiality. I have to invoke my constitutional right."

"To what, act like an ass? I'm looking for a killer."

"And I guess I am, now, too." He twisted to peer through the glass at the Murder Board. "Any developments?"

"Do not press it, Rook."

"You're freezing me out?"

As angry as she was, Heat knew that Rook, although a pain in the butt—frequently delivered solutions to cases. She would be spiting herself to close him off as a resource, even though he wasn't playing fair. Her phone rang. It was Lauren Parry. Nikki asked her to hold. "This could be about Lon King's autopsy," she said to Rook. "I need the office to myself. But don't leave the building."

"I'm under arrest?"

"You're underfoot, as usual." As he rose, she added, "There's a complication here. Our little drama aside, you could be material to this investigation."

"How cool am I?"

"And since Roach is officially in the mix, they're going to need to interview you."

"Nothing to say. It's all puddin 'n' tame with me. Ask me again, I'll tell 'em the same."

"You have fun with that," she said, and he left her to her call with the medical examiner.

The sunniest voice at the Office of Chief Medical Examiner greeted Nikki when she picked up. "Rockin' that uniform look this morning, Ms. Heatness. It's like you were all Beyoncé, but without the shoulder pads."

"And the half billion net worth."

"If that's what you're into." After they shared a laugh, Nikki could hear crisp strokes on a keyboard and pictured the ME perched at the office window overlooking the basement autopsy room. "Headlines first, report to follow, cool?"

"Ready, Doctor."

"Not going to be a surprise here. Pending toxicology, of course, I'm finding cause of death to be traumatic brain injury due to gunshot wound."

Nikki flipped to a clean page and jotted "COD = GSW" in her reporter's spiral notebook. "You retrieved the slug, I assume."

"Correctly. Retrieved it first thing so I could expedite it to Jamaica Avenue. Ballistics is all over it, and you should have a prelim from them soon."

"Give me a preview." Heat couldn't keep the urgency out of her voice. "Fragged or in one piece?"

"Intact .22 caliber."

"Mushrooming?"

"Negative. Either a lucky—if you'll pardon that term in a homicide—or precise shot that met minimal bone resistance. Entry point was on the nasion, just superior to the rhinion (the bridge of the nose, to you), and inferior to the glabella, which is the lower forehead." The macabre image of the small hole between Lon King's placid eyes resurfaced, and Nikki drew a simplistic Charlie Brown face. When she marked it with a dot, her own brow sympathy-tingled. "We've both seen bullets do significant damage or sectioning of the brain due to hydrostatic shock or internal bullet deflection. Not this time. This .22 created a narrow wound channel on a trajectory to what became a direct hit, severing the brain stem. The slug came to a stop at the back of the skull."

In the silence that followed Nikki gathered herself and

tried to remain clinical about this victim. "Would that trajectory fit a suicide?"

"Anything's possible, Nikki, but I'd bet no. To hold a weapon in front of you at that height, exactly on the proper angle? I can't see it. Plus there would have been significantly more flash burn and muzzle residue at that proximity. Also, no GSR on the hands. And with a quick rate of incapacitation and mortality like this, he could never have shot himself and then taken off gloves."

Captain Heat's first incoming call ever on her new department-issued BlackBerry startled her when it rang. She pulled it out of her pocket and read the caller ID. "Listen, Lauren, I've got a bureau chief calling."

"Take it."

"First, let me ask a quick one. Could King have been shot elsewhere and placed in the kayak, already dead?"

"No. Livor mortis indicates that he died seated in that boat."

Nikki didn't bother with a good-bye, just scrambled for the incoming before it dumped to voicemail. "Captain Heat."

"You didn't waste any time catching a hot one your first day," said the chief of detectives without a hello or introduction. Heat guessed he had figured out that she was a detective and could read a caller ID.

"No, sir."

"In about ten minutes, I'm riding with the commissioner to a strategy session on these protests over this college kid from Syria. That shrink was one of our own, and the commish wants a briefing in the car. What do you have?"

She jumped to her feet for an unobstructed view of the Murder Board and began to PowerPoint him, fighting off the squeeze of accountability tightening a corset around her rib cage. Just breathe, Nikki told herself as she spoke. Heat had been in gunfights and felt more at ease.

In two minutes, she had summarized it all, ending with the autopsy findings. "And those just came in when you called, so you couldn't be more current."

"Is that supposed to impress me?"

"Sir?"

"I'll fluff it out for the boss, but sounds to me like you're still clearing your throat. Captain, I want you to move off the prelims and generate some activity. Give me some meat to report, or—preferably—closure. And soon. Am I understood?"

"Of course. Yes, Chief." Heat didn't know if he had stayed on the call long enough to hear her answer. But he was a detective. He could figure out what it was.

Nikki found Raley and Ochoa at a table in the break room interviewing Rook, and, to judge from their expressions, getting about as far beyond his journalistic privilege as she had. "Boys, let's convene."

"Sounds good," said Rook, hopping to his feet with a grin, rubbing his hands together vigorously.

"A meeting?" asked Ochoa from his chair. "Early on, don't you think?"

His partner didn't get up either. "Kind of still tasking."

The air of disagreement hanging between the cops sent

Rook to the door. "You guys work this out. I'll be in the bull pen."

"Seriously," said Ochoa after Rook had left. "We spend more time in meetings, we'll never get traction."

So this is what it becomes, thought Nikki. A battleground of preordained roles. Detectives wanting more time. Downtown wanting more results. Precinct commander caught in the vise grip in between. One slot Heat refused to fill—especially on day one—was that of a skipper harried by her superiors into pushing the pressure down the line. She also didn't want to be perceived as susceptible to that pressure herself. The flop sweat of Captain Irons was still stinking up the halls of the Twentieth. So she didn't mention the hotfoot she'd just gotten from the chief of detectives. "Meeting in five minutes" was all she said, then left them to work it out.

With no sign of dissent, her interim homicide squad leaders had gathered the crew by the time Captain Heat entered the bull pen from her office to begin the meeting. Rook, busy in the back of the room at his squatter's desk, finished pulling a shot of espresso from his machine and joined the semicircle around the Murder Board.

Nikki began with a recap of Dr. Parry's autopsy results, which led to a handoff to Detective Ochoa and the report he had just received from the ballistics lab.

"As expected, we were looking for a small-caliber GSW. The vic's autopsy yielded a .22 slug. Rounded, non-hollow-point."

Feller finished a note and commented, "The .22 is an interesting choice, considering the conditions."

"In an alley fight, I'd want a .9mm or a .44 Mag," said Inez Aguinaldo. "But when I was military police, there were a fair number of fatals with .25s and .22s. Your critical factors are always distance, angle, and location."

"Dr. Parry tells us factors two and three were spot on," said Heat.

"Ballistics gives us an estimate on the first, distance," said Ochoa, going for his notes. "Assuming a long-rifle cartridge and forty grains of powder, the lab puts the muzzle at a range of two to three feet. One yard, max."

As Heat's dry erase squeaked that detail onto the whiteboard, she asked, "Any conjecture about the weapon?"

Detective Ochoa nodded. "Good odds it was a handgun. Slugs from a rifle have a nasty habit of creating more mayhem inside the skull than those from a revolver or pistol. They not only tear up the tissue but create a lead snowstorm in the brain. This bullet is misshapen, but intact. Unfortunately, no prints. And it's a plain-wrap, over-the-counter, retail bullet. However, they said they did get good striations for a future match. Of course, they're running it through the database to see if they get a nexus on priors."

"Excellent, Miguel. Glad I came." Heat arched a teasing brow and got back a half smile from Ochoa, plus another from Raley, which she decided to add together, yielding her one more smile than she had seen going in.

Ochoa continued. "I've gotten in touch with the RTCC detectives. They're running all shooters favoring .22s, with a sub-run for headshots as MO."

Raley read some secret partner signal and took the handoff. "They're also doing a search for me on a shady guy who popped up on video from King's medical building."

"You mean other than the shady journalist who popped up?" asked Heat. Everyone's laughter—including Rook's—went a long way to diffuse tensions. Elephants can't take a joke. When you've got one in the room, sometimes an honest ribbing clears it out.

"This dude's even shadier. If that's possible," continued Detective Raley. "Male, Cauc, early thirties. Made several camera passes over several days this week without entering the office."

Heat asked, "You get a face?"

The King of All Surveillance Media shook his head no. "Kept his head down and wore a brim."

"Question."

"Go, caller," said Raley.

"Shady Jameson from Tribeca; first time, long time. If you got no face, how are you going to run him? Tattoo? Scar? I'll hang up and listen to your answer."

"The answer to your question is gait analysis."

"There's an app for that?" asked Rook.

"There's an app for that," answered Raley. "Real Time Crime techs are using new software, initially developed for Homeland, on the premise that gait—the way every person walks—is unique and can be broken down into algorithms. It's not as accurate as fingerprints yet, but neither was facial recognition when it started."

Inez Aguinaldo had just interviewed Sampson Stallings, the romantic life partner of Lon King, who had come directly from JFK to meet with her in the station's conference room. "The man's in pieces. He and the victim were a couple for almost a decade and were talking about a wedding."

"How was the relationship?" asked Ochoa.

"Like I said, they were talking about a wedding."

"All fine," said Feller, "but look at reality. Weddings bring out the bad shit. People work in one last fling and get caught, or get cold feet and choose a deadly way out, or all the fear and tension around the big step makes one of them crack, and— *pow!*" He caught the stare he was getting from Nikki and added, "Clearly, your engagement is the exception."

"In fact, Mr. Stallings did admit they had been quarreling lately over his partner's gambling debts," said Detective Aguinaldo. "But he told me Dr. King had recently joined GA and was taking steps to get a handle on his habit. As for the rest of their relationship, they had no infidelities, King had no enemies or known threats against him, no changes in routine or behavior, no drugs, no drinking, nothing that would point to this."

Heat asked, "You check his alibi? He said he was in Vermont, but Burlington's only a one-hour flight or a six-hour drive."

"Affirm. During the TOD window, Mr. Stallings was in a portrait sitting with a United States senator."

"I'd go for more cred," heckled Rook.

Detective Feller bent his report through the prism of frustration after spending the day dogging the Harbor Unit and USCG with no accounts of unusual activity concerning a lone kayaker. "I did get some tide info. Yay. Coast Guard ran a computer model factoring in ebb and flood, wind, and drag on a rudderless vessel of that size. Their best guess is that the kayak came downriver, north to south."

"That would fit," said Inez. "Stallings said Dr. King stored his kayak at a boathouse up in Inwood and would have put in there."

"Which Detective Aguinaldo was kind enough to phone to me since the kayak was my assignment," added Rhymer. "I got the call at the REI in Yonkers, where he bought it and took paddling classes. No regular float buddies, according to the manager. In fact, he recalled how King made a big point that he wanted to take up the sport for the solitude."

Nikki reflected on her sessions and his tranquil demeanor. After a day of listening to people talk, she imagined the quiet probably kept the psychologist sane.

"I hit the Inwood Canoe Club on my way back to Manhattan," Rhymer continued. "It's on the Hudson between Spuyten Duyvil Creek and the GWB. The vice commodore got me in touch with a member who saw King put in late yesterday afternoon, about four-thirty."

As one, the entire squad noted the wall clock, no doubt hatching the same thought. About twenty-four hours before, a man had put on his life jacket, thinking he was going for a carefree paddle on an April evening.

Detective Rhymer, who had paused in deference to the collective impulse, resumed, consulting his notes. "The member, an HR exec named Abira, said she had a friendly exchange with King, giving him shit about the hazards of floating solo. Ironically, his last words were, 'If I die, you can have the last laugh.' She had an appointment and left as he was paddling upriver. According to her and the vice commodore, one of his favorite courses was to make a loop: Harlem River to the University Heights Bridge, and back.

"Detective Feller," said Heat. "While there's still daylight, get on your contacts at Harbor Unit for a scour of that stretch." While he moved off to his desk, she called after him, "Fishermen, boaters, birdwatchers, pot smokers hanging at the water, ask Harbor to check them all out." Without turning, he waved in the air to acknowledge.

"How do we feel about Fat Tommy?" asked Ochoa. "After your meet, do you like him for this?"

Heat recapped her meeting at Fortuna's Wheel with Nicolosi. When she finished, Raley observed that she didn't seem convinced that he was involved. "Sean," Heat said, "everyone has to be on the table until we close this. But his motive isn't strong."

"He said it himself," added Rook. "Bad business to kill people who owe you."

Detective Rhymer flipped his notebook closed. "Makes us mighty lean on suspects."

Ochoa crossed to the Murder Board and tapped the break-in at Lon King's office. "This is our hottest lead right now. And those A-through-M patient files that got ripped off? Our killer could be one of them. Maybe there was a patient with something in his file he didn't want known. Something he admitted to the shrink and regretted later."

Raley joined his partner's speculation. "Or, maybe something the shrink blackmailed him with to get money to settle his debt."

"Viable," said Feller, returning from his call.

Nikki shook her head. "I know I said everything has to be on the table, but that doesn't seem in character to me."

Feller scoffed. "People surprise you." Rook and Heat traded some drive-by eye contact and looked away. "So can we get a list of the A-through-Ms? Start getting warrants so we can do some interviews?"

"There is no list," said Ochoa. "The files were stolen and so was all the documentation from the office. Hard drives, date books, everything. It's a dead end."

"Did Lon King keep a patient list at his home?" asked Miguel. "We should find that out."

"I already asked." Detective Aguinaldo riffled through pages of her notes. "According to his partner, they shared an office-slash-studio in their second bedroom. King mainly used it as a retreat, where he read psychology journals and worked on a nature book he was writing. The only way Stallings saw him consult his case notes was with the paper files he brought home."

"His receptionist mentioned thumb drives," Heat said to her.

"I'll follow up."

Rhymer raised a polite hand and waited for Nikki's chin to tilt his way. "Here's one solution. Make our own list. Have Personnel generate a roster of all the department referrals that have been made to Lon King by NYPD."

"That's a great idea," said Roach in a near-chorus.

"It's a fucking needle in a haystack," said Feller. "Come on, man, how many referrals have there been? How long do you go back? It's a nonstarter, if you ask me."

Rhymer, self-advocating for a change, said, "You got something better?"

"Wheel spinning, Rhymes."

Detective Rhymer flared. "Hey, dickhead, just because you didn't think of it doesn't make it a bad idea." Feller was too shocked to fire back. The rest were too shocked to do anything but stare in disbelief at the soft-spoken, sweet-natured, almost courtly Virginian. Squad politics had just gotten ugly—Opie had called Randy a dickhead.

Heat wondered if she had brought this on by not making that clean squad leader appointment and stifling the flames of rivalry right away. Or had this been boiling underneath the whole time and the change simply made it blow up? She studied Rook. While everyone was beating the bushes for a clue, what the heck was he sitting on?

Then she banished that thought—for now. It wasn't going to lead her anywhere good.

Lon King, PhD
Counseling Transcript
Session of Feb. 22/13 with Heat, N., Det. Grade-1,
   NYPD

LK: It's been a while, Nikki. Let's see, last time we talked, you had gotten pissed off and baptized Jameson Rook with your cocktail.

NH: A tequila shot, yeah.

LK: How is it going for you two?

NH: We're engaged.

LK: Congratulations.

NH: Thank you.

LK: How is it going for you two?

NH: You just asked me that.

LK: You answered with a fact. How about a feeling?

NH: Isn't that in the fact?

LK: I'd like to know.

[No reply]

LK: Nikki, when you made this appointment, you said it was just— What did you call it?

NH: A tune-up.

LK: Very nuts and bolts. Which is fine. It's your style. Or your comfort zone. Is there more? You like things concrete, tell me if there's a specific issue that you're confronting.

NH: Well . . . Yeah, I guess. [Long pause] . . . Living together.

LK: You mean before the wedding? I thought you said you and Rook had been sharing space for a few years.

NH: I mean after the wedding. And the issue isn't living together, of course we'll live together . . . It's a question of where. [Long pause] You're going to make me say this, aren't you.

LK: I'm listening.

NH: OK. OK . . . It's just, the whole idea has me all

stressed. We can't be the first couple to choose whose apartment we live in and whose we . . . give up.

LK: You're correct, it's not uncommon. Although I see it more frequently with couples coming into a committed relationship from divorce, where one partner feels like a guest in the other's home. One remedy is to get rid of both places and—

NH: That makes no sense. Rook has this ginormous loft in Tribeca. Lots of space, plenty of room for both of our stuff . . . [Silence]

LK: Interesting answer. So it seems that the issue is giving up your apartment, Nikki.

NH: [Pause. Seeks composure] I grew up there. I . . . lived my life there. [Very long pause]

LK: Your mother was murdered there.

NH: Can we . . . ? [Stands] Can we deal with this later?

LK: Sure. Let's plan another session. Is that what you'd like?

NH: . . . I think I need to.

"Captain? . . . Captain?" Raley and Ochoa, both in her office. Both calling her name. Nikki startled out of her blank stare at the streetlight on 82nd and turned to them.

"Got something," said Raley. "I asked Personnel to gather that list of patient referrals made to Lon King."

"The idea being," continued Ochoa, "that a cop psych referral would be the shortest distance between no client list and a pool of likelies for us to work from."

"What did you get?"

Ochoa gestured with a thumb and Heat followed the partners to Roach Central, where their paired desks were shoved in one corner of the bull pen. Miguel gestured to his task chair, and Heat rolled it up for a view of his monitor. A color NYPD identification photo stared out from the top quarter of the screen. On sight, she profiled the man as a handful. Every cop got told not to smile for their ID pics; this one had followed procedure but managed to dab a hint of a smirk on his face. Or maybe it wasn't the mouth so much as the wise-guy squeeze of his eyelids.

"Detective Third-Grade Timothy James Maloney," said Raley.

"Actually, homes, it's *ex*-grade-three." Ochoa double-tapped the space bar, opening the next page, which was watermarked in red as confidential. It was a single-spaced report on the events leading to the suspension of Maloney for numerous complaints of excessive force, followed by a mandatory referral to a department psychologist after the detective cleared the desk of his Burglary Division squad leader with the sweep of an arm.

"A little tightly wound, wouldn't you say?" said Heat.

Raley said, "You don't know the half of it. Go to the next screen."

On page three of Maloney's digital Personnel file was a list of suspected multiple tire deflations and auto-paint scratchings of his Burglary lieutenant's personal vehicle, a pickup truck. None of the vandalism could be unequivocally attributed to Maloney. Heat tapped to the next page, which displayed the transcript of an anonymous text message to Lon King from an untraceable burner cell phone:

> You are the worst kind of coward. You always sit there pretending to care, always acting like my friend when I open a fucking vein to you, but it's all more Department Bullshit. The fix is in. As always. You're in their pocket. You think you can squeeze my balls just because you give blowjobs to the Commish? Well, here's a dose of honesty, which you NEVER showed me, you sanctimonious prick. I know where you live. I know where you park. I know about your stops on the F Train. I know about your dick-substitute canoe. I know about that organic café you were at last Friday night with your boyfriend. Now who's paranoid, motherfucker?

Heat swiveled to Roach. "Personnel knows this was from Maloney?"

"Knows. Proving is something else," said Raley.

"Why him?"

Ochoa gestured to the bottom of the screen. "For one thing, date of the text. Same day Lon King wrote Maloney up, recommending he be permanently removed from duty."

"Lon King got him fired," said Raley, with the distinct sound of advocacy.

"We have an address?" asked Heat. When Raley held up his notepad in reply, she stood. "Let's make a house call for the doctor."

***

When Rook saw them saddling up to go, he had the good sense, for once, not to call shotgun, and he let the homicide squad co-leaders compete for Heat's passenger seat. Ochoa won a curbside round of Rochambeau with a surprise repeat of paper to Raley's rock, so Sean rode in back with Rook on the brief ride uptown. "Careful he doesn't yack on you back there, Sean," called Ochoa over the headrest.

"Not to worry," said Rook. "Yes, I am prone to motion sickness, but I know better than to spoil the new car smell in the captain's sweet ride."

A blue-and-white from the Twenty-Eighth was waiting for them at West 128th, just outside the south entrance to St. Nicholas Park, a block from Maloney's Harlem brownstone. Heat pulled up, driver's window to driver's window, thanked them for their precinct's cooperation, and coordinated with the pair of uniforms to cover the back of the building and its fire escape while her crew doorstepped him from the front. The officers held up cell phones to confirm receipt of her text of Maloney's ID photo, then split off to their position.

As the four of them got out and mounted the stoop, Rook asked Nikki, "By the way, what got this guy in hot water in the first place?"

"A volatile disposition and citizen complaints about back-alley beatdowns."

Rook stopped and took a few steps backward onto the sidewalk. "May the excessive force be with you."

The three others also exercised prudence, but in a different way. Heat, Raley, and Ochoa rested their hands on their holsters as they took positions beside the door. After several knocks and calls through it to Maloney without a response, they returned to the car to wait for the search warrant they had requested.

"If he skipped, I'm blaming Personnel," said Raley.

"Freakin' A," echoed his partner, cleaning up his language in deference to Heat. "This homicide report went into the system at six-thirty this morning. Dude's had a twelve-hour head start because they didn't notify us of his threat. Aren't we allegedly in this together? What the hell happened to sharing information?"

"Sure makes you wonder," said Nikki. She found Rook in her rearview, but he was occupied watching an elm's spring leaves rustle under the coppery street lamp and missed the dig. Either that, or he was just ignoring her.

"Update from Forensics," announced Raley, scrolling an email on his phone. "Says, 'the forward deck of the kayak also showed gunshot particles that were adhering to a fresh coating of a small patch of an undetermined oily residue.'"

"That's weird," said Ochoa. "Oil on a paddle boat? Like olive oil from a sandwich?"

"Nah, Detective DeJesus says that it's a machine lubricant of some kind. Thin, like someone might use for a gun."

"Or a fishing reel?" asked Heat.

"Yeah, but—remember? No fishing reel, no fishing tackle. Plus it's in an odd pattern, diffused in a fine spray. Forensics is going to lab it, but also send off a sample for analysis at the National Lubricating Grease Institute."

That brought Rook's attention back from the treetops. "There's an institute for lubrication?" he said with a naughty grin. "Imagine the possibilities."

Raley, Ochoa, and Rook all exchanged smiles, all imagining. Heat said, "Boys? Don't even."

"Agreed," said Rook. "It's a slippery slope."

Ochoa said, "Got our man."

The others followed his gaze up the block. Timothy Maloney was approaching with an unhurried swagger, his eyes inside a Popeye's takeout bag. As they prepared to move, he paused at the curb a few yards ahead, across from his brownstone. He pulled out an onion ring and munched it. "Soon as this van passes," said Heat with a side-glance at the approaching headlight in her mirror. But when it came alongside her, Maloney dropped the Popeye's and bolted into the street in front of it. The van screeched to a stop, blocking Nikki's door and Raley's behind her.

"Go, go, go!" shouted Raley to his partner.

Ochoa leaped out and scrambled around the front of the car, but the confused driver of the van lurched forward, nearly hitting him. With their doors clear, Heat and Raley jumped out, scanning the block for Maloney. "Got him," called Raley. He and Nikki dashed off up the middle of the street toward their suspect, who disappeared at a sprint into the shadows of St. Nicholas Park.

Heat and Raley made a sharp turn between the waist-high wrought iron fences that bordered the footpath and bounded up the double flight of concrete stairs. In the darkness, Raley jammed a toe into one of the steps but grabbed the pipe railing before he went down. "I'm good," he whispered without her asking. She didn't turn. Her focus was straight ahead.

At the landing, they paused to get their bearings and to listen. At that hour of the evening, right near the entrance the park, street noise dominated everything. If there were footfalls, they were lost in the city wash of car horns, megabass, and a basketball slow-dribbling somewhere in the night. Detective Ochoa arrived, and Heat told him to radio the unis covering the rear of the apartment.

"Done and done," he said as they moved forward. "They're flanking in the cruiser to the entrance on a Hundred Thirty-Fifth and will work their way down to us on foot. Hopefully, we'll box him. They're also calling in air support."

The box tactic was a sound one, thought Nikki, as the trio fanned out in a sweep line heading north, but ex-Detective Maloney had the same training that they did. At night, in a twenty-three-acre wooded park with thick stands of shrubs, jagged schist outcroppings, and hilly meadows, it wouldn't be hard for their quarry to vault iron to the street, or just go jungle and hide in a laurel or rhody until they passed. He could also be armed, which must have crossed Raley's mind as well, because he cautioned Heat to watch herself under the approaching lamplight in her white uniform shirt.

Just as Heat was about to ask Ochoa if Rook was coming, a flash of silver caught her attention. "There." She pointed to the reflective safety strips from Maloney's running shoes that were disappearing fast around the bend a hundred yards ahead. Nikki sprinted after him with Roach only one yard behind.

Alert for an ambush, they rounded a curve that offered too much cover from hulking sycamores. Nikki palmed the grip of her Sig Sauer but kept it holstered. They came to a basketball court where a high school kid was practicing threes in the urban lightbleed and stopped. "NYPD," said Heat. "You see a guy?"

The kid hesitated, then straight-armed to their right, down a sloping grade, at a dense thicket, darker than the night surrounding it. The three cops took the incline slowly, then stopped at the edge of the brush to listen. They got nothing, only the approaching footsteps of their uniformed comrades, completing their pincer move. The pair held up, waiting on the path above them. Heat hand-signaled, using the spread of her arms to define the area of brush where Maloney had last been seen. One of the patrolmen whispered something in his walkie. Fifteen seconds later came the whine of a jet engine and the swirl of rotor blades, and the area got doused in the blazing searchlight of an NYPD chopper.

Heat, Roach, and a dozen supporting officers from the Two-Eight spent a half hour walking grids, systematically scouring the brush under the floodlight from the Aviation Unit's Bell 429. When they came up empty, Nikki shook the hands of the officers in thanks for the assist. The helicopter killed its Nightsun and returned to base. With a pair of cruisers assigned to patrol the park the rest of the night, there was nothing for Heat and Roach to do but bag it. As they retraced their steps out of the park, they noted that Maloney had had both local knowledge and a head start to help him evade and squirt out the east side of the park. "Or that Melo wannabe lied," said Ochoa.

"Saw you take your pratfall here, homes," said Ochoa when they reached the stairs at 128th Street.

"That? Yo, that was an evasive maneuver. Made me a moving target."

"More like a Rook maneuver, you ask me. Like that time he tripped on a rug when we raided that house in Bayview?"

"And almost crashed through the hole in the floor, ass first? Good times." Raley tilted his head to Heat. "No offense, smack-talking your fiancé."

"I am truly offended," said Nikki. Then she couldn't resist. "I hope if he stayed in the car, he had the smarts to crack a window open for air." They all enjoyed a tension-release chuckle at Rook's expense.

But that got cut short when they saw him halfway up the block. All three drew their weapons and ran, shouting "NYPD, don't move!"

FOUR

Keep your hands where they are!" shouted Heat.

Roach joined in, both guns on Maloney, overlapping each other, barking, "Keep them where we can see them!" and "Not an inch, not a muscle!"

Nikki said, "Rook, step back."

"You sure?"

"Yes, step back—now."

Rook, who had been holding Maloney facedown on the hood of Heat's car, wavered a beat, then did as he was told. Raley and Ochoa moved in to handle the suspect. He didn't resist.

"You hurt?" asked Nikki.

"No, I'm fine. Piece of cake. Before they cuff him, tell me, how'd I do with the position?" He indicated Maloney's hands, which were still clasped behind his neck. He'd been splayed that way, cheek to metal, elbows out, legs apart, bent over the fender.

She paused, then said, "Perfect. But how'd you . . . ?" She studied him. "*You*?"

"Please. Give me some credit. All these years of ride-alongs have some impact, Nik. A man learns a few things. Plus MeTV is rerunning *The Streets of San Francisco*. Surprisingly authentic."

"How 'bout I didn't resist," grunted Maloney. He sized Rook up, shoes to smile. "Piece of cake, my ass. You think I couldn't have had you any time I wanted?" He winced as Ochoa squeezed the cuffs on him. "A little courtesy, Paco?" Then he fixed the detective with an intrusive grin.

"Seriously, Rook," said Heat. "How did you do it?"

"The suspect returned to the scene unaware of my presence. When he attempted to retrieve his bag of onion rings and Louisiana Tenders, I made a citizen's arrest, locking him into a surprise hold, which proved very effective. Thank you, nineteen-seventies Michael Douglas."

A gentle breeze lifted Rook's hair and set it back down in a tousle that could only be described as carelessly sexy. Perfect, thought Nikki, I want to be—in fact, I am—so pissed at this guy that I want to kick his ass around every acre of St. Nicholas Park for taking such a risk, for acting so cavalierly, for hiding behind damned journalistic privilege, for seeing my shrink on the sly, but instead, I can't stop staring at the fall of his stupid bangs, or noticing the streetlight across his brow accenting that self-proclaimed rugged handsomeness, or feeling a warmth inside that makes me want to throw myself at him and bury my face in his chest right here and now.

He caught her staring and asked, "Is that a look of reprimand or adoration?"

"Yes."

As Raley gave Maloney a once-over, he asked, "Did you pat him down?"

Rook scoffed. "Please. Of course."

But then the detective came up from Maloney's ankle

holding a black Smith & Wesson J-Frame. "Oops," said Rook. "Missed that."

"Five buddies in the cylinder." Maloney winked at him. "Anytime I wanted." Rook's grin lost its cockiness. Raley dragged Maloney two paces back and planted him against the side of the vehicle.

Suddenly feeling the slither of his nerves in hindsight, Rook said, "I've been hollering for you the past fifteen minutes. Good luck with that over the chopper. I tried calling your cell phone, Nikki, but then I heard it ringing. Where? In the car." Heat patted her pocket for it, then saw her BlackBerry on the front seat, where she'd left it behind in the chase. "A bit of a lapse, eh, Cap? Understandable given the hot pursuit. But what about you two? Don't you answer your calls?"

"Didn't notice," said Raley, checking his phone and spotting two misses.

Ochoa got off a walkie-talkie call and checked his own iPhone, which, like his partner's, had been on silent for the stakeout. "We were sorta busy."

"Well, as you can see, so was I."

"Warrant cleared," Ochoa said to Heat, brandishing the radio in his hand.

"Timothy James Maloney, we have a warrant to search your apartment."

The ex-cop smirked and shrugged. "All you had to do was ask, Captain."

Nonetheless, Maloney made them wait for the formality of the paper to arrive from the DA's office. Forty minutes of

Heat's overtime budget eroding while their prime murder suspect, a man with a history of violence and insolence, stood docilely enjoying some private amusement as he sucked his teeth.

Heat, Roach, and Rook ascended the steps to the front door with the writ and Maloney's key. Nikki paused before she opened the door. All four shared a silent collective memory of Captain Irons grandstanding his way inside a dangerous suspect's house not too far from where they now stood and losing his life to a booby trap. She turned to the street where her prisoner stood flanked by patrolmen. "Maloney. You first."

He entered without hesitation and with a stride about as cocky as a person can manage with his hands bound behind him. "I'd offer you chips and dip, but I'd need a little help opening the bag."

Nikki and her crew ignored his comment, cleared the two-bedroom and one bath, then slipped on evidence gloves while CSU followed them in with their tackle boxes of swabs, powders, and camera gear. Three unis placed Maloney in a kitchen chair in the center of the living room and stood by while he relaxed to some inner monologue. Heat caught a glimpse of the tableau. It looked to her as if the jester had taken the throne.

"Records search shows you have numerous guns registered to you at this address," she said.

"Correct. Key word, registered. All legal. Just like my ankle carry. I'm in a dangerous line."

"Were," snapped Ochoa, poking his head around an open closet door.

Heat referred to the list on the warrant. " 'A pump-action twenty-gauge shotgun, a Glock .44 Mag, a Glock 26, a Sig Sauer 9mm, a Smith and Wesson .500 Mag . . .' "

"Big Poppy," he said with a proud nod.

"Here's what especially interests me: 'One Ruger SR-22 long rifle, one Walther P22, and one ISSC M22 with laser sighting.' "

"For puttin' it where ya want it."

Heat folded the pages in three and held up the warrant. "You want us to rip this place apart, or just show me where they are?"

"They're not here, that's for damn sure." He chuckled. "But I can tell you where to find them. Each and every one."

"You have a storage unit somewhere?"

"Even better." He almost told her. Then pursed his lips and simply sat back. "Later. Maybe."

Back at the precinct an hour afterward, Heat and Rook stood in the Observation Room looking through the magic mirror at Timothy Maloney as Raley and Ochoa conducted his interrogation.

"You're not getting shit from me until you cut me loose from these." He jerked his manacles upward, filling the ob booth with rattling metal and prompting Nikki to turn the mic volume down slightly.

" 'I wear the chain I forged in life,' " said Rook, in a ghost's voice. "Or was that forged in Pittsburgh?"

"Still waiting," said Ochoa. "Tell us where you were

yesterday between three and eight P.M."

"Listen, Paco, you can ask me ten more times. We're not talking."

"What about me then?" asked Raley.

"What about you? You're what, the Lucky Charms leprechaun?"

An administrative aide entered, handed Nikki a file, and left. She opened it and skimmed. "Well, this makes sense. Lon King's diagnosis of Maloney was paranoid personality disorder."

"Wait, his name starts with *M*. I thought those files were stolen."

"They were. This is a copy of the psych eval King sent to Personnel. The report that got him discharged from the department," she said as she continued to read. "'Detective Maloney exhibits the classic signs of PPD, including repressed anger, cognitive dissonance, rage, unjustified blaming, impulsively violent behavior, and oversuspicious projection.'"

Rook cupped a hand over one ear, announcer style. "If your projection lasts more than four hours, consult a physician."

"Come on, Tim, you were on the job, just like us," said Ochoa, playing the blue card. "You know where this is going, so give it up now."

"Just like you," Maloney repeated with disdain. "You mean they hired me from the sidewalk outside Home Depot to fill a quota, too?"

Raley slid in. "When was the last time you fired one of your weapons?"

"Your peons did my paraffin test. You tell me."

"What about your guns? Where are they?" countered Ochoa.

Maloney wagged his palms with a jangle of chain links, then let them drop. "I want the lady cop. The captain. I want someone with rank."

The risk of giving him what he wanted was that it would empower him and feed the beast. The potential advantage was that it might shake something loose if he did feel he had some leverage. Heat tagged in; Roach tagged out.

She began in silence, immersing herself in his file, letting the hunger for validation he had just exhibited push him to talk. Five minutes can be a long time in a room. But at last, her tactic did its work.

"So, was that your boyfriend?" Maloney said. "The one I let take me down?"

"Perceptive." Then she poked at him. "I bet you miss being a detective."

"Hey, fuck you."

"Sore spot? Not surprised. All those years out the window?" She could see a hint of turmoil fermenting under the surface pose of arrogance and dug at it. Her approach was to knock Maloney down off his stone wall by using his own volatility against him. Nikki glanced at the file and chuckled, shaking her head. "And you never made it above grade three. What's that about?"

"You know what that's about."

"How would I?"

"Because you're with them."

"Please."

"Don't deny it. That's the way it always comes down. Lies get put in my file, and I have to sit and deal with the bullshit. My loot had it out for me, and now you're taking it all on his word."

"Your loot. You mean . . ." Heat ran her finger to a signature on the page. "Lieutenant Branch?"

"Asshole tanked my whole goddamned career."

"Why would he do that?"

"The fuck I know. He just got it in his head I rubbed him wrong and he started jerking my shifts around, like putting me on the cabaret shift just when I got a new girlfriend. He wanted to ruin my love life, so he put me on the eight P.M. to four-thirty A.M., and it worked."

"Why would he want to ruin your relationship?"

"And then when I called him on it, everything I did started getting written up."

Nikki consulted the file again. "You mean like these excessive force complaints?"

"The lieutenant fed them that. Told them what to say. He even worked out a secret set of hand signals. They did what he said, and guess who's taking the weight."

"You want me to believe that your loot fed false information to three different citizens? Using secret hand signals?"

Maloney slammed a palm of the tabletop. "See? You're one of them. Everyone I talk to in this department means one more screwing."

"Did that include Lon King?"

"Fucker double-tapped my career."

"So you tapped him?" Heat's strategy had been working

so well, building the pace steadily, encouraging Maloney's recklessness and eliciting knee-jerk emotional blurts from him, making him careless.

Until then.

The suspect paused and canted his head to the side. A wide-open grin unclenched his red face. The blush faded and the freckles came back to it. "Ach! So close, huh, lady captain?" Links of chain scuffed the edge of the interview table as he swept an arm toward the mirror and called out to it. "You all catch that in there? Huh? See one more One PP stooge trying to sink me? Fail!" He mouthed a video game fizzle sound effect and sat back, self-satisfied, and looked at Heat. But then the amused stare became a glower—invasive and sinister—and even more menacing because he was still grinning. He leaned forward and said in a whisper, "You. Will regret this."

Chilled, Nikki maintained her detachment and tossed it off. "Are you actually threatening me?" It was her turn to gesture to the mirror, and she did.

"That would be, what? Crazy." A twinkle came into his eye. "No, I'm just pointing out that your bad judgment today will bother you. Definitely bother you." He was too smart to be blatant and turned his implied threat into simulated advice. But Maloney's words came wrapped in hostile intimidation. In anyone else, they would come across as a lame attempt to save face. The psych eval under Heat's clasped hands told her they spoke of something more. Personalization.

Maloney's attorney arrived, looking as if she'd been yanked out of a spin class, and took a seat beside her client.

"Mr. Maloney will not be answering any more questions," she began, straight out of the jailhouse lawyer's playbook.

"Of course, that's his right," said Heat, "but it's my job to keep asking them. Do what you will."

"Thank you, Captain. Now, a question for you: Are there any charges against him?"

"Not at present. He's a person of interest in a homicide investigation."

"Did he resist arrest?"

"No. But he evaded."

The attorney examined the arrest sheet. "My client states that he ran because he was in fear, not knowing you were police."

"Oh, please . . ."

"And the confiscated ankle weapon was registered and conceal permitted?"

"Correct. But I still want to know about his whereabouts during the time of the murder. I want to know about the threat texted to his psychologist. And what I really want to know is, where are all his weapons?"

Maloney gave a side wink to the lawyer. "Tell her."

"My client has already answered all of these questions today."

"Excuse me?"

"Internal Affairs came to Mr. Maloney's apartment this morning, confiscated all his guns, and brought him downtown for an extensive interview, including a paraffin test." She read Nikki's expression. "You didn't know?"

"I . . . No."

"You people. Get your shit together." The lawyer stood. "IA had no grounds on which to hold my client, and they released him. Unless you have something they don't, so will you."

Heat tried not to look at Maloney. She didn't need to. She knew the grin would be aimed at her. And that his eyes would be reminding her that she would regret this.

She already did.

Nikki stormed back and forth with the landline receiver to her ear, pacing along the glass wall of her office like an animal trapped in a zoo exhibit. After a series of clicks and transfers, she heard background sounds of silverware rattling and loud diner chatter as a familiar voice came on the line. "Lovell."

"Detective Lovell, I'm not sure you remember me. This is—"

"I know exactly who this is. Detective—and, as of yesterday—Captain Heat. So you took the gold bars. Good for you."

"Maybe not so good for you, Detective Lovell." She had first met the Internal Affairs man three years before in the very office where she stood at that moment. And, as during that first encounter, she now could barely control her anger at him.

A snort of air, his version of a chuckle, came over the line, followed by, "Well, we'll see about that." Nikki could picture him. Skeletally skinny, a creased, angular face that belonged to a Triassic flying dinosaur, and so tall, he must have ducked to pass the department's height requirements. And, like most of his IA pals, not just a bully; a bully with actual clout. No wonder he sounded so unfazed.

From the guest chair, Rook gave Nikki a supportive fist pump, a go-get-'em. She unloaded: about working a homicide with inadequate information that had been withheld by IA; about Lovell usurping her jurisdiction by shaking down her prime suspect without consulting her beforehand or at least informing her of his meddling after the fact; about confiscating Maloney's weapons without telling anyone, causing lost time and wasted effort; about springing the ex-cop without an advisory. "Basically, Detective, you and your division have made me and my homicide squad spin our wheels and trash day one of our investigation."

"So what do you want, Heat?"

"Let's start with an apology."

After another snort from that pterodactyl nose, he said, "What else you want?"

"Everything you've learned."

"The truth? About the same as you. Otherwise you wouldn't be calling me, all pissed off." He covered the mouthpiece of his phone, although Heat could hear him ask for ketchup. When he came back, he said, "Listen, we do what we have to, the way we have to do it. I'm not making any apologies to you or anyone for employing tactics that work."

"Is that your apology, then?"

"Let's stay focused. We swooped in, hoping to jam his ass unawares, but he's a slippery dude. Case in point, that text-message threat. No-traceable to him and, if you read it carefully, contains no threat of specific action." Heat nodded, recalling how well-parsed his threat to her had been minutes before in the interrogation. "He's clean on weapons. Of the guns we seized, all are registered. Ballistics is running them now."

"What do you mean, '*of* the guns'?"

"One's unaccounted for."

"Let me guess," said Heat. "A .22 long rifle with a laser sight."

"He claims he lost it on a hunting trip."

"Yeah, during shrink season," she said.

"Be as mad as you want, Captain, my crew did its job once. We weeded a bad apple off the force. A homicide conviction in a court of law's going to take a lot more."

"Well, then help. Stop making my investigation more difficult."

"We done?" was all he had to say to that.

"One more thing. What else don't I know? Are there any other crazed cops in Lon King's practice?"

"You mean besides you?" Then she heard an actual laugh before he hung up.

When she banged the receiver down, Rook crossed his arms and tsk-tsked. "Infernal Affairs. Whatever happened to the left hand knowing what the right hand is doing? One hand washing the other? Where's the spirit of cooperation? Unity of purpose? And what's that scary look you're giving me?"

"Are you hearing yourself? I should get a mop in here, you're so dripping with irony."

"What?" He frowned in disbelief. "Certainly you're not equating the obstructive tactics of those empire builders at

Internal Affairs with my reporter's unfettered pursuit of the truth?"

"You're hiding behind your journalistic prerogative—

"It's in the Constitution—"

"Like it provided you some invisible cloak, if such a thing could exist."

"Oh, they exist, all right."

"Rook, I'm not talking about Harry Potter."

"Let us not speak disdainfully of a cultural icon and, all right, my sometime alter ego."

"Or is it just ego?"

"Know your problem, Nikki? Your problem is, you don't entertain the conspiracy theories enough. You could benefit from a soupçon of paranoia in your Occam's razor–sharp mind. Maybe it wouldn't be such a bad idea for you and Tim Maloney to hang out. Spend a day. See what rubs off. Suddenly, black-ops projects like time travel, acoustic weapons, and cloaks of invisibility wouldn't seem so far-fetched." His iPhone sounded to signal an incoming email, and he stood while he read it.

"Let me guess. Summons from Dumbledore?" But after Rook's playful nerdist rant, Nikki could see him turn sober and contemplative. "Everything OK?"

"Hmm? Oh, yeah, sure." He slipped his phone into his pocket, gave her a kiss, and told her he'd see her later back at his place.

Heat perched on a file cabinet in Roach Central and briefed Raley and Ochoa on her conversation with Internal Affairs. "Think it did any good?" asked Raley.

"Like scratching after poison ivy, Rales. Kinda feels good, only makes it worse."

Ochoa said, "I want to put a plain-wrap car outside Maloney's apartment. He's been a cop, he'll make it. He made us. Lets him know he's still on our radar."

"You just want to spend my OT," she teased.

"That there—that's captain talk," said Raley. "First day as precinct commander's not over, and you're busting our balls over the budget."

"Go ahead. Order the car." Then she added, "More poison ivy, but why the hell not?"

Miguel glanced up at the clock. "We've got another good hour to go here. But you oughta call it."

Nikki almost said good night, then sat back down. "I need to talk about something."

"Anything," they said in unconscious unison.

"Lon King." She cleared her throat. "I may have led you to think I only had my introductory visit with him. Actually, I had about ten sessions with him over the past few years. I don't know why I held back. It's personal, you know? Not the sort of thing you advertise." What she meant was, not the sort of *vulnerability* you advertise. And Roach's nods indicated they got it. "But this is a homicide we're dealing with, and I don't want to keep secrets from you."

"There's enough of that," said Ochoa. He had second thoughts about that and backpedaled. "I mean IA."

Heat made it easy. "And Rook. We all know that."

A still moment passed among the three of them in the empty bull pen. "Must be tough," said Raley at last. "You and Rook. Both have big jobs. Stressful jobs. Competing jobs, sometimes. Like now. Guess it's bound to happen, right? What you need smacks head-on into what he's holding. Guess he's lucky it's you, and not IA."

And in that instant, clarity came to Nikki. This situation was all very complicated, but also very simple, if she let herself see it objectively. "Fellas?" she said. "He knows something about this murder and he's getting a pass."

"A press pass," joked Ochoa.

But the quip was lost on Nikki, who stayed her pensive course. "Let's be honest. It's not just because he's a reporter, it's because of our relationship. If he weren't my fiancé, I know exactly what I'd do. As my duty to the case. And to the victim." She rested her hands flat on her thighs to steady herself. Then she said the words before her newfound clarity could be muddied by emotion: "Budget one more undercover car. I want you to put a tail on Rook."

FIVE

Guilt, second thoughts, self-reproach, more guilt. Like drop-in company, all the unwelcome demons paid Nikki a visit after she ordered a tail on Rook. It bothered her so much that, twice during the night, she even picked up her phone to email Roach and call it off. They would understand. Or they wouldn't, and they would just have to live with it. Precinct commanders made iffy decisions and reversed themselves all the time. However, Heat didn't know the stats on such things on her first day in command.

Every time she weakened, though, something would reset her resolve. Like watching Rook furtively respond to a text at dinner without regard to her, and, after hitting send effortlessly resuming his theory on A-Rod's shelf life in pinstripes. Or when he excused himself to the gents, only to veer instead into the restaurant vestibule for a quick but intense call that was unacknowledged when he returned to the table. Mostly, however, what kept her from rescinding her order was the ineradicable image of Rook on that security video, striding with impunity into Lon King's office—the safe place where she had gradually learned to let her guard down and bare her soul to a stranger with a trust that did not come naturally to Nikki Heat. So she held firm.

But resolve is not closure. To her, it felt more like a frayed bungee cord straining against the lid on Pandora's Box.

At the end of the evening, as she tucked into her precinct paperwork instead of their bed, she told herself that she wasn't doing that to avoid Rook. Being Captain Heat meant keeping up with new responsibilities—memos, emails, and reports. A quick kiss, and it was back to grand-larceny spreadsheets for her; a trip up that hall with the new le Carré for him. But the distant whir of his electric toothbrush triggered a pang of melancholy that led to a confrontation with the truth—which was that she wasn't retreating from Rook, but from herself. And that she harbored qualms about her own duplicity. Their lovemaking included looking each other in the eye. Nikki was afraid of what he might see in hers that night.

Heat needed to move the needle, or at least to try. She quit her laptop, rose from the dining table, and discovered yesterday's celebration bottle of the Sancerre in the fridge. After pouring a generous glass, she folded herself onto the couch in the library, a cozy alcove Rook had defined with freestanding bookcases, and stared out over the Tribeca rooftops. Between her and Battery Park, almost close enough to touch, the new One World Trade Center's upper floors illuminated an engulfing cloud, making it look like an angel's halo.

Nikki set her wineglass down untouched and admired the spire of steel and light, a gleaming, necessary statement about resiliency, bravery, and pride. Heat's impromptu pause to consider its significance didn't solve her problems, but it sure put them in perspective. At the very least, she decided, she would not end her first day as commander of the Twentieth Precinct in a self-manufactured funk. With a new understanding of the burdens that weighed upon the shoulders of the PCs she had served under, Wally Irons and her mentor, Captain Charles Montrose, Nikki raised her glass. Her silent toast took her back to a time when Montrose had broken out a bottle of Cutty from his desk drawer and they clinked coffee mugs at the end of a shift. She recalled his words then as if he were there to remind her of them now: "No mystery to this job, Heat. Embrace every problem. Because they *are* the job."

Easier said . . . The pressures of command relentlessly carved out chunks of her beloved skipper's soul, and it also didn't escape Heat that she was filling the shoes of two men who had both died on said job. So there was one thing to avoid.

Maybe Nikki couldn't exactly embrace the Rook problem, but she would have to live with it. Raley had nailed it: Their careers were bound to make them smack heads sometimes. And that gave Heat a choice. Live in constant inner hell or accept the fact of an occasionally conflicted life.

OK, fine, she thought. But why today, my first day?

With a sense of renewed balance, if not of buoyancy, she drank her wine standing in the great window, taking a quiet moment to watch the streets reflect neon candy colors as a soft shower passed through Lower Manhattan. Nikki brought her glass up to drain it and, when she brought it down, caught sight of a man in a baseball cap standing on the near corner, staring up at her. She couldn't make out his features, which were cast in silhouette against the shimmer from the wet streets. She wondered if Detective Feller had begun his assignment of tailing Rook early. But Heat couldn't be sure that the figure had Randall's physique, even though there was something familiar about him.

Maloney?

Heat retreated one step back into the shadows and observed the man. In that light, she couldn't be certain, but he seemed to be still watching her. Nikki picked up her BlackBerry from the coffee table and texted Roach, asking whether they had Maloney under surveillance. Raley and Ochoa immediately group-texted that he hadn't returned to his apartment. Apparently he had slipped his leash. By the time Heat looked up from the screen, the man was gone.

The next morning, Rook was already in the kitchen when Nikki came out from her shower, dressed for work. "You're not fooling me, you know," he said as he leaned across the counter and poured a cup of French roast into the mug beside his. Nikki tensed a little, wondering if he had overheard her call to Feller giving him a heads-up that she and Rook would be leaving separately, and that Rook would probably hail a cab or hitch a Hitch! But then he came around to her beaming a self-satisfied grin. "I pay attention. No uniform today. How good am I?"

"Plus-ten for you, Rook." Heat slipped her Sig onto the waistband of her jeans and gave the holster a security tug.

"What's the matter? Didn't like the way the kids made

fun of you at school yesterday?"

"Oh, please."

"One mobster says you look like you're in the St. Paddy's Parade, and you change everything? I thought you were made of stouter stuff, Ms. Heat. Or is it still Captain Heat? With all the denim and cashmere you have going on there, it's, frankly, fried out a few of my circuits."

"It's a choice I made."

"And you're allowed to just do that? Aren't there regulations about what you folks wear?"

"Sure, but there's room for discretion." She added some Equal to her coffee; he stirred it. "Spending another day doing detective work in full regalia isn't something I'm going to do."

"So it was Fat Tommy's smack talk."

"Fat Tommy can bite my ass."

He gave his eyebrows a Groucho flicker, and bent for a salacious look-see. "And in those jeans, who wouldn't want to?"

"Rook."

"Fat Tommy'd have to take a number. And who'd be first? Me. Doing an Ickey shuffle like the big man himself at the cold cuts counter. 'Whoo! I'm next. I am gonna bite Nikki's ass.'"

Heat laughed so hard she had to set her mug down. And while she caught her breath, the thought surfaced again about calling off the tail. A short-lived waver, as it turned out.

"Listen," he said, "I'm going to have to split off from you today. Don't ask why, OK? I'm not answering."

"Are you shopping for a wedding venue?"

"No." He slapped his forehead with the heel of his hand. "Dang. Got me. I said I wasn't answering." But Rook's impishness faded when he saw her all-business stare.

"You do what you have to do, Rook. And I will do what I have to."

"Ooh. Chilly in here."

"Just giving you fair warning. This cuts two ways. You're holding. I'm digging. Someone put a bullet in a member of the police family. My shrink. And your . . . ?" She left the thought hanging there, giving him ample chance to Mad Lib the blank. But he didn't, so she pulled a go cup from the cabinet and poured her coffee into it.

"You're not staying for breakfast?" he asked.

"I have a breakfast meeting with a business leader from the precinct." She slid on her blazer and gave him a kiss. "Guess I'll see you when I see you."

"I like it better when we do this together."

"Me too," she said. And meant it.

On her way out the door, her BlackBerry chimed with a text. She read it and popped her head back in. "If you're interested, Lon King's partner just came home from a run and found someone inside their apartment."

"Interested," he said, and pulled down another go cup.

The sidewalks were fresh smelling and still damp from the overnight rain as they walked from his building, both working their devices. He was moving his mystery meeting to later; she was calling off her breakfast and getting ready to text Randy Feller about the change of plans.

"Nothing like an April shower to wash that urine-y fragrance away, huh?" he said as he pocketed his cell. But then Rook stopped short. Nikki jerked to a halt beside him. Both stood astonished by what they saw.

Around the corner on Reade, where they had left it parked after dinner, someone had key-etched the paint on Heat's new Malibu and flattened all four tires. She recovered quickly and checked the doors, which were still locked, and found that nothing inside had been disturbed. Heat turned around in a circle, first to see if any other cars had been vandalized (none had been) and second, to see if the perpetrator had hung around to enjoy the impact of his work (nobody took any notice except passers-by).

Heat was mainly interested in one person. And she would personally brace ex-Detective Timothy James Maloney about this later.

"Want me to hitch a Hitch!?" asked Rook.

"Yeah, maybe we should. Or just hail a cab."

"Never mind. Look," he said then whistled and waved both arms. "There's Randall Feller. How fucking lucky is that?"

Heat tried to act surprised as Detective Feller—totally made—responded to the street hail and pulled up beside them in his undercover Taurus. Jameson Rook, the conspiracy theorist's conspiracy theorist, said it must be Kismet—as he called shotgun.

⁎

The only one who seemed to be enjoying the ride was Rook.
Nikki hid under the radar in the backseat, finding it easier
there to mask her tells—to avoid inadvertently revealing by
her expression that it was in fact no coincidence that, with
508 linear miles of road in Manhattan, one of her detectives
had just happened to be happening by the spot where they
had been standing. Feller worked his jaw muscles behind the
wheel, no doubt calculating how long it would take to live
down getting eyeballed on a stakeout by the journalist
everyone knew he had written off as a dilettante showboater.

When Rook asked what had brought Randy to Tribeca,
Nikki jumped in like a rodeo clown. "I'm going to have to
call in the ten-thirty-nine on my vehicle."

"Yeah, and who fucks with a cop's ride?" asked Feller,
continuing the redirect.

Rook, now on their track, speculated. "Maybe he or she
didn't know it was a police car."

"First of all, bro," said Feller, "let me explain something
to you. They call these undercover? But get real. Every
miscreant on the street knows what they are a block away."

"Plus I had my courtesy plaque on the dash," Heat said,
adding, "I think I know who it was." The two up front
listened intently as Heat described her sighting from the
window the night before.

"You should have called it in," said Feller.

"I did. At least I know Roach did right after I texted
them to see if Maloney was buttoned down or not. Before I
went to bed I saw three cruisers from the First Precinct
gridding the neighborhood."

Rook said, "He must have done your car beforehand."

"Or after," countered Feller. "Maloney's a sick fuck, but he's got skills. I heard from the Spliff about how he outplayed you in the park uptown. A guy with a head like that probably saw the blue-and-whites and figured he'd leave his mark, and fuck you."

"The Spliff?" asked Rook.

"Roach," explained the detective with a sneer of condescension.

"Ah . . . a nickname for a nickname." Rook nodded and smiled. But then he twisted around to one side of his headrest to address Nikki. "But why do this to you?"

"I think it's kinda in the diagnosis," she said. "Paranoid personality disorder?"

"But wait a minute. It was my loft he was outside of in the middle of the night. You don't suppose he's got some fixation on me because I took him down, do you?" When Feller cackled, Rook shot back, "That's right, Randall, I took him down. And now, he's put me on his crazy payback list."

"But it was her car."

"Let's all be clear, I'm not sure it was Maloney I saw. And whether it's me or Rook or both of us he wants to hassle, I say, bring it on."

Roosevelt Island takes some work to get to, which is part of its appeal. The needle of land in the middle of the East River has one F train subway stop and an aerial tramway hoisting passengers across the river from 2nd Avenue. But if you want to arrive by car, the only option is to drive over the bridge from 36th Avenue out of Long Island City. Detective Feller's Taurus came off that span and made the turn north on Main for the quarter-mile ride to Blackwell's Landing, a luxury apartment tower on the island's north end.

They found a spot beside the pair of patrol cars in the parking lot and walked a flagstone path lined by daffodils and tulips toward the lobby. "Definitely a two-income building," said Feller, taking in the neatly groomed lawn, the blossoming trees, and the whisper-quiet grounds that surrounded the high-rise of tinted glass and modular concrete panels. Like most of the residential complexes on the island, this one felt like a suburban college campus or an Olympic Village.

The concierge regarded their badges gravely as they entered and escorted them across parchment-colored terrazzo tiles to the elevator, saying only "Tenth floor," in a tone of profound sadness that could only have come from hospitality training.

When Heat and Rook stepped into the elevator, Feller palmed the door open from the outside. "Listen, you got it from here, right?" He punctuated the remark with a glance toward Heat and added, "I got a thing I gotta do."

"Yes, the thing," she said. "Go to. We'll find our own way back to the precinct."

"Oh, but I'm not going to the precinct after," said Rook. "I, too, have a thing." The buzzer started to protest their holding the door open. "Never mind, I'll work it out. See you, Randy."

As the elevator door closed, they heard Feller mutter, "Maybe. Maybe not."

A sergeant from the Public Safety Department let them into the apartment. Because the city leased Roosevelt Island to the State of New York, the crime scene fell under its jurisdiction, and Heat was there as a guest. After she had badged and logged in, a Roosevelt Island Public Safety Department detective led her and Rook from the foyer to the living room, where they found Sampson Stallings hunched forward on the couch with his back to them. The room was a sunlit and airy showplace with a high vaulted ceiling and broad windows that looked onto a breathtaking panorama of the river and the Upper East Side to the west and the landmark Octagon to the north. Both views were lost on Lon King's partner, whose head hung in grief.

Stallings rose to shake their hands and invited them to sit. Heat, who had her own connection to violent loss, expressed her condolences, which only caused his bloodshot eyes to glisten anew. He smiled bravely, but his lips, framed by the tight salt-and-pepper curls of his goatee, quivered, betraying the miserable imprint of heartbreak.

Rook stayed out of the conversation, letting Nikki lead Stallings to share reminiscences about his life partner of a decade. Business would come soon enough; she understood that every investigation had a heart, too. "Thank you for listening to me go on," he said, plucking a tissue from the box on the coffee table, which caused Nikki to observe that Lon King had set up his living room a lot like his practice, right down to the Kleenex placement. "It feels better to talk."

"A page out of the Lon King playbook."

He gave her an appraisal. "You knew him?"

She smiled. "Probably more accurate to say he knew me. Dr. King didn't give up a lot."

"You should have tried living with him." Stallings let out a laugh, then retreated from it as if in shame.

"So he never mentioned me?" When he shook his head no, she said, "What about other patients, clients . . ."

"No, as I mentioned to the detective yesterday . . ."

"Detective Aguinaldo?"

"Yes, nice woman. As I told her, Lonnie was very discreet. Oh, once in a while, he'd share a story—a doozer, he'd call them, usually funny—but never a name. It wouldn't have meant anything to me, anyway."

"He never mentioned them, even if they threatened him?"

"Lon kept it all locked down, you understand?" He made a tamping gesture with his slender artist's hands.

Rook joined in with a question that seemed to Heat more than just something out of left field. "Sampson, did Lon ever mention someone offering him money to talk about his clients or cases?"

"Well, he had some serious debt issues, we know that. From his gambling. But he would never, never cross an ethical line and sell out his patients."

"I believe that," said Rook. "But my question is, did anyone ever try to induce him to?"

"Not that I know of."

Rook nodded to Heat, signaling that was all he wanted to

ask. His question gave her pause. Why the hell was he sniffing around a potential bribe? Was this related to some critical piece of information he was holding back on? Her anger started to rekindle, but she set it aside. Something to deal with later. Nikki brought the conversation back to her own agenda." Do you mind going over what happened this morning again?" Stallings shook his head no and sipped some water from a CamelBak bottle. Heat gestured to the RIPSD man sitting on the barstool near the kitchen. "I know you already told the detective."

"That's fine, I understand."

"The report I got was that you confronted an intruder here?"

Stallings nodded and gestured to the running clothes he was wearing. "This morning, I got up and laced up my New Balances." As if to excuse this self-indulgence, he explained, "We all handle our shit differently. When he got stressed, Lonnie paddled. Me, I pound pavement. He used to call it my cleansing run. So I went out, did my route—well, as much as I could." His lip trembled again. He diverted their attention by gesturing across the river. "I do a circuit from here to the tram to warm up, then along the East River Walk over there just past Gracie Mansion, and back. It all came crashing down on me on the tram and I couldn't stop weeping. I got off and hopped on the next one back. When I went to put my key in the door, it was ajar." He measured a quarter inch with his thumb and forefinger. "I thought, maybe I got distracted from the trauma and all, and got careless, but when I pushed the door, some guy's right there.

He trips me and shoves me to the floor and books it down the stairwell. I'm pretty fast, but by the time I got it together to chase him, he was gone."

"And nothing's missing?" she asked.

Stallings shook his head no. "Before you arrived, the detective and I did a walk-through of the whole place. I don't see anything disturbed, and the burglar didn't have anything in his hands."

Nikki asked him for the beginning and end times of his run and, after she made a note, asked, "You called it your circuit. Was it your routine every day?"

"Yeah, five days a week. I'm sort of compulsive about it."

"So, it's possible," said Rook, "that someone was watching this place to get to know your routines and thought he had time to get in and out. But you surprised him by cutting it short, and he didn't have time to get what he wanted."

"Or he got it, and it was in his pocket," added Heat. "Do you know where Lon kept his flash drives?"

Stallings escorted them to the second bedroom, which was King's office on one side and Stallings's painting studio on the other, and which smelled pleasantly of resin and oil paint. At the desk, he reached to open a wooden Levenger box, but Heat stopped him and gestured to the RIPSD detective, who was already wearing gloves. He lifted the lid. The box was empty.

"He kept a dozen or more thumb drives in there," Stallings said. He surveyed the desktop. "His iPad Mini's missing, too, now that I really look."

"Our lab will dust soon as they get here," said

the detective. "And ask Mr. Stallings to write up a methodical inventory."

Stallings drew his brow low, trying to digest the concept. "Why would someone be watching this place, our routine, coming in here? He was the man who killed Lonnie, wasn't he?"

"Mr. Stallings, is this the man who was in your apartment?" Heat brought up Maloney's pic on her BlackBerry and held it out for him to study. The RIPSD detective moved closer to shoulder-surf it.

"No, definitely not him." But when Nikki started to take her phone away, he said, "Wait, wait." He examined the picture again and handed it back. "I have seen him, though. Lonnie and I went out for duck last week at Le Colonial, you know, on East Fifty-Seventh? We had a window table, and I saw a guy walk by—this one—and start staring in from the sidewalk. When Lon spotted him, the guy just made that double finger point thing to his eyes, and left."

"Did Lon say who he was?" asked Heat.

"All he said was 'ex-client.'" He snickered. "Paging Dr. Taciturn. I used to tell him that if he was any more chill, I could use his face as a canvas."

"His name's Timothy Maloney. Did Dr. King ever mention that name?"

"Not that I recall."

Heat turned to the Roosevelt Island detective. "He's ex-NYPD. I'll email you this pic and his sheet. Meanwhile, we should get out a description of the intruder."

"Going to need some NYPD co-op, Captain, if you don't

mind. The building's cams are down for upgrade and we don't have a sketch artist."

Nikki turned to Sampson Stallings. "Actually, I believe you do."

Smiling his first true smile in a day, one fueled by purpose, the renowned portraitist sat at his drafting table, opened his Strathmore pad to a fresh page, and began work on what could be his greatest work of all: the one that could lead to his partner's killer.

Sampson Stallings worked with silent intensity in flowing, sure-handed strokes. Heat had to fight the same urge she battled whenever she walked by the row of souvenir street caricaturists on the east side of Central Park; the overwhelming desire to stand behind him and stare over his shoulder. But she respected the artist's solitude and, in mere minutes, he had finished. Stallings carefully tore the sheet off his gummed pad and presented it to the detectives. As Rook came up behind Heat for a glimpse, both reacted immediately. "It's him," said Rook. "The dude we surprised in the basement on York Avenue."

When they got back to the lobby, Rook admired on his iPhone the photo Heat had just broadcast of Stallings's intruder sketch. "You know," he said, "if it weren't for the grief part, I would have asked Sampson to give me the original. With a signature, of course."

"Nice. The day after his partner is murdered."

"I did respect the grief part, remember? I distinctly said

that. Why are you being so crispy with me?"

"Because you're being so—obstructive."

"How? What did I do?"

Nikki clenched her teeth, then thought, No, out with it. "Your question about King getting offered a bribe."

"That was a perfectly proper question."

"You're not working with me, Rook. No, worse. You're working against me. If you know something, share. What's more important, your article or finding the killer?"

As he pondered his answer—hesitating in a way that further pissed Nikki off—his phone chimed. He checked the screen and grinned. "My Hitch! is arriving." They turned toward the street, where a giant plastic thumb could be seen approaching, floating above the trellises in the community garden. "I push a button, and a car comes. This could be what the Internet is all about."

"So you're not going to help? Not going to answer?"

"Nikki, this is all going to work out for both of us, you watch. Now, if you'll excuse me, I have some legwork to do." And then he was gone. Without a hitch.

"What do we know, Miguel?" called Heat from the doorway as she strode into the homicide bull pen. Detective Ochoa snagged a deli coffee from his desk and met with her at the Murder Board, which she scanned for fresh ink.

"All right, as you can see we have the sketch you just got from Sampson Stallings out to all units, plus media."

"I knew that when I sent it out," she said, making a

mental note not to send her anger at Rook sideways to others. Especially not Ochoa. A little more softly, she asked if he agreed that this was the runner they had encountered the day before charging out of Lon King's medical tower.

"Most definitely. Oh, and since you wanted to hear something you didn't know . . ." His cheeks dimpled—obviously he was slightly amused by his little bit of pushback—then he continued, "An eyewit on York Ave gave us a partial plate on that MKZ he fled in. Crunched it down and traced it to a gypsy cab reported stolen from East Harlem yesterday morning. Traffic Division spotted it, abandoned, blocking a hydrant down in the Alphabets."

"Any chance for prints?"

"Forensics is dusting now. It's going to take some time to isolate all the prints. They said it was like *Hands on a Hardbody* down there."

"Well, we now have a face to go with those hands. Maybe we'll get a positive. What about Tim Maloney?"

"Still no handle on him, Cap," he said, addressing her by rank for the first time. "We've still got units watching his place, but no activity. I even sent a bogus mail carrier to knock on the door. Nothing. He could be in there, just trying to jerk our chains, but we can't go for a warrant."

"No, not without probable," she agreed. "What's your deployment?"

"We're down an asset, as you know, with my most able street detective on Rook's tail. That means spreading things a little thinner." He pointed to Rhymer's initials in a circle beside the Spuyten Duyvil–Harlem River notation on the board. "Raley sent Opie out with Harbor Unit to troll for eyewits or any sightings of King's kayak, night of his murder."

Heat read something dark in Ochoa's expression. "Something wrong, Detective?"

"It's nothing. Just a little disagreement with my pard."

"For putting Rhymer on river watch?"

"For not talking to me first. Sean made the assignment before I got in, and didn't consult. I get here, Opie's gone, and my so-called squad co-leader has also assigned Detective Aguinaldo to run license plate checks from the Roosevelt Island Bridge cam." Ochoa shook his head mildly to himself and said, "Glad you asked?"

Nikki felt the heft of one more rock getting piled on her shoulders to go with the burden of the others: problems with Rook; pressure from the chief of detectives; hassles with IA; a nut-job ex-cop who might have killed her shrink and seemed to have slipped off the grid; and now a turf battle between her squad co-leaders. Day two was shaping up to be an extension of day one. "Is this an issue I need to step in on?"

He shook his head no. "We'll work it out. You just caught me while it was still up my ass. Pretend you didn't hear it."

"Where's your partner now?"

"In his kingly realm." The detective tilted his head to indicate the closet Raley used to screen video. "He's scrubbing this morning's F train and tram cams for the dude in the sketch."

"How about you? Free for a detail?" Heat couldn't let go of Rook's question to Stallings about whether Lon King had been offered a bribe in exchange for information about a patient. As irritating and undisciplined as he could be,

Jameson Rook was a talented investigative journalist with two Pulitzers, both well earned. Whatever story he was working on, Nikki's own investigative antenna told her that his question had been a giveaway, and that the angle he was working involved money and corruption. So, if Rook was taking advantage of information he was gathering from her case, turnabout would be fair play. "Miguel, I'd like you to run a complete financial check on Lon King."

He nodded with some uncertainty, but opened his notebook. "Sure. What am I looking for?"

"What else, the Odd Sock. Something out of pattern. Especially big infusions of cash. He would, I imagine, be running low because of his gambling losses. A spike is going to tell us something." And because nothing and no one could be ruled out, she added, "And do a check of his partner, Sampson Stallings. He's an artist, so his income pattern may be more erratic, but give it an X-ray, anyhow."

Randall Feller checked in later on from the field, and he wasn't happy. "Captain Heat, I'll let you guess where my tail-and-surveil of Jameson Rook has taken me."

"I don't know, Detective. Has he bought you a Mister Softee cone because he made you again?" Nikki played it as a joke, but only as cover for her genuine concern and curiosity about what Rook was up to.

"No, I have not been detected. My subject is too focused on his mission."

"Out with it. Where is he?"

"On Warren Street down near City Hall." While Nikki mentally street-viewed the area, trying to conjure up a notion of what that mission could be, Feller filled in the blank. "He's in a pen store."

"You're kidding."

"I am outside the shop window now."

"The Fountain Pen Hospital," she said. Heat could picture Feller's view because she had been there so many times before to Rook's Mecca for vintage and collectible fountain pens. "He's at the repair counter, right?"

"You don't need me. You have, what, psychic powers?"

"I wish. Last week he was cleaning his limited edition Hemingway Montblanc, and it rolled off his desk and landed point first on the floor. Rook is dropping off his prize pen to get a new nib."

After a long pause filled with the *doop-doop-doop* of a truck backing up, the detective said, "I don't wanna second-guess, but is this really the best use of my time while we're working a homicide? I mean, your boyfriend's getting—a nib replacement?"

"First of all, you are second-guessing. And also, he's not my boyfriend, he's my fiancé. Stay on him."

"You got it." He didn't sound thrilled.

"And Randy? Keep out of that window. Wouldn't want you getting made or anything."

About an hour later, a call from downtown pulled Heat out of a visit to the Burglary Squad room, where the new captain was getting her update on their activity. She strode into her office and waited with a gnawing in her gut for the operator to transfer. As it finally rang, Nikki rested her hand on the receiver and cycled through the ramifications of blowing off the senior administrative aide to the NYPD's deputy commissioner for legal matters. It had been he who had championed her through the system to become a captain and precinct commander. Maybe he was just phoning to wish her well now that the placement was official. One ring before the voicemail dump, she lifted the horn. "Captain Heat."

"I understand you're off to a shaky start," said Zach Hamner. No Hello. No Good afternoon. No Did I interrupt anything? None of that. Zach, the Hammer, was living up to his blunt-instrument nickname from his opening volley. Heat imagined sex with him must be very much about getting it done. She couldn't believe she was wondering about sex with what amounted to a reptile in a suit.

"Thank you, Zachary. Nothing more bolstering than a call from you."

"If you want touchy-feely, try Media Relations. Here in Legal it's all tough love." She could picture him at his desk down at One PP, smugly enjoying his self-defined status as department ball-buster—the guy they send when they just want it done. Never destined to be the front man, Hamner would always be Merlin, one of those pasty slicks with passive faces and thick briefcases who lean forward to whisper strategic answers in the ears of the top-liners. "I'm getting some negative reports and, since I feel a personal responsibility for getting you appointed, I'm doing a little intervention."

"Lucky me."

"Where do I start? Dissing Internal Affairs? No, how about embarrassing the chief of detectives?"

Nikki realized that she should have let the call go to voicemail. "The chief and I hashed that out yesterday, Zach. Old news."

"More like a close call. Think. Be proactive. On this level accountability goes up the chain and information is the currency."

"You should stitch that on a sampler."

"Heat. Do I sound like I'm looking for entertainment?" Heat rocked back in her executive chair while he delivered his department-line reprimand for mixing it up with Detective Lovell at IA. It was useless to argue, so Nikki signed papers while he rambled on. "And what were you doing being seen in uniform, consorting with a known mobster?"

She stopped signing and stood up. "I was not consorting, I was interviewing him as a potential suspect in the murder of Lon King."

"You couldn't haul his ass into the box? You were seen going into his illegal gambling parlor in broad daylight."

"That's where he was."

"Heat, you're a precinct commander. PCs can't mingle with mobsters. It's not PC." As with so many administrators and gray bureaucrats, The Hammer had no idea what police work was all about. She thought of giving him a lecture about that when Ochoa showed up in her doorway with an urgent look.

"Zach, listen, something just came up on a case, I've got to go." And, having a second thought, she added, "Thanks for the good advice," just before she hung up.

"We have a new vic," said Detective Ochoa.

Nikki came around the desk, sliding an arm through a sleeve of her blazer. "Where?"

"Staten Island."

That slowed Heat down. "Not our precinct, why's it our victim?"

"Because Feller called it in."

Heat's face lost some color as she processed the connection, not liking anywhere it was leading. "Feller . . . ?"

"He was tailing Rook. Rook found the body."

SIX

Heat let Ochoa drive, which bought her valuable time to pound out administrative emails and work her phone during the otherwise dead hour getting from Manhattan to Staten. "Two-minute warning," said the detective as he steered off the SIE into the bleak terrain surrounding the Goethals Bridge. Nikki set aside her multitasking, surveyed the patchwork of scrubby marshland and the hard-core industrial zone lining the banks of the Elizabeth River, and wondered what the hell Rook had been doing out there.

If Staten Island was a bedroom community, this was its mud porch. On her right sprawled a massive containerized cargo depot. To her left, the corroded cylinders of a gas tank farm rose at the edge of tidal wetlands marked by acres of cord grass and cattails, hardy survivors of the chemical age. Across the river, a refinery plus even more and even bigger tank farms girdled the New Jersey Turnpike. "If you lived here, you'd be home now," Heat said.

True to Ochoa's estimate, about two minutes later the Roach Coach drew up to the gate of an isolated, cyclone-fenced industrial site between the swamp and a graveyard for old school buses. Back in the 1920s this property had been an airstrip. Flat, and with plenty of land remote from residences, Edda Field became a favorite of private pilots and hobbyists until it closed in World War Two, when civilian flying over the East Coast was forbidden. By the time the ban was lifted, newer airfields, closer to town, with blacktop runways instead of gravel and turf, had opened. Within a few years, the strip was defunct. It was eventually sold to a movie company that used its giant hangar to shoot noir detective films, until the studio head pulled his own caper and left for Rio de Janeiro with the company profits and a stuntman. Then the real estate sat idle, a magnet for weeds, illegal dumping, and taxes until the mid-nineties, when the vast acreage and the enormous hangar caught the notice of a forensic consulting company that purchased the land and developed the site as its vehicle safety proving ground.

Once they had passed the guard shack, Ochoa was able to cut across painted rows of empty parking spaces, making a beeline for the half-dozen NYPD blue-and-whites and plain wraps rimming the hangar. Detective Feller stood inside the semicircle of police cars, clowning with a homicide team from the 121st Precinct. He glimpsed Nikki when she got out of the Roach Coach, quickly broke away from the group, and crossed to meet her, adopting a more sober tone with every stride closer to his captain.

"Help me, Detective," she said when the gap between them closed enough so that only he could hear. "I want to learn what's funny about a dead body. Day I'm having, I could use a laugh."

Sheepish, Feller tried to minimize his lack of decorum at

a murder scene, something Heat had cautioned him about so many times in the past. "This? This was nothing. Just fostering relations with the homeys, you know, since we're visiting their turf."

"I see. Professional interaction," she said. But he heard her don't-bullshit-me subtext loud and clear. Point made, she let the matter drop, especially since Ochoa was joining them. "What are we looking at?"

"Body's in the hangar." He indicated the triple-wide garage door cut into the side of the hulking gray warehouse. The van from Staten Island's Medical Examiner's office sat to the side right underneath the Forenetics, LLC company logo.

"Now there's a picture," said Ochoa. "Definitely not one you want on your corporate homepage."

"What about Rook? Where's he?" Nikki asked, feeling one part concern, one part annoyance, not necessarily in that order.

Feller tilted his head toward his Taurus twenty yards away, where Rook sat in the open passenger door with his head between his knees. "As you might have guessed, he found the vic. And even I won't fault him for ralphing. One of the ME assistants almost barked up his bran muffin when he went in there."

Rook tilted his gaze upward when he heard Nikki approaching, then let his head sag into his palms.

"You all right?" she asked, resting a hand on one of his shoulders to give it a gentle squeeze.

"Yup." But when he got to his feet to prove it, his face blanched and his eyes drifted under half-closed lids. "I'm good. Really."

Not entirely proud of herself for doing so, Nikki decided to exploit Rook's moment of vulnerability. "So tell me how it came down. What were you doing all the way out here at this place? Foren"—she looked up at the sign—"Forenetics?"

But even with his defenses down, Rook's instincts as an investigative journalist kept a toehold. "Nothing out of the ordinary, really. I sort of had an appointment." He took the bottle of water Ochoa held out and cracked it open.

"With the victim?"

He took a sip and nodded. When Rook saw that he wasn't going to get away with a mere head bobble, he allowed, "Yes. I had an appointment. With Fred Lobbrecht. He works here." He blanched again at an inner vision and corrected himself. "*Worked* here."

Unsure now whether Rook was obfuscating or traumatized, Nikki cut bait. She told him they would continue the conversation later. She logged into the crime scene and led her group past the empty coroner's van and inside the building.

Heat had never before set foot inside a vehicle crash test facility, but the scene felt immediately familiar from so many all the *20/20* investigations and car commercials she had seen, as well as all the ghastly videos they had forced her class to watch back in Drivers Ed. To her right, inside the cavernous half acre of the impact laboratory, a two-tiered modular structure sat against one wall. The first floor of the glass booth appeared to be a command center full of electronic gear set into consoles and equipment bays. Up top, accessible from a steel staircase, a line of camera tripod mounts formed a picket fence along the outwardly slanting window of an observation deck. Both booths were empty of life, as was the rest of the facility, except for emergency responders.

Embedded in the concrete floor in front of the control room stood the firing mechanism for the vehicle propulsion system used to catapult cars and trucks the same way fighter jets got launched from aircraft carriers. At the fire command, compressed nitrogen would blast the test vehicle the length of the hangar at up to seventy-five miles per hour. To enhance the video image, the floor was painted snow white and punctuated at strategic intervals by yellow-and-black checked stripes and reference markers. To Heat's left, at the far end of the track, almost the length of a football field away, a small Japanese import had smacked into three hundred thousand pounds of concrete and steel at full speed. Even from a hundred yards away, she could see where the rusty cloud of brain matter and now-dried blood had spattered the impact barrier like a Jackson Pollock. No wonder Rook was so shaken.

"Anybody bring a spatula?" asked the medical examiner, popping up from his kneeling position at the front end of the squashed car. Nikki had not seen Stu Linkletter—or heard his grating cackle—in the four years since he had transferred from the Manhattan ME's office. She counted each year as a blessing.

Detectives Ochoa and Feller clearly shared the same sentiment and muttered the "Fu-u-u-uck" that Heat was only thinking when the ass-hat in the contamination suit popped up from his crouching position like a gopher.

"By the way, anybody up for lunch after? I don't know why, but I'm thinking pizza."

And with that, Nikki forgot all about her inside voice. "Fu-u-u-uck."

"Oh, I hear ya," said Linkletter, oblivious. "It's not like a Road Runner cartoon, is it? You don't go straight through the wall leaving a perfect cutout of your body. Not even at seventy-five miles per hour." He turned to the splotched wall, then back to his colleagues with a grin. "Am I right?"

"How about just giving us a briefing," said Heat.

"What's the fun in that?"

Even Randall Feller, Mr. Gallows Humor, had had enough. "Linkletter. Save it for open-mic night at Governor's."

It took the sober glowers of three cops and one investigative journalist to get Linkletter down to business. "Victim was not wearing a restraint and became a projectile, ejected from the front driver's seat of the vehicle upon high-speed impact with the fortified concrete barrier. Preliminary cause of death: blunt impact injuries of head and torso. Temp, lividity, plus the degree of congealing and dryness at the edge of the blood spatters all lead me to estimate the postmortem interval at twenty-four to twenty-eight hours."

"This happened yesterday?" asked Heat.

"Twenty-four to twenty-eight hours. Am I not being clear?"

"Do you have positive ID of the victim?" asked Ochoa.

"We are unable to confirm anything other than race and gender." The ME indicated the bloodstained gnarl of clothing and flesh fused with the crumpled hood. "Lower body is still largely discernable, therefore, male."

"What about driver's license, wallet?" asked Heat.

He let out a petulant sigh. "First you reject my pleasantries and press for my report. Now you interrupt by pestering me with questions." A photographer from his team flashed a picture of the victim. Linkletter whirled to face him. "Mr. Roe. Cease photography."

"Proceed," Heat said, politely, but vowing never to work a death scene in his jurisdiction again.

"In his wallet, a New York State driver's license for: Lobbrecht, Frederick van; male; cauc; brown over hazel; age thirty-eight. DL photo and name matches the Forenetics laminated ID retrieved from the victim's tissue, identifying him as a 'crash reconstruction expert.' Am I the only one thinking, 'No shit?'" Linkletter cackled his strangled-goose laugh again, but when he saw the stone faces of Easter Island staring back at him, the medical examiner continued, "Given the catastrophic trauma to the head and upper body, positive ID will involve fingerprints. Failing any record of those, we'll go for dental records or a chest X-ray, assuming he has one in his medical files. Of course there's DNA, but you're looking at time and taxpayer moola."

"I'm good for now," said Heat, eager to put space between herself and the annoying ME.

"Oh, sure," he called out as they walked away, "now that you're a captain, you're too big to slum with the grunts in the field."

"E-mail me your report," was all she said in reply and

without even turning to him as she moved off.

"What an asshole," said Feller.

Ochoa added, "Dealing with dead people's the perfect job for that guy."

"Not even," said Rook. "No corpse-side manner."

"You're back." Heat smiled warmly and gave his forearm a squeeze. "Welcome."

"I told you I was fine."

"Yeah, and you looked it," said Ochoa. "Get any on your shoes?"

Heat and her crew met at the other end of the hangar with their counterparts from the One-Two-One to piece together what they could about the crash. "A couple of things I don't understand already," she said, kicking things off, "besides wondering how something like this could happen in the first place. First, how could it go unnoticed for a full day?" Nikki scanned the cavernous space and added, "I mean, where is everyone?"

One of the Staten Island detectives said, "This facility is sort of like a football stadium. Nobody's really around unless there's a game."

"Kind of an expensive piece of property to sit idle," said Ochoa.

"Oh, they make their money, believe me," said the SI cop's partner. "Car makers and insurance companies pay big for these tests. And it's plenty busy here when they do one, about forty of them a year. We come by sometimes to watch—I mean, wouldn't you? Lot's empty now, but on test days, you can hardly find a parking place."

"I called the Forenetics company headquarters in Stamford while I was waiting for you and Ochoa to get out here," said Feller. "Their president told me they were scheduled for an impact test on that import tomorrow. Lobbrecht was the project manager and came in yesterday on a scheduled rig of the sensor cables in the vehicle for Rickles."

"Rickles?"

Feller pointed to the corner beside the catapult where a crash test dummy stood strapped into a dolly. "Irony. Rickles is the dummy."

"It's all part of the timeline they follow. Sort of like a NASA launch."

Heat said, "They have a security guard in the shack at the gate. Didn't he think it was odd that Mr. Lobbrecht came in but didn't leave?"

The lead detective from the 121st shook his head. "The guard says just the opposite. That Lobbrecht only started coming here six weeks ago, but, in that time, was a 24/7 guy whenever there was a launch. Worked all hours, brought his lunch, always pulled all-nighters. It was not out of pattern for him to show up and not clock out for two days. And this place is soundproofed, so they'd have no clue out there across the lot, especially with a radio or TV going."

They all looked downrange at the crash site, where Linkletter and his team were gathering what teeth they could find. "So what do you think, misfire?" asked Ochoa. "Or this guy Lobbrecht pushed the wrong button or plugged the wrong cable in the wrong socket while he was setting up?"

"Could be," said Feller. "Systems fail."

But Nikki had her attention on Rook and could see that he wasn't buying an accident. Neither was she. There are coincidences in life, but in Heat's experience, very few in murder investigations. His connection to two corpses in as many days flashed some mighty big strobes in her brain. "Are you ready to tell me what you were out here to see Lobbrecht about?"

Rook turned slowly away from staring at the crash, but he couldn't meet her eyes. He stared at the bright-white floor and said nothing. Nikki considered a moment. But it didn't take her long to make a decision, painful as it was. In truth, she had made it already the evening before when she ordered the tail on him. This would just be the extension of that call. "Detective Feller?" she said. "I want you to drive Mr. Rook back to the Twentieth."

"Can't I ride with you?" Rook asked. "Tell you what. I won't even call shotgun."

But Heat wasn't smiling. "You're not riding back to the precinct. You are being taken there." She turned to Feller. "He travels in the back. And when you get there, put him in Interrogation One." Nikki gave Rook her all-business glare and walked out with Ochoa, leaving her fiancé behind.

Lon King, PhD
Counseling Transcript
Session of Feb. 26/13 with Heat, N., Det. Grade-1,
   NYPD

NH: Thanks for fitting me in again. I'm sorry about last time.

LK: I could see you were working through something. Are you ready to talk about it now?

NH: [Long pause] There's not really much to talk about. [Longer pause] So you're going to make me talk about it, aren't you?

LK: Would it help if I brought us back to where we left off? In my notes I see that you were beginning to talk about the difficulty of surrendering your mother's apartment—I mean, your apartment—and moving into Rook's. Am I right?

NH: Is that stupid? I mean, we are getting married.

LK: The things we feel are never stupid. They are simply what we feel. What we try to help with here is to find out why you are feeling them. If your feelings are holding you back from life or keeping you upset, then it's constructive to explore them. Do you want to explore this?

NH: Yes, yes, I do. I just don't know where to start.

LK: Why don't we start with these feelings?

NH: Oh, God . . .

LK: What is this bringing up in you? Can you name it?

NH: I know it's logical that I should just move into Rook's loft. Maybe I should just do that.

LK: Nikki, you're going back to logic, your safe ground. Let's get you back to your emotions and explore them.

NH: I'm just trying to picture moving day. Looking back

inside before I close the door on that empty place where I've lived so much of my life.

LK: And where you mother was murdered.

NH: Yes. And where my mom was murdered.

LK: There are many reasons we form attachments to places or things. Is that why that place is so significant? Your loss? And if so, why do you feel you need to hold on to loss?

NH: I feel like I would be . . . I don't know. I just feel like I would be . . . quitting.

LK: Help me understand 'quitting.' You found her murderer. You honored her memory. You did your job. She would be proud, don't you think?

NH: [Nods]

LK: And yet you still feel conflicted.

NH: [No response; long pause]

LK: Sometimes an attachment isn't what it appears to be.

NH: I feel like I know what it is.

LK: Well, maybe there's more to this.

NH: Oh, I am completely committed to Rook.

LK: Interesting.

NH: What?

LK: I didn't mention Rook.

Heat felt the familiar tug on her eardrums as the air seal broke when she pushed open the door of the sound lock that separated the Observation Room and Interrogation One. Completely foreign to her, however, was to see Jameson

Rook waiting for her in the interviewee's seat, elbows on the metal tabletop, anticipating his promised third degree. She dropped a blank notepad and a stick pen at her place and sat down across from him at her customary spot for examining suspects, conspirators, and persons of interest. He kicked things off, but not with any information, only to state the obvious. "This is nutty."

"You think?"

"Usually, when we're sitting across a table, there's far less fluorescent lighting and usually a better class of beverage." He knuckle-tapped the water bottle before him, making the water inside ripple.

"We are in here because this is not a game, Rook, and I chose a more formal setting to make sure that you know that."

"Oh, trust me, I know it," he said. "How could I miss it? Hell, my fiancée had me tailed by an undercover detective. By the way, how cool is that? I'm definitely going to have to work that into the toast at our wedding reception. By the way, speaking of: I talked to my buddy Alton Brown of the Food Network. For the event, he is sending me his secret recipe for Jameson Irish Whiskey Punch. He says it follows the classical paradigm of one of sour, two of sweet, three of strong, four of weak. Which I think also describes the Knicks this season."

"Rook, will you stop? Just. Fucking. Stop." While Nikki watched his face grow more sober as he left off his posturing, she chastised herself. On her walk down the hall to I One, her self-talk had been all about not letting this turn emotional; about not buying in. About using this setting as a wake-up call to get him to see what was going on. To give him an opportunity to say, This is real. I need to lay off with the high-and-mighty stance. And here, thirty seconds into the interview, she had risen to the emotional bait and even cursed aloud for the second time that day. Nikki vowed to get it together and to stay up on the moral high ground. If there was any hope of getting Rook to open up and not damage her relationship with him, she had to be the grown-up.

"Can I have a snack?" he said.

"No." She continued in a more measured, even tone. "Rook. Let's put a Tweet-size summary on what we're staring at here: In a twenty-four-hour period, we have discovered one homicide victim and one highly suspicious death with one common denominator. You."

"Should I ask for an attorney?" He chuckled, then dropped it when he saw the pair of lasers she leveled at him.

"Let's be clear," she said. "At this point nobody assumes you had anything to do with these deaths. But let's walk it through. Yesterday morning we find a body with a bullet hole in his forehead. And it's my shrink. Who works for the police department. You say nothing. We visit the practice of the victim and you're there all through our investigation. You say nothing. You show up on video surveillance as having recently been to that very place—the practice of my shrink, the gunshot victim. You said nothing. Today, we track you to the auto safety proving ground all the way out in Staten Island. There, we come upon the suspicious death of the person you had an appointment with. You said nothing. Two deaths in two days. Rook, it's time for you to say something."

He paused to reflect, then shrugged. "Do I need to repeat myself? I am a working journalist, an investigative reporter. Yes, I am working on a story. And yes, I have been acquainted with both victims. But, Nikki, don't you hold things back when you're working a case? Well, I am working a story. I still don't have all the pieces of the puzzle put together yet. It's still a jigsaw scattered all over the rec room. I've seen bits and shapes, but they haven't taken form yet. I need to continue my investigation—my way—and to do that, I need to be independent."

"How can you say you need to be independent when you're benefitting from all the information my squad and I are digging up? And you are sharing nothing."

"Well, that's a little harsh. I did lead you to the second victim. Wasn't that helpful?"

"No, that wasn't helpful!" she shouted in the voice she had promised herself she wouldn't raise. "All it gave me was another body. And less to go on, not more."

"Hey, know what I just thought of? What if I became a private detective? Jameson Rook, PI." Then he dismissed the notion with a "Nah" and rose to go. "Well, keep me posted if you start to make more progress. And if anything lights up on my end—that I can share—I'll be sure to let you know."

"Sit down." Heat let him settle back in his seat, then broke the silence. "I think you had better get a lawyer."

"Why? A minute ago you said you were ruling me out as a suspect."

And then the penny dropped for her. Nikki Heat had found her point of leverage. Something that would really go to the heart of Jameson Rook, two-time Pulitzer Prize–winning investigative reporter. "Maybe I'm not so sure of that now."

He laughed. "Nikki, come on. Let's not do theater here. What are you going to pull? Threaten me with the Zoo Lock-up?" Rook asked, referring to her technique of scaring naive and newbie interrogation suspects inexperienced with the criminal justice system into thinking that, if they didn't cooperate, they would be locked into some subterranean Devil's Island cage with society's most violent, barbaric, and unclean criminals.

"Oh, I know the Zoo Lock-up wouldn't bother you, Rook. In fact, you'd probably find it very colorful, make a lot of friends . . . perhaps even develop new articles to write for your magazine." Heat cocked an eyebrow and smiled at him. "No, I think I would give you your own cell. A very quiet place. Far from others. Far from conversation. Far from your cell phone. Far from the Internet. Far from your ability to get out and interview subjects." She could see his eyes widen.

"You wouldn't."

She smiled again. "Let me ask you a question. How's your investigative report going to proceed when I hold you off the street for seventy-two hours, isolated from what's going on, sequestered from information?"

She could see his wheels turning. It looked like she had him. But then he said, "That's a nice bluff."

"You willing to try me?"

"My lawyer would spring me."

"If he could find you. You like to play games? I'll play Hide the Client. It's been done. The New York jail system is one massive bureaucracy."

They held a mini stare-down. Before either could blink, Detective Raley pulled the door open and stood half in the sound lock. He wore his excited face and gave Heat a beckoning nod. When she joined him, he spoke in a low tone. "Thought you'd want to know right away. Got a hit on the gait analysis we did on that dude on security video at Lon King's medical building."

Behind her, Heat could hear a chair scrape the floor tile. When she flashed a quick glance to the magic mirror she caught Rook leaning over the table, straining to hear what they were saying. Not only, it seemed, was Raley her King of All Surveillance Media but his timing couldn't have been better if his interruption had been planned. "Who's our dude?" she said, then she made an obvious turn to shoulder-check Rook. "Wait. Let's step out so we can have some privacy."

Inside the Ob room, Raley showed Nikki the prison mug shot of the man matching the result of the gait analysis. Her first thought, a disappointing one, was that Joseph Barsotti was not the same man who had broken into Lon King's and Sampson Stallings's apartment that morning. But at least she had a name for one of the two unnameds circling this case. "Is this high-confidence?" she asked.

"Very. They had him banked in numerous surveillance videos—both RICO and NYPD Organized Crime Unit—

walking the walk at meet-ups in Howard Beach, Belmont Park racetrack, even at a mob funeral. He pinged multiple matches for the swing phase of his stride and a telltale . . . let me get this right . . ." Sean paused to look at his notes. "Here it is: a 'telltale circumduction of his right leg.' That means he rolls it out slightly with each step."

"You have an address?"

The detective shook his head. "Last residence is now vacant. We're running down other leads. Including known associates. You ready for one of them? Tomasso Nicolosi."

"Fat Tommy?" Heat raised her eyes to the glass and caught Rook, fidgeting, eyeing the door. "Good work, Rales. Let me know right away when you have a line on him."

Heat strode back into the box and found Rook trying to act nonchalant but not pulling it off.

"Who was the dude with the telltale gait? My money's still on John Cleese," he said with that grin that usually melted her from half a block away.

But this was about as far from usual as they could get. Nikki remained circumspect. She gathered up the pad and pen she had left behind and said, "The booking sergeant will be in to process you in a few minutes."

"Wait. You're serious?"

"If it helps, there'll be some good sex waiting for you when you get out. I still loves me a bad boy."

Heat's hand was six inches from the doorknob when he called out, "Wait." His head was bobbing when she turned back. "OK," he said.

Nikki sat across from him again. "I think your

cooperation with my investigation will be noted as a timely show of good faith."

"You're twisting the knife."

"I know." She uncapped her ballpoint. "You want to be in the game, you can't sub on the other team."

Rook made a small nod to himself and began. "Just so you know, I have been holding back because I had a nervous source. I've gone through hell trying to secure his cooperation, and I didn't want to jeopardize my access when it was in such a fragile state already."

"Let me ask you, Rook. How many times have you sat in this very room and watched me conduct interrogations?"

"Lots."

"Then you'll understand when I say this. Get the hell to it."

And so he did. "Maybe I can't fit it into one-hundred-forty characters, but I'll do my best. A few weeks ago, I got a tip on something big. I mean third Pulitzer big. A safety cover-up in the auto industry. Something that has cost lives. Many lives."

As Nikki made a note on the top line of her pad, Rook's visit to the auto safety proving ground snapped into place. She wanted to ask more but knew better than to interrupt, so she just wrote "Forenetics?" and let him continue.

"Over the past few years cars have been flipping or rolling over sporadically. Nik, imagine driving the open road—la, la, la—and, with no reason, the steering wheel jerks from your grip, the suspension on one side takes a huge bounce while the other side drops, and next thing you're on the Tilt-a-Whirl. That's what's been happening. Causing accidents. Lots of injuries, lots of fatalities."

"Why haven't I heard this on the news?"

"Exactly," he said. "Well, I am the news. And I am doing an exposé on it. Or trying to. And when I say it's a huge story, here's why: The defect is not limited to one automaker; it's across car brands. But random. It's Rollover Roulette for most makes, models, price ranges, foreign and domestic. My early research indicates it's not the car itself and not the computer that's the problem. The strong indicator is that it is the result of a mystery glitch in the software, in the app that tells the stability-control mechanism when and when not to fire. It's a long story of who and how, but there is a very credible allegation from an industry safety expert that information about this defect is being suppressed. There is a cover-up afoot." He paused to take a slug from his water bottle.

Heat so much wanted to ask what all this had to do with her shrink but again decided to leave it with a note to herself, a reminder to follow up. She printed the initials "LK" on the same line with "Forenetics" and drew a double arc between them, a rainbow over a question mark. She did, however, ask, "Was your expert the one we found today on Staten Island?"

"Getting to that," he said. "The industry insider I'm talking about is the point man of an auto safety research team, and now that he has all the scientific evidence he needs, he is ready to blow the whistle on the cover-up. All very juicy. All the elements of a Jameson Rook *First Press* cover story that kicks off things like massive recalls and congressional hearings. But"—Rook flashed a smile—"in spite of your belief that I've never met a conspiracy theory I didn't love—and oh, do I love them—as an investigative journalist it is my responsibility to fact-check all the angles. Not just the nuts and bolts of the story but the players. Stories like this are never about hardware or software; stories are about people. And motivations. So I have been performing my due diligence. And my research led me to one member of my whistle-blower's safety team: Fred Lobbrecht."

"The dead crash-reconstruction expert," said Heat, drawing a circle around the company name, Forenetics.

"Fred was a tough nut to crack. He was extremely reluctant to talk with me. Even off the record. As a reporter, I'm used to that, but he was skittish and high-strung, lots of insecurities—said he'd talk, then would cancel, that sort of thing. Week before last, he calls me up with a proposal. Would I consent to sit down with his shrink and let him sort of couples-counsel us through the process of making him feel OK about spilling secrets to a journalist?"

As one stunning piece of the puzzle fell into place, the connection between Rook and the two victims, Nikki felt a tiny spark of exhilaration. This was the first moment on this case when she had felt a sense of traction, even if she was still far from closure. Then came a second thought. "I just hit my first bump. Why was an auto-safety expert seeing a police shrink?"

"Because," said Rook, "Fred Lobbrecht was an ex-cop. He retired a couple months ago from NY State Police, where he was on the force's top Collision Reconstruction Unit— you know, the CRU, the Forensics squad that investigates

accidents. And, I guess you didn't know—why should you?—
Lon King had contracts to provide counseling services to the
NYPD, Port Authority PD, and to NY State, plus
Westchester and Nassau counties.

"At first, I worried that Lobbrecht was just a neurotic
flake and that this would be the unraveling of my story. But
when I got into sessions with him and Lon King, it was clear
he was solid and knew his shit. He was jumpy because he
was a man with a code. And spilling secrets to me would be a
violation of that code."

"I understand that," she said. "Even for the greater good.
It's a tough call."

"Agreed," said Rook.

But, thought Heat, it was clear that Rook only understood
that code in the way all non-cops do.

"By our second session," Rook continued, "I had gained
his trust, just about come to a breakthrough. Then Lon King
washed up in his kayak."

"And his files were stolen, A through M, which
includes—"

"Lobbrecht," said Rook. "Notes and transcripts of our
sessions, plus whatever else he told Lon King before I came
into the picture." He grimaced. "Day before yesterday, he
told me to come to the proving ground on Staten Island and
bring my digital recorder."

Nikki thought about the timeline, since it was possible,
given the TOD window, that Lobbrecht could have been
killed before her shrink. "Did you call Fred to confirm your
meeting after we found Lon King's body?"

"Thought about it. Then I decided, no, it might give him a chance to cancel. So I just showed up." He gave her a conciliatory look. "And now you know."

Heat amended that. "And now we've *started*. I want to meet your whistle-blower. Now."

"Hey, come on, he's my secret source."

"Whose life may be in danger, did you think of that?" She stood, preparing to go. "Besides, I want to question him myself. And because you've had the good sense to cooperate, Rook, you can come along."

They drove to meet the whistle-blower in the new vehicle the motor pool had issued Nikki. After she adjusted the mirrors and the seat, Rook said, "So you get, what, a new car every day for life? Is this like winning the lottery?"

"Oh, yeah. And the department is very pleased I'm eating up the transpo budget." When she had signed for it, the motor sergeant had told her that replacing flat tires was no sweat, but that they couldn't have a captain driving the city in a vehicle with "Snitch Bitch" etched into all four doors.

Heat turned her replacement car onto the ramp for the West Side Highway, but not without craning to look over the concrete guard wall of the traffic circle to see the banks of the Greenway, which showed no sign of the previous morning's crime scene shutdown.

"Funny thing," said Rook, who was also rubbernecking the Hudson's edge. "Just a touch more breeze from the north, or a skosh more ebb tide, and that kayak would have made landfall downriver in the Eighteenth or maybe the Tenth Precinct, and this would never have been your case."

"Lucky me." Nikki ruminated a bit before adding, "Otherwise, I never would have learned you were hiding all this from me."

"Hey, now. I came clean. Don't I get a good-citizen's pass?" He gave her that damned charm face, which made her fix her eyes on southbound traffic so he wouldn't be able to see how vulnerable she felt right then. She concentrated instead on processing the updates she had gotten at the Murder Board right before leaving the precinct.

Randall Feller had arrived, fresh from the proving ground on Staten Island, where the president of Forenetics and his operations staff had briefed him on the likely scenario that led to Fred Lobbrecht's death. The vehicle prep was a ritual he always insisted on performing himself. Lobbrecht would arrive on the day before each test to ensure that the car was in the correct position to be engaged by the catapult and would set up the driver's side of the car to receive the dummy, which he loaded in as the final checklist item. "Everyone agreed it's pretty much a solo task," explained Feller. "Mainly plugging in a gang of harnessed cables that snake through the backseat from the black boxes in the trunk and then connecting those color-coded leads into the matching colored sockets. Blue, to the dashboard; red, to the interior cameras; finally, yellow, to the dummy itself. Obviously, he never got to yellow."

"Man . . . What a way to go," said Ochoa, feeling the

dread that was clawing at everyone else's gut, too.

"Randy, did they say why the launch mechanism fired?" asked Heat.

"They have no idea. And our CSU is on scene and not letting anyone from Forenetics touch anything, for the obvious reason that one of them could be responsible, either by accident, or . . . whatever." As the team digested that, he added, "Kind of ironic: a forensics consulting firm getting investigated by NYPD Forensics."

Since everyone else on the squad had past experience with Stu Linkletter, it had fallen to the newest detective to liase with the Staten Island medical examiner. "Kind of a dick," Inez Aguinaldo began. "Am I allowed to say that?" After unanimous agreement, she relayed the salient parts of the ME's report. "Skimming past the abrasions, contusions, and fractures to the mandible, maxilla, and nose, as well as lacerations to the scalp and multiple skull fractures, the COD story is that the victim suffered fatal injuries to the brain, subgaleal, subdural, and subarachnoid hemorrhages, injuries to cerebral blood vessels at the base of the brain, and dislocation of the C-one and C-two vertebrae, with injury to the underlying spinal cord."

"You hardly looked at your notes," said Raley, impressed.

"I had medic training when I was an MP," said Aguinaldo. "Dr. Linkletter wanted me to stress that this finding is still preliminary, since he hasn't run blood and tox yet. He also wants to check the victim's records to see if he had signs of depression that would indicate possible suicide."

"Did you tell him those records were stolen from his

murdered shrink?" asked Rhymer.

Detective Aguinaldo nodded and said, "I also told him suicide didn't seem likely, because of one of his other findings." She now had the attention of the entire bull pen, including Nikki, who felt pretty smart right then for having recruited Inez from a suburban police force in the Hamptons. "Mr. Lobbrecht had open compound fractures of his right distal tibia and fibula: his ankle bones."

"Indicating he was trying to brake," said Rook. "Like mad." A silence fell over the squad as they all imagined that moment of launch followed by the poor man's final seconds—all panic and futile action—rocketing closer to the wall of death . . .

"Nikki, Nikki!" cried Rook.

Heat slammed on her brakes, getting the finger from the driver of the gypsy cab she had just nearly rear-ended at a red light near Chelsea Piers. "Sorry about that." She laughed it off. "Last thing I need is to requisition yet another car." Nikki drove on, a lot more carefully, but still distracted. The puzzle pieces—"the jigsaw," Rook had called it—were still not speaking to her. It all still felt like the early part of the investigation instead of the homestretch, but patience always served her well. Pushing evidence to suit a theory only resulted in dead ends and time lost, not saved. This, like most murder cases, was one she had to loosen the reins on and ride to see where it led. Her challenge would be to get there in one piece.

***

The man in cargo shorts and a beard that might be described in Brooklyn's outré circles as hipster-ironic pushed through the glass doors of the Hudson College Practical Science and Engineering Annex on Thompson Street and brushed past Heat and Rook without a glance of recognition, snapping as he went by, "Follow me, four paces, no closer." He walked briskly, his long black hair brushing his shoulders as he led them past a twenty-four-hour underground garage, two Thai restaurants, a classic-vinyl-and-video shop, and The Little Lebowski, a paraphernalia and souvenir shirt boutique dedicated to The Dude, distinguished by a life-sized cutout of Jeff Bridges abiding on the sidewalk. He headed north at a brisk pace, rapidly traversing the block and a half to Washington Square Park, where he chose a spot on the convex curve of a serpentine stone bench that angled him toward the fountain. He crossed his bare legs and adopted an impatient pose while he picked something out from between his big toe and the footbed of one sandal.

"Nikki Heat, meet Wilton Backhouse," said Rook.

She held out her hand, but he didn't shake it. Instead, he remained intent on Rook. "I told you last time I didn't want you coming to my office." Then he seemed to become aware of Heat. He dropped the unidentified sandal matter he was twirling between his thumb and forefinger and shook her hand. Nikki resisted wiping the dampness off her palm afterward. It wasn't easy. She noted that Backhouse's forehead glistened at the hairline and that he had half-moon sweat marks under the arms of his red Cornell Engineering tee. Maybe, for him, it wasn't too chilly for shorts. He appraised her briefly and announced his finding. "Yep. Cop."

Since he wasn't going to invite her to, Heat sat on the bench beside him. But not too close. It wasn't hard to profile Wilton Backhouse in return: a lab geek with poor socialization. "Glad to meet you, Dr. Backhouse. And, as for dropping into your turf like this, that's on me, not Rook." He listened to her, *studiously*—that would be the word, Heat thought. But in spite of his rapt attention, he gave no interpersonal feedback, no clue as to what direction his response would take.

"You should drop the 'Mr. Rook' shit. It's not like I can't tell you're sleeping with him. Just so you know, I don't care either way. I just don't like artifice. It's insulting."

Rook chuckled. "Well, we're getting to know each other pretty quickly, aren't we?"

"Why?" he asked.

"I'm not sure you heard this, but apparently one of your colleagues—"

"Fred Lobbrecht?" he interrupted. "You think I didn't know he was killed? Your news is four hours old." He patted the block of his cell phone inside a cargo pocket. "What century do you think we're living in, Captain?"

Chants and bullhorns caused them to turn and look across the square. On the far side of the iconic Stanford White–designed marble arch, several dozen protesters had assembled, shouting, "Free Mehmoud! Free Mehmoud!" and carrying picket signs bearing Arabic inscriptions. Theirs was part of the growing angry response in the wake of the NYPD's Organized Crime Unit's busting a ring that had been taking advantage of diplomatic ties to smuggle counterfeit currency into the US through Syria. Mehmoud Algafari, the son of a Syrian UN mission employee, had been arrested as part of the ring, and the controversy concerned whether, as the relative of a diplomat, he was protected by diplomatic immunity, or whether his arrest constituted a US kick in the teeth to Assad's regime, using Mehmoud as a scapegoat.

"NYU undergrads organizing a feel-good march up to the UN because that diplomat's kid, or whatever, got busted," explained Backhouse with a shake of his head. "Like that's going to fucking do anything." Without seeming to have turned a page, he casually added, "Freddy Lobbrecht was murdered. Please tell me you know it wasn't any accident."

Heat glanced at Rook then back to the engineer. "We . . . see that as a possibility."

"A possibility? My respect for you is this close to Hindenburging." He tilted his head up to Rook, who was still standing. "Have you paid attention to anything we have discussed? Do you have any idea what they will do to keep this evidence under wraps?"

"Now you're getting to why I needed to see you," said Heat. She had decided to play into what she read as Backhouse's compulsion to know better, to know more than anyone else, by subordinating herself. "Rook has been tight-lipped. He keeps his secrets. I need to ask you to enlighten me. Help me understa—" Nikki stopped because she had lost his attention, and not just a little. Her studious listener had broken eye contact and was staring over her shoulder in the same direction as Rook, whose attention had apparently been drawn there first. Heat turned to see what the hell they were so intent on. She heard it before she saw it.

It could have been a swarm of bees. But as it drew closer, Heat was reminded of the purring hum made by a Weedwacker, though no gardeners were trimming the edges of the lawns that day. And the buzzing came from somewhere above.

"Eleven o'clock," said Rook. Backhouse stood first, then Nikki joined him, both scanning the far side of the park. A small dot resolved out of the bright western sky, gently hovering between the Judson Memorial Church steeple and the brick apartment tower on McDougal.

"How cool is that?" Backhouse, more engaged than before, stared in awe. "Never seen one of those in an urban area before."

"Is that a drone?" asked Heat.

"Hmm, respect is rebuilding, Captain Heat," said the engineer.

Rook made a visor of his hand to shield his eyes from the sun. "I've seen drones in the Middle East and in the Caucasus, but they were military grade. Bigger, you know?"

"Yeah, like flying torpedoes," agreed Backhouse, whose inner nerd was somehow even nerdier than his outer persona. "This one is hobby grade. You should definitely check them out on YouTube, they're like flying Roombas."

With some pride, Rook said, "I fly a hobby helicopter."

"Do you, grampa?" Backhouse snorted a laugh. Rook's expression lost all its joy.

"It's moving toward us," said Nikki.

Gradually, smoothly, the drone decreased altitude and

floated gracefully, passing over the hexagonal-brick-paved plaza surrounding the fountain until, about ten yards away from them, it slowed, maintained its position, then drifted forward. Rook sang the five-note signature motive from *Close Encounters of the Third Kind*, eliciting an appreciative guffaw from Backhouse. The drone's four small rotors sizzled in the air, maintaining a steady, measured course as the quadcopter progressed toward them. "It likes you," said Rook. Indeed, Wilton Backhouse's enthusiasm for the drone was not only contagious but magnetic. The craft settled at eye level and moved within feet of him, then hovered there.

That was when Heat's fascination turned to alarm. Beside a camera lens she saw what looked like the muzzle of a small-caliber weapon fastened to the bottom of the drone, and it was aimed right at the whistle-blower's forehead.

SEVEN

Gun!" she called. Rook instinctively whipped his head from side to side, scanning the park for a shooter. Backhouse, still mesmerized, held his gaze on the drone. Heat broke his geeky trance with a hard shove and a leg sweep to the back of his knees. He howled in alarm as he went down. His yell was punctuated by the sharp crack of a .22 round fired from the quadcopter and the unmistakable sound of a bullet ricocheting off the wrought iron fence behind them.

They landed in a tangle. Surprised and disoriented, Backhouse began to curse and push Heat off him; meanwhile, she was trying to reach her gun, but his flailing arms were in her way. Rook, still on his feet, tried to make sense of the scene. Heat hollered, "The drone! It's armed. It's shooting." Nikki gave Backhouse a push and rolled clear of him, coming up with her Sig Sauer braced, but the drone had pulled back and twenty yards to one side. Her shot would have been in line with the crowd of protesters. A miss, or even a hit that ended up as a through-and-through, could easily strike a bystander. She holstered her piece, clawed a handful of Wilton Backhouse's tee, and pulled him with her. "Run."

But when Heat and Rook ran right, he tried to go left,

some primal instinct telling him to beat it back to his cave—in this case, his university office. "Wilton, don't!" she called. "Too open." He halted, assessed the clear air space between him and Thompson Street, heard the buzz of the quadcopter coming back for another pass, and followed Nikki.

"There's cover under those trees," said Rook, not waiting, quickly cutting a turn east, away from the fountain. The other two fell in with him, racing along the walkway, all of them stealing panicked glances back over their shoulders at the drone, which continued to follow them, locked in with unnerving menace.

"Zigzag," said Heat. "Be a moving target."

They wove from side to side, scrambling around an undergrad—probably an NYU music major—in a tux jacket, jeans, and Chuck Taylors, pounding out Rachmaninoff's Piano Concerto no. 2 on an upright he had parked in the center of the walkway. The kid was so lost in the music, he never noticed the downdraft from the aircraft rustling the dollar bills in his tip jar as it relentlessly followed its prey.

Rook had been right; the overhanging sycamore limbs challenged the drone's navigational ability and, by the time they reached Garibaldi's statue, the drone had slowed as it tentatively sought a lower altitude—at least for the moment.

Heat still felt too exposed. She pointed to a nearby food cart offering stainless steel for protection and a wide green-and-white umbrella for camouflage. "The vendor," she said.

They ducked down, crouching on the far side of the cart, pulling the NY Dosas vendor down with them. "NYPD," said Heat. The mustachioed old man nodded with the equanimity of a seasoned immigrant who takes the New York streets in stride. "Will this be long?" was all he asked in a thick accent.

Heat's attention was on Backhouse. He was only, maybe, thirty-five, but didn't strike her as a man who got much exercise. He was drawing audible breaths. Plus those sweat half-moons had grown from gibbous to full. "You OK, Wilton?" He didn't answer, only shot her a glare halfway between annoyance and the verge of tears.

In a caricature of a rural twang Rook said, " 'Funny, that plane's dusting crops where there ain't no crops.' " But he got only blank stares from Nikki and Backhouse.

Then the food vendor grinned. "*North by Northwest.*"

"My man," said Rook. He turned to Heat. "By the way, I get to be Cary Grant. Obviously."

Backhouse had gathered himself enough to speak. "Is it gone?"

Nikki cocked an ear to listen for the buzz. "I can't hear over the piano." She raised her head to chance a peek over the steaming masala potatoes and lentils. "Looks clear."

Cautiously, they all rose and scanned the sky above the square. "Is clear," said Rook. They began to retrace their steps warily, relieved to see no trace of the drone and to hear only the adagio of Rach 2 and the disappearing chants of the protesters as they headed uptown toward the UN, lofting placards and Syrian flags.

A gentle voice asked, "Excuse me. Is that yours?"

They turned around. The NY Dosas vendor pointed to the growing dot bearing down on them from behind. Still half a block east, the drone was coming in fast and at a low level—head level.

"This way!" hollered Rook. He seemed to know what he was doing, and Heat and Backhouse followed him, weaving again as they ran, trying to make themselves harder to draw a bead on.

Heat protested when Rook brought them to the fountain and turned north. "What are you doing? You're taking us into the open."

"Trust me. Just keep up."

But the whistle-blower's sandal snagged on an uneven paver, and he fell. As he hit the ground the drone fired again. The slug hit one of the hexagonal bricks about a yard ahead of him with a small explosion of stone chips and dust. After its flyby, the quad banked to make another run. Nikki hauled Backhouse to his feet and charged off, following Rook toward 5th Avenue, hoping he had something more than one of his theoretical notions in mind.

The whir of the four rotors grew louder. "Don't stop to look." Heat nudged Backhouse. "Just keep going." He did as he was told, and soon they had joined Rook at the west leg of the marble arch. "Rook, what are you doing?"

"Oh, if I had a nickel." Then he beckoned her closer. "Bet you didn't know there was a secret door to get inside the arch. I saw it on PBS."

"Thanks for the trivia lesson, but it's locked."

Backhouse shouted, "Here it comes!"

Heat shepherded him and Rook around to the other side of the arch's leg as the quadcopter whizzed by. As soon as it passed, Rook returned to the door. When Nikki joined him he said, "Shoot the lock."

"I can't just go firing a gun in a park."

"Why not? That thing sure can."

"Rook, there are people around here." She indicated a nanny parking her stroller and sitting down on a bench with a pizza box.

"Coming around again," said Backhouse. The drone, lethal though it was, made a graceful turn just above the jets of the fountain and aligned itself to attack again. Rook took three steps back and kicked at the lock, a strong deadbolt set in a steel box. It made a sensational noise but did not give one bit. Rook cursed.

Backhouse continued his color commentary. "Thirty yards, I'd say."

Rook dashed over to the nanny. "Pardon me, I'll reimburse you, promise." He snatched the pizza box from her and took out the personal-size pizza within. As the drone closed in, slowing to hover near Backhouse, who retreated until he bumped into the arch's façade, Rook Frisbee'd the pizza right at the aircraft, grazing one side of it, causing it to shudder and veer away before recovering. As Rook celebrated inwardly, watching the thrumming copter fly off to regroup, a loud cracking sound made him turn.

Heat was kicking in the door to the arch. Well, not the door itself. There was a square louvered ventilation screen set into the thick wood, which disintegrated under three expertly placed blows from the sole of Heat's shoe, creating a hatch for them to crawl inside. "Hey, it's like a doggie door," said Rook in admiration.

As Heat guided Backhouse through the opening on his hands and knees, she said to Rook, "Rule one: Never attack the strongest part of your target." And before Rook climbed in behind him, she added, "Bet they didn't teach you that on PBS."

Fifteen minutes later, Heat climbed inside the police van safely parked outside the privacy gate of Washington Mews and slid in beside Rook. She hooked an elbow over the seat back and addressed Wilton Backhouse where he sat on the middle bench. "No sign of the drone anywhere, so you can relax a little."

"Yeah, that makes me feel fucking great." He craned his neck to look out the rear window, past the pair of unis posted beside the van, and into the park, where other officers from the Sixth canvassed the square for eyewitnesses. "What happens when the blue crew leaves for Donut Planet?"

"We'll provide you police protection, if you want it. I suggest you want it."

"What do you call what I just had?"

Rook said, "Hey, Wilton. You're alive, right?"

Since Nikki wanted to finish the interview that the attack had interrupted, she worked to engage Backhouse. She knew it wouldn't be easy. He wasn't so much uncooperative as asocial, enough to make her wonder if the engineering professor wasn't on the autistic spectrum somewhere—Asperger's, possibly. "For the record, the cop-donut thing? So done. It's Cronuts now, grampa," she said. That elicited a hint of a smile that came and went as fast as a wince. "One eyewitness—the nanny whose pizza I replaced, which Rook owes me fifteen bucks for—says she saw the drone gain altitude and rapidly exit the park to the west."

"That fucker was all over me."

Rook said, "I know a thing or two about those things. I've been thinking about buying one." He said that as news for Nikki to digest. She did, and rolled her eyes. "The range of the controllers on the latest versions is up to a mile."

"But it was so precise," said Heat. "I was thinking it must have been controlled by someone on one of these tall buildings around the park. Either the NYU law school or those apartments bordering the square."

Rook wagged his head. "Wouldn't be necessary. That thing was rigged with a high-def camera. That's all the real-time visual feedback a controller would need. Draw a one-mile radius around the fountain, it could have been someone with an iPad in a parked car, a storefront on Canal Street, even at a picnic table outside Shake Shack."

"Not making me feel any better here," said Backhouse. "Especially after Fred. Man . . ." He hung his head, and his face fell behind a curtain of long hair. Just when Heat thought she had been premature with her Asperger's diagnosis, she realized he wasn't mourning, but texting. "Canceling a class. Not happening today."

"Wilton," Nikki asked, "can you tell me how Fred Lobbrecht was connected to you?"

"You already know that." He nodded toward Rook. "He told you, so why ask?"

"Because I want to hear it from you."

"I'll have to backtrack."

"I have time."

He sighed. "I'm a gearhead, surprise, surprise," he began, as if reciting a memorized text. "Did engineering, got my BS. Did even more engineering, got my PhD. But please do not call me Dr. Backhouse. Ever. I'm a professor at Hudson, laboring in the long shadow of NYU, teaching undateables in Comic Con souvenir wear about automobile and truck systems forensics plus a Saturday seminar on metallurgical failure analysis. Yes, it rocks. My university contract allows me to moonlight, and I have a lucrative parallel life as a forensic consultant in accident causation factor analysis (read: expert witness) in all performance-related vehicular matters, principally accident litigation."

"So you consult for Forenetics?"

He gave her a thumbs-up. "Ding-ding. I'm a loathsome consulting expert, in and out, mail me my check. Fred Lobbrecht, ex–Collision Reconstruction Unit state trooper—you know all that—was on salaried staff of Forenetics. Started back in February. Good man."

"I'm sorry for your loss. Truly," said Heat. After a decent interval, she moved on. "Fill me in on this whistle-blow issue."

The professor's eyes flared at Rook. "You said this was going to be in confidence until publication. Who else knows—besides her?"

Rook pushed back. "You tell me."

Nikki intervened. "Mr. Backhouse, this is a police matter. Two people have been killed."

"Two?" He reared back like a horse that just caught a whiff of smoke in the stall. "What the fuck is happening?" Then he scanned the windows of the van, looking for fresh danger.

Although Heat hadn't intended to probe him yet for what he might know about the first murder, now that it was on the table, she followed that thread. "There was a suspicious death that may, or may not, be related to Fred Lobbrecht's. Have you ever heard the name Lon King?" She watched him process the name blandly but saw the corners of his mouth turn up slightly. "What?"

"L-O-N K-I-N-G. It's an anagram of *Klingon*. Sorry, it's a thing I do, I can't help it. Word scrambles." He tapped his temple. "It's busy in here."

"Did you ever hear of him?"

"No."

"Did Fred Lobbrecht ever mention him?"

"If he had, I would have heard of him; ergo, no."

Heat decided to leave the matter for now. "I want you to tell me about the whistle-blow."

"There was a team of us who were tasked to investigate an alleged wrongful death due to a defect in an automobile's stability-control system. The company I consult for, Forenetics, got hired by the lawyer representing the family of the victim. Just when we started to make some progress—even doing our own autopsy on the car—the family settled out of court. End of case, end of investigation." Backhouse sat up tall, becoming animated. "But see, it got under my skin. So I had my team keep digging. We saw two patterns. First, a little bulge on the scale of accidents reported to the

National Highway Traffic Safety Administration involving spontaneous vehicle rollovers. And second, a matching pattern of out-of-court settlements."

Nikki finally felt a connection with Wilton Backhouse. His investigative process consisting of observing patterns and breaks in those patterns was what she was all about. "So, lots of cars flipping for no reason, lots of money going out."

"That's only part of it," said Rook. "I've looked into this in my research. When there are settlements like these, the parties sign nondisclosure agreements. Let's call them what they are, gag orders. So the companies, by paying cash settlements, are essentially buying silence. It hides the defect under a lid."

"That's it, totally," agreed the whistle-blower. "What happens with this rollover protection system is this: The vehicle's onboard computer is programmed with software that senses when it is about to tip over going around a curve and basically knocks the car back down to prevent the roll. But when these stability-control systems don't work—for instance, when the antiroll sensors spontaneously engage a vehicle's suspension and steering at highway speeds when it's *not* in a curve, bad things happen. People have died. Lots of people.

"So my group of consulting experts studied other accidents nationwide for a year and presented our test data to our bosses, Forenetics management. We showed them incident by incident how there was a massive public safety hazard due to a defect in the software of the stability systems."

"In which cars?" asked Heat.

"Only about three-quarters of newer cars, trucks, and high-profile SUVs, that's all."

The scope and gravity of that sunk in. "And Forenetics didn't respond?" Heat asked.

"Oh, they responded," he said. "They told us it wasn't their responsibility. There was no commission for the study, no client. Therefore, it wasn't sanctioned."

Rook asked, "Is that policy, or do you think they were paid off?"

"There's plenty of money, no doubt about that. So we said to each other, let's be bold, and we had an off-the-record meeting with the NHTSA. They're no longer seen as Detroit's lackeys, yet we got nowhere. They're concrete thinkers. They wanted more evidence. But all those lawsuit records were sealed because of the settlement gag orders. Am I a quitter? No. I took it to the next level. Right to the company responsible for the defect. Their engineering and software developers watched our presentation, asked questions, accepted copies of our findings, and told us they'd get back to us." He paused for effect, then continued. "The next day my entire team was called into the Forenetics boardroom. The president of our company told us the developer of the defective software was threatening a major lawsuit. My boss called us an 'unauthorized splinter group' and warned that if we didn't drop this, we'd be fired. So we let it go. For almost a day.

"I rented a cabin up in Rhinebeck for a weekend and called my team up there for what I dubbed the Splinter Summit. It was one rough weekend, man. I pushed them. I said this was all about lives being lost because of a failure to act. I said that if we were real about what we do and who we are, we needed to man up and walk the walk. I said, 'Maybe the cars are rolling over, but we can't.' By Sunday night—thank the Lord for vodka—we voted unanimously to join together and blow the whistle." He settled back on the bench, self-satisfied. He turned to Rook. "You shoulda been taking notes, dude."

But Nikki had been. She glanced up from her pad and said, "I have to ask you a question. Why haven't you blown the whistle then?"

"OK, fair enough," he said. "First off, I am so carefully writing this report so that it is iron-fucking-clad. And I have it in the hands of my attorney. If I'm putting my nuts on the block, I don't want to give anyone an axe. And second, I now have a problem. Since word got out about Fred today, everyone else in the Splinter Group is spooked. They're all balking. They're scared. It's one thing to lose your job . . . you know?" He scanned 5th Avenue again and added, "And what do you suppose they'll do when they hear that *they* also came after me again?"

"Explain 'again.' This wasn't the first attempt on you?"

"No. One night I'm coming out of the bar at The NoMad, and the fucking CEO of that software company I investigated tries to run me down with his SL. There's a police report. Do your homework much?"

"Thanks, Professor," said Heat. "I'll do some independent study. Count on it."

Discord has a sound: a tense whispering. Captain Heat could hear it the moment she stepped into the Homicide Squad

Room back at her precinct. Each unhappy workplace sounds unhappy in its own way, thought Nikki, adapting a maxim from one of her favorite novels, as she surveyed the bull pen.

Her team's body language told her everything that no one was saying out loud. Detectives Feller, Rhymer, and Aguinaldo looked up as she entered. But Raley and Ochoa not only both kept their gaze down, they had shifted their chairs apart from the side-by-side position they usually adopted for a squad briefing. There it was: Trouble with the Roach. A split of the Spliff.

For now, Heat decided to ignore whatever beef Sean and Miguel were dealing with. "Quite a day in the great outdoors," she said when she got up to the Murder Board.

Feller said, "Yeah, understand you took up a new hobby."

"Dodgedrone," added Rook as he rolled over his orphan chair with the crappy wheel.

During the chuckles that followed, Heat turned to write "Drone" on the whiteboard under the "Lon King's Mode of Death" heading but saw that it had already been posted in Ochoa's handwriting. She made a quick scan of the boardscape and saw that Miguel had updated numerous items. There was no visible ink from Detective Raley, his squad co-leader. She tapped the MOD entry and said, "As usual, I see Roach is way ahead of me. Nice going, you two." Both nodded joylessly. "Of course it's not a lock yet, but a shot from the drone logically tops the list."

Detective Aguinaldo said, "Plus that would account for the mystery lubricant on the deck of the kayak. I called Forensics, and they said it could definitely be a match for the weight and viscosity of oil used on a quadcopter to lube motor bearings and the driveshaft."

"Mmm," said Rook. "Lubricant."

Heat gave him an admonishing glance. "Rook."

"But I'm talking about shafts."

Without missing a beat, Feller and Rhymer chimed in with, "Then we can dig it."

Their laughter faded to background noise for Nikki, whose memory of her own encounter with the drone that day made her reflect upon the last moments of Lon King's life. She imagined him alone, enjoying a splendid evening on the water, seeking that elusive equipoise, the state in which a tranquil outdoor setting matches a feeling of inner peace. Then the quiet hum of the drone. Soft, as it approached. A strange sight, at first. Then, knowing Lon King as she did, he would not feel fear but an odd fascination as he watched the craft draw nearer and nearer to him and hover a few feet from his face. Heat saw in her mind's eye the small muzzle beside the camera lens and wondered if he had even heard the shot that killed him.

Nikki briefed her team on the events in Washington Square and her interview with Wilton Backhouse, who had accepted a patrol to monitor his apartment and workplace. "Detectives Raley and Ochoa," she said, seeming to startle them both. "Did you make contact with the remaining members of Backhouse's so-called Splinter Group whose names I texted you?"

"In process," said Raley.

"Speed it up. They are likely under threat, so offer

protection. I'd also like them interviewed, and soon. Also make the usual checks of drone sales and local quadcopter clubs. See if any familiar names stand out."

"All over it," said Ochoa, jumping in ahead of his partner, as if they were in some sort of competition for Heat's attention. Raley lowered his head and gave it an exasperated shake.

"So what do you think?" asked Detective Rhymer. "Is this smelling like a contract hit from that software developer to keep the whistle from blowing, or what?"

"Of course, it's an obvious possibility," she said. "I'll tell you this for sure: I want some face time with the CEO of that company."

Rook scoffed. "You'll never get it. I've been banging on that door for the past month. Tangier Swift has got more stone walls around him than Fortunato." As he surveyed a sea of blank stares, he added, " 'The Cask of Amontillado'? Edgar Allen Poe? Anyone?"

"Breaking news." Nikki turned around from stuffing files into a shoulder bag to find Randall Feller wandering into her fishbowl office, reading something on his cell phone. "This a bad time?" asked the detective.

"Not for breaking news." She slid her laptop into its neoprene sleeve. "I'm off to One PP in a few minutes. My first CompStat review."

"And not in uniform. Bold start, Captain Heat."

That morning when she got dressed, Nikki had shrugged off the worry about going to her inaugural CompStat in civvies. She decided that her casework for the day, not some administrative meeting, however venerated by the brass, should dictate her wardrobe. Besides, she had heard how stressful the CompStat gatherings were and wanted to be comfortable. They involved more than just reporting figures: you had to defend your numbers as a yardstick of accountability for performance. Rumor had it that a precinct commander had fainted the year before while being harangued by the commissioner about insufficient activity in some of his arrest categories. Forty-eight hours in, Heat didn't own the Twentieth's performance numbers yet, and therefore she wasn't stressed enough to pass out. But if she were to faint, better to suffer the indignity of being revived in jeans and a sweater than in uniform. "If I get fired, it's been a great two days. Whatcha got?"

"Our Forensics team at the Staten Island test facility says the test-car misfire is looking good for sabotage." While he read, Feller's fingers sprang up one after another to enumerate each bullet point. "One: car was seated and locked into firing brackets on catapult, against procedure. Two: catapult monitor showed a false Safe Mode reading on the master control panel. Three: color-coded wires were apparently tampered with and reversed. When Fred Lobbrecht plugged the blue one in, it ignited the nitro and fired the vehicle, turning him into a human crash test dummy."

Heat knocked on her window. All heads turned in the bull pen, but she beckoned only to Raley and Ochoa to come in. When they had joined the meeting, she said, "I want you to assign someone to get to Fred Lobbrecht's home immediately.

Do a search for anything related to this rollover investigation."

"Done," said Raley. "You go, Feller."

Heat gestured to the door, sending Feller scooting off on his assignment.

"And I have the DA cutting a warrant for his office and lab at Forenetics," said Ochoa, with an inflection that to Heat's ear suggested competition rather than teamwork.

"Sounds like you two have it worked out." She paused, appraising the pair. "Why don't you work out whatever else you need to work out?" With that, she slung her bag over her shoulder and strode out past them.

Detective Aguinaldo called Heat's name when she was halfway through the precinct lobby on her way downtown. "Kind of on a mission, Inez."

"You're going to want to hear this, Captain. I had an idea about Tangier Swift. I didn't want to speak up until I had something."

The weight of bagfull of CompStat files was digging into Heat's shoulder, so she set it on one of the cheap plastic chairs near the soda machine and gave the detective her full attention.

"He used to own a mega-estate in Southampton," Aguinaldo continued. "My old stomping grounds. One of those humongous seaside honkers near Beckett's Neck off Gin Lane?"

Nikki recalled her visits there prior to Hurricane Sandy. To this day, she wondered who had the money to afford those American versions of Downton Abbey.

"Well, a gal friend of mine's a real estate broker out there and, last year, she managed the sale of Tangier Swift's property. In the process, they sort of had a little thing—it happens—never to me, but it does. One of those romances that's over, then it's not over—you get the idea. Anyway, they still keep in touch, and so I phoned her just now."

"Tell me. You got a line on Tangier Swift?"

Inez Aguinaldo simply smiled.

Thirty minutes later, standing in the shadow of Gracie Mansion on an eight-by-twenty-foot slab of concrete sticking out into the East River at Ninetieth Street, Nikki gazed anxiously upstream. Rook leaned in, blocking her field of view, and asked, "One more time before it's too late. Are you sure it's smart to skip your CompStat?"

"Of course it's not smart. But I am. It's called following the hot lead."

"But couldn't you send Roach?"

"Rook, will you stop?"

"It's divide and conquer. You perform your sworn duty as precinct commander; they get a field trip to rebond and work out the kinks in their relationship. If you ask me, those two lugs need some us-time."

"You do know that if I sent Raley and Ochoa to do this, you couldn't ride along."

That stopped him. He turned and craned around to look upriver, too. "Command decision. I fully support you." But then he seemed to have second thoughts. "Is your plan even going to work? It could be a lot of One PP risk for zero NH reward."

"Says the man who waved the white flag about meeting Tangier Swift."

"I did not surrender. I merely pointed out that our elusive billionaire CEO was heavily insulated. I had not given up."

"I won't, either. And since Mr. Swift's corporate handlers blocked all my straightforward approaches, it's time to innovate." She tipped her forehead northward; Rook turned again. This time he saw the NYPD patrol/rescue vessel passing under the Wards Island Bridge and heading toward them.

The boat throttled down to a stop, sat down in the water, then drifted neatly to the edge of their small dock, where two Harbor Unit officers helped first Heat, then Rook aboard before the captain engaged the twin ten-cylinder diesels again and the craft continued downriver.

Heat and Rook donned their life vests and stepped to the rail, admiring the sixty-one-foot Gladding-Hearn craft, one of the biggest in the Harbor Unit's fleet. "Didn't they have anything smaller?" Rook asked. "This is one big boat."

"It's a ship," corrected Heat. "A boat can fit on a ship. A ship can launch a boat."

"You're making my point. If we show up on something this size, won't it be overkill?"

She didn't answer, just smiled at something private and watched the FDR go by. A lone runner pounding out his miles on the East Side recreational path held a hand waist high in a too-cool-for-school wave, which Nikki returned. Then she grew somber as she reflected on Sampson Stallings making that very circuit sorrowfully past his murdered partner's medical building.

"You know how you pissed me off by holding back?" she asked as they passed the UN, where protesters, probably the same ones from Washington Square, were shouting and waving Syrian flags, red-white-and-black-striped with two green stars.

He stroked his chin. "I seem to have a vague recollection."

"Good. You can make it up to me by briefing me on Tangier Swift."

"And that'll make it up to you?" he said with a smirk.

"Call it a start. If I know you, writer boy, you've obviously done some research on him."

"I have. This will be without notes, though, so apologies in advance for any rambling." He crossed his arms and leaned against a bulkhead door, rough-drafting from memory.

"Let's see, Tangier Swift. First name given by his parents in honor of one of the early settlers of New Amsterdam— that would be Manhattan—apparently an ancestor. Harvard wunderkind. Rare combo of gaming-obsessed funster and MBA standout. Made his first half billion, that's with a *b*, at age twenty-two, developing an eponymous app named SwiftMoji, which morphed user photos into cartoon images they could use as emojis.

"In his thirties, he expanded his company— SwiftRageous—from gaming to industrial software design and struck platinum again with the automobile stability-control application his company developed.

"He's forty now and obsessed with pushing limits. He's driven to be the next Bill Gates or Paul Allen and obsessed with making Steve Jobs into Steve Who? A disciple of the management cult of poster motivation—that's my own term for MBAs who love them some homilies—who are obsessively guided by the kind of inspirational motivational quotes you see on posters, usually involving soaring eagles and mountaintops. He's all Malcolm Gladwell, Franklin Covey, and Googlisciousness."

Heat flipped her notebook closed. "I can now see very clearly what Tangier Swift is all about."

"Why, thank you. At my second Pulitzer ceremony the presenter did say I was known for daubing tight lines and shadows with a painter's eye for prose."

"No, Rook. Your rundown was OK. What I mean is, I can actually *see* what he's all about." He turned to follow her gaze. Rook's jaw didn't exactly drop, but there was definitely some involuntary hinge action when he reacted to what she was indicating.

Ahead of them to starboard, just beyond the Circle Line docks and the Intrepid, one of the largest private motor yachts Rook had ever seen sat berthed at the Manhattan Cruise Terminal. The *SwiftRageous*, which Rook estimated to be over three hundred feet long, was docked at Pier 90, which was normally reserved for cruise ships. As their captain dropped speed to approach the wharf, Heat and Rook tilted their heads back to look up at the pair of MD600N helicopters looming four stories above them from the stern helipads of the *SwiftRageous*. Rook rubbed the kink out of the back of his neck and turned to Nikki. "You're gonna need a bigger boat."

***

Churning up a swirl of brackish foam, the NYPD skipper backed the stern of his ship quickly and surely right up to the water-level transom of the *SwiftRageous*. When Heat leaped onto the other vessel and then stepped aside for Rook to join her, she expected to be met by security, which she was. Four very athletic men in matching khaki slacks and green polos assembled, forming an impressive line of muscle between them and the Hudson River. What she didn't expect was to be greeted personally by Tangier Swift. Although it wouldn't exactly be called a greeting.

"What do you think you are you doing?" said the CEO as he descended the open staircase from the sundeck.

"Tangier Swift?" She reached up to part her blazer to show him the shield at her waist. As she did, all four security men immediately placed a hand on their fanny packs. "Captain Nikki Heat, NYPD." Even after she had flashed tin, not one hand ever left the proximity of its sidearm.

"Heat . . . You're the one who's been calling my office." Two of his bouncers parted to let him through the line and he lifted his shades to appraise her. "Have you got a warrant?"

"I don't need one, Mr. Swift. This is a Harbor Unit snap safety inspection of your vessel." She pointed between the Zodiac and the Sea-Doo GTX attached to the port side of the garage deck. "For instance, does that fire extinguisher have a full charge?"

Swift tipped his wood-and-titanium Maybachs up onto his shaved head and made a sour face. "You're joking."

"Sir, I assure you, it's all legal. We have the authority to board and conduct our inspection." She beckoned to the three waiting Harbor Unit officers, who stepped from the Gladding-Hearn onto the yacht. "I suggest your men move their hands away from their weapons. This is not something we take lightly."

"Captain Heat, this is completely over the top."

"And totally avoidable if you had cooperated with my request for a meeting."

The billionaire seemed more amused by Heat's audacity than he was perturbed by the intrusion and signaled his detail to stand down. "How did you find out I was here?"

Rook spread his arms wide to indicate the ship and said, "Duh. The James Bond–villain boat with your name on it was kind of a hint."

"It's a ship, not a boat."

"Don't need to tell me. You could fit Mick's, Bono's, and Madge's yachts on here and still have room for David Geffen's hot tub."

"Who the hell are you? You're no cop."

Heat stepped in. "This is Jameson Rook. He is fully authorized to be a civilian ride-along with me."

"The writer? Fuckin-A, it just gets better."

"Mr. Swift," said Nikki, "I only have a few questions to ask you. If we had just addressed them, I'd already be gone by now."

Seeing that someone with the balls to successfully board his ship was not about to go quietly, he flipped his mirrored shades back down on his nose. "You want a soda or something?"

**

It turned out that Rook had underestimated the length of the
SwiftRageous by four yards. The luxury motor yacht
measured 312 feet, with five decks, including a master suite
and staterooms on the top level, and a salon (aka: living
room) complete with a wood-burning fireplace of French
limestone that separated it from the formal dining area. In
the forward area one deck below, across the passageway from
the twenty-seat movie theater, a state-of-the-minute gaming
parlor with night-effect lighting was jammed with big
screens, gaming stations, both Internet and satellite
connectivity for remote play, and the latest in interactive
voice and motion-sensing platforms. Rook peered longingly
from the doorway and couldn't resist. "Please tell me you
have Dance Dance Revolution." Swift didn't acknowledge
the question and ushered them on. "It's addictive," said
Rook. "I am this close to Maniac Level."

As they rounded a corner, Swift nearly collided with four
Asian men in dark suits, one of whom, who looked to be in
his sixties, beamed and said in accented English, "Mr. Swift.
We are ready to meet when you are."

Swift's return smile was unconvincing, and he seemed
agitated. "I'll need a few moments." Then he head-signaled
up the hall. A trio of his polo-shirted handlers stepped in,
ushered the suits back in the conference room, and rolled the
pocket doors closed. "Chinese industrialists," he explained
without being asked. "More money than sense. They want to
buy my yacht." Gesturing aft, he followed Heat and Rook
toward the sun deck.

Male and female wait staff served sparkling Saratoga

waters and kale chips as they sat down in a cluster of deck chairs beside the swimming pool. "I have to say, this is quite overwhelming, Mr. Swift," said Heat. Since he had relaxed his stance, she had tried to relax along with him, hoping to get more information by adopting a less adversarial stance.

"To be overwhelmed every day. That's the guiding beacon of my life."

"That can't come cheap," said Rook. "Just operating this thing, you've got a crew of—what?"

"Thirty-five."

"That's a lot of polo shirts. And it can't be inexpensive to tie up your modest *pied à l'eau* here on Luxury Liner Row."

"If you really want to know, it's not that bad. Two grand a day. Better than a hotel, and worth it for the convenience of location." Swift added an inch to Nikki's glass from the blue bottle. "Except when that means getting stormed by zealous cops reenacting a scene from *Captain Phillips*."

"I wouldn't have done it if it weren't important, Mr. Swift."

"And you should call me Tangier. And that's not because I'm a nice guy. Those dudes who founded Google got it right when they created an atmosphere for moon-shot thinking, and I'm not above modeling myself after mold breakers."

Nikki recalled Rook's rundown on Swift, how he was a motivational zealot.

"Oh, I gave it my own spin, calling my hierarchical structure a Flat Pyramid, but I'm really chasing their unicorn. No neckties; messy offices, a plus; first names only—including the CEO; transparency, and direct access—including the CEO."

"Is that why it was so easy for me to see you, Tangier?" Nikki asked, making a calculated back-to-business jab to forestall his hijacking her meeting with a wharf-side Tony Robbins seminar.

"Nikki, is it?" He set his glass down on the river-stone-covered tabletop, top-decked his designer sunglasses again, and fixed her with a steely gaze. "Nikki, maybe you had better ask me those questions so you can be on your way. That transparent enough?"

Heat didn't flinch. "Glad to. First, I'd like to ask if you know the name Lon King." Swift rolled his eyes upward, then shook his head no. She opened her notebook and popped the cap on her $1.28 stick pen. "How long have you been berthed here?" Beside her, Rook turned to look upriver, where he could see the George Washington Bridge spanning the Hudson, right where Lon King's kayak would have been adrift the night before.

"Ten days, why?"

One way to keep control of an interview, Nikki had learned through the years, was not to respond to questions. Especially with a smart, strong personality who was accustomed to getting his way, it was too easy to have the meeting wrested from her grip if she let it become his conversation. "When was the last time you used those toys on your transom, the Zodiac and the Sea-Doo?"

"Hmm. Not since Bermuda. Before we put in here. What does that have to do with anything?"

"Has anyone else used them here in New York? Someone on your crew, maybe?"

"No."

"And you also have those two helicopters."

"MD660Ns."

"Do you fly them yourself?"

"I'm rated for fixed wing only. I'm learning though. Spending a lot of time in the copter simulator in the game salon."

"Those things are great," said Rook. "I fly the radio-controlled copters. You ever fly them?"

Swift squinted at him as if he thought Rook must be high. "No."

"Ever fly the drones?" Rook asked. "You know, the quadcopters?" Rook caught Nikki's eye, and in that nonverbal micro-instant she marveled at how in tune they were. And how deft he was at playing the exasperating court jester one moment, then coming in sideways on a point she was going for.

"No," he snapped. "Are you writing fucking hobby profiles now?"

Heat took advantage of Swift's irritation to jerk the conversation in another direction. "I have another name to ask you about. Fred Lobbrecht. You may also know him as Frederick or Freddy."

"Sorry, no matches. Who are these people you keep asking me about?"

"What about Wilton Backhouse?" Swift was about to speak, then held back. Red blotches appeared at his collar and spread toward his jawline. "Wilton Backhouse," she repeated.

"Shit disturber." He reached across and tapped a forefinger on her notebook. "You can quote me. Shit disturber. And neurotic. Oh, and narcissist," said the man with the 312-foot yacht named after himself.

"So. You know him," said Rook.

The irony escaped Swift. The flush had splotched his cheeks by now. "You know what that guy really is? A gadfly. No, worse than a gadfly. A gadfly may be a pain in the ass, but at least a gadfly is operating from a sense of conscience. Wilton Backhouse is all about Wilton Backhouse. Fame, gaining wealth through extortion. He creates nothing. He adds no value. He is a self-important leech who would be better off—" Swift caught himself. "Oh fuck, he's not dead is he? You're a homicide detective, and I'm shooting my mouth off about— Is he dead?"

"No. But he swore in a complaint that you once tried to run him down with your Mercedes outside the NoMad."

"I didn't see him. Until I swerved to miss him."

"I read the police report. Eyewitnesses said you were laughing afterward and told Mr. Backhouse that next time you wouldn't miss."

"I can be immature sometimes. No charges came of it, right? And he wasn't harmed. And certainly not killed."

"No. But the two other people I mentioned were. And you still say you have no relationship with them?" Heat showed him Lon King's picture on her cell phone. He shook his head no. Then she swiped to Lobbrecht's. That one made Swift pause and think. Or pretend to think—Nikki couldn't be sure. Finally he gave a no to that picture, as well.

Heat pocketed her phone. "The second picture is of Fred Lobbrecht. He worked at Forenetics with Professor

Backhouse on a special study involving your software."

"That fucking committee. This is what I'm talking about. Backhouse, trying to build a brand by squeezing my balls over some phony claim about a faulty stability control system."

The investigative journalist weighed in. "And you assert that the claim is untrue?"

"Absolutely. I would be happy to go further, but there has been litigation and I am bound by the same settlement gag order as the complainants when it comes to the rollover lawsuits. Neither side can talk about it. It's a two-way street."

"And if we are on that two-way street," asked Rook, "are we OK if one of your apps is in our car?"

"Hey, fuck you."

Nikki worked him from the other side. "Tangier. You maintain that you have had no contact—directly or indirectly—with any of these three men?"

"If you are accusing me of something, you'd better say it." Swift stood. "But you are going to be saying it to my lawyers." Then he stormed up the staircase to the upper deck and disappeared.

"I'm telling you, your new buddy Tangier's lying about hitting the river," said Rook as they pushed through the front door of the Twentieth. "He seems a little wussy for the Sea-Doo in spring weather—even though he can probably afford a mink wet suit. But he could have easily made it up to Spuyten Duyvil in the dry comfort of that Zodiac, popped Lon King, and been back in time to catch Matt Damon duct-taping Jimmy Kimmel to his chair."

The duty sergeant two-finger-saluted the captain as she moved past the bulletproof glass, then buzzed her through the security lock. "Rook, you're assuming Swift would have done it himself. Or would have needed proximity. I'm buying into the drone as MOD, and that could have been controlled onshore."

"Or from a Zodiac," Rook insisted as he scurried to keep pace with Heat as she raced up the hall and into her office.

Heat kept the conversation going while scanning the stack of message slips on her desktop. "Besides. As usual, you're jumping from zero to sixty on this case."

"You don't think Tangier Swift has a perfect motive?"

"I'm sure that busting the colorful villain CEO as our double murderer would make great copy for your article—"

"That's cheap—"

"And fuel your next Pulitzer—but for now Swift is only top of my list as a person of interest, not as a suspect." To be honest with him, she had to add, *"Yet."*

But something seemed off with this case. Few homicide investigations ever rode an express train from the discovery of the victim to conviction of the murderer, but this one was giving her a particular sense of unease. Heat had a strong sense of an inconsistency trying to bust through the early noise of this investigation. If only she could hear what it was trying to say through the static.

Acquiescing to the pull of her administrative responsibilities, Heat spent the next half hour catching up on paperwork while Rook sat quietly nearby, going over his notes. She put her best foot forward, but it still felt like a chore—and a distraction from the case that was preoccupying her.

It wasn't all mindless work, however. A red-banded priority bulletin from Commander McMains of the Counterterrorism Task Force flashed on the NYPD intranet alerting all precinct commanders of a credible, nonspecific threat of retaliation sparked by the diplomatic conflict over the arrest of Mehmoud Algafari, the Syrian counterfeiter. Captain Heat issued an email memo to all her department heads in the Two-Oh to brief their personnel on the threat and to report related activity immediately.

On the flip side, however, were the workaday requests for overtime and time off, the usual citizen complaints about noisy nighttime trash collection on Columbus Avenue, and an earful from the businessman Heat phoned to reschedule the breakfast meeting she had postponed that morning. The owner of two Indian restaurants in her precinct insisted on face time to demand that she do something about a rash of bicycle thefts from his delivery men. She booked him again for the following morning, secretly hoping something else would come up.

Detective Rhymer stuck his head in to update her on the other Forenetics whistle-blowers, starting with Abigail Plunkitt, the biomechanical engineer. "According to HR at Forenetics," Rhymer said, "Ms. Plunkitt resigned her consultancy and told them she was moving to Naples, Florida, to work with a conservation group on saving the manatees. I tried calling her, but she may still be in transit. Meanwhile, I'll try to get a contact number for her there."

"And what about the other one, the test driver?"

"Right, Nathan Levy. He is out of town, too, but not for long. Upstate at some private resort that has its own race car track, can you believe it? We've texted and will set up a meet when he gets back."

Just as Rhymer left, Ochoa summoned her to the bull pen with an urgent wave. "Just got a check-in from Detective Feller out on Staten Island."

Heat made a silent bet with herself about what the report would be. She wasn't wrong.

"Fred Lobbrecht's house in Dongan Hills? Thoroughly tossed. Somebody got there first and ransacked the whole joint. Files gone, computer missing, even the telephone. You get the drill."

Rook sidled up and joined them. "Tangier Swift was with an NYPD captain at the TOD. Guess he has a watertight alibi."

"Maybe not," Ochoa said. "A neighbor spotted a cargo van leaving his driveway at . . ." He surfed his notes. "Eleven-thirty last night."

"When Lobbrecht was already dead," Heat said. "Any description of the driver, passengers?" She won another bet with herself when Ochoa shook his head no. "Where's your partner?" she asked.

"Right here." They all turned to find Raley occupying an empty desk instead of his usual one in Roach Central.

Rook piped up. "OK, you two," he said. "Am I going to have to do some couples counseling, or should we just go over to Central Park and let you have a duel?"

His attempt at levity was wasted on them, as it was on Nikki, who knew she would have to confront this rift sooner rather than later. But not right then. "Rales," she said, "where do we stand on bringing in your gait-analysis suspect?"

"Joseph Barsotti. Still searching for him. I've got Rhymer and Aguinaldo canvassing his known associates for an address or hangout."

"And what about the dude who broke in to Lon King's apartment?" asked Ochoa.

Heat registered Raley's irritation at being pressed by his own partner in this way, which went beyond a simple request for information to touch upon the dynamics of their relationship—making her reconsider the wisdom of asking both of them to share the job of squad leader.

To his credit, Detective Raley remained professional, swallowed his anger, and swiveled to his computer. "Real Time Crime said they'd help run facial recog from the F train and tram cams. They should have gotten back to me by now. It's not like them." He tried to launch the intranet, but all that came up was a bouncing app icon, and the page failed to load. "That's weird. This usually comes right up."

"You probably screwed it up when you moved your computer," said Ochoa. He moved to the computer on his own desk while Raley worked his jaw muscles and watched the spinning hourglass on his screen. "Huh," said Ochoa. "Not getting anything here, either."

Annette Caesar, the precinct switchboard operator, made a tentative step into the bull pen. "Excuse me, Captain Heat? There is a problem with the computers."

"Here, too," said Nikki. "Would you please put in an urgent call to MISD?" With so much reliance on technology, the department's Management Information Systems Division—cop jargon for IT—was generally first-rate. Whatever this glitch was, they would be all over it.

"I did. They said the entire department is crashing. They're not sure why, but they said it could be a hacking attack. Either way, all of NYPD tech is shut down, citywide."

EIGHT

ntranet's back!" Raley hollered from the hallway. Nikki was in her office, vainly attempting to get a call connected to her district commander. She raced back into the squad room, where an antsy cluster of detectives and Rook stood around a desktop monitor as if witnessing the historic first broadcast of color television.

Just as Heat joined the semicircle, something happened to the screen. The dark blue top banner of the NYPD intranet homepage began to pixilate and the white-and-gold letters of its slogan, "The Nation's Premier Crime Fighter," digitally melted and began to streak down the right half of the display like candle wax. The screen went black, then flashed rapid-fire images of raised fists, bright flames, and a close-up of a human eye. Middle Eastern music blasted, and Raley reached out to turn down the ear-splitting volume on his external speakers.

Ochoa gestured around the room. Every flat screen was playing the same thing in unison. "What the fuck is this?"

The distorted music blared on, but the video gradually pulled back from the close-up of the human eye until a young man's face came into view, trapped behind Photoshopped black bars of a jail cell, with bold script in both English and Arabic flashing over it: "FREE MEHMOUD!!!"

Detective Raley, ever the King of All Surveillance Media, circulated around the office, dialing down the tinny musical assault, but leaving the screens alive so that they could be monitored. But everyone knew what they were witnessing, even if they could hardly believe their eyes. The NYPD had been hacked.

As commander of the Twentieth Precinct, Captain Heat took immediate action to assess the impact on New York City's technology infrastructure. It wasn't easy. Trying to get in touch with One Police Plaza resulted in nothing but call failures on all cell phone numbers and busy signals on the landlines. In these early moments of a crisis, even though she wasn't certain how deep it went, one thing Heat knew for sure was that no police force in the world would be better prepared or more quick to respond to any incident than New York's Finest. This was the stuff they spent countless hours prepping for—drawing up scenarios, crafting contingency plans, running drills. Mobile command center RVs would roll out, personnel would be deployed, rapid-response teams would spring into action.

Now if Nikki could just get someone to answer a telephone.

When the department's crisis contingency logistics finally engaged—translation: when old-technology landlines got plugged in downtown—Heat's official telephone briefing from the Incident Response command basically only confirmed what everyone had known the instant *Habibi*

Bass kicked in on the secure NYPD intranet: New York City was under orchestrated cyber attack, making good on the threats of retaliation for the arrest of Mehmoud Algafari.

The impact was still being assessed, but the early news was stunning: the NYPD intranet, the official platform used by the 53,000 members of the force to communicate, send department email, broadcast bulletins, post crime alerts and stats, run vehicle checks, and make reports had been completely disabled; MISD also indicated that all department-issued personal devices—including BlackBerries, tablets, and laptops—were inoperative. One PP was a mess. Although headquarters was finally able to accept and make landline calls, service was sporadic because of the overload. Worst of all, perhaps, the databases of the Real Time Crime Center, the Enterprise Case Management System, and the Crime Data Warehouse had all been shut down. Also disabled was ShotSpotter, a network of audio sensors that detected and mapped gunshots in real time throughout the city. Since the repercussions of the problem had not been fully evaluated, it remained too early to tell if any information in sensitive files had been compromised. That would be sorted out later.

The police department wasn't the only victim. The mayor's office, the City Council, the DA, and courts were also hobbled, as were all city surveillance and traffic cams. But not all services were affected: 911, FDNY, emergency paramedics, city hospitals, subways, and traffic lights were fully operational. So far, consumer Internet and cell phones were still up and running. Same for the IT capability of the financial markets. At the headwaters of money's digital river, Wall Street was still buying and selling, in a blink, around the world.

"Welcome to 1965," said Heat, trying to play it nonchalant and stay big picture in the Homicide Squad Room but, inside, knowing that whatever its cause, there could not be a worse time for this blackout of tech resources. Nikki didn't care that more than four million transactions and investigative searches were made on the NYPD's system every year. Right then, all she wanted was for nothing to stand in the way of finding a killer who had murdered two people and could be in the early stages of a plan to kill more. "Until this gets fixed," she said, "we are going to have to try to catch our bad guy with Cold War technology."

"Actually, it's kinda cool." Heads turned to Rook as he waltzed in from the break room with his hand buried in a bag of kettle corn. "It's like we've hopped into a classic YouTube clip and we get to be that cool collection of private eyes on *77 Sunset Strip.* Or that sixties TV lawman who was so formative in my development as an investigator."

"Barney Fife?" asked Raley.

"Zing. No, I am speaking of none other than that two-fisted loner, Peter Gunn."

Ochoa said, "I prefer the seventies. I always saw myself in *Starsky & Hutch.*"

"Except you'd want to be both," muttered Raley, obviously still harboring some serious resentment toward the other half of Roach.

Rook set aside his snack and grew serious. "This has been

a shoe waiting to drop. We live by technology, and now technology is the new battlefront in state sabotage. China hacked the Pentagon's contractor networks, the Russians breached two systems in the White House—the White House, for God's sake—by gaining entry first into the State Department's computers. The Iranians just hacked a casino in Vegas. So Clooney's got his plot for *Ocean's 21*. The Iranians are highly skilled hackers, and are allies of whom? The Syrians. And here we are, all because young Mehmoud got busted for passing bad currency. So find your carbon paper and stop and smell the mimeo machine. This could be a rough one."

In her decade-plus at the Twentieth Precinct there had never been a general roll call until Captain Heat ordered one that evening, the first, they said, since 9/11. In the hour since the cyber shutdown, not only had more information come in but public safety and that of her officers, detectives, and staff made it important for Nikki to provide information, direct resources, hear concerns, and answer questions. In other words, to lead.

She held her meeting in the precinct lobby because it was the only indoor area large enough to accommodate all the personnel. It also allowed Annette Caesar to stay at the switchboard behind the glass and get the same information as the uniformed patrol officers, detectives from various squads, traffic unit, civilian clerks, administrative aides, jailers, and interns. "Let me begin by saying this is about two priorities: safety and communication. I am going to ask all of you to keep in mind above all that you can't have one of those without the other." For a packed room, it was church quiet. Clearly the group wanted to hear all they could about this bizarre occurrence. There was also a sense of appraisal, and Heat could feel her words and comportment being judged, even if in silence.

"As for safety, until further notice, I want all uniformed patrols to be in threes only. No pairs, no lone wolves out there. Whoever is watching your back is going to have his or hers watched, too. All days off and vacations are canceled, TFN. We need all personnel available. One PP has reaffirmed high-alert status. And, given the bulletin from Counterterrorism, be extra vigilant about potential terror activity now that we are vulnerable." Of course, Nikki—like just about everyone else assembled there—had her own private suspicions that this hacking incident *was* terror activity.

"Obviously this event has left us communications challenged. You already know what is not working; here is how I would like us to adjust. I think you'll see it's pretty much common sense." She referred to talking points she had listed on a single sheet of her reporter's notebook. "We all need to switch immediately to personal e-mail. As soon as this meeting is over, please email each other so that everyone has only to hit Reply to stay in touch. Same applies to cell phones. I am ordering everyone immediately to begin using your personal smart phones and likewise to send email and texts so communication is seamless. In your squads and units, please create text groups right now so everyone can be text-alerted at once and at all times."

A patrol sergeant raised his hand. "What happens if this thing grows and knocks out our personal electronics?"

"There's always a party pooper," said Heat, winning some relieved chuckles from the group. "We don't know what course this is going to take. And we live in an era—and a city—not equipped for this. Can anyone here remember the last working pay phone he or she saw?" Nikki held up the walkie-talkie she had placed on the table beside her. "In the meantime, Sergeant, to answer your question, two-way car radios and walkies are still good to go. But that's going to mean more air traffic, so be mindful of who you are stepping on, and keep it short. As for here in this building, we have located additional landline telephones in the basement and they are being brought up. Hopefully, we'll have enough jacks." A glance at her crib sheet. "Oh, for those of us who were here in 2009 and used to make fun of the department for forcing us to still use typewriters to fill out our Complaint Informational Follow-up forms . . ." She paused while an amused murmur about the old DD5 Pinks circulated among the cops. "You'll be happy to know that there are about a dozen typewriters with some of your fingerprints on the keys headed up from storage for use in completing reports. What can I say? Even a cyber blackout can't defeat a bureaucracy." After the chorus of moans had faded, she added, "For now, we are going back to the way cops did it in the old days."

"Graft?" said Detective Feller.

***

"We're going to have to resort to some retro work-arounds," Heat told Raley and Ochoa when she called them in to her office after her roll call. "Fewer instant searches and more shoe leather, for starters. Sorry, Your Highness," she said to Rales. "No surveillance cams makes you a peasant like the rest of us."

"We'll find other ways, like you said."

"And what about you two?" Estranged as they might have felt, the longtime partners continued to share nonverbals. For instance, at that moment, each shifted his crossed legs at the same time. "Well?"

"You don't need to worry about us," said Ochoa.

Raley nodded. "We're all about the job."

Nikki knew the difference between game faces and masks, but before she could go deeper, they dove in and laid out their plan to deploy their squad, adjusting for the blackout. Detective Aguinaldo would drive down to RTCC and retrieve the raw license-plate video from the Roosevelt Island Bridge cam, hand-search all tags recorded that morning, and run them through the DMV. State cyber structure, so far, remained unaffected by the hacking. With all police databases kaput, Rhymer would go analog and hit the mug books, armed with Sampson Stallings's artistic rendering to search for the intruder at Lon King's apartment. Since Joseph Barsotti had gone MIA, Randall Feller would pack a thermos of coffee and an empty milk jug for an all-night stakeout of Fortuna's Wheel in case the mob soldier showed up to talk with his boss, Fat Tommy. Roach's own task would be to continue reaching out to the other members of Wilton Backhouse's cadre of whistle-blowers. When Raley and Ochoa had finished, rather than poke at the wound, Heat just said, "Team Roach," and let them go to it.

"What's your take on Tangier Swift?" asked Rook after he had checked in at the hostess station for their ten o'clock reservation at ABC Cocina.

"And . . . he's off!" Nikki said with a grin.

"What?"

"What what?"

As the hostess ushered them through the lively late dinner-and-bar crowd, Nikki said, "This is so you. You want me just to race out and arrest him without evidence." When they reached their table, she took the banquette side against the distressed brick wall, not for the cushion but following her cop's habit of always maintaining a full view of her surroundings. They accepted their menus, then Nikki waited for the hostess to leave before she continued. "I can't go around busting people for murder just because Wilton Backhouse pointed a finger and Swift reminds you of Largo from *Thunderball*."

"See, this is why I'm crazy about you. Excellent recall of Bond villainy."

"I can't help it. It's catching." She rested a hand on the center of the table, palm up, and as he gently lowered one of his to complete the sandwich, Nikki felt his warmth flow into her. "Are you trying to distract me from my point?" He shrugged impishly. "Well, I can hold hands and still advocate."

"And a man's dream comes true."

"Unfounded allegations and dick measurement by motor yacht are not sufficient cause to break out my cuffs. That's a luxury you have as a writer that I don't. I need evidence." Heat studied him. "Unless you know something and are still holding back."

"I think we're past that, aren't we?"

"Are we?"

"Look, Nik, I'm sorry I kept a secret from you. But not so sorry. It sure wasn't to hurt you, and certainly not to impede your investigation. But, c'mon, everybody has secrets, right? In fact, what do the two of us do for a living? We dig out the truth behind people's secrets. We uncover the stuff they're hiding for one reason or another."

"Well, let me make something clear. I don't want to have to dig out yours."

"Oh, you made that very clear. I believe you invoked a threat of jail with a denial of my constitutional right to due process."

Nikki held up her menu to study it and smiled. "I have my moments."

They both ordered margaritas, which Rook, as he always did, declared to be the best south of 'Cesca and east of the Zuni Café. The Jean-Georges kitchen turned out chic Latin American and, even though they had both said they would mix things up, they went for their standbys. He ordered the glazed short-rib tacos with habanero relish, and she went for the charred octopus with guajillo vinaigrette.

"Do they even have mug books anymore?" Rook asked as they traded bites.

"They'd better, because Detective Rhymer is going to be spending all night flipping through something." She explained to Rook that, as high-tech as the NYPD was, they had had enough foresight—or, maybe, stubbornness—to have paper backups of everything. "That's the good news. The bad is retrieval. We've all gotten used to our instant info at the swipe of a finger. Some foreign hacker with a grudge decides to teach New York City a lesson, and suddenly we're back to paper-based everything."

"Which only makes me yearn all the more for my Montblanc."

"Rook, nothing's keeping you from your computer to write."

"True, but when all technology fails us, and someday it will, I shall have my pens. My mother bought that Hemingway for me when I was in school to encourage my writing."

"And how'd that work out, you of two Pulitzers?"

"Do you know, back then Mother paid six hundred dollars? On eBay now bids on the Limited Edition Hemingway top out at thirty-five hundred. Although I'd never sell."

Nikki leaned in close to his face. "I'll go thirty-six and a sexual favor of your choosing."

"Sold."

They laughed and she picked up her margarita glass. "One more of these first."

He cackled. "Joke's on you. That pen's going to be community property soon enough." But the smile had fallen from her face and, in the pool of light from the votive candle between them, her complexion had blanched to the color of a white-marble tombstone. "Maloney," was all Heat said before she dashed for the front door.

A table full of hedge-fund boys rose and stood in her path to check their smart phones, oblivious to the server with the tray waiting to get by and the police captain hemmed in by them all. She found another path, side-squeezing between the chair backs of other diners, then hurried past the bar overflow and dashed through the reception area to the street.

Heat rotated east, then west, scanning 19th Street for a sign of him. To the east, the sidewalk was clear, except for an old recycling picker pulling empties out of a stack of curbside garbage bags. A taxi turned onto the block from Park Avenue South, but its vacancy light was lit, and Nikki could make out no passenger inside as it approached. From the opposite direction, four laughing women formed a chorus line as they marched toward her. Heat's view behind them was blocked. She scanned both ways again, then asked a couple braving the night chill at one of the cocina's outdoor tables if they had seen a guy staring in the window a minute before. They both gave her New York signature you-fuckin'-kidding-me? looks and went back to their conversation about somebody getting beaten by his own selfie stick.

Nikki heard Rook call her name as she jogged west, giving a wide berth to the *Sex and the City* reenactors, but she kept going, choosing that direction because it had the blocked view. Heat scanned a stoop behind a big carpet store and an alcove across the street. Other than that, there were no nooks or crannies to hide in. When she reached the corner at Broadway, moviegoers had just begun spilling by the dozens out of the AMC Loews. If Maloney was around, he could easily blend in. And would. She had gotten a firsthand lesson in his evasion skills the previous night in the park.

Heat threaded her way through the crowd anyway, searching, sweeping—what else could she do? When she caught a favorable red light, Heat took a step out onto Broadway to do an uptown-downtown check, but came up empty there, too. On the green, a lead-footed cab driver nearly brushed her with his car. He gave her a honk with one hand and a finger with the other as he went by.

Rook was waiting for her on the corner holding her walkie-talkie when she stepped out of the street. "You sure it was him?"

The image of Timothy Maloney standing outside the restaurant on the sidewalk, arms defiantly crossed, just waiting for her to make eye contact with him, was as vivid as it was unnerving. "None other."

He held up the two-way. "Think you should call it in?"

The effects of the cyber shutdown made her worry about stressing the system with her sighting when there might be more urgent police concerns. Nikki scanned the area again, knowing she did so just for drill's sake, and said, "He's long gone."

A light drizzle started to fall during their walk to her apartment, only two blocks away off Gramercy Park. In the mist, people started waving wildly for cabs and running with hunched

shoulders or holding copies of the *Post* over their heads.
"Answer me this," Rook said as they moved along at a relaxed
pace. "When did weather become something that happened
to us instead of just something that happened?"

"Sandy wasn't just something that happened," she said.

"Agreed. Once in a generation."

"What about Irene, the year before?"

"OK, if you're going to resort to facts, I see no future in
this conversation." Rook put his arm around her at the corner
and they folded into each other, a perfect fit. While they
waited for the signal, he caught her doing a recon up and
down Park Avenue South. "Maybe you should just call it in.
At least let Roach issue a BOLO."

"Much as I love it when you speak acronym, a Be On
The Lookout is going to be a drain on resources when
Maloney either had a car waiting or hopped a subway down
at Union Square."

"With this guy's history of paranoia and stalking, I think
you should be a little more mindful of your own words at
roll call today. Safety and communication." Rook's point
was one Heat was already mulling over herself. True,
Maloney had slid down her roster of potential killers, but he
was still short-listed. And now Nikki had what she believed
was her second sighting of him in as many nights—stalking
via a restaurant window, no less—the same MO Maloney had
used when he crashed Lon King's dinner with Sampson
Stallings at that Vietnamese place.

"Maybe I will," she said. "Soon as we get to my place
where it's dry."

In the elevator to her floor, Rook said, "You know what? This weekend we should just bite the bullet and haul all of your stuff to my loft. Some things here and some things there is kind of scattered."

"Or I should just buy a spare charger to keep there." This trip to her place was initiated by the hacking attack, which had transformed her department-issue BlackBerry into a designer paperweight. With her iPhone now her primary handheld, she needed to pick up her power cord. As Nikki unlocked her front door, she needled him. "If you're feeling too scattered, maybe we should just spend the night here tonight. I've got cold wine, you've got clean clothes, I've got dirty thoughts."

"Captain Heat, you're trying to seduce me. Aren't you?"

"Is that what you want, Jameson?" She let him in and they kissed in the foyer. Heat pushed her door closed with her back as he pressed against her. When they parted she whispered in his ear, "I guess you do want that."

"I didn't answer."

She tugged at the front of his jeans. "You didn't have to."

Nikki flipped on the lights in her kitchen and started to uncork a bottle of Gavi she wanted to try. From the living room, Rook said, "Now I know the real reason you wanted to bring me here tonight."

"Not sure what you mean."

"What did you get me? Let me guess." He appeared at the counter carrying a Godiva gift box with a stick-on bow. "Chocolates?"

"I didn't get you anything." A flood of adrenaline

released in her. "Rook, don't open that!" Heat dropped the wine bottle, which shattered on the floor, and raced around to him where he stood frozen in place. Speaking more calmly, even though her hands were quaking, she said, "Slowly, carefully, set the box down."

He squinted, bracing for something terrible, eased the box onto the countertop, then gradually drew his hands out and away.

This time Heat didn't hesitate to grab her walkie-talkie. She used it to call the bomb squad.

NINE

The Emergency Services Unit had evacuated the tenants from Heat's building and the apartments flanking it to a safety zone around the corner on the west side of Gramercy Park. The mist had let up, but everyone was still milling around in front of mid-1800s Mayor James Harper's landmark brownstone with bodies hunched and arms gathered close to their chests as if it were still drizzling. No doubt those folks, many of whom had pajama bottoms protruding from their coats, were not only feeling the chill of the evening but also of anxiety. Nikki certainly felt a deep shiver of her own.

A rumor was emerging among the chattering crowd that the incident was an act of terror committed by the same group that had blacked out the city's technology. As wild and misinformed as some of the conjecture got, Heat had to admit that nothing fueled speculation like standing on a wet street for a half hour at night in your jammies with an armored ESU bomb disposal vehicle parked in front of your home.

Those who already knew their neighbor was a cop, or else had glimpsed her shield, engaged her from behind the tape, asking Heat what was going on. She thought back to a bull-necked detective she knew from the Counterterror Unit who made it his stock practice to answer all such questions by saying someone had called 911 about spotting an alligator, and they were checking it out. "You'd be surprised how many people that shuts up," he had said. "They'll swallow anything if you act like it's true." Believing she owed her community more than cynical pragmatism, Nikki answered honestly, but revealed as little as she had to. "A suspicious package," she repeated for the umpteenth time. "Just a precaution."

The package was more than suspicious, it was brazen, and Heat had quite a good idea where it had come from. So did Rook. Without articulating that suspicion, Rook was scanning the night for the suspect's face, just as she was. Both knowing they'd never find it. They had a better shot at spotting an alligator.

Two words—a matter-of-fact "All clear" from the ESU commander on her walkie—sent Heat hurrying back to her stoop with Rook following in her wake. They passed the Emergency Services truck with its bomb disposal chamber hitched to the back, which always reminded Heat of a small cement mixer in tow. Officers on the lee side of the vehicle began heading over to release the evacuees. In her vestibule Heat and Rook stepped aside for a K-9 sniffer coming out with his handler. Upstairs CSU had already begun to suit up in her hallway. "Bootie call," muttered Rook as they approached some techies slipping on paper shoe covers. Even he didn't smile at his own joke.

The bomb sarge had his protective hood off when they came in. His short hair was pasted down by sweat. "Thank you," was the first thing Heat said. She could only imagine the bravery it took for him to wake up every day and face the unthinkable, especially in these times. This unit called itself the "tip of the spear," and they were.

The sergeant gave her a half smile and a salute with his thickly gloved hand. "Shame about your bottle of wine." But Heat's attention was focused inside the armored box in which the disposal expert had placed the suspicious package. "We ascertained pretty quickly it wasn't an explosive device," he explained, tugging his hands out of his Kevlar oven mitts. "We did an X-ray, and saw no wires, timers, caps, et cetera. Exterior swab, neg. K-9 was also negative—same for the rest of your apartment, by the way."

"I can't tell you how freaked I was," said Rook. "I kept thinking, 'Forrest got it wrong. Death is also like a box of chocolates.'"

"OK to have a peek?" she asked.

"You bet." The containment vessel sat on the floor under the overhang of the kitchen counter. Boards under the rug creaked under the weight of the sergeant's suit as he led her to it. Nikki's limbs lost strength when she looked inside.

To Heat, it might as well have been a bomb.

Rook, immediately sympathetic to the impact of what she saw, draped a hand on her shoulder that Nikki never even felt. She was too transfixed by the contents of the Godiva box. The candies had all been removed to make room for two items: a spice jar full of cinnamon sticks and a chef's knife.

The bomb sergeant said, "When I saw this I thought, 'OK, somebody's playing a practical joke on you.' It wouldn't be the first time we rolled out to a prank." Then he studied her and, seeing her reaction, gave her some quiet space. He didn't know the symbolism of these everyday items. He didn't know that on her freshman Thanksgiving break from Northeastern, Nikki was helping her mom do some baking and left the apartment to buy cinnamon sticks at the Morton Williams up the block. He didn't know that while she was out on her errand, someone attacked her mother with her own chef's knife and left her for Nikki to find her dying on that very kitchen floor. He didn't know any of that. But the person who had put this package together, then broken into her apartment, then left it in her living room, did.

Closure is more than elusive, it is an illusion. But in the years since her mother's murder, thanks to the healing of time and by ultimately solving the case, Heat had made a tenuous peace with the formative tragedy of her life. Now, in an upending instant, the act of a sick mind had ruptured that detente.

"Captain Heat," said a CSU technician peeking around the corner from her entrance hall. "Something for you to see." Nikki and Rook joined her in the foyer, where the evidence specialist indicated a folded piece of paper on the Oriental runner. "This just floated down on your rug when I opened the closet door to lift prints off the knobs. It must have been wedged up high in the door crack."

"By someone who knew it would be dusted," said Rook. Nobody disagreed.

Heat snapped on the pair of blue nitriles offered by the technician, who then handed her the slip of paper. Nikki unfolded it carefully, even though she knew there would be no fingerprints on it for her to spoil.

The single sheet of plain, multiuse paper contained a brief message printed on an inkjet or laser. It contained no greeting, no salutation, no addressee. The writer got right to it:

So Blackwell's Landing this morning, huh? Yeah, I saw you. Did you and King's boyfriend have a cry and sniff his sheets? I had a gut feel about you and King. And now you think you can pick up where he left off. Fucking me over. Think again. You don't know who you're fucking with. But you will.

Nikki felt a lurch inside, as if she were rocketing skyward in the Coney Island Cyclone. But her alarm and anguish quickly resolved into anger at Timothy Maloney. Anger served Heat well. It gave her something to do instead of something to feel.

As CSU continued its work, Heat sought some physical outlet for her as-yet-undirected energy. She threw herself into cleaning up the broken glass and wasted Gavi on the kitchen floor while Rook sat at the counter absorbing the download of her ricocheting thoughts. "Want to know the big message from all this?" she asked.

"You mean Maloney's big subtext of, 'I can have you anytime?'"

A dustpan full of glass shards clanged into the trash can. Heat banged the broom head against the rim to shake off any slivers embedded in the bristles. "He's going to have a challenge there, trust me." She crouched and swabbed the wine and stubborn bits of glass up from the tiles with a wad of paper towels. "No, my big takeaway is to see Maloney in a different light in this case."

"You mean killing Lon King? I thought he had slid down that totem pole."

"He had. Especially after you brought the whole automotive safety conspiracy into this." She tossed the wad of towels into the trash, and a shower of bits of glass plinked against the big chunks of broken bottle like sleet. She grabbed for another fistful of paper towels. "Now I'm renewing my interest in him."

"You know me, I love a big, juicy, rare hunk of speculation," said Rook. "But, purely from my take on the guy? A drone shot doesn't seem like Maloney's MO. A little too much finesse. Agreed?"

Nikki didn't reply. She had paused, absently fixing a blank stare on an area three tiles over from where she was mopping—the spot where she had wiped up her mother's dried blood almost fifteen years before—and yet, it seemed, only yesterday . . . Then she resumed cleaning. Out, damned spot. "I don't know what he's capable of, although I got a good idea tonight."

"You mean mind-fucking you with the Godiva box?"

"I mean by knowing what to put inside it." She stood up, chucked the towels in the rubbish, and slammed its lid. She dropped her voice low so it wouldn't carry to the Crime Scene Unit. "Rook, I think he did steal King's files. Those details, the cinnamon sticks, the knife—hell, even my mother's murder, in the first place, I talked about those things in my counseling sessions, and those would have been in Lon's notes."

Rook said, "May I point out that the facts were also in that cover story I wrote about you in *First Press*? And that includes the cinnamon sticks, the knife, and dozens of other case details in that article and the follow-up, both of which not only were available at any newsstand but are still there online. Except, of course, in most offices of the NYPD tonight. So now it's my turn to tell you not to jump to conclusions or speculate wildly. What's wrong with this picture? The shoe's on the other foot, and I like it!"

Nikki rocked her head side to side as she considered all that. "Maybe. Maybe not," was all she'd give him for now.

"By the way, thank you for trusting me enough to share your conversation with your shrink. It means a lot." Then he couldn't resist. "What else did you talk about?

She smiled. "I think we'd best leave it there. Some things are just mine to know."

"Fine, absolutely." But he couldn't help himself. "Did I come up?"

Before CSU left, Rook gave them a set of prints to eliminate his from the batch they had collected. They asked for Heat's, as well. Even though Nikki's were on file, nobody knew how the hack attack would affect prints searches, so having hers at hand would save time. It really didn't matter. They all knew the intruder had left no fingerprints or fibers.

"Don't forget to bring your iPhone charger," said Rook as

he grabbed his jacket. "Forgetting it would add insult to injury."

"I'll take it in the morning. I want to stay here tonight."

"Really? After what happened? It doesn't creep you out or make you feel unsafe?"

"Why, does it you?" She unwrapped an alcohol wipe and used it to clean a smudge of ink off his thumb. "Because I'm fine with it. In fact, I think staying here tonight will make a little statement."

Rook hesitated, then took a turn around the room. "How do you suppose he got in without a key?"

"Listen, if you are scared—"

"Not scared, definitely not scared—"

"Feeling cautious, then. The district commander is posting a car out front tonight."

"To stop a nutjob ex-cop who's got the balls—and the skills—to let himself into your place, undetected, and threaten you?"

"Yeah, pretty much."

He returned his jacket to the back of a chair at the dining table. "This little statement you want to make by staying here. It *is* directed at Maloney, right?"

"Who else?"

"Just wondering out loud. I would be lying if I didn't tell you I am getting a definite sense of foot-dragging when it comes to our living arrangements."

"Let's not get into this. Not tonight."

"It never seems to be a good time for you to get into this. Ergo, foot dragging." She ignored him and pulled the liner out of her trash can. But he pressed on. "By the way, about this apartment? I don't know if they keep official stats, but you must have the home invasion record in this building."

"Oh, nice, very nice." She bow-tied the liner's gray drawstrings and cinched the bag extra tight. "How can you stoop to glibness at a time like this?"

"I see we have gone from foot-dragging to diversion tactics."

Nikki leaned a hip against the range and crossed her arms. "All right. You want to deal with this? Look around. This isn't just real estate to me."

"Nik, as far as I'm concerned, I can be happy wherever we settle down. Hell, we could even get side-by-side bathtubs on a lake just like in that commercial." He grinned, but when he saw how deeply she was dug in, he came around the counter to join her. "If this is about your freedom, your independence is something you never have to worry about. Not with me. You do know that, right?"

"Sure. Of course. Look, can we put a pin in this subject? It's all been a bit of a drain, especially with Maloney all paranoid that I'm out to get him."

"Which, of course, you are."

"I am now."

At a quarter to six the next morning Heat left her building with two fingers looped around the hook of a clothes hanger that held her captain's uniform in dry-cleaning plastic. The outfit wasn't going to Rook's loft but uptown with her to the Twentieth, where she could keep it handy in her office with the other backup clothes she kept stashed there. But they were civvies, same as she was wearing again that day, held at the ready in the event of the inevitable coffee spill or bloodstain. It made sense to keep her uniform handy just in case her duties unexpectedly required it. She and the other detectives used to bad-mouth the late Wally Irons, the Camera-Ready Captain, for always keeping a fresh uni on his coatrack in hopes of a press conference or photo opportunity. Now, here was Nikki, doing it herself. " 'And we become what we hate,' " quoted Rook on their elevator ride down.

"Nietzsche?" she asked.

"Screeching Weasel, Chicago punk band."

Both had their heads on a swivel after the previous night's incursion, and when they crossed the street toward her car, Rook noted the black SUV parked in front of it and said, "You're starting to rate, Nikki Heat. It appears you not only got a car spotting you, it's an undercover detail."

But caution rose in Heat, and she slowed to a stop. "Something's not right." All four doors of the Ranger Rover HSE popped simultaneously. She turned to survey the area for cover and slid her free hand to her holster. "Stay close."

Nikki directed Rook between the trunk of one car and the grill of another, figuring they could at least put some metal between themselves and the men in suits getting out of that SUV. But then she recognized one of them. So did Rook. "Kuzbari," he muttered, ID'ing the security attaché of the Syrian Mission to the UN. Heat didn't know whether to feel relieved or more concerned.

"Captain Heat, please wait," Kuzbari called with a hand raised.

Just then the NYPD blue-and-white posted on her block roared up. The siren burped, the car screeched to a halt, and the officers bailed out and braced drawn weapons atop their open doors. "Freeze!" they shouted, and "Nobody move!" But the security beef protecting the security attaché took its role seriously, too: *security*. All three went for their weapons.

In the maelstrom of shouts and threats from both sides in different languages, Nikki tossed her uniform to Rook and waded into the mêlée. "Stand down!" she called first to the police officers. Then to the foreign protection detail, she added, "You, too. Everybody back off. Now."

Fariq Kuzbari said a few quiet words in Arabic, and his men, albeit hesitantly, reholstered their weapons. Heat met the Syrian leader's eyes and what she saw in them made her turn to her own crew. "Guys? Thank you, but this is an order. It's all good."

Minutes later Heat was sitting alone with Kuzbari in the tranquility of his HSE. Outside, his men stood in a line with hands at the ready, facing off against the blue unis, similarly ready to respond to trouble. Rook, excluded from the meeting, kept himself occupied with his iPhone camera so that he could capture the standoff tableau.

Fariq Kuzbari had changed very little since Nikki last encountered him. A few years before, when she learned her mom had once been a spy who infiltrated the homes of diplomats and foreign agents by giving piano lessons, one of her mother's clients was Kuzbari's family, so he had come onto Heat's radar as a person of interest in her mother's murder. In the end, he was not a suspect, but he and Nikki had formed a bond of mutual respect with an overlay of healthy suspicion.

"I didn't intend to alarm you or to spark an international incident, Captain," Kuzbari began. His English was excellent, just as she had remembered it, with a touch of a British accent that, along with his looks, reminded her of Sir Ben Kingsley. She also noted his use of her new rank in addressing her. Either he had spotted the pair of gold railroad tracks on the collars in her dry cleaning or he had serious access to intel. Heat would go with the latter.

"There's a lot in play here you may not know about."

"Something I don't know about. Refreshing." He sounded like he meant it. With everything in the news about the civil strife, including atrocities gone wild, in his country, Nikki could only imagine the information he had thrashing about in his head. She wondered how he felt about it all. Was he a partisan, a party to the abuses, or a man in a frightening position threading the needle until he could disappear from the nightmare with a set of Louis Vuitton full of gold bullion? Was this gentle side she was witnessing the real Fariq, or was he just another thug in a bespoke suit?

"I'll make this brief then," he continued, "as we both have a great deal to attend to. In the world of diplomacy, this is what's called a back-channel outreach. As I know you must be keenly aware, there is an issue of tremendous import and great sensitivity between our governments."

"The counterfeiter we busted."

He paused as if he had a reply to that, but moved on. Apparently mixing it up with New York's Finest over semantics wasn't on his agenda. "The tension surrounding Mehmoud Algafari is what I am referring to, yes."

"Pardon me, Mr. Kuzbari, but what does any of this have to do with me, aside from the fact that the safety of my city has been compromised by your Free Mehmoud cyber attack?"

"You cut right to it, don't you?"

"As you said, we both have a great deal to attend to."

"I am reaching out to you because of our unique relationship. Although our occasional dealings over the past few years had a degree of healthy friction, I have always found you to be forthright, trustworthy. Also, I confess I have am sentimental because of the kindness your mother displayed to my children when she was their music teacher."

Nikki wanted to add, Even though Mom was spying on you, but kept the thought inside.

"So, my point—or shall I say, my message—is that I would like you to hear directly from me that the Syrian government has no official connection whatsoever to the disruption of the technology infrastructure of this city."

"You're telling me this, because . . . ?"

"Because I know you will believe me and because I have faith that you will inform others in your metropolitan government, hopefully with some advocacy."

"And if not officially the Syrian government, then who? Rebel insurgents? Dissenters? Human Rights Watch? Anonymous? Mehmoud's counterfeiters?"

Fariq opened his car door. "You see? I may have reached out to just the right person."

"The Syrian's playing you, Captain." Detective Ochoa pulled his bag of Earl Gray out of his chipped old friend of a mug and watched it twirl, waiting for the drips to subside. "He's pulling your chain."

"I told her the same thing." Rook stepped on the pedal of the break-room garbage can. The lid yawned back to make a landing zone for Ochoa's teabag. He turned to Nikki. "What were my exact words? Allow me to refresh your memory. 'The Syrian security thug wants us to take his word for it that it's not them but some prankster in a Guy Fawkes mask? I don't think so.'"

"Settle down, fella," she said. "I never saw anybody so needy about being right."

"Aha, so I am right!"

"Only in the sense that I haven't proven you wrong yet." She flashed Rook a quick smile and picked up her coffee cup. "There's time."

Heat moved along to the bull pen to bring herself up to speed on the Murder Board. In the short time since she had gotten back to the precinct she had already called the bureau chief of intelligence down at One Police Plaza to report her encounter with Fariq Kuzbari and relay his message. The chief had seemed to be more intrigued by why Fariq had chosen a police captain as his lucky target than by the actual content of Heat's encounter. She hung up feeling as if her call had been nothing but bureaucratic wheel spinning. A pair of incoming calls from the same building was more blatantly unsettling. In the first one, her district superintendent reprimanded her for blowing off the CompStat meeting. Heat's defense that she was following a hot lead on two murders led only to a fresh rebuke for not balancing her duties. Of course when the chief of detectives phoned minutes later, the axe he had to grind was a demand for more results on the double homicides. And soon. While he filled her ear with not-so-veiled threats about stepping in himself, Nikki's gaze drifted from her cluttered desktop to the coatrack holding her uniform shrouded in plastic. Staring at the gold captain's bars on the collar, Heat thought that they perfectly summarized the job: heavy metal.

Raley joined her to stare at the board. It should have been a roadmap to the killer of Lon King and Fred Lobbrecht. Instead it was more like roads under construction. "Whoever is behind this Big Hack Attack, it's killing us," he said. "We're spending man-hours on things that used to take seconds. Feller has been smelling his own BO all night on stakeout hoping to nab Barsotti, and Rhymer, he's getting carpal tunnel flipping mug book pages. Opie says he'd have a better chance of finding the dude who broke into King's apartment by walking 5th Avenue, scoping out pedestrians face by face."

"Tell him when he runs out of mug books to try it," she said. "Whatever works."

"Here's what we should be doing with our manpower," said the detective. "Putting some of us on you to make sure you don't get your day spoiled by Maloney."

"He's an ex-cop, he'd spot the tail," said Detective Aguinaldo from her desk.

Heat nodded in agreement. "Which is why I want to change things up. A BOLO is not going to turn him up, especially with our street cams all blacked out. And Inez is right, he's too savvy to get caught following me."

"And cocky," added Rook. "I'm sure he followed us to Cocina last night, and when he saw us ordering a meal instead of just drinks, unhooked us from his leash, walked five minutes away to Nikki's apartment to leave his surprise, then came back and made sure she saw him in the window just to mess with her head."

"Now I want to mess with him," Heat said. "No more passively waiting for a random sighting. Let's do some digging of our own so we can take it to him. Roach, I want you guys to see what more we can find out about Maloney's life that might start blazing a trail to where he is or hangs out. His habits, his likes, maybe some known associates—that would be good. Does he have cop buddies? Any pals from school, the military?"

"Military service in Nevada, according to this." Ochoa, who had already opened up Maloney's personnel file, put his finger on a page. "A posting at Creech Air Force Base."

"I know Creech, it's just outside Las Vegas. When I was an MP I did a training cycle there," Inez Aguinaldo said, giving Heat a significant look. "Creech is where the Air Force flies its drones."

***

Maloney and drones. It might have still been a Murder Board full of roads under construction, but the potentially tantalizing connection between the clinically paranoid ex-cop's military background and the murderer's apparent MO brought a sudden burst of energy to the bull pen. For Heat, who had still harbored a nagging voice that doubted Maloney's viability as a suspect in Lon King's murder, this fact now jacked him up the totem pole, as Rook described it. Her instinctive misgivings had been based on the murderer's means more than his motive. Simply by adding "Drone?" under Maloney's name on the whiteboard, the odds of his being the culprit seemed to rise. The discovery of this nexus also relieved Heat's other hesitation, her fear that their pursuit of Maloney was motivated by her own personal vendetta and was siphoning minds and talent from the main event, the double murder. Even if this proved out to be a dry lead, the experienced cop in Heat knew that you have to play all the leads out until you find your hand on the right one.

Detective Aguinaldo set aside her prior assignment, screening license plates from the Roosevelt Island Bridge cam, and moved to making long distance calls to Nevada to find out what she could about Timothy Maloney's service at the USAF's Unmanned Aerial Vehicle Battlelab, where service personnel in high-tech warehouses used big screen TVs and sophisticated electronics to control American drones in Iraq and Afghanistan, 7,500 miles away. In addition to his service duties, the detective was to also gather as much information as she could about Maloney himself, especially friendships or romances that might lead from the desert years before to New York City today—an idea no more unlikely than that of firing a missile from an unmanned aircraft half a world away with, basically, a big-boy video game controller.

Raley and Ochoa, still not seeming as Roach-like as usual to Nikki, set about finding similar liaisons within Maloney's prior precincts from their newly separated desks.

Ochoa interrupted his serial dialing around to NYPD station houses and Internal Affairs, his task chair rolling into the wall with a slam as he jumped up and hustled to Heat's door. "Captain. Just got a call. Shots fired at the home of Nathan Levy. He's one of the whistle-blowers from the Splinter Group."

Rook came along in Heat's car to where the Bronx meets the water's edge on a tidy residential avenue of freestanding duplexes, single-family two-story Capes, one- and two-car garages, clean yards, no shortage of wrought iron fences painted white, American flags on display, and a portable basketball hoop parked in the gutter about every half block as if by city ordinance. "Here we go," said Rook, as if Nikki could miss the three radio cars and the Crime Scene Unit van in front of the cream-and-beige clapboard surrounded by Do Not Cross tape.

They pulled into the space created by the departing ambulance, which left with no lights or siren on. A traffic officer gestured for clusters of looky-loo neighbors to clear the street to let it out. On the walk up to the door, Nikki drew in a chestful of clear air that tasted of the sea. On a warmer day, with fewer murders and less bureaucracy on her back, she might have gone sailboarding. As she exhaled, Nikki told herself the fact that she had not one second to consider that was probably the very reason she should just go do it. Someday, she thought. But not today.

When Heat and Rook had cleared the vinyl tape and approached the red brick driveway they found Nathan Levy seated with his legs dangling over the open tailgate of his silver F-450 swigging a bottle of Brooklyn Lager. He gave Rook a head dip of acknowledgment, which seemed to be as far as Levy wanted to go with him. Heat flashed tin and ID'd herself. Levy brought the bottle down and said, "Open container, but it's my own property, so cool, right?"

"We're not here to enforce Quality of Life on you, Mr. Levy."

"Good, because I fucking need something to steady my nerves."

On first meeting, it didn't seem to Heat that he needed an excuse. She could see evidence of his drinking in the puffy eyelids and the meaty complexion that didn't go with the cross-fit build. The Mardi Gras beads dangling from the pickup's rearview mirror also suggested a party-hearty lifestyle. "Were you hit? I heard you weren't hit."

He shook his head no. "Ambulance was just a precaution, I guess. Or what they do. Hell if I know. I don't even know what I fucking know anymore."

Nikki waited for him to tip back another swallow of beer. Even in his loose tee shirt, the solidness of his upper body was evident. It was hard to be sure, the way he was seated on the tailgate, but she made him out to be on the short side, yet in the way that athletes such as divers, soccer players, and yes, race car drivers, are: compact, lean, agile. She imagined his hands on a steering wheel testing tight turns on the proving track, flexing against G-forces and winning. "Do you mind telling me what happened?"

He barked out a laugh barked, and she could smell hops. "Somebody fucking shot at me, that's what happened." Shock did funny things, so she waited him out. He set the bottle on the truck-bed liner beside him and explained. "I was coming out to go meet my buds for a rehearsal. Out of fucking nowhere, I hear this—bang!—gunshot. Something zips past me. A bullet. It smacks the garage behind me."

Both Heat and Rook turned behind him. In the gap between his performance pickup and the white M3, a single bullet hole punctuated the frame of his garage door, right above his saxophone case, which lay sideways on the bricks where CSU was setting up shop.

"Close," said Rook. "You see where it came from?"

"I was a little busy trying not to piss my pants." And once again dialing down the asshole factor, he went further. "I wasn't paying much attention. I've been kind of distracted since Fred Lobbrecht bought it. It really hit me."

Rook, not hiding his annoyance at Levy's snarkiness, said, "So much so that you were going to jam with your buds?"

Levy frowned at Rook. Then he took another swig and continued his account. "So I duck. And here's the freaky part. I come up and see this flying saucer, you know, one of those drone things at the end of my driveway, zipping off."

"Which way?" said Heat and Rook in unison.

Levy pointed over the roof of his house.

"Can we look?" Nikki asked.

The houses in that neighborhood were narrow but deep, like shoeboxes. With a slight limp, Nathan Levy led them through the breezeway between his home and his neighbors'. When they reached his backyard, they mounted the cedar deck that overlooked the bay formed by the mouth of the East River. "This is where it went. Where it flew to or from is anybody's guess."

Immediately to the left and right were more decks and more backyards, nothing special. Peering beyond, Heat and Rook could see, to the north, the Throggs Neck Bridge to Queens, crossing above the SUNY Maritime College on its way over the water. To the south lay the new Trump golf course at Ferry Point and the Whitestone Bridge beyond that. Plenty of open land, lots of open water, and no sign of a drone or its controller. Rook observed, "With the one-mile range, that thing could have gone anywhere."

"And be long gone," agreed Heat.

"Early in the season to have a boat in." Rook had his eye on the red-and-white speedboat tied to Levy's dock.

"Only if you're too prissy for cold weather."

Nikki was trying to figure out if his antagonism was a sign of test-driver testosterone, beer-fueled, trauma-induced, or a cover for something. "You sure you didn't get injured this morning?"

"No, why?"

"I see you're favoring your right leg."

The man stood a little straighter. "It's nothing. Just racked it up. Playing handball. I've got a Saturday group at my gym and one of them got stupid."

Oversell, though Nikki. Usually a hint that there's a lie receiving compensatory cover. She filed that away and asked Levy if anyone had threatened him, even in an indirect way. He said no. He also told her he hadn't had any sightings of any strangers or unknown cars around. The block was low-crime, and with so many kids around, folks tended to beat the jungle drums when there was any unusual stuff going on. Heat recalled the crowd behind the crime scene tape and got the idea.

"Just one more thing for now. Do you recognize any of these men?"

She showed him a headshot of Timothy Maloney. Levy shook his head no. Same for Joseph Barsotti. When she offered Sampson Stallings's drawing of his apartment intruder, he said, "A cartoon? What? The Syrians hack the memory out of your camera, too?"

"Just yes or no is fine. Does he look familiar?"

"No."

To wrap it up, she flashed him a screen grab of Tangier Swift from his corporate website. "You're kidding, right? That's Swift, the fucker killing everyone with his shitty software." Levy fixed Rook with a glare, as if he should have known that, but said nothing more.

"Has he approached you, directly or indirectly, with any threat or intimidation?"

"The asshole breathes intimidation, that would be nothing."

"What about threats then?" continued Nikki. "We know about your Forenetics Splinter Group."

Levy's head snapped toward Rook again. "I see. You interview me, then go to the police. Fuck you."

"It's a murder case now," said Rook.

"Fuck you sideways."

Heat tried to reel in Levy with questions. "Do you think today's attack was linked to your whistle-blowing?"

Levy seemed about to go on, but turned aside dismissively. "I never should have gotten into this."

"Why not?"

"I'm done talking about it, OK?"

Rook said, "Your hands are shaking."

"Wouldn't yours be? Look what the hell's happening. Look what they did to Fred Lobbrecht. And I heard from Abigail they tried to get Backhouse, too. *With* a goddamn drone." He handed Heat's cell phone back. "Today I got lucky. I know from driving cars, luck only gets you so far."

"Mr. Levy," said Heat, "you're not being totally open with me about something, and if you're really worried, I advise you to start sharing, so I can help."

Levy said nothing, only watched a dot over the water that turned out to be a seagull, not a drone. Heat wasn't sure if this evasiveness was the man's panic response to getting shot at—completely understandable—or if there was something he was trying to keep hidden, something bigger that might have taken on a life of its own. For now, all she could do was wonder, and keep pushing to get her own answers. Nikki handed Levy her card and said, "Whenever you're ready to talk, here's how to reach me."

As they started to go, they caught a flash of white as Levy tossed her card on the ground. "Nice fella," said Rook, which actually made Heat laugh.

The blue-and-whites had departed, the neighbors had gone back to call each other to gossip, and Heat pulled away, leaving the dour victim of a near miss watching her go from his driveway. "I'm surprised you two aren't tighter. Aren't you a beer-for-breakfast dude?"

"Sure, if I wake up at five P.M. in the tropics. But in the tropics I'd have fresh oranges to squeeze, so I think the whole Jameson Rook–Nathan Levy buddy film will never get ma— Turn around!"

She glanced over her shoulder.

"Not you," he said. "The car. Stop the car. Turn it around, hurry." Heat braked and, as she paused, waiting to make a U-turn in the middle of Tremont Avenue, Rook added, "That car that passed us going the other way, toward Levy's . . . The guy in the sketch was at the wheel."

At that, Nikki made the U-ey, running one front tire over the curb before she sped off in pursuit.

TEN

East Tremont is a nice, fat, wide, old-fashioned four-lane, which made quick work of putting pavement behind Heat. She wove at a decent clip around a slowpoke who was texting and a plumber's box truck, coming up in no time to Nathan Levy's street at the T intersection. Unfortunately, a food service van idled at the stop sign.

"What the hell's he doing?" said Rook.

Nikki spotted the rolling gate begin to open at the catering business across the intersection. "He's blocking the lane waiting here to get in that driveway there. Simpleton."

"You do realize we are one *Muppet Show* opera box from becoming Statler and Waldorf," he said.

Heat lit up her LEDs and gave her siren a short, guttural burst. The driver's arm emerged from the van's front window and windmilled to tell her to go around him. She pulled up to a fast stop beside him and made her turn toward Levy's house.

Rook pointed to the Impala two blocks ahead. "Dark-blue Chevy."

"Got him." Heat keyed her microphone. "One Lincoln Forty, in pursuit of blue late-model Chevrolet sedan, southbound on Schurz Avenue, cross street, East Tremont." Dispatch came back and asked for the plate. She was close enough now see it and read it off. "Driver is wanted for possible ten-thirty-one, request backup."

"Ten-four, One Lincoln Forty."

She dropped the mic in her lap and said, "Watch for peeps. Don't want to be on the *Eyewitness News* tonight for mowing down any citizens." Then, something unusual ahead. The Impala showed brake lights. It was Nikki's turn to ask, "What the hell's he doing?"

The car slowed, its right blinker came on, and their prey pulled over to the curb, parked, and shut off the engine.

Rook turned to her. "To state the obvious? Worst car chase ever."

Heat's attention was too focused on the job at hand to even hear what Rook had said. She called in her location and popped her door, approaching the vehicle from the driver's blind spot with her hand on her holster and alert for sudden moves. But the first thing she saw was both of his hands gripping the steering wheel at the classic ten and two o'clock positions—keeping them right where she could see them. Nikki surveyed the backseat to make sure he was alone, also saw that there were no weapons around him. She didn't notice any drones, either. When Heat looked at his face, he was smiling. She was struck by how much he looked just like his sketch.

Eric Vreeland seemed quite at ease seated with his hands loosely clasped on the table in Interrogation One. He wore a well-cut off-the-rack suit and one of those French-blue shirts that you still saw around but which had been more standard issue for the MBAs who had been released to roam lower Manhattan about ten years before. His hair was the shadow of another time as well, and the way Heat handicapped it, she figured he was about a year from either plugs or a shave, with a possible intermediate stop for Julius Caesar bangs before a confrontation with denial forced the Big Decision.

"Are we just going to sit here like this?" he said at last. "I'm not getting any younger."

It's like your reading my mind, Nikki thought, noticing the horizontal line above his gut, a dent made by the male shapewear she had felt when she frisked him back in Throggs Neck. "Ball's in your court, Mr. Vreeland. All you have to do is start answering some of my questions, and we can move this right along."

His response was to scope himself briefly in the magic mirror, then study his hands. Nikki made out the ghost of an absent wedding band, completing her midlife assessment of one Eric Vreeland.

One the other side of the mirror, in the Observation Room, Rook stepped in to find Raley and Ochoa watching the interview through the glass. "Aw, hell, she started without me."

"Snooze, you lose, homes," said Ochoa.

"For your information, home-away-from-home skillet, I was anything but snoozing. I made a call to one of my contacts to see what I could scare up about Timothy Maloney."

"Whadja get?" asked Raley.

"Time will tell. Just laying my groundwork." The lull in

Interrogation One matched the uncomfortable silence between the partners in the Ob room. Rook turreted his head back and forth from Raley to Ochoa, who had mutually created a gulf between them by standing at opposite ends of the window. "Anything I can do to help you guys?"

Ochoa said, "Just keep turning over rocks with your contacts like you are. Maybe one will pay off."

"I don't mean help you with the case. I mean help you with this." He held his hands apart as if to measure the distance between them. "You think nobody notices the tension? Maybe you two need to go out and get drunk. Or go to a movie. Or get drunk *at* a movie, I've done that—although, it was at a porn theater, purely for research on an article. I mean, why else would I pay money to see *Lord of the Cock Rings*? That's not even subtle, is it?" He paused. "I seem to have lost you."

"It's not that you lost me," said Raley. "I just don't want to talk about it. Some things are not for open conversation. For instance, you don't see us commenting on whatever's going on between you and Heat."

That took Rook plenty aback. "I don't know what you're talking about."

Raley smirked. "There you go. That's how you keep people from getting into your shit. Deny and clam up."

Eric Vreeland's voice came on the speakers, and they turned their attention back to the box. Rook, however, did so with his attention suddenly divided by Raley's remark.

"My lawyer's on the way. You think I'm going to say anything about anything without her here?"

In fact, as patient as she was playing it, hoping the man would feel uncomfortable with the silences, Heat was quite aware of the ticking clock, and of the need to move things forward before the attorney showed. She transitioned to impatience. "That's how it works for you scumbags. Do what you please, create your own morality, even break the law because you have something bigger on your side: money and the lawyers it buys."

"What the hell?" Finally some reaction. He put his hands in his lap and dried his palms on his thighs. "I am a licensed private investigator."

"On record as being on retainer to SwiftRageous, LLC."

"So? Just one of many clients. And what's with 'scumbag'? I have no problem with what I do."

"Let's talk about what you do."

"Not going to happen."

"We'll see. What is your interest in Lon King?"

"Who?"

"Sampson Stallings?"

"Who?"

"Nathan Levy."

"I'm lost here."

"Nathan Levy. I just followed you on his street."

Vreeland's face was all innocence. "Did I even know that? I was going for a drive. Nice day, thought I'd check out that new Jack Nicklaus course The Donald is building. I saw you following me—an obvious cop, come on—so I pulled over. Now, for reasons I don't understand, here I am. Waiting for my very, very good lawyer."

Conversation wasn't going where she wanted it to, but at least he was talking. Heat kept pounding. "What did you do with the materials you stole from that apartment on Roosevelt Island?"

"Whose apartment? What materials?"

Before she could press more, the door opened and Helen Miksit tromped in. She didn't bother to sit. The blockily built lawyer had accessorized her tweed St. John with a matching frown, and it was all Nikki's. "Heat, I thought I trained you better than this. Hey, Eric. Don't get too comfortable." As a former hardball prosecutor and now as one of the city's top criminal defense attorneys, Miksit was a badger in court, and in Nikki's unhappy personal experience, bare knuckles in the station house. "This interview is over."

"Not your call, counselor." Heat remained seated facing Vreeland, signaling a delicate operation that could not be interrupted. Nobody told the lawyer.

"Bullshit. You have charges?"

"Not yet. But a man who encountered your client in his apartment is coming down to ID him."

Miksit brought out her crass sarcasm. "Oh, so you've got him tried and convicted already. Why don't we just hook him up to Old Sparky and fry him for the Lindbergh kidnapping?"

This time, Heat rose and turned to face the hard-ass squarely. "He's not going anywhere, Helen. Not until I place him in a lineup for my eyewitness."

"That's fine." Miksit plunked her giant briefcase on the table and took a seat. "We'll just wait out your little process so we can bail him."

Heat sat back down. "I want to talk to him first."

"You already did. Thank you for your interest." The lawyer reclined in her seat with a smug grin that made Heat hate all lawyers. For now, this one would do.

Heat told Raley and Ochoa to set up a lineup to include Eric Vreeland, PI for Sampson Stallings, then went to her office to put in a call that begged to be made.

"Will Mr. Swift know what this call is about, Captain?" asked the assistant.

"You writing this down?"

"Go ahead."

"Tell Mr. Swift I just arrested his private investigator for breaking into the home of a homicide victim and I want to know why he sent him there." There was a gap of dead air and Nikki thought she heard a click. "Hello, did you get that?" Heat assumed she'd been hung up on, but then there was a sudden rush of street bustle followed by the voice of Tangier Swift.

"Nikki Heat, you should work for me in sales. You sure know how to get your foot in a door."

"So does Eric Vreeland," she said, neither flattered nor charmed. "And since he does work for you, we need to talk again. And soon."

On Heat's drive to Tribeca for her second meeting with Tangier Swift, she mulled the notion of Eric Vreeland as a possible killer. On one level, it felt so right. High-level men like Swift relied on lowlife cockroaches like Vreelend to do the heavy lifting. So the PI—or operative, or fixer, or whatever the polite designation was for the scummy art of "making it so"—had instantly become the shortest distance between the combative software magnate and the inconvenient whistle-blowers who were threatening to shut him down.

But what seemed initially such a good fit raised doubts on examination. Eric Vreeland was unarmed at his capture. His hands and clothing tested negative for gunshot residue. He claimed he knew nothing about drones other than seeing on TV that they might be delivering pizza someday. Whether that was a lie or not, there was no drone or drone controller in his car. Plus, he was apprehended heading to Levy's home *after* the attack. Was Vreeland going back to finish the job, or was he simply planning surveillance or light break-in work on his boss's behalf?

Heat couldn't recall a case with so many moving parts, so many orbiting elements begging to connect without hinting at their apparent relationships. The whistle-blowers going after Swift—the alleged auto-safety violator—was clear enough, of course. But why would a high-stratum billionaire bother killing his accusers when he employed lawyers to handle such problems as a matter of course? And how did a mobster like Tomasso Nicolosi figure in? He was plenty lethal, for sure. But murder to collect a gambling debt could be ruled out by his own logic. Even if he were brought in to arrange a contract killing by Swift or someone else, both the drone and the proving ground car crash seemed well above Fat Tommy's beer-fart level of sophistication. What Heat did know was that the only way to find the links she needed was to keep asking questions and continue observing. And keeping her head in the swirl of everything else going on during the first week of her new job.

Which would break first, she wondered, the case or her?

Heat skipped the valet, slid her NYPD dash talker under the windshield, and left her car curbside at The Greenwich. Robert DeNiro's upscale hotel was an easy walk from Rook's loft and, over the past year, the two of them had eaten their weight in papardelle with lamb ragù at the embedded restaurant, Locanda Verde.

The Drawing Room at The Greenwich lived up to its name: quiet, tastefully decorated, and for guests only. Tangier Swift must have had a room there, or just booked one for the day so he could have the meeting where his whim took him. The concierge ushered Heat in, and she found the tycoon in the corner nook by the fireplace speed-swiping his iPad screen. He set it aside when she approached. "Don't mean to put it in your face. Unlike New York City's, my technology still works. Let me know if I can Google anything for you."

Nikki didn't miss a beat. "Sure thing. Why don't you run a search for private eyes who do B&E work for dot-com billionaires? See if you get any hits."

"You won't be deterred, will you?"

She sat down and looked at him with a level gaze. "Count on it."

"I'm surprised you came alone. Is Jameson Rook out beating the bushes and/or cesspools for new targets of his 'journalism'?" Swift actually made air quotes around the word with his fingers. Heat didn't need to spend her interview capital defending her fiancé, and stayed on point.

"The next time we meet, Mr. Swift, we may not be in such an agreeable setting. The way I see it going, you may not even be wearing a belt or shoelaces."

"Oh, man, that's hilarious. Are you really trying to intimidate me? Really?" He uncrossed his legs and leaned forward. "What world do you live in, Captain?" He didn't form air quotes around her rank, but it sure sounded like it. "Do you even think this is *your* meeting? That I wanted to sit down and let you browbeat me with your fantasy probes and conspiracy theories?"

That made Nikki wonder why he had agreed to meet. She turned to see if she had been set up for something. They had the room to themselves . . . and rough stuff at The Greenwich? Not likely.

"Here is how I will enlighten you. When you dare to walk the global stage as I do—And yes, I began as a dot-com billionaire, what can I do?—You build it, they come, they pay. Oh, mama, do they pay. Anyhow, when you have a profile like mine you are a constant target for unrelenting bottom-feeders out to suck up a chunk of your hard-won fortune. It comes in many ways, and it is nonstop. Patent trolls, intellectual-rights theft, class action lawsuits, and yes, spurious claims about wrongful injury and death caused by one of my myriad products. Key word here: *spurious*. So what do I do? I write a lot of checks. My lawyers call it go-away money, to make the bottom-feeders do what? Go away.

"But some claims are so egregious that I need to take extra steps to protect myself, and I do that in a number of ways, one of which is to engage the services of what is called a fixer. You might say 'an operative.' You might say 'private detective.' I say, prudent. So let us leave it there with the understanding that I am not going to yield to you—and certainly not to the litigation trolls—and apologize for taking prudent action against bogus attacks by employing an interventionist."

"Are you saying that's what you did? That you"—Heat made her own air quotes—"'intervened' to shut down inquiries into your faulty software system?"

"That's a lie. My system is not faulty."

"It sounds like you're admitting you set your fixer loose to fix the problem. Was Fred Lobbrecht a problem? Lon King?"

"You are not hearing me."

"Wilton Backhouse?"

Swift cast an obvious glance to someone behind her. This time, when Nikki turned, someone was moving toward her. But it wasn't muscle. At least not in the physical sense. The man with the silver hair gripping his cane so firmly that his knuckles whitened with every labored step was United States Congressman Kent Duer.

Wary, but unable to fight her instincts, Heat stood out of respect as the septuagenarian representative joined them and, without more than a crisp nod to her, let himself drop with a heavy exhalation into the red leather chair beside Tangier

Swift. "Too pretty to be a cop," said Duer as an aside to his host. The sly wink made it feel like anything but a compliment.

Heat had grown up in New York seeing the congressman in newspapers, on the TV news, and lately, on the Sunday talking-heads shows from inside the Beltway whenever the subject was military budgets and the powerful head of the House Defense Subcommittee was the Big Get. Congressman Duer looked her in the eye for the first time and said, "I came a long way for what's going to be a very short meeting. Fine with me, as long as you get the message loud and clear. This ends now." In the red leather chair beside him, Tangier Swift's face was etched by a smile. Suddenly finding herself outgunned, rather than cave, Heat did what she would have done in a street fight: buy time to assess the situation for optimal tactics.

"I'm not sure what you're talking about, sir."

"I believe you know exactly what I mean. Need I spell it out for you?"

Tangier Swift rested a hand on Duer's knee. The easy familiarity wasn't lost on Nikki. "Kent, you don't have to."

"No, it's all right. I want to make sure the lady understands." The representative cleared his throat and continued in a quiet but determined way. "Not only are you misguided in following the road you are on but—for reasons you cannot know—you are also creating a potential threat to national security." He let that rest, then added, "That light up the marquee for you?"

"So I should just drop it."

He chuckled and turned to Swift. "Smart, too."

But Heat wasn't done gauging what she was up against. The invocation of national security seemed like overkill in a double homicide and a probe into auto safety. "Congressman Duer, I'm afraid I'm going to need more to go on than that."

"Maybe you're not as smart as you seem. So let me come at it another way. You think you know what you're doing, but poking around blind like you are, all you're going to do is end up sticking your hand in a sack of rattlesnakes." Satisfied with the picture he had painted and the clear warning he had delivered, Duer studied the burnished eagle's head on his cane, the one he had been given the day he was released from Bethesda Naval Hospital after losing a foot in the battle of Quang Tri. "That give you plenty to go on?"

Heat digested all this and said, "Congressman, I have the utmost respect for you, your office, and your committee."

The lawmaker shook his head. "Here comes the *but*."

"However, I don't take orders on conducting homicide investigations from anyone other than NYPD. Surely, you can understand."

"Unfortunately, I do. All I'm going to say is I suggest you think long and hard about this." He turned to Swift, signaling that he was done, then back to her. "And now, since I'm through explaining, why don't you put those getaway sticks to use and move along."

As she stepped onto Greenwich Street, Nikki was too busy pondering the ramifications of that conversation to feel objectified. Or to care. This was one of those moments that came in a case where she wasn't sure if she was walking out of a meeting with information or disinformation. One thing

Heat knew for sure was that there was no such thing as a simple murder. Double that for two. Now, one of Washington's most powerful players trying to knock her off her investigation had added a new layer of complexity. But it had done something more: fueled her determination to dig even harder for the truth.

The not-unexpected bad news in the Homicide Squad Room back at the Two-Oh was that Tangier Swift's fixer had gotten sprung. "Eric Vreeland was not only released," reported Ochoa. "No bail, no charges."

"What happened with your lineup?" asked Heat. "Couldn't Stallings ID Vreeland?"

Raley said, "Oh, he picked him out. Right away. But the PI's bulldog of a lawyer gets to Stallings on the side and plants uncertainty in him about whether Vreeland was out in the public hallway or inside the apartment itself."

Nikki said, "But Stallings told us he ran into the guy inside, in his foyer."

"You know how it goes," said Ochoa. "Fog of war, heat of the moment, seeds of doubt. Take your pick." In fact, Nikki had seen it often, as every cop had. Otherwise-reliable eyewitnesses conflate or confuse details that seem indelible to those not caught up in the trauma of the incident. Criminal defense lawyers have seen it, too, and Helen Miksit jumped at the opportunity she had created.

"Also, with the backlog of craziness from the cyber attack, the DA's office didn't want to spend the effort on an uncertain complainant." Detective Raley spoke for them all by adding, "Sucks big-time."

"Always does," said Heat.

But Rhymer was taking it almost personally. "Doesn't seem right. I pull an all-nighter, nosing through mug books, and the dude's out of here before I get back to even see what he looks like."

"About like this." Ochoa held up the sketch Rhymer had been working from, and they all got a laugh.

When Heat filled the squad in on her encounter in Tribeca, the roomful of born skeptics didn't buy the national-security no-fly zone any more than Nikki did. "If there's a security threat, it's from a doucher with a politician in his pocket," commented Rhymer. "I mean, I can't say one way or the other whether Kent Duer is crooked, but at the very least, with what campaigns cost now, I'd lay odds the congressman's getting some major fund-raising done at a one-stop shop."

"And what does Tangier Swift get?" asked Raley.

"Exactly what he got today," said Ochoa. "Bigfoot comes to call."

Heat stepped up to the Murder Board. While she printed Congressman Duer's name in her neat block letters, she said, "Well, whether we buy national security or not, we have to keep it open until we can get better information."

Behind her, Rook said, "I might be able to help with that."

Nikki, who hadn't seen him since she had left for her meeting at The Greenwich, continued her writing and asked,

"Let me guess. One of your sources from Area Fifty-one?" She turned to the room with a playful smile that froze when she saw who Rook was standing a little too close to in the doorway.

"I'm not sure," he said, turning to the woman in the business suit. "Which black ops agency are you with now? CIA, NSA, NRO, GDIP?"

"Let's go with Area Fifty-one," said Yardley Bell, holding a shush finger up over her perfect grin. Then Rook's old girlfriend stepped forward with a manicured hand extended to shake. "Hi, Nikki, great to see you again. Jamie says you made captain. Yay!"

"And look, your own office," said Agent Bell after Heat had ushered Rook and his ex out of the too-public bull pen. Yardley had what Nikki referred to as a realtor's smile. Could be genuine, could be for show, could be masking a thousand unkind thoughts or beaming as many points of light. When they had crossed paths on a case a few years before, Nikki had seen the dark side of that cheer and knew there was plenty of toughness and severity accessible at the flip of a switch. Ultimately, the two women had forged a sort of peace after a bumpy initial experience. They exchanged kinder words, had a lunch once (or was it brunch?), and made promises to stay in touch, vows that represented a fusion of vacant insincerity and politeness. The last time they had spoken was over the phone just after Hurricane Sandy, when Yardley had done Nikki a favor, helping her leverage a case-breaking confession out of a foreign mercenary.

As she sat across the desk from Heat, blowing ripples across the Americano Rook had made for her, Nikki tried not to be too obvious in her appraisal of the only other woman with whom her fiancé had had a serious relationship. Her hair had changed from brunette to a tasteful light caramel with tawny lowlights. Her slender build seemed fit as before, perhaps from some yoga mixed in with the strength training, to judge from her dancer's posture—unless that was just to show off her chest for Rook. There was always that possibility.

Yardley crossed her legs and rested the coffee cup on her knee. "I hear congratulations are in order."

"Yes, that's right," Nikki said. "Thank you . . . You'll come—we hope."

"Sure thing. When's the big day?"

"August—"

"Something," finished Rook. "Mark the date. August-something."

"We're still working it out," Nikki added quickly. Bell just stared at her, taking her measure. Yardley's eyes were arresting—model gorgeous. But they took everything in, and gave so little back. Heat wondered if Rook had seen something more in them. And under what circumstances. But then Heat let go of that line of thinking. Therein lay self-torture and madness. She advanced the topic to less perilous ground. "So five minutes into a conversation about national security, you materialize. You spies are better than I thought."

"A little credit here?" said Rook. "I reached out to Agent Bell this morning."

A small gnawing took hold under Nikki's sternum. "You reached out?"

"That's correct. Shined my Batman signal on a cloud."

"And here I am." Bell laughed and held out a fist to bump with Rook. He obliged. The impact of the bump registered in Heat's stomach.

"At our briefing this morning, when we learned Timothy Maloney had been stationed at a drone base, I thought I could cut through the process by asking Yards to access his military records."

"You didn't know?" asked Bell.

Not wanting to appear so out of the Rook loop, which was becoming increasingly more difficult to do, Nikki shrugged and said, "It's divide and conquer around here."

"Nikki's a captain now," added Rook. "She can't be in every conversation, so initiative rules." Annette, the switchboard operator, came in and handed a folded message slip to Heat. "See?" he said. "Nary a moment to herself." Nikki unfolded the note. It read, "Zachary Hamner, One PP—3rd call. Insistent." Only when Annette was sure Nikki had read it did she leave.

"I can see you're scrambling, so I'll just share and be on my way," Bell said. Without notes or hesitation, Agent Bell recited, "Timothy James Maloney, Basic Military Training, Lackland AFB in San Antonio. Following BMT, stationed at Sheppard, also in Texas, for six weeks of occupational training, then transferred to Creech AFB in Nevada."

"And it's our understanding," said Heat, "that Creech is a drone base."

"Yes. That's not classified. Creech AFB is a mission site for RPAs—that's Remotely Piloted Aircraft. The MQ-1 Predators and the MQ-9 Reapers performing recon and tacticals in the Middle East and . . . Well, the Middle East."

Rook groaned melodramatically. "O-o-ow, darn. You almost slipped. You were going to tell us where else the drones fly."

"Was I?" she said with a wink.

Nikki broke up the playfulness. "I'm not that interested in details of our covert ops. Was Maloney trained as a drone operator?"

"No. Maloney was an enlisted specialist in munitions systems. He might have mounted some Hellfires onto drones, but he wasn't trained to access what the RPA pilots called the Game Room."

Heat's earlier excitement over connecting Maloney with drones plunged. But she also knew that any information was good information, even if it wasn't what she had hoped for.

Rook must have been feeling the same thing. He asked, "But it's possible he maybe developed an interest in drones."

"Anything's possible, Jamie. We know that." She toasted him with her Americano and took a drink.

"Since you're here," said Nikki, "mind if I ask you what you know about Kent Duer and a man named Tangier Swift?" Heat bullet-pointed the facts and events of the double homicide they were working, taking the agent right up to the congressman's intervention an hour before.

"Interesting," Bell said, but in a way that Heat felt showed she was masking something. Was Nikki getting better at reading the agent's tells, or was this just more wishful thinking? "SwiftRageous," Bell repeated with her eyes closed, as if committing the company name to memory. "I'll check it out." Again, this struck Heat as theater, but for now she would have to be happy with that—and for the fact that "Yards" was preparing to leave.

"Appreciate the help," said Nikki as she and Yardley clasped hands on the sidewalk outside the precinct. "I assume you are here about the cyber attack. What can you tell me about it?"

"Not my area of expertise, but we have an army of people at Langley and Fort Meade chasing their tails on it. If I learn anything, I'll definitely share it with you."

Heat chuckled. "Guess by now I should know better than to assume. I thought you were in town because of the hacking."

"Oh, I wasn't in town. I was in DC when Jamie called." Heat could feel color drain from her face and couldn't do anything about it. Yardley gave Rook's arm a squeeze. "You know how it is with this guy. Anything I can do. It also helps that the agency had a G-Four sitting at Andrews, fueled and unspoken for."

Rook waved, but Agent Bell had her head canted down in the classic texting pose in the backseat of her Yukon as the driver whisked her off on West 82nd. "That was nice of you to walk Yardley out," he said. But when he turned back and registered the stony face of Nikki Heat staring at him, he furrowed his brow. "What?"

"I came out here because I don't want to have this conversation in a fishbowl."

Now it was his turn to turn pale. "We're going to have a . . . conversation?"

She jerked her head eastward and started off toward Columbus Avenue. Within three of Nikki's long, angry strides Rook was beside her, keeping pace. "What is wrong with you?" she said.

"OK, less of a conversation and more of an appraisal of my deficiencies. Am I right?"

"What do you know, Rook? You do have some social radar, after all."

"Enough to know we have now transitioned into pre-argument mode."

She came to a halt at the corner. "Will you stop? Put a sock in the stupid banter for one second and talk to me."

He reflected a moment. "I think I had better just listen instead."

"Good idea." Nikki waited for a twin stroller to go by, a sleeping one-year-old on one side, a grinning pug on the other. "I don't know what's going on. You have been pushing every button of mine you can push the past few days. You're keeping secrets, you're hassling me about spending one night in my apartment, and now what do you do? Spring a surprise visit on me from your old flame."

"Where the hell is all this coming from?"

"My feelings, exactly."

Rook worked his jaw a little. "May I respond?"

"Love to hear it."

"This idea you have that I am keeping secrets is, well, it's ancient history. I had my reasons, but didn't I share?"

"Because I threatened you with jail."

"Never the sign of a healthy relationship, to state the obvious, but the point is, I opened up." His eyes rolled skyward while he retrieved his second point. "Oh, and the apartment. Didn't I relent and stay anyway?"

"It's not only about that one night."

"It was to me. I had plausible safety concerns following the break-in by that stalker you picked up." He winced. "Wait, that came out wrong."

"Are you actually suggesting I chose to have Maloney follow me?"

"No, no, no, of course not. It's just something that happened, I get it. You hang out at the circus, you're going to meet a few bearded ladies."

Nikki cocked her head back. "What the hell does that mean?"

"It's an analogy." Rook held out one open hand. "Here is Lon King's shrink practice—aka: the circus." He held up his other in balance. "Maloney here is the bearded lady."

"That not only unfairly characterizes psychotherapy and patients, it's callous to me."

Seeing that he was only digging himself deeper into his hole, he said, "Maybe we should move on to Agent Bell."

" 'Yards.' " The nickname had been roiling at the back of her throat and she spat it out. Petty, but sometimes petty feels awfully good.

"This is the easiest one to defend," he said. "We are shorthanded and oversubscribed on account of the cyber attack, plus you are taxed to the gills with your new administrative duties. I saw nothing wrong with being proactive and getting a consult from a top intel insider. It's just the way I work a story."

"Revealing choice of words. Your story versus our case."

"Semantics. We're in this together."

"Are we? It feels more like parallel play." Nikki could have left it there. Some instinct told her she was overwrought and should just cool off and disengage. It felt too much like the night when she gave Rook a rooftop baptism with a shot glass of Patrón.

But then Rook said, "I know what this is. You're jealous of my old girlfriend," and a smoldering ember inside Nikki flared as he continued. "Which I sure as hell thought you'd be past by now. And you should be. You may look at Yardley and see hot, dynamic, and fun. I see a disconnect from emotional access that I couldn't handle. Yards and I are over."

"I am not jealous of her."

"Good. Then what is this tension? The promotion?"

"Are you serious?"

"I've seen how the pressure of the new job has been working on you."

"Don't do that. Minimize me by saying I'm not up for my own job now."

"It's only human. Heavy is the head that wears the crown, and all that. It has to go somewhere. I can take it."

And with that came ignition. "Well, aren't you the noble martyr. Rook, this isn't bimbo jealousy, or work stress. You know what it is? Me, sick of you acting out like a sophomoric prince, feeling no accountability and taking no responsibility. As usual, it's all about you."

He held up a palm. "Hey, now—"

"What, coming a bit too close to home?" Nikki still could
have stopped, but dry acreage was being consumed and she
had crossed the firebreak. "If all this crap you're pulling is the
death rattle of your bachelorhood, I don't want to have to
stand by and watch it. Let me know when you're done, or let's
ask ourselves where this relationship is really going."

Heat left Rook slack-jawed and speechless on the corner
while she stormed back toward the police station, the sting
of regret already spreading in her heart. Halfway there, she
slowed and almost turned back. She thought about running
to him for a reset, to start the conversation again and work
this out. But Nikki couldn't bear to have him see her tears.

When Heat stepped out of the women's room from washing her
face and composing herself, raucous laughter drew her to the
homicide bull pen. It sounded as if Detective Feller was being
taunted by the squad. But when she entered, he was the one
laughing the loudest as Ochoa pinched his nose theatrically
and Raley and Rhymer fanned the air around Randall with
open manila files, calling him "Sasquatch" and "stink ape"
and chuckling like frat boys on keg night.

Glad to see some tension getting siphoned off, Nikki eased
into the squad room so she wouldn't quell the fun with the
shadow of her authority. But watching Feller's pals needle him
over his grubby beard, ripe clothes, and greasy hat-hair from
his extended stakeout only brought more weight to Nikki's

sadness over her blowup with Rook. Things settled, either because they were all laughed out or had caught sight of their captain. "Don't let me interrupt the horseplay," she said.

"Horse is right," called Detective Rhymer. "You getting a good whiff of Secretariat here?" Which kicked off another volley of name-calling and guffaws.

When that had died down, Feller told Heat that his lack of grooming came with a payoff. "I got me my man," he said with some pride. "Fat Tommy's persuader."

"You nabbed Joseph Barsotti? Good for you," she said. "He finally show up at Fortuna's Wheel?"

"I gave up on that place after the first night with no action. I figured Fat Tommy had probably let it be known there'd be some attention after Lon King got killed." He paused. "I really do stink, don't I?"

Heat took a half step back. "You're . . . fine."

"With RTCC and the other databases down I couldn't check on vice harassment complaints, so I went old-school and started making a surveillance circuit of some of the skin clubs Fat Tommy has a hand in. This afternoon, broad daylight, during the generously titled Gentlemen's Fashion Lunch at one of the titty bars in East Harlem, I spot Barsotti in the parking lot kicking the snot out of some showgirl in a bathrobe. The dancer's up at Metropolitan getting stitches. Barsotti's in Interrogation Two."

Through the glass of the observation room Joseph Barsotti projected the calm you only see in the conscience-free. Dead eyes, a dead stare, and a mind that had parked its body and gone elsewhere because whatever had to be endured would simply be endured as the bargain made with life and the capo. "How'd you like that to be your collection agency?" asked Feller. It wasn't likely that the enforcer could hear through the mirror, but Barsotti rotated his chin toward them and, with those vacant eyes, it felt like he took an X-ray through the glass to add targets to his list. Randall shivered. "Whoa, chilly."

Heat felt her iPhone vibrate. To her relief, Rook had replied to her previous text message suggesting that they meet for dinner. "To continue the conversation," as Nikki had put it. Her torment easing slightly, she set aside her cell and said, "Randy, I want you to have the honors."

"Truly?"

"You bagged him, you work him."

This gesture by the captain, stepping aside to let the detective handle his own interrogation, added an inch to Feller's height. "Thank you. He's only going to keep it shut, you know."

"You never know. Maybe he'll buckle under the stink." She left for her office to return calls and make a dent in the mountain of forms she had to complete on the typewriter that had been resurrected from the basement. At least it was electric.

As a professional courtesy, the USPS cop watching the postal truck garage on the north side of Roosevelt Station waved Captain Heat into the driveway and pointed her to a safe spot to park beside one of the idle loading docks. Nikki didn't like to call in PCs, but relentless administrative grappling hooks had snagged her on her way out of the precinct, and she didn't want to keep Rook waiting while she hunted for a public space. Or, to be more honest, she wanted to get there first so she could settle herself down. Shame had started to shuffle into her emotional mix, as if sadness and regret about her outburst weren't enough.

A chilly fog had settled over Manhattan, and Nikki waited for the cone-shaped beam of headlights to pass before she jaywalked from the Midtown East mail center across 55th Street to the restaurant. P. J. Clarke's, a landmark Irish pub frequented over the years by everyone from Sinatra to Hedy Lamarr to Buddy Holly, occupied the ground floor of a two-story brick building squatting between modern high-rises on 3rd Avenue. Less known, and in Heat's view, the better for it, a sister restaurant, a warm, clubby steakhouse named the Sidecar, lived on the second floor at P. J. Clarke's. Part of its mystique was the speakeasy entrance on the sidewalk near the back marked by a small, unassuming sign jutting out above a black door. It gave Nikki a Gotham-throwback feel every time she approached the nondescript entrance, pressed the silent door buzzer, and presented her face to the lipstick camera until the hostess upstairs buzzed her in.

Nikki climbed the double flight of stairs past the curated memorabilia adorning the walls beside vintage Yankees team photos and framed newspaper pages of Mayor LaGuardia, big-band crooners, and last-century prizefighters. Nikki pushed open the door from the stairwell into the festive, muted bustle of the restaurant. The hostess greeted her warmly, but Heat looked past her, surveying the dark wooden bar and the banquettes for Rook. Both disappointed and relieved, Heat said she'd wait to be seated until her other party arrived. The woman moved off to retrieve coats, and Nikki reflexively checked her watch. Somehow, she'd gotten there a minute early. She heard the nearly inaudible purr of the door buzzer and craned over the podium at the surveillance monitor, and there he was, Jameson Rook, smiling up at the lipstick camera, from Heat's perspective, directly at her. It beat the look she'd gotten from Barsotti thorough the interrogation glass. It beat a lot of things.

Then everything changed. And in a hurry.

On the monitor, Rook swiveled casually to look back over his shoulder, as if making room for other diners, who were out of the frame of the picture. But, as he turned back, two pairs of hands reached in to the frame and grabbed him. The whole thing startled Nikki for an instant, as if the speakeasy monitor had flipped channels to some primetime cop show. But the image was both real and in real time. As Rook struggled and was dragged out of the picture, Heat shouted, "NYPD, call 911!" and yanked open the door.

Hopping down the stairs two at a time, Nikki raced down the first flight but missed a step on the turn and stumbled onto the floor of the landing. Without bothering to stand up, she let the momentum of the fall carry her on a roll down the lower flight, regaining her footing on the fly halfway down, and was quickly out the door and on the sidewalk.

Her first glance was to the left, in the direction where she had seen Rook being dragged away. But there was no sign of him there, and no reason to think that was the right direction

to go—unless they had taken Rook into the lobby of the
office building next door, which seemed unlikely. When she
swung her view right, she heard yelling and a woman
screaming just as she saw the backs of two large men
struggling to drag Rook around the corner of 3rd Avenue.

She sprinted after them, calling behind her, "NYPD!
Officer needs help!" in hopes that the postal policeman would
hear and respond. But city buses were parked along that block,
and she couldn't count on being heard—or seen—over them.

Heat came upon the two men, working to get a hard-
fighting Rook into the back of a family-style van. He had the
sense to spread his arms and legs to make it more difficult for
them to get him inside, even though the big men would
eventually surely prevail. Heat drew her Sig Sauer and, just
as she was about to call for a freeze, a pro wrestler–sized guy
standing beside her, one she hadn't counted, spun, executing
an arm bar that clotheslined her to the pavement and sent her
pistol clacking into the gutter. She went for the man's legs
instead of her weapon, but her angle of leverage sucked. It
felt like slamming into a tree trunk. He slipped free and
brought a leg back to deliver a kick, but she log-rolled to one
side and his shoe only grazed the meat of her upper arm.

The blur of feet and pants legs at ground level told Nikki
they had gotten Rook inside the vehicle. She lunged for her gun
and took a soccer kick behind her ear. Heat's vision faded out.
Her head came down on concrete, and in her swirl of nausea
and blindness all she could hear was running footsteps, a door
sliding and slamming, and the squeal of tires disappearing up
3rd Avenue with Rook inside going God knows where.

ELEVEN

Nikki Heat burst through the door of the homicide bull pen full bore, calling out assignments even before she had cleared the threshold. Even though it was after 10:00 P.M., Raley and Ochoa had mustered the entire crew and the squad was operating at full capacity. Rhymer and Aguinaldo had canceled their evening plans to rally for the captain. Even Detective Feller, bleary, unshaven, but in fresh clothes, had zombied in and was already working the phones. Nikki would take him on his worst day. Or, in this case, hers.

"Roach. The BOLO on our silver minivan hasn't turned up crap. Call in an extra shift of blue-and-whites to get out there and supplement existing patrols. Screw the overtime, I want eyeballs on the streets. Now." Raley rushed to his desk to make the call. Heat turned to Ochoa. "Miguel, air support. Verify how many copters they have working this. If there is even one chopper sitting on the ground, let me know, and I'll call the chief personally. We've already got two bodies, we are not going to let this man be a third."

As Heat continued barking out assignments, everyone sprang to action; no one was bothered by the hard edge she had brought into the station house with her. Rook had been violently abducted. Rook. One of their own. Their friend. Her damn fiancé. Every detective knew this was no time for niceties; these were the critical hours to beat the bushes for leads. Everything else was wasted energy that could cost him his life.

"FBI for you, Captain," said the night switchboard op from the hall. "I put it through to your office phone."

She lunged across her desk to grab the phone. "This is Heat, who have I got?"

"Captain, it's Special Agent Jordan Delaney, FBI."

"I called you people twice."

"I'm in my car now heading to Federal Plaza to meet my task force. I just got the case. And I'm with you. We don't want to burn any time."

"Then let's not." Nikki was redlining at top rpm's and wasn't about to slow for anyone, not even the FBI. She bulleted Delaney through the event as it had gone down, detailing the before, during, and after of the 3rd Avenue street grab along with all the descriptions she had, including two of the abductors and the partial plate she had been able to spot from the gutter. "Detective Raley from my precinct is en route to the restaurant at this very moment to secure their speakeasy cam video."

"I want it, too," said the agent.

"Done. You'll have a copy within the hour." She then filled Delaney in on the measures they had taken so far: the BOLO, the canvassing for eyewitnesses near the intersection where the grab had gone down, the extra manpower on the streets, plus the frequent calls they kept making to Rook's cell phone. "I've assigned a detective to go to his loft to get his laptop so we can activate the Find My iPhone feature."

"Save him the trip. We've already pulled Jameson Rook's cell number and run our own ping on the StingRay network," said the FBI agent. "Nothing. Apparently his SIM card's been disabled or removed from the device." The implications of that shot a lightning bolt of fresh panic through Nikki. She nearly had to sit down but clamped a lid on that shit and kept it together. "Captain, are you there?"

"What about street cams?" She came back with extra bite in her voice—trying not to see the mental picture of those goons wrestling Rook's cell phone from him. "The cyber attack has rendered our cams NG. Do you feds have any visual tracking capability?"

"No."

"Or aren't you cleared to tell me?"

"I understand your frustration."

"Like hell you do."

Either this guy Delaney was an experienced agent or he had no pulse. He paused to absorb her rebuke, then continued evenly. "It's put us in a box, too. I understand you have a close relationship with Mr. Rook, am I right?"

"He's my fiancé."

"Damn. Then let me assure you, Captain Heat, you have my word—this is family—I'm not going to hold anything back."

"Thank you, Agent Delaney." Her conciliatory tone barely masked the flames of urgency blazing underneath.

"You got it." He paused, and she could hear his turn

signal before he continued. "Your fiancé is quite well known and, unfortunately, journalists are big targets these days, and not just on foreign soil."

Heat's patience for a what-if dance of potential scenarios was zero, so she interrupted. "Let me save us both some time here and get to it. This was not some symbolic jihadi grab of a reporter. I know exactly what triggered this."

"Go," said Delaney.

Nikki told him about the case her team was working, and especially encouraged the agent to make a hard run at Tangier Swift, who topped her list for motive and means. As a longshot number two, she included Timothy Maloney, who had been stalking her and had motive to harm Rook as a means of personal retribution, crazy as that would be.

"Let me do some seat-of-the-pants profiling," said Delaney. "You're talking about a lone wolf ex-cop with psych issues. Paranoia, for starters."

Heat nodded to herself. "I'm right there with you. I'm not seeing Maloney with the organizational chops to pull off an operation like the one I witnessed."

"But he's viable as a number-two. Got it." Nikki heard the turn signal again. "Listen, I'm about to hit the parking garage downtown. Get me that speakeasy video. My crew specializes in missing persons and abductions, and we're going to put a monitor on your phones in case contact gets made—hopefully by Mr. Rook—otherwise, anyone asking for ransom. Oh. Do you need a sketch artist to work up your kidnappers?"

"Ours just got here."

"Shoot me the pics. And Heat—fly close."

Minutes after she hung up, her landline rang again and, as always when the incoming was from Zachary Hamner's number at One Police Plaza, she hesitated before answering. But, whether she liked the political survivor–slash–hatchet man or not, he was high up in the department, so Heat answered. And when she did, Nikki heard something she had never before heard from The Hammer: compassion. "I'm reaching out to tell you how sorry I am about Rook. But beyond that, I want to give you my pledge that we are all over this. I've reached out to the FBI, but I hear you've already engaged—good. Keep doing what you do, we'll do the same. And if I hear anything at all about him, you're my first call. And if you hit any departmental obstacles, any at all, make me your first."

She thanked him and, as she replaced the phone on its cradle, she thought Zach had sounded almost human.

Sitting with the police sketch artist tortured Heat with a double dose of agony. First, it forced her to sit idle for twenty minutes—excruciating, even though she knew the importance of getting the faces of those kidnappers out there. But the interval also gave her too much time to grapple with the thoughts she'd been able to avoid by keeping busy. Was he still alive? Was he suffering? Would she ever see him again? And through it all ran the deep anguish she felt over her last conversation with Rook having been a bitter argument. Out there on Columbus and 82nd, Nikki had slipped her emotional chain and gone off on him. Losing Rook would be unbearable enough. Living with a harsh quarrel as their last words would be a crushing weight borne eternally.

She had to make sure that didn't happen.

As soon as the sketches were finished, Nikki bolted into the squad room, only to encounter a surprise. Raley was back from his video errand at P. J. Clarke's, and he and Ochoa had transformed the bull pen into a Rook-abduction war room. They had called in extra detectives from Robbery-Burglary plus an extra shift of uniforms and administrative aides to facilitate logistics, make calls, and act as runners. In tandem, Roach brought Heat up to speed on status and assignments.

"We're going at this with a dual strategy," began Detective Ochoa.

Detective Raley took the handoff. "We decided our best shot to break this is to break it down. So we're operating on two fronts: First is the immediate search for Rook. Here's where we are with that." He indicated a list they had posted on a new whiteboard they had rolled in. "An aide is calling his cell every ten minutes. Even though you said the SIM is inactive, it's an easy base to cover—so why not? Next, we've contacted his credit card companies to monitor any usage and get us an instant alert of where and when."

"Same for his bank card?" asked Heat.

"Affirm," said Rales. "If Rook—or anyone—taps an ATM for his cash, we'll know in seconds and have cars and a chopper swarm it. We're sending a detective from the First Precinct to check out Rook's loft in case there's been a forced entry or signs of it being tossed."

Flywheels were spinning so fast in Nikki's head that, in her impatience, she started to read ahead on the board so she could assess the coverage without waiting through Raley's recitation. The list felt comprehensive: Run silver minivans through the DMV. Check for minivans reported stolen, starting in the last twenty-four hours (painstaking without access to the database, but they would assign the manpower to do it by hand). Assign an administrative aide to call the Crime Stoppers anonymous tip line every half hour. Get in touch with 911 Dispatch for any calls reporting fights or ... gunshots.

With that the to-do list had taken a sharp left into corrosive areas. Nikki's mouth went dry, and she crossed her arms so she could wedge her hands into her armpits and hide how much they were shaking. At the end of his bullet points, Raley concluded with, "That's one front we're hitting."

"But we're hitting a second front just as hard," continued Ochoa. "And that's to step it up and push harder on the Lon King and Fred Lobbrecht murders." He must have caught Heat's reaction to that and started to explain. "Our theory is—"

"The murder case is tied in to his kidnapping," Heat said, interrupting. "Solving that case equals saving Rook."

"Exactly. We don't know how—"

"But we know they're linked," said Raley. "So the last thing we can afford to do is drop the ball there."

Heat nodded. "Agreed. The clock is running."

Detective Ochoa indicated the busy squad room. "That's why we called in extra investigators from Robbery-Burglary.

So our squad can keep flogging the homicides. Meantime, everyone has canceled their lives for this. We are going to find him, Captain."

"And if we don't have solid leads—" added Raley."

"We are going to follow up on every single weak one no matter how tangential it looks until we get Rook back safe and alive," finished Ochoa.

The alternative sickened Heat, so she told herself for the hundredth time that there *was* no alternative. "Keep it rolling, bring him home," she said. The thank-you was implied; making it explicit would only cause them to lose a step in a fast race. But on the way to her office, Nikki paused for the briefest second to appreciate the fact that her squad co-leaders had set aside whatever differences they had for the sake of the mission. The fact that they were back together working as the Roach machine gave her heart hope that they actually might find Rook.

Heat closed her office door and placed another call—one that pride had made her procrastinate over, but pride would not help find Rook. It went to the 703 area code, and the operator in the big glass building in the woods Nikki pictured outside Washington, DC, answered on the first ring. After a short interval—mercifully without lite jazz—there came a double click and a single electronic purr. "You've reached voicemail for Senior Agent Bell. You may now leave a message."

Figuring that the encrypted line would be secure enough, Heat left a lengthy message describing Rook's kidnapping to Yardley and urging her to call so they could talk more about

Tangier Swift. Trying to keep the throat squeeze of desperation out of her voice, she said, "It's ten past one A.M., but call anytime with anything." Before hanging up, she added for emphasis, *"Anytime."*

So much for hiding her desperation.

Lon King, PhD
Counseling Transcript
Session of Mar. 21/13 with Heat, N., Det. Grade-1, NYPD

LK: You've been away for some time.

NH: Not so long.

LK: You canceled your last session. And the makeup one, as well.

NH: Best of intentions, but real life intervenes. Casework, the usual. You know.

LK: It wasn't discomfort over our prior conversation?

NH: Of course not. Just busy.

LK: Then you won't mind if we go back to where we left off. In my notes here you were just about to talk about commitment to Rook. [Note—NH avoiding eye contact, restless] I'm sensing this might be a sensitive area for you, Nikki. Is it?

NH: No. I mean, we are engaged. That's commitment, right?

LK: Is it?

NH: Yes. Absolutely. We are going to do this.

LK: Very concrete. As a high achiever, I have no doubt

you are committed to the event. My question is, how
does it make you feel?

NH: Like it's the time of my life. [Long pause] Crap. I'm
sorry. I just got a text from the precinct. I have to go.
Sorry.

LK: Duty doesn't call anymore. It texts. But this is
something you need to explore. Your comfort zone
when things get too emotional is your task orientation.

NH: It's a big job, and I'm dedicated to it.

LK: Yes, it's quite a drive you have. The thing I would ask
you, is are you driving toward something, or driving
something away?

Just before dawn after a night without sleep, Nikki sat on hold
with the graveyard-shift DMV supervisor she had chased
down in Albany to gate-crash the Records Section and run
out a list of silver minivans for her. While he slowly—so
damn slowly—took down the information, Heat tried to pry
open the bottle of Tylenol she had found in the break room's
first-aid drawer so she could tame the throbbing knot behind
her ear where the goon had soccer-kicked her. Nikki's
quaking fingers managed to pop the top, but the force of the
action sent all the tablets clattering over her desktop to the
floor. Screw it. Heat selected two off her blotter and dry-
swallowed them.

As she wrapped up her call to the DMV, she heard
someone walking on gravel and turned. But it wasn't gravel.
It was Detective Ochoa treading across Tylenol. His face

registered something she had not seen all night: hope. Then he said one welcome word: "Tipster."

"Tell me," she said, rising to her feet, adrenalized. With a cop's reflex, she noted the time: 5:42 in the morning.

"Just came in. A guy in town for dinner last night from Port Chester saw Rook get taken. He said it didn't look right, and tailed the silver minivan as far as he could."

"He credible?"

"Gave the full plate that matches your partial."

"Why'd he wait so long?"

"Said he was with someone he wasn't supposed to be with, and didn't want to get found out. Guess he got a conscience."

"Let's hear it for cheaters," Heat said, pulling on her blazer. "Have him show me."

To make sure he didn't wiggle off the hook, Detective Feller picked up Alvin Speyer outside his Times Square hotel and chauffeured the philandering plumbing contractor to where he had last seen the kidnap van. They followed Montgomery Street under the FDR into the parking lot of Pier 36, where Detective Heat was waiting between the cargo warehouse and the big Parks & Rec basketball complex. Raley and Ochoa wanted to be there, too, but she had come alone, not wanting to overwhelm an already apprehensive eyewit with a heavy turnout of detectives.

Heat crossed the blacktop to her tipster after he got out of the passenger seat and gave him her most welcoming smile and a friendly handshake. She had already slid her badge further back on her belt so that he wouldn't spot it and freeze up. She made out Speyer to be about forty-six to forty-eight, with the kind of cheerful bad-boy face that some women find irresistible, and the faded-glory level of fitness you see in suburban sports coaches. Nikki wondered if the previous night's Gotham slumber party had been with a soccer mom or a lucky customer, then banished all that as distracting. "Hi, Mr. Speyer, I'm Nikki," she said, careful to keep it informal. No sense introducing rank-caused jitters. "I want to thank you for your cooperation, and I want to assure you, right off, that your assistance will remain just between us."

"Good. 'Cause I'll end up in court if it gets out I was here. According to my wife, I'm supposed to be in East Meadow on a big condo contract all this week."

"Your secret's safe with me." In order to move away from the subject of adultery before he retreated, she added, "Why don't you describe exactly what you saw."

Speyer massaged the back of his thick neck and said, "Sure. We were heading to dinner up at Neary's, you know, that Irish spot, when this asshole in a silver van cuts me off and hits the brakes right in front of me. I give him a dose of horn, but then I see these three big dudes coming, and figure I'd better cool it. Then I see they're wrestling this guy who no way wants to go with them. My lady says we should get out of there, but my dad was a fireman, you know? It's in the blood to help. I tell her let's just follow and see what's what, you never know. Then when I see this lady get dropped in the gutter, I say, 'No brainer, we're on these dudes.'"

Speyer described the route, and Heat was happy to see

Randall Feller taking notes behind him, out of his view. From the East Side they had taken the FDR south past the Williamsburg Bridge, finding their way to South Street and then to the place where they now stood. "We didn't want to get too close. Who knew what the fuck they were up to. Or carrying. So I hung back there near the street and watched. They pull up to that ramp down there." He made a chop with one hand toward an incline to the East River. "Then they drag the same guy out and take him down to this motorboat that's waiting. They load him in and it takes off."

With her heart lashing her rib cage, Nikki asked, "What about the man? Did he seem all right? Hurt? Was he struggling?"

"Naw, he wasn't fighting at all. He seemed sort of out of it. Upright, but these guys were big, and they were basically carrying him one on each shoulder."

"Drugged?"

"I'd say so. Or they'd fucking cold-cocked his ass. He had a lot of blood on his shirt."

Nikki felt herself lose feeling in her hands and feet.

Feller picked up on it and stepped in to distract her. "Tell us about the boat."

"Not much to tell, and we didn't hang around, I'll tell you that."

Every detective knows that when an eyewitness says there's not much to tell, it's only because they haven't been asked the right questions yet. Randall had a few. "Did it have any numbers? Maybe a name or markings?"

"I'm sure it had numbers and such, but it was too far to read."

"Could you see what color it was?"

"It was night, much darker than now." They looked east. The sun was not yet up, and oystery clouds hung low.

Heat had regained her equilibrium and joined in. "But I see some lights there on the pier; they're still on."

"Hmm, I'm thinking blue. The boat was blue."

"Good," said Feller. "All kinds of blue, Alvin. Navy, powder, light, dark?"

"Light and bright. Kinda like the sky, I'd say."

"Sky blue."

"Yeah, I'd definitely call it sky blue. Open boat, too. Like a skiff. Big outboard. That thing hauled."

"So you actually saw it leave?" asked Nikki. "Did you see where it went?"

"It was foggy, so I lost it. But the direction was sort of that way." He straight-armed toward Brooklyn.

Nothing definitive—but more than they had had five minutes before.

Detective Feller didn't even need to be asked. He had made some good contacts in the Harbor Unit and Coast Guard earlier in the week in chasing down leads on Lon King's kayak and volunteered to hop on them right away to check boat registries and set up patrols of the waterfront for a sky-blue skiff, especially concentrating on a zone from Williamsburg to Red Hook.

Heat called the description in to Ochoa so helicopters could cover the harbor as well as streets and backyards, in case the skiff had been trailered and hauled. The detective said he would alert cruisers to be especially watchful for the silver minivan in Brooklyn, in case that was its destination, as well.

On her drive back to the precinct, Nikki's panic dueled with hope. But there was nothing like a lead to bring faith, so she clung to that. For dear life.

The King of All Surveillance Media had seen happier days. Heat popped into his screening room up the hall from the bull pen, where he was painstakingly scrubbing his copy of the footage from the Sidecar's speakeasy cam, which so far had offered no good imagery of the abductors. The frozen frame on his monitor was of Rook, wincing in reaction as hands clutched him from behind. Nikki had to look away from that picture of him and hurried out.

She had just entered her office when Detective Rhymer beckoned her through the glass to come into the squad room.

Opie stood at his desk, indicating four thick manila accordion files stuffed with documents that were marked with a rainbow array of sticky tabs. "Roach assigned me to dig deeper into financial matters for our decedents. Lon King came out pretty much as projected. Big dips to cover gambling debts until there was no more to dip from. I'm sure he was living off his artist partner's commissions. With the cyber snafu, I had to go old school looking into Fred Lobbrecht. That meant going the paper route. Hard copies, so nothing got sucked into the ether." He patted the files. "Just came from his bank branch. Very interesting. Here's a guy who went along and along on his state trooper salary.

No spikes up or down. Nothing out of pattern—until . . ."
He drew a printout from one of the accordion files and
displayed it for Heat. "Until a month ago, when the last ten
years of his mortgage suddenly get paid off."

"A definite spike," said Heat.

"The Odd Sock, Captain," saidOpie, tossing Heat's own
lexicon back at her. "Now where do you suppose a guy who's
been a career state trooper gets that kind of money without
buying a Pick 10?"

"I don't know. Rich uncle? Perhaps one in the automotive
biz?" Of course, a huge windfall never smelled right in a
murder investigation. But what did it mean? A big lump sum
could point to any number of things: a bribe, hush money,
compensation to a mole among the safety watchdogs, even an
extortion payment squeezed out of Swift by Lobbrecht.
What Rhymer had turned up in that bank statement could
even reframe the actions of some fellow whistle-blowers who
had suddenly changed careers: one to decamp to the
Everglades on a manatee rescue mission, the other to drive
fast cars and live out a Clarence Clemons fantasy in Bronx
rock 'n' blues bars. Heat knew that kind of independence
either comes from a life change or ready cash. It was time to
go back to the whistle-blowers to ask a few more pointed
questions about their dead colleague—and to see if they
passed the smell test.

Detective Rhymer set out for Throggs Neck to
reinterview Nathan Levy. Detective Aguinaldo was tasked
to stir up Abigail Plunkitt, who still had not checked in from
Florida. Heat made a call downtown to set up a forensic

accounting study of both Tangier Swift and of his corporation, SwiftRageous, hoping to find some telltale payment that coincided with Lobbrecht's windfall. It was going to take some time, they told her. The cyber intrusion had overwhelmed their office, but they would do their best. The bureaucratic response hit Nikki like a kick in the gut. Rook's life hung in the balance. She damn well needed more than a checked-out worker bee doing her best. She hung up and dialed One Police Plaza to cash in the offer from Zach Hamner to kick some municipal ass.

After that, Heat headed to NoHo to see what there was to learn about Fred Lobbrecht at Hudson University.

The officers in the blue-and-white detailed to Wilton Backhouse confirmed to Heat that the professor was inside the Practical Science and Engineering Annex. Before she stepped away, the driver raised a clenched fist and said, "You hang in, Captain."

She returned the gesture and said, "Always."

Crossing Thompson Street, Nikki was amazed at how word spread, even when the department's intranet was down. The small gesture also gave her greater hope that more eyes in that city were alert for Rook than she had imagined.

Heat startled Backhouse, who was in his office with the door open to the hallway while he collected materials for a morning lab. "Embarrassing," he said when he had recovered his composure. "I've been jumping at everything. Noises, even freakin' door slams get me."

Heat understood why his nerves would be frayed and

tried to assuage him. "It's all good."

"Are you shitting me? Are you serious? You don't think I know about Nate Levy? He calls and tells me about the goddamn drone taking a shot at him, and you're saying it's all good? You people can't even keep your computers running, and I'm supposed to feel safe and snug because there's two cops playing Sudoku in a police car out front?"

"We're doing everything we can to bring this to a close." This guy needed to be calmed down, so she tried enlisting him. "Help me do that. Do you have time for a quick chat?"

He flicked a glance at the Pebble on his wrist. "Ten minutes, anyway. I've got a session on impact elasticity and coefficients of restitution." He seemed put off when Heat took it upon herself to close his door, but set down his laptop and files and settled onto the yoga ball he used for a desk chair.

The rest of his office looked lived-in, but more utilitarian than homey. The window behind him looked out to a dark air shaft between buildings through bent venetian blinds. The overhead fluorescents gave light that was good but too bright for Nikki's headache. Technical books stuffed with papers filled gray metal shelves on two walls; the rack above his desk held DVD collections of *Bladerunner*, *Lord of the Rings*, *The Matrix*, and *Firefly* bookended by a pair of miniature blue British phone booths, which she recognized from Rook's obsessive viewing as being from *Dr. Who*. That jibed with his tee shirt, which read, "Daleks Do It with Directed Energy." She took in the unframed wall art behind him. Side-by-side posters of Benedict Cumberbatch: one as Kahn from *Star Trek Into Darkness*; the other as Julian

Assange, the famous whistle-blower, a role Cumberbatch had played in *The Fifth Estate*.

The whistle-blower across from Heat said, "Where's your pal, Jameson Rook?" The question hit her like a jolt of electricity. "He hasn't been scared off my story, has he? This needs to get out. Lives are at stake, do you get that?"

Heat kept it together while listening to Backhouse whine, thinking, who was more keenly aware of lives being at stake at that moment than she was? Rook was out there somewhere, and she didn't even know if he was alive. But after witnessing the prof's jumpiness, she thought better of agitating him with the real reason the journalist wasn't there, and answered with truth by omission. "No, trust me, Rook is still completely immersed in this story." Heat wanted to get Backhouse's impressions of Fred Lobbrecht's sudden wealth, but decided to hold off on that topic and switch first to Backhouse's own area of focus. "Can you help me drill down more on Tangier Swift?"

"You kidding? Let's do some fracking."

"What do you know about his relationship with a congressman, Kent Duer?"

"The defense industry hawk? Not much. Why?" He started bouncing ever so slightly on the yoga ball while Nikki described her encounter at The Greenwich. When she had finished, he spotted an elastic band dangling from a pen in his pencil cup and used it to put his hair back in a ponytail as he spoke. "I don't have any specifics, but here's all you need to know. Tangier Swift is an empire builder. His whole reason to get up every morning is to surpass the legacy of

Steve Jobs. He's got a hard-on to expand his tech impact across every possible platform, so I'm sure he's doling out campaign contributions with both fists to grease the skids. With Tangier, it's all about ego."

Heat's gaze moved from Wilton Backhouse to his Julian Assange poster; she decided that the CEO of SwiftRageous didn't hold the monopoly on narcissism. "This may be sensitive," she said, "but I need to ask you about Fred Lobbrecht."

He finished fooling with his hair and regarded her warily. "Yeah . . . ?"

"We reviewed his financials, and there's evidence Mr. Lobbrecht suddenly came into some money last month. A lot of money."

Backhouse's expression changed from caution to revelation as he whispered, "Fuck . . ."

"What do you know about this?"

"God, it's just like Nate suspected. Levy thought Fred Lobbrecht was dirty."

While relived memories appeared to play across the young professor's face, Nikki flipped up the cover of her spiral notebook. "Explain why Levy thought that."

Her question brought him up short, and he shook his head slightly. "I don't want to get into it. It's nothing. Forget I said it."

"Wilton. Look at me. Do you really think I am going to forget you said anything?" She waited, and made it clear she would wait as long as it took while he bobbed up and down on his bouncy chair.

At last, he blinked. With a resigned sigh, he said, "I didn't want to go there, but there was some ugly shit going on between Lobbrecht and Levy."

"How ugly?"

"Butt ugly. It was over solidarity, whether our Splinter Group should go forward with our whistle-blow. Fred had been all gung-ho, then suddenly got all 'Let's put on the brakes, here.' Nathan got royally pissed and accused Lobbrecht of being on the take. Freddy punched him out and Levy threatened to kill him, after all they'd been through, sticking their necks out."

"Nathan Levy clearly threatened to kill him?"

"Exact words."

"Did anyone else witness this?"

"Lobbrecht. But he's dead. Levy, of course. And Abigail Plunkitt. Abby had to help me pull the two of them apart. Ask her. I don't think she's going to forget that."

"And where was this? At Forenetics?"

"At work? Oh, hell, no."

Heat thought back to her interview with Backhouse after the drone attack in Washington Square. "Sounds like you, Lobbrecht, Levy, and Plunkitt were all together in one place. Was this at your Splinter Summit in Rhinebeck? You did say things got rough that weekend."

He nodded. "You have some memory."

"It's yours I'm interested in. When was this again?"

Backhouse narrowed his eyes and searched the acoustical tile overhead. "Six . . . seven weeks ago?"

"Is that scuffle how Nathan Levy hurt his leg?"

"I told you, it was one intense fight." Backhouse tapped

his watch and rose to go to his lab.

"One more thing before you take off." Nikki took out her iPhone. "Look at these and see if you recognize any of these three men." He gave a quick study to each face she showed him: Timothy Maloney, no. Joseph Barsotti, no. Eric Vreeland, no. "You're sure. Do you need more time?"

"Not really. They don't look familiar."

"I'm especially interested in this one," she said, holding up Eric Vreeland's headshot. Nikki held back his association as Tangier Swift's fixer, but told Backhouse, "This man was seen in the vicinity of Nathan Levy's home after his drone attack."

A look of concern clouded his face. "And this fucker's out there somewhere? Why don't you bust him?"

"We did bring him in for questioning. His . . . um, lawyer got him released."

"You people are inept." He gathered his laptop and papers again and opened his door. "You are not making me feel any safer, do you know that?" Then he did a hallway check and strode away before Nikki could give him an answer. Which was just as well, because she didn't really have a good one.

First thing before she got on the elevator, Heat made another scan of her emails and texts for word on Rook. The passage of time brought a fresh stab of worry with every hour. Knowing that everything that could be done was being done was not enough. On the ride down, Nikki shut her eyes, seeking calm, reminding herself what she and Roach had said in the bull pen, that keeping busy working the homicides was the same as looking for Rook, because she was convinced they were related, even if not sure how.

Armed with new information about Levy's death threat, Heat speed-dialed Inez Aguinaldo to have her ask Abigail Plunkitt about the incident in Rhinebeck. While the phone rang, the captain decided that, whether it was in her precinct budget or not, she'd put the detective on a plane to Florida that afternoon if her witness was incommunicado somewhere in the middle of the Everglades.

When Detective Aguinaldo answered, there was some urgency in her voice. "I was just taking out my phone to call you, Captain. Abigail Plunkitt is not in Florida. She's here in New York. Dead."

TWELVE

The traffic officer recognized Heat's car as a plain wrap when she pulled up, so without having to badge herself through, Nikki got waved to a spot in front of the coroner's van on East 3rd Street, down in the Alphabets. A patrolwoman stood at relaxed sentry beside the front door of the apartment building, an unremarkable tan-brick structure sandwiched between a laundromat and a cross-fit gym advertising its grand opening. The uni gave Heat a smart nod as the captain signed in to the crime scene. Following a five-story climb up through the old walk-up, Heat stepped out through the propped-open service door onto the rooftop.

Across the flat expanse, which had been painted white, per the latest eco-trend, Lauren Parry and a crew from the Office of Chief Medical Examiner had set up shop near the victim. Detective Aguinaldo stood with them, taking notes. Nikki paused, performing her usual ritual of respect and remembrance, then let her eyes soak up the area as she approached the body.

Every murder scene is memorable in its own way. The lasting impression made by Abigail Plunkitt was that she didn't appear dead at all from the rear, but simply like a woman seated in her patio chair, enjoying the view of the Lower East Side. The laid-back quality was furthered by the glass of red wine on the teak end table beside her and the Kindle that lay sleeping on her lap. Only when Heat came around for a front view did it all change. Dried blood formed a line descending from a small hole where her eyebrows met above the bridge of her nose. The rust-colored stream traced the channel formed between her right cheek and nostril, around her mouth to her jaw, then down her throat onto her pale-yellow tee, where it had been absorbed and spread by drizzle two nights before into an oxidized tie-dye. In that sense, this murder scene was not unique at all. "Same COD as Lon King down at the river," said Heat.

Dr. Lauren Parry peered up at her from her kneeling position beside the corpse. "Normally, I'd say don't rush to judgment, but I can't say I disagree."

"But you'll need to run your tests."

"I will." The medical examiner stood and approached her. "Right now, I'm more interested in you."

"Thanks."

"Any word?" Then she read her friend's face and let it go. "OK, but anything you need. Anything." Sympathetic enough not to push it, Parry focused on the prelim of Abigail Plunkitt. "Obviously small-caliber, single GSW, same POE as King's. Based on his condition, I did a quick field test and see definite signs of residue from gunpowder. The lab will be more definitive, probably reveal some trace metals."

"So, another close-range shot."

"Bet on it."

Nikki turned a 360, then tilted her head to examine the victim's lap. "You're going to find residue from lubricant on that Kindle's screen."

"Already have."

Heat studied the condition of the body, whose bloating and discoloration spoke of a long passage of time. "What's your ballpark on TOD?"

"Going out on a limb, Nikki, I'd say three, probably four days."

"Same day as Lon King."

"Pretty near."

Heat turned to Detective Aguinaldo. "Guess we know why she was unreachable."

"We checked her apartment, we checked her car, we checked her friends."

Nikki reflected for a beat and said, "I guess we learned something then." She left it at that. Inez would be chewing herself up; Heat didn't need to add to the new detective's own postmortem. "Let's move on. What we need to find out now is whether Nathan Levy is the next victim, or our prime suspect."

Detective Rhymer's field report over the phone from Throggs Neck tipped the balance of that scale. "Damn near got myself creamed coming up here," he said. "I'm driving on Schurz, about a block from Nathan Levy's house, when this souped-up 450 comes barreling up the wrong side of the street at me. I swerved, and so did he at the last second, missing me by an inch. I made Levy as the driver and started working a three-pointer when the cruiser detailed to him blows past me running a hot code, nearly taking my rear bumper as a souvenir."

Heat's pulse quickened. Things are breaking, maybe I'll finally get some answers, she thought. "How long ago was this?"

"By now, ten, no, eleven minutes. He led the blue-and-white out on the Neck and lured them into a cul-de-sac off Soundview Terrace. Levy chewed some lawn making his turn, but the unis got boxed. By the time they came out, he was a ghost. Local knowledge and a test driver—I guess you're gonna end up with some *Fast and Furious*." Nikki remembered Levy's built-for-the-job physique and could picture him muscling that performance pickup anywhere he wanted, at any speed he chose. "Called in a BOLO, of course," added the detective. "Could be anywhere by now, though."

Thoughts bounced in Nikki's head, and one of them settled in the clear. "Let's update that BOLO. Radio in a Do Not Apprehend. If they spot him, have them maintain a tail. Just in case Levy is involved with Rook's disappearance, he might lead us to him."

"Copy that."

"And the instant they spot him, I want to be notified. I want to be there, understood?"

Now that Levy looked good as a potential suspect, Raley and Ochoa were already busy shoveling deeper into his past. They were making calls, trying to run him for any jail time or arrests.

***

"While you're at it, a guy who drives like that is going to have some moving violations," said Heat once she got back to the station. "Run them—even parking tickets, now that I think of it. See what addresses he got pinched at. Maybe there's a pattern to a neighborhood or borough where he hangs out."

"On it," said Raley.

Ochoa sucked his teeth. "So frustrating. If the databases were up, we could run this stuff in the time it took to print. Instead, we're calling multiple jurisdictions and waiting for them to do hand searches."

Heat fixed him with a firm glare. "Then that's what we do, Miguel. We do whatever it takes."

"Look what just came in from Ballistics." Detective Raley rose from his desk holding up a printed report.

Nikki rushed across the bull pen to him, her internal voice pleading with every step, Please let this help, please let this help . . .

"It's the finding on the slug found in the garage door frame at Nathan Levy's house," he said. "It was a .38."

"Not a .22?" she asked. "Lon King was killed with a .22. Prelim on Abigail Plunkitt is also a .22."

"Same with the drone slugs recovered at Washington Square," added Ochoa.

"But Levy claims the drone shot at him," said Ochoa. "But that's out of pattern if it's a .38. Which means either his drone weapon got swapped—"

"Or he's lying, and staged the potshot," added Raley.

Heat held up the interoffice envelope which, from all the signatures on it, looked like it had been in circulation since the Kerik era. She read the date of submission, and her chest became a furnace of rage. "Two days it took this to reach us! Goddamnit, if we'd known about this discrepancy even thirty-six hours ago, we could have been all over this guy. Now"—she crumpled the envelope and tossed it in the trash—"right now. Somebody find out if Nathan Levy is registered to own a gun—especially a .38."

Back in her fishbowl, she called Detective Feller, who was patrolling the waterfront in a Zodiac borrowed from the Harbor Unit. He had been working a slow recon of Long Island City all morning and had gotten the notion to mix it up and check the Gowanus Canal, which was where she caught him, motoring in the Brooklyn channel's 4th Street Basin, with no luck, so far. With the ballistics foul-up fresh in mind, she double-checked him on running the skiff through the boat registry.

"Affirm. Boat registration is handled through DMV, and they've still got tech capability—but no matches. I also put it through New Jersey, Connecticut, and Rhode Island. No hits there, either. At least not yet. Of course, it could always be unregistered or stolen. If the RTCC was up, we could do a quicker check. But I have some Harbor Unit pals on it."

"How much more do you have to cover?"

"I never knew there was this much waterfront in this city. It's slow going," he said, "but I'm working it, boss. I'll freakin' swim it, if I have to."

Nikki paced her office, frustrated, panicked, desperate to do more than wait and hope. But what could she do? Thoughts of Rook pummeled her, attacking from every direction. Where he might be. What he was doing. What was happening to him. Whether he was alive. Instead of helping herself, all she was doing was dragging herself deeper into her own vortex of despair and speculation. "Stop," she said aloud. "Stop right there."

What Heat needed was to be useful. And busy. What bases weren't being covered? All of them were; what she lacked was results. She flopped in her chair and put her face in her palms to think in isolation. What any detective does is follow the hot lead. What was it that Randall Feller had just said? The boat. That was the last sighting of Rook. But with five hundred miles of New York City waterfront, even if you carved out everything but Queens, Brooklyn, and Lower Manhattan, that was still quite a haystack in which to find a needle. Assuming the boat was even in the water anymore, and not trailered somewhere inland. Or out of state. If they got lucky with registration, they might get a line on it. But how long would that take?

She balled up her fists against her temples. Think, Nikki, think. When the hot lead is at the end of a cold trail, and the technology you always used as a crutch goes belly up, what can you do? She thought of her combat training. When disarmed, trapped, or overpowered, what is your strategy?

Embrace the obstacle.

She stood up, crossed to the bull pen, and stuck her head in. "Call me if anything pops."

Raley looked up from his desk. "Where are you going?"

"Back to school," said Heat.

⁎

Throughout her senior high years, Nikki Heat had clocked as many as eight to ten hours a week in the last quiet place on earth, the Rose Main Reading Room of the New York Public Library. A cathedral of books, she thought then. Standing in the entry, peering into the vast North Hall, with its long oak tables and stately brass lamps surrounded by walls lined with yards and yards of literature, she thought that now. Heat knew that many greats of letters from Singer to Doctorow had quietly labored under that fifty-foot-high muraled ceiling. She also knew that the true power of the research branch, now named the Schwarzman Building (same lions, new name) came from the librarians who catalogued publications, sought answers, fetched materials, and advised readers, writers, dilettantes, scholars—and teenage girls who just wanted to know.

Carolyn Jay, who had been an inspiration and spirit guide to adolescent Nikki, had become a bit thinner and more angular and had more salt than pepper in her hair than last time they had seen each other, but the playful eyes above the wry smile had not changed, even behind those eyeglasses, which were also a new addition. When Carolyn saw Nikki and came around the dark wooden counter of the research call desk, they embraced as old friends, and it was the librarian who turned heads by being too loud in her joyful greeting. "Let's go down to my office where we won't bug anybody," she said in mock indignation.

The room behind the heavy oak door with the "Staff Only" sign was just as Heat remembered it: a bull pen, smaller, but not unlike the one uptown at the Twentieth. A common space for lots of work and sporadic privacy, with eight mass-produced desks arranged to face the walls. Mrs. Jay still had the same spot, frozen in time. Same single shelf of books overhead, same lamp, same single plastic cup of water next to the pencil mug. The upgraded computer took up less of the desk surface, but that was about it. Heat began by asking about the computer. "Are you guys cyber challenged like we are?"

"Yes, it's really maddening. I still remember my first Internet search. Tom Wolfe wanted to fact-check commercial real estate tycoons in Atlanta. You get so accustomed to answers at the stroke of a keyboard or the click of a mouse. Suddenly I'm forced to go back and do it the old way. Truth be told, I love my technology."

"But I bet you still have your old skills."

"Who you calling skilled?" She laughed then took a moment to study Nikki. "I can see this isn't a social call."

"I need your help, Mrs. Jay."

"Absolutely, you know that. What can I do for you?"

"Find me a boat."

If Carolyn Jay felt daunted by the task, she didn't show it. Nikki showed her the notes from her spiral notebook that included the eyewitness description of the sky-blue skiff from the plumbing contractor who had followed Rook and his abductors to Pier 36. The only time the librarian faltered was when she saw Rook's name and his circumstances. She stared at Nikki, understanding the gravity of all this without needing to discuss it, then put herself to work. Mrs. Jay made photocopies of Nikki's reporter's notebook and made some side notes to herself on slips of paper, which she had made, as she had always done, from the blank backs of printed sheets of paper that had been cut down to scratch size.

She led Nikki across the marble-lined hallway to room 217 to show her how she was going to proceed, but as soon as they stepped into the catalog repository, Heat's cell phone buzzed. It was Detective Ochoa. She stepped back in the hall so she wouldn't disrupt the researchers and answered. "On my way now," she said. Carolyn stood by the door and asked her if she was all right. She had good reason to ask. Nikki looked anything but.

"I'm sorry, I need to . . . Police business." She rushed out, her footsteps echoing on the marble steps. At the lobby, her hurry became a sprint. She had to get to the East River, where someone had reported a man's body in the water.

Two blocks into her drive east from the NYPL, Heat consciously had to tell herself to breathe. The fifteen-minute trip to the river seemed otherworldly, a soundless voyage to the very gates of Hell, insulated from all outside stimulus. Heat drove with her damp palms on the wheel; her lungs felt seared, and it seemed that because of some untimely breakdown of her cerebral cortex, evolved messages of reason and judgment were being skip-wired, while her amygdala served up high-velocity jolts of primal darkness under the banner of "Coming Attractions"—random clips from a jumpy mental snuff film that filled her with fear and hopelessness.

One of Heat's front tires smacked the curb on the right

side of the driveway that cut into the sidewalk under the Queensborough Bridge. The traffic cop manning the entry to the service lane at 60th Street winced at the impact. Nikki bounced in her seat but didn't notice the slam or the reaction. She steered up the blacktop incline running under the bridge and then, after reaching the top of the hill, turned down the other side of the steep ramp. She left her car against the fence of a dog run without bothering to close the door. Willing air into her lungs, sucking her lips in hard over the edges of her teeth, Nikki trudged forward, passing two ambulances, a fire truck, and an FDNY Urban Search and Rescue Team van, until she came to the black iron railing, where she pushed between some first responders in time to see a pair of divers in wetsuits working to attach a flotation harness to the corpse about thirty yards out in the swirling water.

The body's head and shoulders were still submerged, and Nikki bent forward at the waist, hands flat on the cold steel rail, as if leaning six inches closer would give her more information. She caught a glimpse of his clothing, athletic wear of some sort, and dared to believe that it wasn't Rook's corpse floating out there. Unless he had changed (or been changed) out of the sport coat and bloody dress shirt he had had on the night before, it must be someone else. Had to be. Please be. The current had created a rip between the concrete footings of the bridge's piers. The back of the man's upper body bobbed up through the surface foam, revealing brown skin and a glistening bald or clean-shaven head.

Heat's relief that it wasn't Rook nearly laid her flat on the paving stones, and she needed to grip the metal piping when she felt herself go faint and her knees wavering. Composing herself, Nikki said a silent thank-you as she watched the dead man getting reeled toward one of the Zodiacs working the scene. A second boat came alongside to assist with the recovery, and, as he was hauled up, the victim's running shoes emerged from the muddy water with a bright flash of neon green. Nikki had seen shoes like that recently—New Balance Zantes—and, in the blink it took her to access her memory, she recognized the face of Sampson Stallings as his head lolled forward during the transfer into the police boat.

Twelve hours later, alone by the light of a single dwindling candle, Heat blasted "Stay" by Rihanna and refilled a shot glass resting on the rim of her tub with Patrón. Her pouring was sloppy, thanks to a combination of a less-than-optimal arm angle and her blood alcohol level. Nikki overfilled the glass, and the slosh trickled down the side until the tequila met her bath, creating the soft sizzle of bursting bubbles.

She had started with a single glass of wine when she got home, but by the third one, which emptied the bottle, Nikki had put away the Rosa Mexicana takeout menu, deciding there was no point to the enchiladas suizas without tequila, but that tequila was just fine without the enchiladas. Nikki was making all the wrong choices that night and just kept making them.

The trauma of fearing that Rook had washed up off Sutton Place had cored out her insides, leaving her emotions strewn in a bloody tangle. Her relief, however profound and welcome, collapsed at the new shock of discovering that Lon King's loving partner had stopped his daily run mid-span on the recreation lane of the Queensborough Bridge and, according to numerous eyewitnesses, stood on the rail, blessed himself, then let gravity tip him forward with his arms at his sides. The postmortem indicated water in his lungs, so it wasn't the fall that killed him. Nikki knew it wasn't the river either, but the heavy pain of unbearable loss. She submerged herself under lavender froth until she could hold her breath no longer, not to contemplate anything rash, just to see what it must have felt like to Sampson Stallings.

Yes, she was definitely making all the wrong choices.

Her cell phone rang, and Nikki made a SeaWorld dolphin vault out of the tub, naked, in her dash to grab it. She had intended to leave the phone within arm's reach so she could get news about Rook but had been afraid she would drop it in the water. Instead, in her drunken scramble, her wet feet slipped and she fell hard to the bathroom floor, knocking the wind out of herself and sending the iPhone across the tiles like a hockey puck.

She pulled herself toward the john and snatched the phone up before the call got dumped to voice mail. But her screen swipe was clumsy and the phone fell from her hand, clattering onto the floor again. She made a fumble for it and, at last, managed to croak out a hello.

"Nikki, it's me." Lauren Parry. For the second time that day, Heat prayed the topic would not be the discovery of Jameson Rook. "What's going on? You sound like something's wrong."

"No, I'm fi-ine." Heat flinched, hoping she hadn't cracked a rib. The sharp pain gave *fine* two syllables.

"You can't fool me. I called because I'm worried about you. Should I be worried about you?"

Nikki didn't answer. Didn't know how to, didn't have the energy to, didn't want to open the vein. She decided to stay on the floor and rolled onto her back, hoping for some comfort from the rug, but came to a stop half on, half off. She grunted.

"I'm coming over."

"No. Don't. Laur, I'm OK, really. I just . . . I'm OK. You know me."

"Which is why I'm calling. You looked liked hell this afternoon at my office."

Instead of speaking, Heat shook her head no, as if Lauren could see her, though she was very glad this was not a FaceTime call. Finally, she said, "Well, it has been a bit of a strain."

"I can't even imagine. So what are you doing about it? Sitting home, getting hammered?"

Nikki pulled her phone away to examine it to make sure this was indeed not a FaceTime call. She began to tell Lauren not to be concerned, that she had this covered, but as the words formed, they turned into vapor and left her with nothing. Fueled by alcohol and despair, Nikki began to weep.

Her dear friend did the best thing she possibly could have done at that moment. She just listened to the sobs. A minute later, or two minutes, maybe even five, when Nikki whined a high-pitched "I'm sorry . . ." Lauren still didn't intervene, except to say she was there, not to worry.

When she was cried out, at least for that round, Heat forced herself to sit, sliding her backside on the tile until she could rest her shoulders on the toilet.

"You want some company, Nikki?"

"Want to know what I'm doing right now? I'm wet and shivering from the tub, sitting on my bathroom floor naked, using the john as a backrest. I'm kinda drunk and all alone and I kinda need that. You insulted?"

"No, I get it."

"Because if you wanted to come over like Melissa McCarthy from *Bridesmaids* and slap some sense into me, you might not like the result."

Dr. Parry chuckled. "Don't want that."

"No, you don't."

"All right, then, I'll respect your wishes."

"Thank you."

"Wait, wait, don't you hang up yet. Now if I *were* to come over there—which I am not. But if I did, and went all Megan Price on your ass, I would tell you one thing: Be Nikki Heat. Stay strong. Whatever it is, you've got to stay positive."

"That's three things."

"And you can start by corking the wine bottle."

"Oh, that was gone an hour ago. I've moved on to the hard stuff."

"Just promise me, Nikki. You do what I said? And call anytime. Please?"

"Hey, Laur?"

"Yeah?"

"Never call this number again."

The two ended the call laughing—but only Nikki's laughter turned into tears.

She struggled to all fours, found the cork for the tequila bottle on the floor, then hauled herself up using the side of the tub as a handrail. The shot glass must have fallen into the bath water, so she drank straight from the bottle.

It was definitely a night of wrong choices.

The beauty of a hangover, Nikki thought the next morning, was that it did wonders for confusing the source of pain. Was it from the knot on your head some bruiser gave you with his shoe, or from the tender ribs you got hitting your bathroom floor in one of your life's more un-shining moments? Or was it from the hangover itself? As she took a sip of her second vanilla latte of the day, Heat knew where the real pain lived, and that was why she was standing on a sidewalk on Warren Street at seven-thirty waiting for someone to unlock the front door of the Fountain Pen Hospital.

"I left him a voice mail, personally, to let him know it was fixed," said Terry Wiederlight, one of the owners, as he returned from the back room holding a small cardboard box the size and dimensions of a pen. "Always glad to see you, Nikki, but Rook was so eager to get this Hemingway back, I'm surprised he didn't come himself."

Maybe to convince herself as much as Terry, she smiled and said, "He's tied up on an assignment. But he's going to want this when he's free, I do know that."

"That's great, I hope it's real soon. I expedited this. You know how Rook gets when he's obsessed."

"Sometimes all we need is one little thing to keep us going, Terry."

"You are so right. Although this is no little thing, is it?" He uncapped the Montblanc collector's edition pen and let her examine the replacement nib, which looked exactly like the original: gleaming Rhodium-plated 18-karat gold with deco scrollwork engraved around the number 4810, the metric altitude of the eponymous highest peak in the Alps.

"He is going to be so happy." Once again, for herself, she added, "When he sees this."

On her way out, Terry said, "Hey, if you two are getting each other wedding gifts, they also have other limited editions in the Writers Edition series. Maybe the Agatha Christie or the Edgar Allen Poe. Although he's not much of a mystery writer, is he?"

Even with the Montblanc protected to excess in Bubble Wrap, Nikki carried the package in her hand like a fragile keepsake, beginning to worry that this entire errand was acting out some delusional fantasy, as if she were like Miss Havisham, clinging to a pen instead of a decaying wedding dress. Whether it was a positive gesture of hope or an exercise of pure denial, picking up Rook's pen constituted for her an affirmation of his life in the absence of facts. It not only had to do, it needed to do. For now.

As bolstering as Lauren Parry's well-intended words had

been, they were really just a nudge. The actual wake-up call that prompted Nikki to turn the emotional corner came in bed that morning, and from herself. And it came in the same apartment, the same room, and the same bed where, over a decade before, she had begun another climb, a struggle from the depths of a bottomless hole following her mother's murder. Back then, Heat had come to realize that it was not enough to stay positive: She had to *do* positive.

Actions carry great, sometimes mystical power, and back at the start of the new millennium, after Nikki had passed a lost, miserable week cocooned under those covers, the decision to do something rather than wallow had led her to become a police officer. Today, her saving act was to secure Rook's fountain pen—perhaps not as emphatic a life choice as altering her entire path to be a detective instead of an actress, but in one way not so different. Both worked as concrete steps. The one thing Dr. Parry had gotten right was when she had told her to be Nikki Heat.

Nikki Heat was all about action, not wallowing.

On the second level of the parking garage near City Hall, as she remote-clicked the locks on her car and opened the door, she heard a man speak her name softly from somewhere up the ramp. She dropped the Fountain Pen Hospital sack on the driver's seat and turned, ducking into a crouch between her car and the one beside hers, resting her hand on the grip of her Sig Sauer.

She waited, listening.

The only sound came from the morning rush out on Broadway and the annoying buzz of a flickering lamp in the entry to the stairwell. Then he spoke again. Calm, measured, matter-of-fact. "You won't be needing that gun, Captain, I promise you." The echo against concrete in the cavernous space made it hard to pinpoint his location. Heat duckwalked back against the wall in case he was directly above her. No sense creating too much opportunity. "I wouldn't advise you to pull it, anyway. It would not go well."

She chanced engaging him, hoping to draw him into view or give her a ping on his location. "Is that a threat?"

A full minute passed before he spoke again, and by that time he had relocated. He was now nearer, it seemed, but his calm voice was still diffused in the reverberations of the space, defying any attempt at triangulation from her defensive spot, where she crouched between two engine blocks. "I'm not here to threaten or harm you. I'm here to talk to you about Jameson Rook."

Heat's stomach hit the spin cycle. Oh, shit, she thought, is Rook dead? Is he here to tell me Rook's dead? Nikki fought the urge to bolt out into the open ramp and try for a look at this guy. Or to take him. If he knew something about Rook, she wanted it—now. "What about Rook? Tell me!" In contrast to his measured tone, her blurt sounded eager and needy. Because she was.

"I thought you'd be interested, and I can hear that I have your attention. Which is good, because what I am about to say to you is very important." He paused again. Taking his time, running the table his way, and only making it harder on Nikki, who was coping with a turbo pulse and wondering what the fuck was going on. "I need to issue you a caution to stop overreaching in your homicide case. Not only are you trying to go places you shouldn't go but doing so would be harmful to Mr. Rook."

His words smacked Heat with alarm and hope. "Oh, my God . . ." she muttered. "He's alive . . ." She couldn't help herself and shot to her feet, calling, "He's alive?" She got no reply and this time shouted it loud enough to hear her own voice ring back at her in the concrete cavern. "Don't screw with me, is Rook alive?"

Another pause, and the voice came from farther away, as the unflappable baritone with a hint of accent—maybe Oklahoma?—resumed. "I urge you to listen. I know this is very difficult because it runs against all your training and, to be certain, your emotional investment."

"Damnit, tell me. Is. He. Alive?"

In that same soft-spoken tone, he said, "Yes . . . so far."

Her cop wheels started turning. If this guy was telling the truth—if Rook wasn't dead in a gutter somewhere with a bullet in his head—this guy might be able to lead her to him. She stepped from between the cars and shouted again. "Who are you?" Nikki got her iPhone out and texted her location and a 10-13.

He chuckled. "What do you like? How about 'Mr. Jones,' does that work for you?"

The moment she had completed her message and hit Send, Mr. Jones said, "I see we only have a few more moments to spare here, so let me make this as clear as I can. If you continue to press the issue and follow the path you are on, you will be putting Mr. Rook's life in jeopardy."

"If he's alive, prove it. Let me talk to him. Let me see him! Take me to him!"

"You're not listening. And you're assuming I have control of the situation. I am trying to share a clear warning. Unless you want to bring him harm, or worse: Stand down."

Heat's heart raced. He sounded like he was wrapping up, and she needed to do whatever she could to keep this man engaged—for information and to stall him until backup arrived. "If you don't have control of him, who does?" She waited and got no reply. Nikki strained to listen carefully, assuming he was, once again, repositioning. "And where is he? Talk to me!" Still no response. "And who do you work for . . . Mr. Jones?"

Her only reply was the echo of a slamming door, on the far side of the garage and a floor below. The sound was the theft of hope.

When the cavalry arrived, it was too late. Heat gave a report to the First Precinct lead, but they both knew that a neighborhood search without a physical description would be a waste of manpower. And unfortunately, since Heat had parked in a municipal garage, the security cams were blacked out along with the other services compromised by the Free Mehmoud cyber attack.

Heat put her head together with Raley and Ochoa back uptown in the bull pen. "Whoever it was," she said, "it was the second no-fly warning I've gotten. First from Congressman Duer, and now from this 'Mr. Jones.'"

"So do you think this mystery voice guy is with Duer?" asked Raley.

Nikki shrugged. "Hard to say. But—going purely by gut? He had a fed vibe. If he's not Homeland or a spook, he could be former."

"And, therefore, contracted out to anyone from Duer, to Swift, to the Syrians, for all we know," reflected Ochoa.

"One thing, for sure. He was pro. And tapped in. Literally. As soon as I texted my ten-thirteen, he put a clock on our conversation. Which tells me he had access to my phone."

Raley folded his arms and fixed her with a look. "So. Does this guy in the garage seriously think you would stand down?"

"Or that we would?" said Ochoa.

"If he does," she said, "he doesn't know me—or us."

Annette appeared in the doorway. "Zachary Hamner is calling. Shall I transfer here or your office?"

Heat bolted up. Zach had promised to call her the instant anything broke about Rook. "Mine," she said and hurried to the door. On her way out she called to her squad leaders to hang tight.

"Heat." Hamner said it the way people tell Siri to look up a contact: as a fact. Like everything else about the man, his tone was joyless and impersonal. "This isn't an easy call to make."

"Oh, God . . ."

"You might want to close your door."

"Zach, don't torture me. Is it Rook? Just tell me."

"No, it's not Rook."

Gathering herself again from another shot to the ribs, she heard him cover the phone and tell someone that he would call back in three minutes, that he had a thing he had to do. Nikki was too relieved to feel insulted to learn that she was a check-off on someone's to-do list.

He uncovered the mouthpiece and got back to her. "Here's where we are. I am calling to feel you out on stepping down from your command." Nikki stretched the phone cord across her desk so she could close the door. "Are you still there?" he asked.

"Step down?"

"I told you it wasn't an easy call."

"Less so for me," she said. "I've only been in the job a week. Not even."

"Yes, and the push I'm getting is that are there are some issues. Telltales. Shall I enumerate?" He barely paused; the question was rhetorical. "Not informing chain of command about high-profile cases. Upsetting community leaders by brooming meetings. Flouting the CompStat process—the *CompStat* process, for chrissakes—by blowing off the weekly meeting. In your own shop there is leadership unrest due to your perceived lack of commitment to naming your successor as homicide squad leader. And you are spending too much time in the field doing casework instead of sending your people to wear down their shoe leather and report back, like a good administrator should. You still with me?"

"Listening, yes. With you, no." Reeling as she was from hearing that the same guy who had gone out of his way to offer his condolences and full support was now caving to pressure and squeezing her, Heat still managed to keep her head. When she had taken the job, she knew it meant facing down the machine at various intervals, so she saw this as an early test. One she could have done without, but there it was. If Nikki came back at him whiny or defensive, she'd be finished. So she gave professional resistance, aka tossing the ball back in his lap. "You and your downtown buddies are sending me mixed messages. One chief says, Stay on the case so he can brief the commissioner, but then you say I'm not delegating enough. You want leadership? I made a leadership decision to skip those meetings to follow events in the double homicide that the chief of detectives personally ordered me to stay on top of. Which I am trying to do right now. But here's the thing, Zachary. I am not only running my precinct to the best of my ability, I am also working my damndest to save a man's life, and I am going to see that through. If somebody wants me out, I am not quitting. You can fire me and then see where the blowback lands when the press jumps on that, and you know it will."

In the brief interval that followed, Heat was pleased to hear some throat clearing on the other end. Maybe Zach Hamner, senior administrative aide to the NYPD's deputy commissioner for legal matters, wasn't accustomed to pushback from lowly precinct commanders. "Well," he finally said, sounding less like the shark running the table. "This has to be explored further, I see."

"This is a load of horse crap, and you know it." She decided to get something out of this annoying call by asking the question begging to be asked. "Who sent you to see if I'd resign my command? Where is this coming from? Who's trying to get me off this case?"

"That's absurd."

"Not how I read it, Zach. *Who?*"

"Hear this clearly: There is no effort to hinder your speedy closure of this case."

" 'Speedy.' Sounds a lot like Swift, doesn't it?"

He ignored that. "There was merely some concern here at the Plaza that you might be having a difficult time keeping pace with your duties, given the distraction."

"The distraction?" Her foot nearly slipped off the brake, but she kept her cool, even as she seethed. "If you are characterizing my efforts to resolve the kidnapping of a citizen off the streets of New York—regardless of my relationship to him—as a distraction instead of the very definition of my job as a sworn police officer, you need to take a walk out of that administrative dreamworld and breathe some real-world air. And you can start by taking your head out of your ass."

Nikki hung up.

Then she threw her typewriter at the wall, causing faces in the bull pen to whip her way. While she had everyone's attention, she marched to the doorway and said, "Raley. Ochoa. Murder Board update. *Now.*" If ever there was any ambiguity about her resolve, this third attempt to get her off the case had only stiffened it. Her only hope was that her dogged perseverance wasn't sealing her fiancé's doom.

It may have been the first time ever in the history of New York City that a plumbing contractor got whisked through

Manhattan in a police motorcade. But Alvin Speyer, the "pipe fitter," as the stud had been nicknamed in the squad room, interrupted an extramarital tryst to get picked up by Captain Heat in the carriage turnaround of his Times Square hotel and Code Three'd behind a pair of motorcycles to the curb between Patience and Fortitude, the famous marble lions of the NYPL's main branch.

The first thing Heat noticed when they met Carolyn Jay in her office on the second floor was that she was wearing the same clothes as the day before. "Not my first all-nighter," said the librarian with a mock-salacious wink. "Thank goodness I'm on good terms with security and the coffee pot in the break room got fixed."

"But you did make progress, right?" asked Nikki, trying to get to it without appearing disrespectful to the woman who had burned midnight oil to help her.

"It's a process, right? Catalog interpretation isn't like the Map Room, where the answer to every question is a map. But enough headway to ask you to bring . . . Mr. Speyer, is it? Come in, let me show you why I needed to borrow you."

It was early enough that Mrs. Jay had the bull pen to herself, so she rolled two chairs from other work stations beside hers. "Let me walk you through my journey. Succinctly, I promise. Time is critical, I can see it that, Nikki. That's why I bore down. Not so easy with the digital system down, I don't need to tell you."

"And I thank you so much for your efforts, Mrs. Jay."

"Well, hold your applause until we see if it paid off." She swapped her glasses for the readers on the chain around her neck and picked up a yellow lined tablet full of abbreviations, acronyms, and code numbers in her Palmer Method script. "The key to the whole thing, thanks to Mr. Speyer's good citizenship, was to focus on the provenance of that boat. From the description, a wooden eighteen-footer, isn't that right? Please say that's right."

"Yes," said Alvin Speyer.

"Thank God." She went back to her notes. "A search needs a premise. Mine was that wooden boats are so retro, so high-maintenance that, much like a hot rod enthusiast, any owner would be proud of his craft and consort with like-minded devotees. That led me across the hall to room 217 to explore the *Directory of Associations* and appropriate newsletter catalogues shelved there. Here's where I'll skim for you. I spent hours thumbing through the *Oxbridge Directory*, *Benn's Media*, and others, searching for association newsletters, filtered for this region, of clubs catering to the small-wooden-boat owner. I made my short list and moved downstairs to Microforms, where I pulled the annual newsletters of each organization from the last five years—an arbitrary limit, but it seemed a reasonable time frame given the circumstances. Going on and on, that led me to learn of the Great Upstate Boat Show, held annually up in Queensbury, New York."

Nikki opened her own notebook. "And you found a contact we can talk to?"

"That was my intent. Instead, I found these." Mrs. Jay took two color photocopies from a manila file and held them against her chest. "These are prints I made from the boat show's newsletters from 2010 and 2012. Remember what I said about wooden boats being high-maintenance? There are numerous ads placed by repair and restoration companies. And they like to print brag pictures of their work." She then placed both ads faceup on her desk for them to examine. "Mr. Speyer, could either one of these be the boat you saw the other night?"

Heat would have been amused by how much the form of the librarian's question was identical to that of a detective showing a mug shot array to a victim, if she weren't so focused on the pair of advertisements. One was for a wooden-boat restorer in Glen Cove on Long Island, whose display showed a Brady Bunch–style grid featuring grainy shots of a 1962 Penn Yan, an Electri-craft inboard, and a light-blue eighteen-foot skiff rigged for an outboard. The other craftsman was located near Paterson, New Jersey, and his ad featured only one boat, in a hero shot of an immaculately restored sixteen-footer, also in light blue, also with an outboard-motor mount.

Alvin Speyer leaned over the pages and said, "Hmm."

While he picked up each page for a closer examination, the research librarian said to Heat, "Of course, I could have phoned these places myself, but given what's at stake here, I didn't want to take the risk. I'm no detective."

"Could have fooled me," said Nikki.

Carolyn Jay blushed. "Well. More of a Miss Marple than a Nikki Heat."

"This one," said Speyer. He held out one of the ads.

"Are you sure?" Heat asked. "You do know that it could also be neither one?"

"No, definitely this one. It's got the same white center console for the chrome steering wheel. And see the flared lines of the inset for the motor mount on the stern? Never seen that before on a boat. Made me want it when I saw it." He tapped the page with his forefinger. "*This.* I'm telling you."

With a grateful nod to the librarian, Heat took out her cell phone and dialed the number in the ad.

The owner of Natural Neil's Marine Restorations in Glen Cove, New York, didn't need to look up the sky-blue skiff in his records because, as with all the boats there, he had worked on it personally. The eighteen-footer had come in along with a number of small vessels damaged when Hurricane Irene blew through in 2011, and he liked the result of his labor so much, he posted a picture of it in his ads a year later. Once Natural Neil felt sure that Heat was who she said she was, he did go to his records to look up the address of the skiff's owner. Before they hung up, he said, "By the way? It's not really sky blue. In the trade, it's known as *celeste pallido.*"

A half hour later, Detective Feller, in a floppy fisherman's hat with a rod and tackle to complete his cover, steered his borrowed undercover Whaler from the Red Hook channel into Brooklyn's Erie Basin. He chugged the man-made cove lazily, pretending to be as much interested in the gulls and puffy clouds as he was in his true focus, which was the wharf line. The barge company that had made the repair payment for the skiff had an address that placed it on a rectangular inlet off Beard Street, just west of the new Ikea. He avoided the narrow channel so he wouldn't arouse any suspicion, killed his engine, and floated along in the basin, casting his lure and letting his gaze follow the splash, which was always in the direction of the barge dock. After a few casts, he leaned his fishing pole on the gunwale, reached down for his tackle box, and took out a sandwich. On his second bite he put the sandwich down and casually picked up his phone. Heat answered on the first ring. The detective said, "Got your sky blue skiff."

THIRTEEN

Randall Feller maintained a low-key surveillance in case he was being observed, even as he took precautions to cover all the bases. With Heat engaged for at least half an hour of travel time from Midtown, the critical priority was to observe keenly in order to learn whatever he could about what was going on at Channel Maritime, while wrapping a net around the perimeter of the wharf that nobody could slip through. The hard part of that job was not being obvious about it. Do it wrong, and you could excel at keeping the bad guys in, but at the expense of driving away their accomplices if, for example, they had recently taken a ride to pick up a pizza and were coming back with it.

Feller's first goal was to get himself on land. In short order, three vessels from the Harbor Unit responded to his radio call and formed a blockade, keeping out of the sight line of the dockyard. That freed him to reel in his lure and putt-putt across the basin to his car in the Ikea lot a quarter mile east.

He met Heat just as she arrived at the staging area Lieutenant Marr had already been set up around the corner and a block north on Van Dyke in the weed-overgrown parking lot of a deteriorating warehouse. Nikki's first call after getting Feller's confirmed skiff sighting was to Marr, asking the veteran Emergency Services officer to command the raid. Even though he worked out of the 108th Precinct up in Long Island City, she had prior experience with him and, with the possibility of Rook's being held captive in there, she wanted the best: a cool-headed pro who left little to chance and got results. "Shouldn't we get some observers out there while we do this?" asked Feller.

"Already done, Detective," said Marr with a smile.

"I just went by, and I didn't see any."

The weathered corners of the lieutenant's eyes were tugged into a genial squint. "That's good news then. We can relax." He must have noticed the tension in Nikki, and so went right to work spreading an enlargement of a municipal street map on the hood of his car. How the ESU had managed to pull together a strategy map complete with color-coded markings for containment, deployment, and contingencies in under thirty minutes—while in transit from Queens— mystified her. But all that, along with the calm Marr had already bestowed on her and Feller with his light military demeanor, told her she had made the right choice calling in this man.

"We're setting up intercepts on land and water. Detective Feller, you've already taken care of the harbor; what I've done is placed units at these intersections." He took out an old silver-plated Cross pen and used it as a pointer. "Our choke points are Beard and Dwight, Beard and Van Brunt, Richards and Van Dyke. Fall-back roamers will work Coffey Street between Otsego and Conover." He triple-tapped the page. "Nobody's busting out of here without a Double-Oh-Seven jetpack." He gave Nikki a wink. "That'll happen one of these days. Not today, I have a feeling."

"What about air support?" she asked.

"Standby only. Chopper's going to attract media. Don't want that. There's a Bell Four-twenty-nine on routine patrol less than two minutes away in Cobble Hill. If we need a copter, we'll have a copter, and in a hurry." He went back to his map.

"Here's how it's going to come down. On green, the BearCat parked behind us will enter through the front gate, which is padlocked. That is why God gave us BearCats. Simultaneously, our other assault vehicle will pull up to the east-side fence here, where teams will deploy from its roof over the concertina with mats and Telesteps. Harbor Unit will send two boats up the channel to deploy officers and to discourage a water exit. Each team coming in the gate, over the fence, and up the canal will have target assignments." Nikki leaned in as he pointed to each spot, which he had color-coded. "The modular office trailer, the warehouse, barge one, barge two, even the minivan and the skiff—just in case Mr. Rook could be located in either one of those." Reading Nikki's breathing, he added with resolve, "Know what? If he's here, we are getting him out, Captain."

Heat popped her trunk and put on her Kevlar and, while she cinched the tabs, a sour melancholy spread within her, prompted by her memory of Rook, whom she always mocked for vesting up with armor that was stenciled "JOURNALIST" instead of "POLICE" and had two small gold medallions embroidered on it—one for each of his Pulitzers. She would give anything to have him suiting up with her now instead of donning hers to rescue him.

She stuffed the gloom in her back pocket. This was not only the day to do positive, this was the moment.

Heat and Feller crouched behind a small Dumpster, each with one knee down on a street where old rounded cobblestones had reappeared, exposed where the newer blacktop had been worn away. The worn stones—a sign of neglect or nostalgia, take your pick—continued under the front gate of Channel Maritime and out along its wharf, which stretched about two hundred yards toward the Erie Basin. The scene within the property was just as Randall had described from his water surveillance.

A pair of workhorse barges, scruffy boys, each a hundred and forty feet long, were lashed by long sides to the dock, where hawsers wrapped around giant cleats. Between them, a smaller line ran from underneath a stained tarp that took the shape of a skiff bobbing in the gentle tide. The boat itself wasn't visible from Heat's vantage point, but Feller had confirmed seeing a patch of sky blue peeking out from under its drab camouflage. Rotting timbers, the skeletons of old boats, formed a pile against the brick warehouse, a relic of the golden age of shipping in Red Hook, before the containers had taken the business to Perth Amboy. Nearer to them, a sagging modular office trailer with a buckled roof sat close enough to the sidewalk to have gotten tagged with ornate initials and devils' faces right through the chain-link fence. At the trailer's far end Heat could see the hood of the silver minivan nosing out, minus a license plate. She heard a flutter as a plastic shopping bag caught on the top of the fence, billowed in the spring breeze off the water. Then the BearCat roared to life and things started moving.

After a soft squelch, Nikki's earpiece filled with the buttery, reassuring sound of Lieutenant Marr's voice: "Good for green." She and Feller drew their sidearms and fell in behind the armored vehicle, taking cover with the SWAT team. The BearCat never revved, never had to flex a muscle. Over its enveloping rumble came the sharp ping of metal and Heat saw the gate whip open ahead and to her left, smacking into the fence and rebounding, only to be bounced back once more, mere steel shrugged off as the black Cat pushed onward.

The incursion played out like the symphony the field lieutenant had composed: A second BearCat parallel-parked to the east fence deployed a dark-blue waterfall of Emergency Services pros over the razor wire and onto the property; two Harbor Unit Zodiacs cut rooster wakes up the channel, slowing at each barge and the skiff to offload officers; Heat's group branched out, half going for the warehouse to the right, the others, including Heat and Feller, staying in the shelter of the vehicle across the vulnerable open terrain between the entrance and the long trailer. "Window," said Feller.

Heat had already spotted the movement. Someone inside the modular had parted the blinds for a glimpse and closed them. They swung, bent and dirty against the cloudy glass. "Team Alpha, action in the trailer," said Heat into her walkie.

To her relief, Marr came back on immediately. "Team Alpha, holding fire, repeat, holding fire. We don't know who's in there."

The door burst open and a big man rushed out, hopping the pipe railing beside the three steps and racing for the yawning gate behind the team. Just as Heat recognized him as one of the men who had grabbed Rook, he drew a gun from behind his back. "Gun," said Nikki. The man fired one round that smacked the armor plate in front of her.

"Hold fire until he's clear of that hut," came the lieutenant's instructions. Heat and her team countered to the far side of the vehicle for cover and waited.

"NYPD, freeze and drop your weapon!" blasted the bullhorn command from the BearCat. The man ignored that and doubled his pace for the gate, where a rear flank uniform was advancing. The man raised his pistol to shoot. Well clear of the structure, the team unleashed a volley on him that threw his body into the chain link and then to the ground, pouring red onto the old cobblestones.

The backup officer toed the dead man's weapon aside and cleared him with a hand signal to the group. "In the trailer," came the next PA call. "This is the NYPD. You are surrounded. Throw out your weapons and come out with your hands raised." The driver gunned the monster engine as added incentive. No response.

They waited.

But not long. Using hand signals, the Alpha team set up in entry formation, with one cluster taking position behind a concrete ballast block near the steps and the other fanning right to the gap between the silver minivan and the far end of the trailer. Heat joined the squad behind the concrete cube just as they advanced on the door with a battering ram. She waited at the bottom of the steps and, during the ram's backswing, right before impact, she heard glass break. "Back window!" Nikki called, and ran for the gate.

Heat got to the sidewalk just as another huge guy—the same one who tried for a penalty kick with her head—cleared his legs through the shack's back window and started scaling the fence.

If he felt the pain of the razor wire, he didn't show it. He scrambled over the concertina, letting himself fall and land hard in his own blood, which had dotted the sidewalk. Rugged and solid but UFC-quick, he vaulted to his feet and started to run. "Police, freeze!" called Nikki. He slowed and turned to regard her, actually scoffing, while in her earbud, she heard the all-clear from inside the trailer.

No Rook.

In that instant, Heat knew she wanted this one alive. For all she knew, this mouth breather was the only link to finding Rook. Or finding out what had happened to him. She holstered up and charged him.

The shock of realizing that this woman would come at him hand to hand caught the goon so much by surprise that she was able to knock him to the ground with her tackle. He got himself up on one elbow and, flailing with his other arm, tried to throw a clothesline at her as he had on Third Avenue. But she dipped, presenting her shoulder, and his blow struck at an angle that diffused its energy. Heat came back with a quick shot with the heel of her hand up into his nostrils, which brought the sound of crunching bone, but no protest. Instead, he log-rolled away from her and came up kneeling with one hand reaching for his back waistband. In that blink of an eye, Heat heard footsteps racing toward her and overlapping calls of "Gun!" and "He's got a gun!" plus her own voice hollering "Hold fire!" and yelling "Don't!" to him while she drew her piece and then, in a flash of instinct or poetry or just plain damn payback, she kicked him in the head, sending him tumbling back on the sidewalk with his Glock sliding into the weeds.

"Clear," called Heat. Then she rolled him and cuffed him.

As the others rushed up, Nikki stood, bent over her prisoner, repeatedly shouting, "Where is he?" Feller and one of the officers manhandled the guy to his feet, and he gave Heat a stony glower over his swelling nose, but no reply.

"Let me to take this shithead for a ride," said Feller. "He'll talk." He meant it, too. There was a street side to Randall, a part of him that was capable of anything under the right circumstances.

"We don't do that here." Lieutenant Marr's comment came out as an observation rather than a reprimand. Like everyone else, he knew the stakes and understood the need to get information—and quickly; however, the field commander's ethics were not situational. Even so, Detective Feller's eyes probed Heat's in silent appeal. Before she could reply, everyone's two-ways crackled.

"K-Nine Four. Hostage located."

Heat was already sprinting back up the sidewalk and

making her turn at the gate by the time the transmission was repeated by the dog handler. Ahead she saw officers starting to gather around the farther of the two barges, and seconds later Nikki bypassed the gangplank, leaping from the dock to the gunwale, and disappeared down the open hatch into the bulkhead below deck. ESU officers had lit halogen lamps to illuminate the metal hold that rimmed the cargo box like an underground tunnel, with about the same dimensions of a mineshaft. She moved forward, ducking her head under the crossbeams, to where the K-9 sergeant was moving his dog out of her way. When the German shepherd moved aside, she gasped.

Rook was sitting on the deck with his legs splayed out in front of him and his head slumped forward over a bloody shirtfront. His hands were behind him, handcuffed around a steel truss, and one of the officers was crouched there setting to work on the lock. Relief swelled inside Nikki when Rook heard her footsteps and brought his face up and smiled. "Guess I'll need to change shirts," he said. "This definitely falls outside the P. J. Clarke's dress code."

He made her laugh, as he always did, and she brought her fingers over her mouth in case the emotion welling below turned into a wail. "Are you hurt?"

"You mean all the blood? My bad. I made the mistake of going heroic and trying to head-butt one of my captors. The one who looks like an Orc." He pointed with his chin over his shoulder at the cop. "Sir, are you going to get me out soon, or do I have to rip these shackles off so I can hug my fiancée?"

Heat could no longer restrain herself. She knelt and pulled herself to Rook, squeezing him, then pulling back for a deep kiss. When they parted, he said, "Um, a little *Fifty Shades*, wouldn't you say?"

"No," she said firmly with a side-glance at the other cops. And at the dog. "I definitely wouldn't."

"Oh, right." He arched one brow and nodded toward his lap. "Awkward." Then he turned to the others. "But you guys have seen just about seen it all over the years, right? . . . No?" Then the cuffs came off and he folded his long arms around her. They clung to each other while his rescuers wordlessly left them alone for their reunion.

Topside, while Rook refreshed his lungs with sea air and let his eyes adjust to the sunlight, Detective Feller took Heat aside. "What are we going to do with Beckham?" The goon who soccer-kicked Heat now had a nickname. Across the wharf, paramedics called in from the staging area were bandaging razor-wire cuts from his failed escape.

"Kidnapping's federal," she said. "FBI's going to want jurisdiction."

"What do *you* want?"

"To interrogate him myself, of course."

The detective turned to face her. "I don't see any wrinkle-free suits around here, do you?"

"Then I think it's time you hustled Becks across the river and let him wait in our interrogation room. I'll be right behind you."

Randall set off, then turned to her as he walked backward. "Should I red-card him?"

"Enough. Just go."

When she felt she had a sufficient head start on the Bureau, Heat phoned Special Agent Jordan Delaney to inform him of the raid. Vying for first dibs on an interrogation was one thing; Nikki's sense of responsibility wouldn't let her ignore protocol and allow agents and resources to remain tied up on a case she had already closed. Delaney thanked her for the information and asked how she had managed to locate him.

"The New York Public Library," she said, then waited for his long pause.

It came. Then the agent said, "No, really."

"Really." Heat explained that her frustration with the cyber attack had led her to resort to a very low-tech data search. "I didn't just go old school. I went old schoolgirl."

Delaney laughed and congratulated her on the safe rescue of her fiancé. "I'm guessing Mr. Rook came out of it OK?"

"Yes, he did, thank you. As we speak, I'm outside a Banana Republic near Lincoln Center watching him pay for a shirt. One that doesn't have bloodstains." Back in Red Hook, Nikki had offered to have a patrol car drive Rook to his loft for a shower, a change, and a nap. His response was to call shotgun and ride with her to the Twentieth so he could dive right back into their investigation.

"Nothing serious, then."

"Nosebleed. He says they didn't abuse him. Except for poking him with a hypodermic sedative on the way to the hideout."

"I want some one-on-one with him. A debrief."

"Of course." In an attempt to hasten an end to the call before the subject of her prisoner came up, she added, "I'm ten minutes from the precinct. I'll have him call you when we get there."

"Wait. Captain Heat?" She could tell by his tone that her ploy had failed. "You said one of the kidnappers survived. I want to speak with him, also. Immediately, in fact."

"You bet. Like I said, back at the precinct soon. I'll call." She hit End before that went any further.

The good news about doing the right thing by the Bureau was that they were busy running checks on the kidnapper killed in the raid and on Beckham, whose real name was George Gallatin. The not-so-good news was that Special Agent Delaney didn't wait for Heat to make contact on her schedule. By the time she and Rook entered the homicide bull pen, he had already been in touch with her prisoner, who was manacled and waiting in Interrogation One.

Rook enjoyed a round of handshakes and backslaps. Detective Ochoa said, "You're showing me something, homes, coming right from your rescue to this place."

"You kidding?" said Rook. "Wouldn't miss it. Since my kidnapping, the entertainment value of this case has increased dramatically." He then turned to Randall Feller. "Detective, I can't thank you enough for your part in my rescue. Above and beyond. And, as a token of my appreciation . . ." He held out a Banana Republic shopping bag. "I want you to have this. It's my bloodstained shirt." Even Feller had to laugh.

Before she lost her prisoner to the feds, Heat asked Rook

to brief them all on his experience, so the squad could pitch in on what to ask Gallatin when she got in the box with him. Raley handed him a cup of coffee, and he took a seat on Heat's old desk to recount all he could remember from street snatch to rescue. "I have no idea how they knew I'd be at that restaurant. Either they were tailing me from Times Square where I'd been at my editor's office at *First Press*, or they were following you, Nikki, and just hoped I'd come along to snag. The grab itself was pretty undignified." He tipped his head toward Heat. "I could hear you coming for me, but clearly neither of us was a match for that much goon power. They shoved me in the minivan and, after I smashed my nose into one of them, they put a needle in my shoulder. Before I went out, I heard one of them say, 'You'd better check in with Black Knight.'" The detectives exchanged side-glances with each other. "What?"

Heat said, "Rook, are you making this up, because it's OK, it was already an excellent adventure without you—"

"Turning it into a Monty Python remake?" offered Raley.

"OK, first of all, in *Holy Grail*, it was *the* Black Knight, not plain ol' Black Knight. And I feel no need to embellish. It's obviously a code name. Once, while I was cuffed in the barge hold, I watched the big one, Gallatin, dial Black Knight on his cell. I used an old reporter's trick to memorize the phone number by following which digits he tapped on his screen. It's this talent I have, like being able to read somebody's memos upside down on a desk."

Heat turned to a clean page in her notebook. "Great. Give me the number."

"One sec." He smiled weakly. "I forget. Gah! It'll come to me."

"Did you ever see this Black Knight?" asked Feller.

"A guy visited a couple of times to ask me questions, but they put a hood over me for that. Considering my circumstances, I didn't think it would be a good idea to ask if he was Black Knight."

"Weenie," said Feller.

"So all I heard was his voice. It was deep, kind of Southern, but not quite Heart of Dixie."

"Like Oklahoma," said Heat.

"Yes! Or Texas panhandle. How did you know?"

"I think I may have encountered him in a parking garage." She glanced at the wall clock. "Later for that."

"And you were never beaten or threatened? Waterboarded?" asked Ochoa.

"Don't sound so disappointed, Miguel. No. The guy, Black Knight, or whoever he was, just kept asking me a bunch of questions."

Hoping for a link to Tangier Swift, Heat asked, "Was it about the SwiftRageous whistle-blow?"

"Ish," said Rook. "Questions like, Did I ever see Swift meet with anyone other than the whistle-blowers? Was I aware of his recent travel? I don't know what he was digging for." He swirled the coffee in his cup and took a sip. "By the way, let the record show, I gave them nothing." Then he smiled at Nikki. "I don't know if you noticed, but I'm very good at keeping secrets."

***

Nikki didn't like the way George Gallatin had made himself feel
at home in the box when she strode in. The muscleman had
lounged backward in his chair as far as his restraints would
allow and was balancing on the two back legs while he
enjoyed his view of himself in the mirror. "I'd say be careful,
you're going to take a fall, George—but we both know you're
already set up to take one." She let her paperwork drop to the
tabletop at her place and took a seat. Becks seemed
underimpressed and concentrated on his balancing act.

She kept at it, trying to find the pressure point. Heat didn't
want to lose sole possession of her captive before he gave up
who he was working for. "Kidnapping is a Class B Felony
carrying five to twenty-five in this state. Add to that resisting
arrest and battery of a police officer. And I'm going to hazard
a guess that you have a number of other warrants out, which
would fill up your date book deep into this century."

He let himself fall forward on the front legs of the chair,
unfazed. "That guess you're hazarding? It's because you don't
even have a way to look me up on your fucking computers, do
you? Don't bullshit me. You have no levers to pull."

"Mr. Gallatin—"

"You can pull my dick's what you can pull."

Comments like that rolled off Heat. Years in that room
had inured her to abuse. But not prevented her from giving
it back. "From what I've seen, I'd have to find it first. Why
do you think I kicked you in the head instead of between
the legs?"

Amused, he hunched his shoulders and made a primal
yowl that shook the windows and, for a second, did make

him seem like the *Lord of the Rings* Orc Rook had described. She flipped open her manila file and continued, "Your macho posturing will serve you well where you are going. But I am prepared to talk deal with you in exchange for information."

"You could offer me a lap dance right now, and I wouldn't tell you the color of my shit this morning."

Heat had witnessed such posturing many times before. Sometimes they meant it, sometimes it was a pose to keep the upper hand in the negotiation. She proceeded, assuming the latter. "I am willing to call the DA and ask for their best deal. But first I want to know who told you to kidnap Mr. Rook." When he had settled down and folded his hands in his lap, she gave a little nudge. "Think about it, George. You're stacking a lot of years." He gave his chin a ruminating stroke. She could hear the rasp of his stubble six feet away. "It's as easy as answering a few questions. Who is this Black Knight?"

She waited while he considered. Then his shoulders began to shake. Nikki wondered if he was starting to weep—but no, he was giggling. A raspy, *gotcha* giggle. "Wanna know how I'm going to cut a deal?" He picked up his manacles and bit at the chain. "With my teeth." His laughter came harder, in hoarse bursts. He dropped the restraints and the laugh. "You can save your shit to feed some fool. Which I am not." Gallatin leaned forward, speaking casually. "You know who I liked? I liked the FBI dude. He seemed like a nice man. Think I'll take my chances with him instead of whatever bone you and your DA decide to throw me." Then he leaned back in his chair again. "Changed my mind. I'll take that lap dance now."

Special Agent Delaney was on hold in the Observation Room when Heat came out. He was not too pleased with Nikki for dragging her feet but surprised her by not coming at her too hard. "Look, Captain, I've played Hide the Hood plenty of times myself over my career. So I get it. I know you think you can get something before we can. But you've had your fun. Tag, I'm it."

Heat agreed to deliver George Gallatin personally to Federal Plaza within the half hour, but asked if, in exchange, she could take part in the interrogation. The agent sighed and said, "I'm going to agree. But I want something from you then."

"Name it."

"I want to know how the hell you managed to locate that hideout using the damn public library."

While they prepped Gallatin for transport downtown, Heat made a stop in the homicide bull pen for the latest. Detective Feller reported the results of his preliminary inquiries with the Coast Guard and the Port Authority about the barge company. "Channel Maritime, LLC, has a history of safety and immigration violations—all of which just sorta went away."

"Translation:" said Rook, "a friend in government."

Made sense to Heat, and, of course, she thought of Congressman Duer. But she had a hard time imagining a man of his stature bothering with low-level graft in a rusting business. "Let's keep our minds open," she said.

***

To make sure George Gallatin didn't get any heroic notions,
three strapping patrolmen led him in cuffs from the precinct
to Heat's unmarked car, which she had left double-parked
along with a half-dozen other police cars on West 82nd.
One of them palmed the prisoner's head so he wouldn't
whack it when they assisted him into the backseat and
belted him in. "Comfy?" asked Heat, who was standing in
the road with Rook.

Gallatin's only response was to flick his tongue at her in
mock cunnilingus. One of the uniforms handed Nikki a
transfer voucher to sign. "All yours," he said, and closed the
back door.

The window was fogging from Gallatin's taunting breath
as Nikki got out her keys and said to Rook, "You sure you
want to go?"

But before he could answer, the ignition cranked and her
car started. She turned, bending to see who was at the wheel,
but there was nobody in the front seat. "How'd you do
that?" asked Rook.

"I didn't." Nikki was reaching for the driver's-side door
handle when she heard the *thunk!* of the locks engaging. She
tugged at the door. "It won't open. Try your side."

Rook jogged around the trunk to the passenger door and
gave it a yank. "Locked." They both tried the rear doors.
Same. Then the engine started to rev, a few quick *vroom*s at
first, followed by repeated gunnings loud enough to bring
the heads of the three officers back out the glass doors of the
precinct lobby to see what gave. Heat looked around for
something to break the driver's side window when her car

roared off up the street—on its own, driverless—burning rubber at very high speed. As it raced off, George Gallatin twisted around in his seat as far as his handcuffs would let him. He made eye contact with Nikki as the police car roared onward. His expression was anything but cocky.

FOURTEEN

That police car had plenty of horses under the hood, and it gained speed rapidly, roaring directly toward the back of a parked box truck half a block away. Rook hunched his shoulders and half turned away but still peeked. At the last second, though, a hair's breadth before head-on impact, the front wheels turned hard and the car lurched to the left, its side doors making a piercing screech as they were raked by the edge of the truck's steel motorized lift. Astonished, but far from frozen, Heat shouted to the uniforms, "Call it in and get some keys! Go, go, go!" One of the officers was already getting in the blue-and-white behind her.

While he cranked up his engine, Heat's commandeered unmarked busted the red light up at Columbus. Taking the hard right turn at too much speed, its tires squealed and its momentum whip-cracked the rear of the car into a one-eighty slide-spin, smacking sideways into the potted trees that marked the bike path divider three lanes across the avenue.

Heat started sprinting toward the intersection, just in case the car had stalled. She'd shoot the tires if she got there in time. But the thick rumble of the engine vibrated the air again as it revved, then fishtailed off down Columbus, disappearing in a streak of blue smoke. The patrol car sped past her, but in the wake of the driverless car, confusion and alarm had caused a gridlock, and all the officer could do was slam on his brakes and keep burping his siren.

When she reached the corner, Heat stood on a planter to get some height, craning her neck for a view of the car. Rook arrived, and she shook her head, indicating that it was long gone. When she hopped down, he put his arms on her shoulders, stared at her and said, "This never happened."

But it had. And—since it was a first—she had to write the rules as she went along on how to deal with it. Naturally, the APB went right out, although Detective Raley had to repeat himself to the dispatcher who insisted on a description of the driver. Heat requested two helicopters and got them. Another effect of the cyber attack was that the signal from the transponder in her car couldn't be located, so she needed one chopper to fly a grid, hoping for a sighting. The second one she had make an aerial survey of rooftops around the precinct. Assuming that her car was being controlled remotely, whoever was doing it would need to have some sort of visual capability to work the turns, sloppy though they were. To cover possible window vantage points, a squad of uniforms and detectives was walking 82nd, knocking on doors of likely apartment buildings.

It never took long for dark humor to take root in a police station. On the hallway bulletin board, someone had already posted the cover of that month's *Car and Driver* magazine, but defaced with a Sharpie to read, *Car and* No *Driver*. To a cop's mind, there was no such thing as "too soon."

By the end of a very uncomfortable call from Heat to Special Agent Jordan Delaney—who first voiced concern that Heat had invented this story as a smokescreen to delay George Gallatin's handover to the FBI—he had become convinced, saying he found the account too bizarre to be anything but plausible. "Plus, you're not known for playing games." Then he added, "Just be careful this isn't the start of your new legacy," and hung up.

Of course, Heat's suspicions, along with everyone else's, went to Tangier Swift as the man behind all this. "Thinking it's one thing, proving it is another," said Rook after Nikki had red-circled Gallatin's name on the Murder Board and drawn an arc to the automotive software tycoon.

"What the hell is this?" said Ochoa. "When those kidnappers put that hood over your head, did they cut off your oxygen?"

"Really," added Feller. "This is Rook? Cautioning us about caution?"

"Why, because I know we have to make sure we have what we need before you go arresting him? Do you think I've learned nothing hanging out with you these past few years?"

"All the time," said Raley, who looked at Ochoa for appreciation of his jab. But the other half of Roach turned away. Nikki caught that and realized that while they may have agreed to work together, playing together was not happening.

"So how does something like this happen?" asked Detective Aguinaldo. "I mean technically happen?"

"It just can," said Feller. "Because it did."

"That's not an answer, that's a stance," said Rook.

"Hey, some Syrians can hack our whole city, how hard it is to hack a car?"

Heat didn't know. But she knew who might be able to tell her.

***

Nikki's call to Wilton Backhouse went straight to voice mail, but he called back within three minutes, just as she had left the ladies' room and stopped at the bulletin board to check out the latest addition. Someone had pasted George Gallatin's mug shot over Nic Cage's face on a screen printout of *Ghost Rider*. "Sorry, you caught me in a lecture. I keep my phone off." She could hear his sandals flipping on the linoleum floor on his way to his office. "Is there anything about Nathan?"

"No, not as of yet. In fact, part of the reason I called was to find out if he had made any contact with you."

"Uh-uh, I even tried his cell a few times. Nothing. He must have totally freaked when he heard about Abigail. Fuck me, I freaked. And he's not one to sit on his emotions, if you know what I mean."

Heat slipped behind her desk and sat down. "Yes, I do. He seemed pretty tightly wound the time I met him."

"Who wouldn't be?" Backhouse paused and sounded grim. And, for the first time with her, vulnerable. "Can't you stop all this?"

"We're working on it, believe me." In a moment of empathy, she almost shared the ordeal she had just been through with Rook, but stopped herself, figuring it wasn't the best time to introduce kidnapping and a shootout into the conversation. Instead she said, "In fact, you can help us, if you have a moment."

"I'll create one," he said.

She heard him settling in at his own desk. "I want to

know if it's possible to hack a car."

Wilton Backhouse's breath rustled against the mouthpiece as he chuckled. She pictured him on his bouncy ball, grinning. "You're kidding, right?"

"Do I sound like I am?"

"Gotcha." In his brief pause, Nikki heard him suddenly become Professor Backhouse. "The fundamental principles apply to all wired devices. Which is to say that, basically, you can hack anything that has a computer in it."

"And a car . . . ?"

"Is more computer than ever these days. Cars have systems that not only tell them how to function—power steering, traction control, stability control—as in the defective system fucking SwiftRageous is covering up; there are air bags, climate control, they also have GPS, heads-up displays, blindside driver alerts. You get the idea. Cars have computers systems. Systems are made to be hacked."

"How?"

"Lots of ways. There's a receptacle called an OBD-II port under the dashboard. Basically all you need now is a laptop and a cheap USB cable to plug into that and run any program ya got. There's also some new open-source software out there that, once you tap into the CAN bus—that's Controller Area Network—you can have total access to the vehicle the same way auto mechanics run Unified Diagnostic Services software to give your car a checkup. From there you can access or control just about anything you like, depending on your software. Locks, Bluetooth, GPS, phones, headlights, wipers . . ."

"What about the operation of the car itself?"

He laughed again. "Why not?" At least he didn't call her an idiot. "Savvy dudes have been putting performance chips in their own cars for years to increase torque. With new codes, you can pretty much do anything. Brakes, ignition . . ."

"What about acceleration and steering?"

"What do you think?" he said. "Why do you want to know all this?"

Once again, Heat held her panic cards close. She didn't acknowledge his question but instead asked a key one of her own. "And to do all this, could your run-of-the-mill hacker do it, or would it have to be someone who had a strong, sophisticated background in this?"

"Either. But those higher functions would point me to the latter. Is this about Swift?"

Heat said, "Just gathering facts."

"Pure research, it's called. A study without thoughts of an end goal."

"Sounds good."

"But I don't believe you," said the professor.

After Heat had shared Backhouse's information with the squad, Ochoa said, "This guy knows his stuff. And all this expertise about cars came right off the top of his head?"

"It is a rather brilliant head," Rook observed.

"Geek power!" said Heat. Even as she laughed along with them, Nikki found herself fixating on a tiny speck of grit in the back of her brain. Just for the sake of covering all possible scenarios, however unlikely, she turned to Detective Rhymer. "Opie, would you discreetly find out during what hours

Professor Backhouse had his lab at Hudson University today? And if he was present for it?"

"You want to alibi him for the car hacking?"

"I want to be thorough, that's all."

"And after you do that," said Feller, "find out if he can help me rig some sick subwoofers in my Bel Air for Cruise Night in East Rockaway."

At the end of the day, with nothing solved but everything being done that could be, Heat rested a hand on Rook's shoulder and said, "You look like hell."

"Thank you. Words I dreamed of hearing during the dark and wretched hours of my captivity."

"I'm serious. Gold star in your crown for extra effort, but let's get you out of here." He didn't object, so she shut off her office lights and grabbed her walkie-talkie, Nikki's bulky new accessory since the cyber attack had instantly turned her department-issue BlackBerry into a sleek dust catcher. Out of habit, she also reached for her car keys, then scoffed and tossed them back on her desk.

"Motor pool's going to issue you a loyalty reward card if you keep this up," said Rook, hauling himself out of the guest chair with an audible "Oof." On their way out, they passed the bulletin board, and she noticed that a picture of KITT, the artificially intelligent Trans Am from *Knight Rider* had been added to the lampooners' collage along with the cover someone had cut off a paperback copy of Stephen King's *Christine*.

Rook had used his Hitch! app to summon a car service to Tribeca, and the black town car with the ridiculous 3-D thumb on its roof was waiting when they stepped out. "At least it doesn't light up," she said.

"Give them time. This town will be crazy with luminous thumbs."

They were starving, but with both of them longing simply to shut the world out and fold into each other for the night, they did what all good New Yorkers do—ordered delivery without a second thought. Nikki called Hamachi from the backseat, but when she turned to ask Rook what he wanted, he was already dozing against her shoulder, so she ordered for him.

Wordlessly, Heat and Rook drew themselves into each other's arms in his foyer as soon as he had latched the door behind them—a spontaneous magnetic event fueled by their aching need to affirm something as basic and celebrated as their togetherness. They stood there a long time in the dark, silent, clinging, adhering. Chests rising and falling against each other, bodies feeling warmth and pressing closer to get more. It felt like there would never be enough, not after the past two days.

It took the delivery man's ringing the buzzer to break them apart, which they only did because they liked ordering from that restaurant and didn't want to get on its flake list by ignoring the poor guy. "What did you get me?" Rook asked as Nikki unpacked the bag and he uncorked the wine.

"I got you all eel and various roe."

"I hate eel and roe, you know that."

"Next time stay awake." The small things, laughter in the kitchen, takeout sushi, a kiss after the clink of glasses—they both knew how un-small they really were.

While they sat at the counter and he spread wasabi with his chopsticks on his favorite—*o-toro*—Heat told him the details of her search. And how frantic she had got. And how low. And she confessed about the night before last, when she had got herself drunk and nearly given up hope. He didn't answer, but got up from his barstool and enveloped her from behind. The hug was more profound than anything he could have said.

When he sat back down, Nikki said, "Is it an understatement to call this heaven?"

"Let's compare. I woke up sixteen hours ago with my hands cuffed behind me on the wet floor in the smelly hold of a scow. By the way, I'm making a unilateral decision: no cruise for our honeymoon."

She set down her glass and took his hand. He turned to her and felt her eyes painting him. "What?" he said, toying with her.

"You know what."

"I do know." He swiveled to face her. "And it goes for me, too. Absence makes the loins grow hotter."

She put down her napkin and stood, still gripping his hand. "Prove it," she said.

Rook's kiss took her by surprise because he met Nikki's mouth with tenderness instead of the abandon she expected. His adolescent swagger had stripped away and exposed the unguarded man who kissed her softly as if he needed to revisit the hushed magic of their interrupted moment in the foyer—an urgent attempt to finish some profoundly inexpressible thought. The words that would not find his writer's tongue found another way to reach her. Tasting him again, feeling his warmth and strength and vulnerability, sensing how he knew to slow the moment and create their own unique time and place, tapped a well of warmth inside Nikki that made her pulse race and urged her to want all of him, all at once. As if energized by her will, and helpless before it at the same time, she rose on her feet and pressed her body to his, backing him against the counter. His breath caught. He let out a faint moan and thrust himself closer. Then closer still. Nikki pulled her mouth from his, gulping for air. He whispered her name against her ear once, then twice, and she found his mouth again, kissing him hungrily.

They didn't walk to the bedroom, they were transported as if airborne through the fluid darkness, and fell onto the comforter to kiss again and then pause, breathing, wondering at the hoarse cadence their excitement had created and staring at each other, absorbing the power of the moment and what they knew was to follow.

Still locked in her eyes, Rook let his hand drift, exploring, finding her just as Nikki's hand found him. The lust they had been taunting, that deep mortal hunger pulling against its restraints, came to life.

After that, any sense of their being apart was vanquished.

In the murky span of the hammock hours between too late and too early, Heat and Rook stayed awake and talked.

Exhausted, spent, it didn't matter. They craved this as much as the lovemaking they had just shared. Nose to nose on a single pillow, he told Nikki how picturing her face kept him going when he had had no idea what fate would befall him as a captive—where, and at whose hands, he didn't know. Over his storied journalistic career Rook had been abducted and imprisoned before. Once in Chechnya. Twice in Africa. In Paris, it had happened to both of them one night when they got snatched from the Place des Vosges for a ride in the trunk of a car courtesy of a paranoid Russian spy who wanted a secret meeting in the woods outside the city. *"Bon temps,"* she said with a chuckle.

"I'm sorry for the mill I put you through," he said.

"We both had our ordeals. Not the first. I have a feeling it won't be the last." She shrugged and stroked the hair off his forehead with her fingertips.

"That's my tousled look you're messing with," he said. "Part of the ruggedly handsome persona I work so effortlessly to maintain."

Nikki laughed at that, then he nestled his cheek into her and spoke into the soft space where her neck met her collarbone. "It's good to hear you laugh."

"You always get me out of my serious self. That's why I keep you around, if you didn't know."

"Not the sex?"

"Part of the package."

"Pardon your pun."

"Writer boy. Always on the clock." After a minute or so of silence, feeling his chest rise and fall against her breast, she said. "I really did panic that I had lost you. I thought, what if we'd seen our last snowfall together? Or would I ever again watch you do your butt dance Saturday mornings to the WBGO *Rhythm Revue*?"

"That sweet soul music puts a shake in this moneymaker, for sure."

"Or would we ever make it to Nice on a vacation?"

"Hold on," he said. "I thought you said I'd permanently tainted Nice by having a rendezvous there with Yardley Bell."

"And you think I want Yardley Bell dominating my life like that? Removing geographic leisure options?"

"Hey, here's an idea. What about Nice for our honeymoon!" Then he read her. "Right, that would just be creepy."

Scooting up on one elbow, Nikki looked down at him in the duskiness of the bedroom. "Anyway, all this is what put me in such a tailspin the other night. I don't need Joni Mitchell to tell me to appreciate what I've got before it's gone."

Rook frowned. "Canadians. Always so earnest and introspective. I think it's the long winters up there. I prefer to be less about the talk, and more about the action."

"I noticed," said Nikki. "My turn." She rolled him onto his back and got on top.

After her morning shower, Heat dressed to *Eyewitness News*, the local ramp to *GMA*, and the lead was the same as it had been for most of the week: the cyber attack that had left municipal services in chaos. The new wrinkle was the leak from an insider in the city's Management Information

Systems Division who said the feds, admitting complete frustration, had brought in black hatters—unreformed hackers—in a desperate attempt to find the elusive solution to the crisis. Echoing what the FBI had told Nikki days before, the unnamed source said that every time they thought they had a fix, the attack would shift, putting them back at square one. "Sounds like Whack-A-Mole to me," said one coanchor to the other.

Meanwhile, even though Damascus continued to disavow any responsibility, the secretary of state was seen arriving in Paris, purportedly for off-the-record talks with the Syrians. "A long way to fly for the reiteration of a denial," said Rook when Heat recapped the story for him. "They should just tell everyone, whatever they need, just go to the local branch of their public library."

She poured herself a cup from what was left of the pot he'd made an hour before, and asked, "What the hell are you doing there—working out a system for Powerball?" Before him on the dining table in the great room Rook had spread sheets of paper upon which he had been scrawling numbers before crossing them out and starting a new page.

"If you must know, I'm trying to remember the phone number I saw that mouth breather from the barge use to call Black Knight." He slapped his pencil down in irritation and drew a deep sigh. "It's driving me batshit." He brandished some of the pages, which replicated digits from the phone keypad of a cell phone—some of the digits. Each page had gaps and sloppy cross-outs. "What?" he asked.

"Nothing. It just looks a little—"

"Mad?" he said with wild eyes. She couldn't tell if he was goofing or not. She knew that obsessed look from the times when he couldn't get the modem to reset or locate a phantom high-pitched mechanical whine in the alley below his office window.

"Maybe if you let it go—"

"I can't! . . . Let it go." He smiled. "OK, that was a little crazy, wasn't it?" She rocked her head side to side. "Yuh, thought so." He sipped some cold coffee and leaned back, willing calm upon himself. "I just feel like I should have this nailed."

"You're proud of your phone surfing, I know."

"It's not pride. Well, a little. But, what it really is, is wanting to get some damned traction on this story." He corrected himself. "*Case*, I mean case."

Nikki sat with him. "It's all right. It can be both. I know it's a story, too. And I know there might be another Pulitzer Prize for you, that would be nice. You could embroider another gold coin on your flak vest."

He got a chuckle out of that. He wouldn't be Rook if he couldn't see his own folly. Then he said, "Yeah, yeah, we joke about the Pulitzers. The Pulitzers are fine, I suppose. Not that I don't love them. I have two, you know."

"So I've heard."

"But the awards aren't the goal. They just follow. You know I do this because it makes a difference, don't you? I've exposed arms dealers supplying terrorists, diamond smugglers, human traffickers . . . And now I can help blow the whistle on Tangier effing Swift and his safety cover-up. That means I have a chance to save lives. Who can say that about what they do?"

"Doctors, nurses, first responders, suicide hotline counselors . . ."

"OK, yes, this is how we joke about my Pulitzers. Ha-ha, L-O-L, winking emoji, hashtag–you made your point."

"No, I hear you," said Heat. "And love you for that fire you have."

"You have it, too, Nik. It's what we share. And I want to see this through. I may not be able to get justice for those crash victims—or, now, the murder victims—but when my article comes out, there won't be any more lives wasted."

"So go to it. And leave the justice part to me. And if you're going to insist on jotting down your numbers, why don't you do it with something worthy of your quest?"

She went to her coat draped on the barstool and came back with the box from the Fountain Pen Hospital. He took it, removed the lid, and found his Hemingway Montblanc nestled in a felt liner. He carefully unscrewed the cap to examine the new nib, then looked up at her with tender eyes. "I'm speechless . . . I can't believe you touched my good pen."

Heat and Rook had a surprise waiting when they arrived at the precinct that morning. Nikki spotted the red satin track suit through the glass doors while she was still on the sidewalk and gave Rook a muttered "What is this?" to go with an elbow jab. Her curiosity only grew when she passed the Wall of Heroes, got a full view of the lobby, and saw that not only was Fat Tommy there but beside him in the visitors' chairs

sat none other than Joseph Barsotti. In that tableau, instead
of a journeyman mobster and his muscle, the pair resembled
an irascible senior and the dutiful grandson who insisted on
waiting with Pop-Pop to make sure he got on the right bus.

But prudent caution made Heat eye-sweep them for signs
of weapons and ascertain that they were the only ones there,
except for the desk sergeant behind the ballistic glass. From
police stations to shopping malls, no place was truly benign to
Heat anymore, nor was anyone, hospice-bound or otherwise.

"Thank God you guys start early," said Fat Tommy.
"Been a long night at the Wheel, and I'm ready for bed."

"Mr. Nicolosi." Heat calculated her greeting to keep it
cool. Chillier yet for Barsotti, whom she didn't acknowledge.
He was on her shit list for refusing to cooperate after being
such a pain to apprehend.

"Come on, doll, everybody calls me Fat Tommy." He
tugged at the loose fabric of his jumpsuit. "For now." He
hauled himself to his feet with some effort and spread his
arms for Rook. "Come on, big fella, bring it in." After a
careful hug of the frail old man, Rook took a step back, and
Tommy cupped a hand on his jaw. "You had me worried, you
know that? When that detective came to check me out, see if
I kidnapped you, I shit myself. Not literally, but that's
coming next, I'm waiting. Mind if I . . . ?" He indicated the
gaudy plastic chair and Rook and Barsotti eased him back
down into the form-fitting ass mold.

Heat made a clock check. "Is there something we can
help you with? Otherwise, if you came to see how Rook
was doing—"

"Can you help me? You've got that backwards, Nikki Heat. I'm here to help you."

"I'm listening."

Fat Tommy adjusted the angle of his big sunglasses. That seemed to alter his demeanor at the same time. The *Goodfellas* act went out the window, and the mobster grew steely and severe in a way that gave Nikki a minor chill. "I wasn't kidding about getting pissed when I heard somebody fucked with your boyfriend. Rook's always been stand-up with me. We don't need to get into details, but I respect this man. Time for me to show it. Now, I don't know if what you wanted out of my associate has anything to do with whoever kidnapped him. But in case it does, I am here to give you Joseph Barsotti with my blessing for him to cooperate."

Nikki regarded Barsotti, who gave her a shrug of assent. "Well," she said. "That is most appreciated, Fat Tommy."

"Hear that?" said Rook. "She called you Fat Tommy."

"About fucking time." Then, as Barsotti went through the metal detector and into the precinct with Heat and Rook, Tommy called after to her. "And smart move ditching that uniform. You've got too much going on to hide it."

Rook turned to her as the door closed. "Wouldn't it be funny if that's the real reason he came? To mentally undress you?" Nikki gave him a stony look. "Perhaps more ironic than funny," he said. "Let's go with that."

Heat made a quick stop in her office to take a moment to formulate a strategy. Over the years she had learned that the most powerful tool an interrogator has is an objective to work toward. With this opportunity sprung on her unexpectedly, she didn't want to blow it, and so a pause to reflect would be time well spent. Once she had an idea, she gathered the materials she would need into her file, then made a few quick status checks.

Detective Aguinaldo had managed to track down some of her former Military Police colleagues from Creech AFB. "One of my MP buds remembered an incident with one Airman Timothy Maloney. He had been called in to investigate a sexual harassment claim and discovered that the enlisted man had been spying on a female officer—wait for it—with a hobby-grade drone. No charges were filed, because Maloney claimed he'd lost control of it. Nonetheless, they kicked him out of the base's amateur drone club."

So Yardley Bell's information was confirmed, that Maloney had not been a USAF drone op, but he had gotten bitten by the UAV bug at Creech. The question for Heat was whether he had left his toys in Nevada, or brought the hobby to New York—with lethal consequences?

Raley gave her the report that there had been a sighting overnight of a pickup truck matching the description of Nathan Levy's 450 in the parking lot of the Marine Air Terminal at LaGuardia. Port Authority PD had run a check, and it came up registered to a caterer from Edison, New Jersey. Both George Gallatin and her stolen car were still unaccounted for, with the APB still being repeated on her scanners.

Detective Rhymer confirmed Wilton Backhouse's whereabouts the previous day, which didn't surprise her.

"The professor indeed was scheduled for, and personally conducted, a lab at Hudson University at the time he said on the subject—get this: 'Velocity, Spin, Frictional Coefficient, and Impact Angle.'" He looked up from his notes. "Sounds like a porn title."

"Maybe in Virginia," Heat said with a grin.

If it had been anyone other than Joseph Barsotti, a career scumbag, Heat would have set up a more informal interview in the relatively relaxed setting of the conference room. But once on the shit list, it's a complicated process getting off of it. So, after a pat-down to make sure he knew this wasn't a social visit, she and Rook sat across from him in one of the interrogation rooms.

Her plan was to press Barsotti as the prime suspect in the killing of Lon King. Although that didn't seem likely to Heat, given the investment Fat Tommy had in keeping his debtor alive, the enforcer didn't know that, and would be more pliable if he was trying to beat a homicide rap. So that is how Nikki cut the ribbon on the interrogation, coming at him hard with questions about his firearms and permits, his arrest jacket for violent offenses, and repeatedly using phrases like, "the last time you saw Lon King alive . . ." Without the protection of his mob code of silence, Barsotti grew fidgety and his eyes darted around. Heat liked that. And once she had him in a more vulnerable place, she zeroed in on what she really wanted to know.

"If you expect me to believe you didn't kill Lon King,

you'd better give me something I can get my teeth into. Something real. Otherwise, it's you, Joe." Heat knew Barsotti wasn't the killer, but making him worry that he might take the fall for a murder was great leverage to get him to talk about things she needed out of him—and she was going to use it.

"What can I tell you other than I didn't do the guy?" he whined. Nikki always paid attention to hands. Barsotti's were large, be-ringed, and had empurpled knuckles. She pictured him giving the beat-down to that exotic dancer and was glad she'd held a hard line with him.

"You've got to give me everything you saw. How long were you dogging King?"

"I dunno, a few days?"

Heat slapped a hand down, making him jump. "You *dunno*?"

Rook tilted his head toward the man and gave him a sympathetic face. "Trust me, pal. If I were you, I'd start knowing."

"A week. Not every single day. Six. Six days." He looked at Rook and got a reassuring wink in return.

Nikki slid a blank yellow pad and a ballpoint to him. "Write 'em down. Dates, times, places. Soon as we're done." Barsotti nodded. "I also want to know about any unusual activity around King."

"He was a shrink. Everything was unusual."

She heard a soft "Ahem" for her benefit from Rook, but kept her gaze on Barsotti. "You're not helping me, which means you are definitely not helping yourself. Give me specifics. You were pretty much stalking him, right?"

"I wouldn't use that word . . ." He caught Rook's cautioning head wag. "Yes. I watched him. But only so I could pick my spot to persuade him to repay his debt."

"Did you notice anyone else watching him?"

He paused. "Yeah."

"You'd better not be saying this to please me, because if you're lying, I'll know. It won't be good." Heat had him emotionally where she needed him and slid a photo from under the cover of her file. "Ever see this man?"

"Oh him, fuck yeah. He's off the chain." He handed the picture of Timothy Maloney back across the table like he might catch something from it.

"Tell me."

"I made—let's call it an office visit—to provide incentive to Lon King about his gambling debt. When I got there, a big argument was going on in the waiting room. That guy was reaming out King while everyone else freaked."

"Everyone like who?"

"Patients, I guess. I took a hike. But I did hear the fucker say he was going to kill King." He waited and continued. "He said he was going to kill him. You didn't write that down."

Heat flicked a forefinger at the yellow pad in front of Barsotti. "You write it down." Then she took out another photo from her file and dealt it to him across the table. "What about this guy? Ever see him?" He studied it a moment and nodded. "Are you certain?"

"Yes. A couple of times. Basically just hanging out at the

medical building. I thought he was a doctor or something. But I remember seeing him."

"I'm going to ask you to think. Get a calendar if you need one, and give me the dates and times." Heat suppressed the exhilaration she felt, and she could tell from her connection to the man beside her that Rook was right there with her. She took the photo back and left.

Heat and Rook speed-strode the hall and into the bull pen. "We may have just gotten some traction," she announced. The homicide squad gathered around. "Look who Joseph Barsotti just ID'd as someone he saw hanging around Lon King's office multiple times." Nikki posted the photo from her file on the Murder Board. "Eric Vreeland."

"Tangier Swift's PI?"

"None other," said Rook.

Ochoa turned from the picture to Heat. "That's large."

"Extra," she said. "I want Vreeland brought back in. It doesn't make him the killer—necessarily—but it is our first nexus between Tangier Swift, Lon King, and Nathan Levy."

"Two of our homicide victims," said Raley.

Heat's brow pulled into a vertical crease. "Two of our victims . . ." she said, but it sounded unsure enough to be a question.

"Just got the call," said Feller. "They found Nathan Levy's body in his truck fifteen minutes ago."

FIFTEEN

Poetic." That was Rook's first word when they got to the crime scene. And he wasn't too wrong, Nikki thought. An automobile test driver killed behind the wheel might qualify. Except the only rhyme Heat saw was the hole in his forehead, same as two of the other vics.

Heat had gotten there quickly, even before the Medical Examiner, which gave her a clearer view of the site, a self-pay parking lot under the Highline, not far from Chelsea Piers. The patrol team that spotted the performance pickup truck had not only been alert, they were well trained. Rather than contaminating the scene, which happened with maddening frequency, they hadn't done anything more than glove up and open the driver's side door to see if he was alive or not. After that, the officers caution-taped the driveway to secure the zone and did the best possible thing. They waited.

"So the door was closed when you got here?" Heat asked, ever thorough.

"Yes," answered the patrolwoman. "But the side window was down."

Nikki walked back and forth, surveying the open door and the rolled-down window, then peeked inside. "Was the ignition turned on like it is now?"

"Huh, I didn't notice."

Beginner's eyes, Heat told herself. She always came to her scenes as if she were just learning how to do this. Nothing got taken for granted that way. Veterans had a nasty habit of overlooking things. She made a note of the engaged ignition and that the battery seemed dead. The setup suggested Levy probably had been sitting there listening to the radio when he bought it. The seatbelt was unfastened and retracted. As for the body itself, it was facing the open window, but tilted back and away toward the passenger side—an obvious consequence of the gunshot.

Rook said, "May I state the obvious? Unless you can convince me this is a suicide, Mr. Levy's not looking so good as our killer."

Nikki sing-songed, "He's ba-a-a-a-ack." But did it with her inside voice—wise, given the setting and the pair of uniformed witnesses.

"Know what else? I also don't think he'll be throwing those at Mardi Gras this year." Heat followed his gesture to the colorful plastic beads hanging from the rearview mirror. Within the red, green, purple, and yellow strands, something caught her eye. Using her capped stick pen in her gloved hand, she leaned into the cab and lifted a white latex bracelet by one end.

"What is that, a hospital bracelet?" he asked.

Heat turned her head to the side so she could read the band. "With Nathan Levy's name on it."

***

Rook's conjecture about Levy's poor viability as a suspect was reinforced, albeit without the wiseass factor, back at the precinct by Detective Aguinaldo. "When he took off on the run, I decided to establish Mr. Levy's whereabouts during the time frames of our various homicides. You want to hear?"

"I have a feeling there's no stopping you," said Heat, impressed with the initiative. Inez, a talented detective, clearly was pushing harder, trying to make up for her stumble in overlooking a search of Abigail Plunkitt's rooftop.

"During the spans of time around King's and Lobbrecht's deaths," Aguinaldo said, "Levy was up in Monticello, New York, at a meeting about a job as a driving coach at the private racetrack and resort up there."

"That's only ninety minutes away," said Feller.

"Yes, but he had an early interview and spent the night at the Courtyard by Marriott in Middletown. I've confirmed he was physically present at both places. That leaves the period in which Plunkitt was killed. He was away during that time frame, too. He told his next-door neighbor he was in Atlantic City getting physical therapy on his leg."

Detective Rhymer said, "Hold on. Who goes all the way down to AC for physical therapy?"

Aguinaldo grinned. "I checked. The physical therapy wasn't exactly covered under insurance, if you know what I mean. There's security footage of him in the lobby of the place. On two visits."

"Ah," said Rook. "Nathan's massage had a happy ending. His life, not so much."

Heat tore a page out of her notebook. "Detectives Raley

and Ochoa." The pair, who were sitting on opposite sides of the group, raised their heads. "I copied this off a hospital bracelet I found hanging in Levy's truck. Note the patient." She handed it to Ochoa, who was nearer. He read it and passed it on at a signal from Raley. "It's from an ER up in Cortlandt, which is Westchester County. He was there in February, about a month and a half ago. I'm not sure what this will give us—maybe why the limp—but place a call, and let's find out."

"On it," said Raley. "As long as we're gathered, we have a few updates for you. First of all, CSU found George Gallatin's cell phone on the floor in the modular trailer at the Channel Maritime."

Rook grew very excited. "That's great. We can get that number for Black Knight."

"'Come back here, you bastard!'" called Feller in a passable Monty Python impression. "It's only a flesh wound!"

"You mock me, but I'm telling you, I heard Gallatin say he was calling Black Knight." He turned back to Raley. "All we have to do is check the Recents. The number will be there."

"Sorry. History's been cleared. You're going to have to keep noodling. Or give it up."

"No, I'm too OCD for that." Nikki could see Rook's eyes glaze over as he tried to conjure up a replay of that phone dialing.

Raley consulted his cheat sheet. "We also got word about Eric Vreeland."

"I already know I'm not going to like this," said Nikki.

"Well, then you won't be quite so disappointed when I

tell you. It's going to be tough to have him drop by for an interview. His office said he was away on vacation. We checked with Customs and Immigration and they report that Vreeland exited the country on a flight out of JFK yesterday for Croatia."

"Croatia," said Rook with appreciation. "Have you ever been? Croatia has everything. Castles, beautiful woman . . . Stunningly. Beautiful. Women. Oh, and no extradition agreement with the United States."

"The perfect vacation spot for a Person of Interest in a multiple homicide," observed Heat. "Terrific."

As everyone scattered on their assignments, Heat returned to her desk, which had taken on the appearance of an urban curbside on recycling day. The collateral effect of the cyber attack was the rapid, seemingly endless generation of paper. The height of the stacks, however neat, could be measured with a ruler, and they formed a bulwark around Nikki's blotter. On the upside, they served as a graphic example of how the digital age had cut environmental waste. Plus it gave her a degree of privacy in her goldfish-bowl office.

The captain compliantly went about her administrative duties: meetings with the union steward, the vending machine supplier, and the lead officer in the precinct's Traffic Division about staggering the maintenance of the Cushmans. None of these made her feel like she was fighting crime.

Detective Raley showed up at her door, a welcome interruption, with the word on his call to the ER up in the Hudson Valley. "Records indicate Nathan Levy showed up there in the middle of one night complaining of severe pain from an injury to his right leg. He reported that he whacked it on a table. His chart said he had a large amount of swelling and bruising. They did an X-ray that showed he had a hairline fracture of his tibia, right below the knee. They treated him, gave him some crutches, and he self-released."

Nikki sat back and crossed her arms. "That must have been some table."

"Yeah, doesn't pass inspection to my nose, either."

"What do we know about our patient?"

"Our boy liked his cars," said Raley.

"And to drive them fast."

"I'll contact State and County up in that area and see if they worked any accidents around that date." The detective got up from the guest chair. "Not quite sure what it means to us."

"Never know until it does," said Heat. "Or doesn't. But let's at least close the loop." Then, before he left, she snagged him. "Hey, Rales? Things any better between you and Miguel?"

He almost answered, but left it with, "I'll make those calls now," and went back to his desk in the squad room.

The Office of Chief Medical Examiner had been slammed by the hacking event just like other city MISD services, so Lauren Parry called Heat personally with her postmortem results on Nathan Levy. "By the way, how many more of these cranials am I going to be doing?"

"Working on it. Hopefully the last one."

"Good, 'cause I need another one of these like I need a—"

"Lauren, stop. You stop. If you were about to say 'hole in

the head,' cease. I have all I can stand of that with Rook."

"Oh, and now you're complaining about him instead of getting hammered in your bathtub? Besides, I'm working morning and night with dead bodies down here, and I have one chance for a little human interaction, and you cut me off."

"Damn right. You want to amuse me? Brief me on your post."

Dr. Parry's narrative regarding Levy echoed her reports on Lon King and Abigail Plunkitt, as expected. Small entry wound made by a .22-caliber slug, severed brain stem, no exit wound. Also, as with the other two, indication of a close-range weapon discharge, as evidenced by gunshot residue and muzzle burn.

"What about the condition of the bullet?"

"Not bad. I already gave the slug to ballistics."

"Thanks," said Nikki. "I'll task a detective to go over to Jamaica and get the report personally. Last time they practically used a carrier pigeon."

"Still beats my intranet. Other items of note that you'll see in my write-up: I saw a recent hairline fracture—"

"Of the right tibia? Just below the patella?"

"OK, now that's just weird. How'd you know that?"

"See, that's how you create human interaction, Doctor. Take note." After a chuckle Heat told her about the ER report she had just received, and the ME agreed that, although it was not impossible, such a fracture was unlikely to be the result of walking clumsily into a piece of furniture.

"Question," said Nikki. "Oil residue. Any sign?"

"No, and I was looking for it, especially after we found traces on the other two."

"I'm asking because I looked real closely at the door of his pickup, and I didn't see any. I'll check with Forensics."

"I already have. No oil residue." After a long pause, Parry asked, "You still there?"

"Yeah, I'm just thinking about that."

"One of your Odd Sock moments?"

"When something breaks a pattern, that's what we call it around here," said Heat. "A pleasure interacting with you on a human level, Doc."

After Nikki hung up, she started feeling unsettled. And she liked that. Things that didn't feel right had a funny way of turning into clues.

About an hour later, as Heat was returning from briefing the new patrol squad she had formed to discourage smartphone thefts on subway platforms, Raley waved her into the bull pen. "I made the rounds of NY State Police and county traffic enforcement in Westchester and Putnam, which would be nearest the ER in Cortlandt. It's mostly a lot of the garden-variety rural stuff. Rear-end taps, flat tires, engine stalls, missing license plates, broken headlights, kids driving on lawns, failures to yield, and drunk drivers. But there was a fatality."

Without realizing it, Nikki took a seat at her former desk. Rook came over and sat on it. Old habits. "Where and what?" she asked.

"A stretch of the Cold Spring Turnpike between the Taconic and Route 9."

"I've been there," said Rook. "They call it a turnpike, but that's a backcountry road."

"Quite isolated," continued the detective. "And a lot of twisty-turnies. The fatality involved a single-car accident. The driver was alone. She somehow veered off the road and smacked head-on into a tree."

"Impaired?" asked Heat.

"No. And the autopsy showed no physical issue like heart attack, aneurism, or anything like that."

Heat's mind raced to a hundred places all at once. "And it was a solo event."

"That's the conclusion. Staties are sending me the MV-104, but that's their finding. They said things like, it could be a deer reaction or a coyote swerve. Or a distraction. Except the driver had her cell phone inside her purse, and there were no messages or calls preceding the crash. Also no suicidal indicators."

Rook swiveled on the desktop to face Nikki. "Do you think this could have anything to do with Nathan Levy? Let me rephrase that. What do you think Nathan Levy had to do with this? Like, instead of a deer or a . . . I dunno . . . a rabid woodchuck, or Toonces the Driving Cat . . . was he the one who made the driver lose control?"

Raley chimed in. "My contact at the state troopers said their investigation had ruled out a phantom vehicle."

"But still," said Nikki. "A little coincidental, wouldn't you say?"

Bobbing his head, Rook added, "And I know what you say about coincidences. They're like seagulls. You've never seen one that didn't lead someplace fishy."

Nikki winced. "I never said anything like that."

"I'm a writer. Take the sound bite, OK? All yours."

Heat instructed Raley to put in a call to Inez Aguinaldo, who was up in Throggs Neck scrubbing through Nathan Levy's house with the Crime Scene Unit. He briefed the detective on the ER report and the fatal solo crash that had happened the same night. "Which we aren't buying it as solo," Heat said.

"I've already asked Forensics to check his F-450 for damage or recent repairs. Why don't you have somebody up there with you in a bunny suit take a close look at his BMW?"

Aguinaldo called back less than a half hour later. It wasn't difficult for the CSU tech to note that the M3 had a replacement front spoiler bumper cover and brand-new wheels and tires on the front, as well. There was no other evidence of bodywork. The airbags had not been deployed; however, it did look like the factory glove box door had been replaced. "I searched his desk in the living room and dug out a receipt for the work. It was done last month at a specialty Bimmer shop here in the Bronx. The owner remembered the job and said it was a flatbed truck-in."

Raley clicked his pen. "From where?"

"I've got the address. It's a wreck-and-tow service up in Peekskill."

"Hard to ignore how this hooks up," Raley said when he rushed back into Heat's office. "Levy's damaged car gets towed from Peekskill—the town that's right in-between where the accident happened and the hospital where he dropped into the ER."

Not yet knowing if this was a meaningful development or just a seductive trail leading into a dead end, Heat was too seasoned to get excited. And yet, she did give herself permission to feel at least intrigued by the news.

"Next step is to get in touch with the tow company," she said.

"Going to call them now. I just wanted to loop you in first."

"Hang on." Nikki had an idea forming and took a moment to reason it through before she spoke it. "I think we need to get some eyes on this situation instead of just calling."

Raley awakened his phone to check the time. "I could be in Peekskill before lunch. You want me to go up there?"

"No." When he gave her a puzzled look, she tapped her knuckles on her window. Inside the bull pen, Detective Ochoa turned from the Murder Board and came in. "I want you guys to fire up the Roach Coach for a field trip. Your partner has the details." She watched the two of them sweep each other with side-glances.

At last Ochoa spoke. "You think that's a good use of our time?"

Heat already had thought about it. She had witnessed how focusing on the search for Rook had rallied them. Another mission might be just what these two needed: a couple of hours in the car. Together. Raley and Ochoa, just like before. Before her promotion had made them competitors instead of partners, instead of Roach. "Actually, I think it's the best use of our time." Then she added, "I want you fellas to do what you do best. Get a sense of things, up close and personal."

"Oh, I get it," said Ochoa. "This some takeaway of yours from the cyber attack? Be more hands-on?"

"Something like that."

On their way out the door, Raley said, "We're all over this. Like a seagull on a tuna boat."

"Careful, or I'll make you take Rook, too," she called after them.

The young woman with the sad eyes said, "I'm sorry, Nikki, I truly am. You know I'd like to help you, but I can't." They were sitting in Lon King's office. Correction: his former office. Josie Zenger had taken the far end of the couch and twisted to face Heat. The receptionist and office manager for the practice had avoided the shrink's beige lounge chair on the other side of the coffee table. It remained, and would remain, empty as long as it was there, Heat thought. That was a safe assumption. King's desktop, always uncluttered, was cleared and dusted, its contents—everything from surface knickknacks to storage drawers—had been boxed and labeled by Josie and now sat in a double row of containers under the window, every one numbered and marked. The books and awards from the shelves must have been in there, too. If it weren't for the carpet, the room would echo.

Nikki wasn't so sure she wanted to hear any of those echoes.

The place felt so strange and beyond silent to her. When this was all done, another practice would fill this space. Maybe another psychologist. Perhaps a dentist or pediatrician, creating a more active and noisy suite. For now, though, there was the hush. And Josie's sniffle. The box of tissues hadn't been packed yet. Nikki pulled one and handed it to her. Heat waited for her to settle and continued gently, "But you can confirm the incident, right? I have an eyewitness, Joseph Barsotti, who says he walked in on an altercation in the waiting room."

"Yes, two and a half weeks ago," the receptionist said. "I can confirm that much because I was there. It was ugly. But I am ethically bound by the Health Insurance Portability and Accountability regulations not to disclose confidential patient names or records."

"Well, Lon King was there. And you also confirmed that Fred Lobbrecht was there."

"Yes, but they are deceased." Josie choked up a little at that and took a moment to recover. "Our lawyers say it's all right to cooperate about decedents. And I want to cooperate. But I can't give you the names of anyone else who was there because they were patients and are living. Or could have been patients."

"Explain that, if you don't mind."

"Even if someone wasn't formally enrolled, their presence assumes a privileged doctor-patient relationship."

"So you mean someone seeking help? Shopping doctors? A guardian, a visitor, what?"

"You can get what's called an administrative subpoena, then I'd be free to answer all these questions and help you."

"Thanks, Josie, I understand. I'll do that."

"Or, if you'd like, I can contact the individuals and see if they'll give permission."

"No, don't." Nikki said it sharply enough to make the woman flinch. She smiled and softened her voice. "Sorry, I just don't want to set off any alarms for people unnecessarily." Meaning, *Don't tip anyone off.* "I'll look into the subpoena, as you suggested."

Heat paused before she left for one last look at the beige-and-creamy-vanilla room where she had cried, laughed, worried, sighed, and ultimately found a measure, if not of peace, at least of herself. No box could contain that, she thought as she closed the door. Nikki was glad she had stolen a few tissues for herself.

Rook had lunch waiting on her desk when she got back from her visit to York Avenue. "How did you know I'd be starved? And Spring Natural Kitchen, great." Heat lifted the takeout lid. "And you got me my favorite."

"Thai falafel salad, madame."

"And what the hell is that?"

He held up his container. "Continuing today's international salad motif with organic quinoa."

"I have never seen you order quinoa."

"Never knew how to pronounce it. Now that I do, turns out it's delicious."

After a few bites to cushion the dent, Nikki called the DA's office to request whatever paper she needed to get past the HIPAA regs so she could get a full accounting of the incident in Lon King's waiting room. As with the thread that had started with Nathan Levy's visit to the ER, Heat wasn't sure of the importance of Barsotti's information. But the purpose of investigating wasn't to decide instantly which data were important. You had to collect it all first before you knew. Sometimes it meant nothing. Sometimes it meant nothing for years. Heat thought of those twin lions outside the library, Patience and Fortitude. She didn't need to conquer all things; just this one case would be nice.

"Sorry, Captain Heat," said the assistant DA.

"What do you mean, sorry?" Nikki set down her fork and pushed her food away. "It's my understanding this isn't even something that has to get judicial approval. I thought I could just file a written request with my justification and scope, and we're good to go."

"That's correct. The sticking point is in what you just said. The scope is too broad. Looking into a patient, we can do. Like this Timothy Maloney."

"I don't need to know about him, I already know he was there. I want the names of the others in that room."

"You're coming full circle, Captain. The others in that room can't be confirmed as patients—ipso facto, too broad."

"Here's an ipso facto: This is why people hate lawyers." Heat hung up and felt ashamed and oh so good at the same time.

The call had soured Nikki's appetite, and she was marking her initials on the takeout carton before she put it in the fridge when Detective Rhymer skidded into the break room. " 'Scuse me, Captain?"

"Hey, Opie, what's up?" Rhymer didn't have much of a

face for poker and she could read his excitement. Nikki
shoved the refrigerator door closed and strode to join him
even before he had answered.

"Raley and Ochoa on the line in the squad room. You'll
want to take this."

The detectives had conferenced together, and Heat got a
double hello when she picked up. "Hey, an actual Roach call.
You weren't kidding when you said you'd make it by lunchtime."

"Yeah, and damn glad we came up here in person, like you
suggested," said Raley. "Let's walk you through in order."

Ochoa picked up the ball. "We found the wrecker service
here in Peekskill, Dunne Towing. The owner was very
cooperative, called in the kid who drives the overnight hook."

"Name is Dooley," added Raley.

"Dooley worked the haul-out of Nathan Levy's BMW
on Cold Spring Turnpike. Guess where?"

"Around the hairpin turn from the fatal," said Raley.
Heat felt her pulse accelerate, and when she looked at Opie,
he was working his head up and down, knowing, yep, this
was something. "You still there?"

"Yes, I'm just . . . That's big," Heat said.

"Not done yet. Miguel?"

"Dooley reports the damage to the M3 was also solo."

Raley clarified, "Not car to car."

"Skidded into a small runoff ditch paralleling the
shoulder. Bent both front wheels and smacked the spoiler
into the gravel siding. The car was undriveable, so Dooley
flatbedded it back to his repair garage. But Levy was
compulsive about the car and wouldn't let the locals touch it.

So he arranged to have them transpo his vehicle to that body shop Aguinaldo found the paperwork for in the Bronx."

Nikki processed the implications. "This is bizarre."

"Understatement," said Detective Ochoa.

"I mean, you and I both know a fatal accident lights up all sorts of police follow-up," she went on. "How is it that this wasn't reported by the hauler, Mr. Dooley?"

"OK, now we're getting to it. He did report it."

"That makes no sense. The State Police said it was a solo event. How can he say he reported it? Is he credible? Do you believe him?"

"Oh, he's high-cred," said Ochoa.

"Extremely," his partner added. "You see, this is why we're glad you sent us up, first-person. He showed us the paperwork."

Detective Ochoa said, "I'm holding a copy of it now. You ready? It was signed off by a state trooper."

"Holy—" Heat grabbed a pencil out of a cup on Rhymer's desk. "I want to talk to that trooper."

"That won't be possible," said Raley. "According to this report, the state trooper who led the accident investigation was their top collision expert at the time: Fred Lobbrecht."

SIXTEEN

Opie couldn't stop shaking his head. "Isn't this just too weird?"

"Although when you think about it," said Rook as he dragged his chair with the whimpering caster over to Heat and the rest of the squad in the bull pen, "isn't 'too weird' really just another way to say 'too cool?'"

"Definite freak factor," agreed Detective Ochoa, who was still patched in on the speakerphone from Peekskill. Raley, also on the line, grunted his agreement.

Heat was equally intrigued by the news, but her mind was busy wrapping itself around its implications, and she wanted to get the homicide detectives there with her. "Can we generally agree that Roach has rocked our world and settle into making something of this now? Hopefully leading to finding a killer or killers?"

"Oh sure, if that's your thing." Randall Feller put his work boots up on an empty chair and snuck a sly smile. "Guess we could do that."

Rook raised a forefinger. "May I kick things off by noting that this certainly sheds new light on the emotional turmoil Fred Lobbrecht was grappling with. Obviously he had pangs of conscience about whatever unethical crap he pulled at that accident scene."

"Try *illegal*," added Detective Aguinaldo.

"That, too. But my point is, it sure explains why I got pushed into mediation with Lon King to help this guy into a headspace where he could spill his story to me. Even off the record. Lobbrecht's bowels must have been a Vitamix."

Rhymer, who had done the initial bank search on Lobbrecht, leafed through his pages of notes. "And what about our conclusion about the whole lump sum of cash ex-trooper Lobbrecht got right after the accident to pay off his mortgage? What if it was a bribe from Levy, and not the payoff from Tangier Swift, like we've assumed?"

Heat sucked one of his cheeks, ruminating. "If you're right, Ope, that nails him as the source of the windfall, but it then removes a link to Swift's involvement. At least on that score."

"I hate that," said Feller.

"Don't," cautioned Nikki. "Remember—"

"'Follow your evidence, not your bias.'" After Randall had recited Heat's maxim for her, he added, "I know all that. I just felt like we had the sucker."

"And we may still. We just need to be open to all the possibilities. Do I need to mention this is a case with a lot of moving parts?" She turned her attention back to Rhymer. "I wonder if Nathan Levy had the kind of money to pay off Fred Lobbrecht's house. Run his financials. Visit his bank or stockbroker, if he had one. Check for fat withdrawals. Obviously, anything that coincides with the accident date a month and a half ago and Lobbrecht's big deposit."

"Something's a little funky for me the more I chew on it."

Feller crossed one leg over the other and picked at a dangling strand of elastic from his sock. He left it alone and said, "This fistfight between Lobbrecht and Levy. Didn't Wilton Backhouse tell you it came after Levy talked smack to Lobbrecht at their whistle-blower powwow in Rhinebeck?"

"They called it their Splinter Summit," affirmed Heat. "Professor Backhouse's account was that Levy accused Lobbrecht of being on the take from Swift, and Lobbrecht punched him."

Randall went back to tugging the errant string on his ankle. "That's the part that doesn't jibe. If Lobbrecht saved Levy's ass—and got a jumbo gratuity for it from Levy—why would Levy accuse him of taking money from Swift? Unless Levy was cranked because Lobbrecht was shaking him down for more."

Rook wagged his head. "Judging from my sessions with Lobbrecht at Lon King's, Fred Lobbrecht didn't seem like a shakedown kind of guy."

Over the speakerphone, Raley said, "Well, maybe Fred was double-dipping, squeezing Nathan Levy and taking money from Tangier Swift to be his inside man at the same time."

"And nice guys extort, too," added Ochoa. "If a cop's going to take a bribe to cover up a fatal accident, all bets are off for me."

"I'm still trying to hardwire a connection to Tangier Swift in all this," said Rhymer.

"And the congressman," added Detective Aguinaldo. "Kent Duer is a war hero who checks out clean. So far, Captain, his only transgression seems to be a display of throwback notions about women when you saw him at The Greenwich."

Nikki was right there with them all. Additionally, she was groping at a loose end of her own: Rook's kidnapping and how that fit in. It was a phenomenon of contradiction she had experienced in many cases over the years. The closer they got to an answer, the further it took them from other elements of the case.

Rook said, "As long as we're kicking things around, is anybody else seeing the obvious? That Lobbrecht got a job with the same company Levy worked for?"

"Before we found out Lobbrecht worked the accident, I never got bumped by it," said Heat. "I assumed it was a natural progression. Work for the state troopers on the CRU and then, when you go private, consult for a collision forensics firm. DAs become defense litigators, politicians become lobbyists, quarterbacks move to the broadcast booth. It seemed normal."

"Right, to me, too," said Rook. "We all just sort of bought it. But now, there may be more to it. Like the job itself was a payoff, too."

By instinct—and habit—Nikki paced in front of the Murder Board. "OK, moving forward. Here's what we'll do." Not letting her zeal diminish the enthusiasm of her squad co-leaders on the phone, she halted and took a figurative step to the side. "Miguel, Sean. How do you want to deploy the rest of your squad?"

For a half breath, they were taken aback, but Ochoa jumped right in. "I'm feeling like the hot lead is Lobbrecht. What about you, homes?"

"Totally agree with Miguel," said Raley. "Randall, you have prior contact with management at the forensic company Lobbrecht consulted for, right?"

"Affirm. Company's called Forenetics."

"Get his employment recs from HR. Look for basics: salary, whether he got a bonus for signing that might account for the sudden cash, any grievances against him, especially beefs on the job with Levy."

Ochoa picked up without missing the cadence. "We also want to do a thorough vet of Lobbrecht before Forenetics, when he was a statie. If this guy was a dirty cop, I want the paper trail to prove it. Detective Aguinaldo, you reach out to New York State Police. Go for his job file, any IA paper, you get the idea."

"I do," said Inez.

Raley added, "Plus get hard copies of his accident report. Not just the MV-104s, but maps, statements, evidence pictures, the whole jacket."

Detective Feller leaned close to the speakerphone. "What are you two going to do? Besides bark orders at us while you walk hand in hand through apple orchards up there?"

Detective Raley laughed. "Jealousy's an ugly thing, Randall."

"Which explains your face," said Ochoa. As they all chuckled at that, Nikki enjoyed it most because it sounded like Roach was being Roach again. Then Miguel continued, "We're going to have Mr. Dooley from Dunne Towing take us to the accident scene for an eyes-on."

"Then a stop at the hospital on the way back to talk to the

ER nurse and doc who treated Levy," said Raley.

Heat moved closer to the phone. "I'm going to have another chat with Wilton Backhouse about all of the above. Meanwhile, nice work, guys. Don't forget to stop and smell the apples." She hung up before they could say anything.

No voice mail this time. The engineering professor answered her call on the second ring. "Hi, it's Nikki Heat." She kept her tone light and casual. Nikki had some bad news to give him about finding Nathan Levy dead in his pickup, but since Backhouse had proven so jittery, she wanted to ask him first what he had known about one colleague's apparent acceptance of a bribe to hide another colleague's probable involvement in a fatal auto crash. Things like that had a tendency to derail even the most grounded interview subjects.

However, it was a more strident Wilton Backhouse who greeted her. Or, to be accurate, did not greet her, but jumped right to his own hot topic instead. "I'm only taking this call because I want to know why the fuck your boyfriend is dragging his feet on my whistle-blowing article."

"Whoa, Wilton. First off, hello. Let's not get off on this foot, OK? Whatever issue you have with Rook about his article is separate from why I'm calling you." Even as she said it, Nikki stood and waved a signal arm through the glass into the bull pen. Rook was immersed in his laptop screen at his rear desk, but caught her in his peripheral vision and hurried in.

"Your dude was all over me to get access to my research—

my smoking gun that buries Tangier Swift. Honeymoon's over. Now where is he?"

"Hang on," said Heat, switching the call to the speakerphone as Rook took a seat across from her. "You there? I've got Jameson Rook here with me."

"Hey, Wilton."

"Hey, Jameson," Backhouse echoed his cadence back mockingly. "Know what? Since we last talked, there has been one more highway death and two critical injuries caused by Swift's defective system. If you're going to just sit there stroking me with one hand and parking your thumb up your ass with the other, I'll just post this motherfucker on the Web myself. Do I have your attention?"

"Absolutely. But you don't want to do that."

"I think I do."

"I understand your eagerness, but you need cred. My cred. And I have that because I am thorough."

"*Somebody* thinks this has cred. They keep offing everyone involved."

Rook raised his eyebrows and shrugged to Nikki, who hand-signaled him to keep it rolling. So Rook did. "Wilton, if you rush this out—dump it on some, what? blog?—you're running a risk of a major fail. Either you're going to come off as some wacko ax-grinder, or get lumped in with the likes of *Dateline* when they took on GM about exploding gas tanks. The only thing that blew up was the story, in *Dateline*'s face. Or, worst-case scenario: It's not going to get any traction. Let me keep doing what I do: gathering all the facts so I can write a comprehensive exposé that will do the job." He

finished convincingly and waited for Backhouse's response.
When none came, he said, "Wilton, did you hear me?"

A shot—it had to be a gunshot—rang out. Every cop
knew the sound. It turned heads in the bull pen when it came
over the speaker. Heat and Rook heard the sound of
Backhouse's phone receiver hitting the floor. Nikki jumped
up. "Wilton! Wilton, what's happening?"

His voice was quiet. A gasp. "Holy shit . . ."

"What just happened?" Nikki said.

Noise, furniture scraping, came over the speakerphone.
Then Backhouse's voice, weak and bewildered. "The drone.
It was in my office window."

The scanner behind Heat came alive: "Shot fired, Hudson
University Annex, Thompson Street north of Bleecker."

"Stay down. Get under your desk. Have you been hit?"
said Heat. While she listened, she keyed her walkie-talkie.
"One Lincoln Forty. Units responding to the ten-ten at
Hudson University. Possible victim is on floor twenty-two,
room three-A."

Backhouse's phone clanged around as he snatched up the
receiver. The professor's breathing came heavily, rasping
across the mouthpiece. "Is this what you call keeping me
safe? Telling me to sit under my desk? Seriously?"

"Help's coming. Stay down."

"I am not fucking sitting here like a dumb shit. And I'm
done trusting incompetents." He slammed down the receiver
and the call went dead.

***

"He must have taken the stairs," said Officer Tew when Heat
arrived on the scene.

Her partner, Officer Townsend, made a hooking gesture
around an imaginary corner. "Or the service elevator." A few
days before, these cops had given Nikki a supportive fist
clench from the front seat of the radio car outside Hudson U.
Now they were upstairs in Wilton Backhouse's office feeling
embarrassed that the man they had been tasked to protect
had not only got shot at but had slipped his surveillance on
their watch. "To be honest, we were all about getting up here
to disarm a perp."

"I understand," said Heat. "And meanwhile, your perp
could have been a mile away."

"And who knew a drone could fly down that air shaft,
right?" Townsend searched Heat's expression, a patrolman
wanting to be let off the hook by a captain.

"Right," Heat said and watched both unis relax. "I never
would have figured it."

Over at the window, the Forensics technician peered
around the bullet hole and said, "There's more clearance than
you think between these buildings. No crosswinds? A
straight-down descent? Especially with video assist and if
the operator has skills? Cake."

Heat indicated toward the punctured glass. "Looks like
small-caliber. You find the slug?"

"Just did." He walked her over to the shelf above the
professor's desk. "It landed in this bookend."

Rook groaned. "Ooh, shot in the TARDIS!" The tech gave
him a blank stare. "Dr. Who? The seemingly innocent-looking

police call box that disguises a vehicle that travels Time and Relative Dimensions in Space? That bullet could have ended up anywhere from the first settlement of New Amsterdam to the next millennium." The Forensics man reached into the miniature phone booth, tweezed out a slug, and held it up to Rook. "Well. You got lucky today, my friend."

While CSU did its job, Heat and the officers sought out witnesses. Two students and a custodian on the twenty-second floor said they had seen Backhouse on the move. "Like he was running for his life," said the maintenance man. "His backpack flew right off his shoulder, he was hauling it so fast to the stairwell." None of the eyewits had seen any sign of injury. That assuaged Nikki that he didn't seem to have been hit. On the downside, it closed options for tracking him through ERs, which are legally required to report gunshot victims.

But Backhouse found her. No sooner had Heat and Rook stepped out onto Thompson than Nikki's cell rang with no caller ID. "It's me."

"Wilton, where are you?" Out of habit, she three-sixtied the block, but without sighting him.

"On a pay phone, but not for long."

"Where?"

"No chance. I'm thinking somebody did more than hack the NYPD. I think they're listening in on your phone."

Heat could hear the paranoia rising in his voice. She could also understand why. A second drone attack in the space of a week would do that to anyone. "Come to my precinct. I'll arrange more protection for you."

"I don't think you can. I trust you—personally, I mean—but I have nil faith in police protection. So I'm going to get as far away from needing you guys as possible until you figure this whole thing out. Taking myself off the grid's the only way I'm going to live." Before she could protest, he hung up.

Weeks before, Rook had committed the two of them to dinner with his literary agent at La Esquina but, given the volatility of the case, he canceled. So instead of hip Mexican among the A-listers, they settled into his loft, where he cooked while she balanced CompStat reports with status checks on Wilton Backhouse. "Still not picking up his calls." Nikki lobbed her iPhone onto the sofa cushion beside her and ran a yellow highlighter across a line of figures comparing weekly Drunk and Disorderly arrests during the past quarter.

"He's not answering for me, either," called Rook from the kitchen. "Although, truth be told, not the first college professor who stopped taking my calls."

Nikki marked her place with a Post-it flag and crossed to the counter. "Did you have a particularly tough prof in school?"

"No, she was easy. It was when we stopped sleeping together that things got ugly." He double-flicked his brows and picked up his whisk. "You ready for some of my famous Morning-After Hotcakes? Or is this the night before? That's the beauty of life, you never know."

Nikki went to town on those pancakes. He had added bananas and macadamia nuts in the shape of a smiley face to his recipe and swapped out maple in favor of coconut syrup.

The effect was a comforting experience that tasted like vacation in Maui. For now, that was as close to a respite as she was going to get. She swallowed a bite and said, "So I got confirmation from Hudson University that Backhouse no-showed his scheduled lecture this afternoon. Feller says he also blew off a mandatory staff meeting tonight at Forenetics without any notice, something he has never done." She pressed her Home button to check for text badges; there were none—same as her last check two minutes before. "Nobody answered at his apartment. Since we have probable cause for concern about his safety, the super let detectives Rhymer and Aguinaldo in, and he's not there. Opie said that in the hall closet there's a gap among his suitcases, and all his toiletries are cleared out of the bathroom."

"What about checking with Backhouse's friends, colleagues, associates?"

"One of whom 'hit the wall'—literally—and the other two have bullets in their heads, which is what he is trying to avoid—in a very ill-advised manner."

"By going off the grid? I don't know . . . If I thought I was on somebody's list of inconvenient truth tellers, I might pull a Dick Cheney myself and hunker down in an undisclosed location." Something in what he said rekindled the latent thought she had been trying to access. It still teased her from afar. He studied her. "What?"

"Just thinking."

"You're beautiful when you do that. Even more so when you tell me what it is." She picked up her phone again and touched Redial. "You're not going to share, are you?"

"Soon as I have something to. Unlike others, I don't hide information in this relationship." She put the phone to her ear, heard Wilton's outgoing message again, and ended the call. "This guy'd better hope we find him before they do."

"'They' being who we think it is?"

And can't prove, thought Nikki. At least not yet.

After too many hours of paperwork, they cleaned up the kitchen together to *Nightline*, which included a special report on the ongoing cyber attack on New York City. Rook, who said he was tired of living it and didn't need to see it on TV, too, wanted to switch to some Bourdain. Any Bourdain. But Heat's sense of needing to know all she could won out, and they left it on.

The piece did have a sense of churning instead of learning, as Rook liked to phrase it. "Speaking as someone who knows a bit about journalism, there comes a point in a news cycle where the public appetite for the topic is hotter than the information flow. So you get recap and talking heads and very little that's new."

To underscore that, the network rolled archival footage of the Free Mehmoud pickets, blending with archive video of the Free Mehmoud hack message, and the press conference in which the Syrian ambassador to the United Nations (with a circumspect Fariq Kuzbari stationed in the background) demanded that Mehmoud be returned from custody, all the while denying his nation's involvement in the unfortunate cyber event. In a jailhouse statement issued through his attorney, Mehmoud Algafari declared himself to be not a criminal but a prisoner of conscience. Nothing new in that, either. A black hat expert on hacking, who was photographed in silhouette with his or her voice electronically altered, told Nikki something she didn't know. The hacker said the MISD vulnerability stemmed from the fact that New York City doesn't employ developers, but mainly expert caretakers. Competent, but not elite code writers. Sounding a lot like Darth Vader because of the vocal processing, he/she said, "Most of the applications the city's MISD network uses come from a hodge-podge of third-party sources, and that's why they haven't been able to execute a unified solution. It's like herding cats."

When the commercial came on, Nikki said, "You ready for bed?"

"Sure." Rook furrowed his brow gravely. "But one can't help but wonder. Is this the night before the morning after?"

Nikki swatted his ass with a dish towel and said, "One way to find out. I'll be right in."

"You're only going to get his voicemail again. This is very OCD of you."

"I'll be right there. Don't start without me."

Rook made her laugh, performing an over-the-top sexy model's runway walk up the hall, and calling over his shoulder, "Gait analyze this."

Heat did redial Backhouse's number, with the same result. Then she switched off the TV and stared at its blank screen a few seconds in contemplation. She picked up her cell again and scrolled to Sean Raley's number. "Hi, did I wake you?"

"Mmm, no."

"Of course I did. I have an assignment. As King of All

Surveillance Media, it may be the greatest challenge of your reign. You ever try herding cats?"

An administrative aide took Heat's CompStat homework first thing upon her arrival the next morning, bound the spreadsheets with thick rubber bands, set them inside a cardboard box, and gave them to an officer for hand delivery downtown at One Police Plaza. "As long as you're keeping stats," observed Rook, "the true crime is you having to do the bean counting by hand like that."

"No intranet, no electronic data. We can't risk emailing sensitive attachments like that on public domains."

"Sure, but come on. What's next, sleeve garters and a green eyeshade?"

Nikki gave him a side-glance. "Is that on your list of turn-ons now?"

"No." He paused. "Yes."

The homicide detectives started gathering in the bull pen. Heat quickly signed vacation authorizations for some patrol officers and staff, accepted an invitation to speak at a school assembly at P.S. 199, and then hurried into the squad room to join the briefing.

She hadn't missed much. Raley and Ochoa, back from the previous day's field trip to Peekskill, were getting filled in by Detective Rhymer on the Wilton Backhouse incident and his self-imposed exile. Rook added that both he and Heat had been dialing the professor's cell phone compulsively, as well as emailing and texting. "No pickups, no call backs, no texts, and the emails are now bouncing back with an I'm-out-of-the-office message."

"Dude's not careful, it's going to be an I've-been-offed message," said Feller.

Inez Aguinaldo took her seat. "Cranky Randy this morning."

"It's my default setting. You'll get used to it."

"Let's get into Fred Lobbrecht," said Heat. "Inez, you covered the accident report, right?"

"Yes. I made friends with a clerk at the DMV in Albany who overnighted a photocopy of the MV-104 and Trooper Lobbrecht's notes, diagrams, and photo documentation of the scene." The detective moved to the side of the room and brought up front a bulletin board on which she had posted enlargements for the meeting. "I'll walk you through a couple of items of note. First, this accident scene didn't fall in Trooper Lobbrecht's jurisdiction, which was Troop NYC, posted in Richmond County which, as you know, is Staten Island, a long way from Peekskill. When he called in the crash, he said he happened to be in transit on that road and observed the victim's car smashed into the tree."

"Already hinky," said Rhymer.

"Agreed. It was the middle of the night, just after three A.M., and he told dispatch at Troop K that, as long as he was there, he'd run point on the investigation, and they agreed. Why not?" She moved from the Westchester County map to a one-sheet printout of a report. "I pulled this page from the Forensic Science Lab findings. Most cars these days have sophisticated computer systems."

"No kidding," said Heat, leading to a burst of laughter.

When it settled, Inez continued, "Among the things onboard this victim's car was the black box, which records a loop of twenty-five seconds of data for steering, acceleration, and braking. It lets Forensics examine the pre-impact actions of the driver. Like, was the driver slamming on the brakes or swerving to avoid something?" She tapped the page. "Forensics found that the black box was clean."

"Clean how?" asked Rook.

"Simple trick. Ask anyone in the motor pool or traffic detail," said Detective Feller. "All somebody would have to do—and by somebody, I'm thinking Trooper Fred—all he had to do is go up to the victim's car, reach in, turn the key off, then turn it back on, count to twenty-five, and you have now recorded over whatever was on the EPROM chip and replaced it with a bunch of *nada*. So the data weren't erased, just replaced by nothing. It's a crude but effective way to create erroneous data after an accident."

"That's why it's procedure to pull all keys after a fatal, to prevent that from happening," said Aguinaldo.

"It's also procedure when there's a decedent to canvass all body shops and tow services in the vicinity for the phantom vehicle." Opie shook his head in scorn. "I guess our friendly trooper who was in charge of the investigation made sure that one got overlooked, too."

Nikki, who had been making her own notes, set her pen down. "Let me get a picture of this. If the victim swerved or braked to, say, avoid Nathan Levy coming the other way in his Bimmer, that would leave skid marks."

Ochoa raised a hand. "It did. Even now, Raley and I could see scuff patches on the road. We haven't had much snow since then, so they didn't get totally plowed off."

"Not according to this." Detective Aguinaldo indicated some photo blowups of the crash scene. Everyone rose and gathered around for a better look. The pictures showed the familiar Forensics spray-paint markings on the victim's tires and on the ground beneath each one. But the official photo documentation of the roadway itself was devoid of any skid marks.

Raley took out his cell phone. "Compare that with the shots I took yesterday." He had shot an angle of the road similar to one on Inez's board and held it up side by side. Same road, two conflicting images: tire scuff marks on Raley's; none on Trooper Lobbrecht's.

Ochoa rapped a knuckle on the Forensics print. "This sucker's been Photoshopped."

"You mean Freddyshopped," scoffed Detective Feller. His tone conveyed the disdain clean cops have for dirty cops, which was shared by everyone in that semicircle.

As they found their seats again, Heat addressed Roach. "Your eyes-on up there was worth the trip. Good work." They nodded in unison and even half smiled. Progress, she thought. "What did you learn at the ER?"

"About Levy's leg injury? Pretty much as described," reported Raley.

"But," said Ochoa, "talking one on one with the ER nurse and the doctor, this dude was out of it. Drunk, sloppy drunk. Belligerent . . . They had to put a pair of orderlies on him just to keep him in line."

"From the twenty minutes I spent with him, I can imagine the aggression," said Heat. Then one of those tiny detail questions arose. So small, she almost didn't mention it. But Nikki gave it voice anyway. "Kind of granular here, but if Nathan Levy was so plastered, how did he get to the ER? Too far to walk, drunk and on a bad leg. Not an ambulance—that would bust him for sure. And clearly Trooper Lobbrecht had damage control to do at the accident scene, so he wasn't going to leave. Did this tow driver, Dooley, run him down to the hospital?"

Ochoa looked to Raley. "Didn't occur to us."

"Find out. Never know, it could be something. And let's run down all the auto-body parts from Levy's M3 repair. Spoiler, rims, glove compartment cover . . . Whatever we can locate, rush it to Forensics for a go-over."

One secondary consequence of the NYPD's hamstrung tech infrastructure was that more transactions were getting done personally. For the commander of the Twentieth Precinct that meant increased phone calls, more face-time appointments and, worst of all, a spike in drop-in visitors. Maybe that human touch was all for the better. But it had scattered Heat's focus, no matter how hard she tried to maintain it. Now, with a sense of critical elements being suddenly in play while new revelations were breaking at a fast clip, Nikki selfishly (or, maybe it was more out of enlightened self-interest) isolated herself from her workaday distractions as Captain Heat to do the one small thing she had been neglecting: quieting her detective's mind to contemplate the fragmented pieces on the Murder Board.

The exercise of sitting alone in the silent Homicide Squad Room in front of the whiteboard had served Heat well in past investigations, especially when the volume of facts was creating chaos instead of narrative. All those names, dates, places, events, color-coded markings, photos, arrows, and encircled questions were hailstones in a rain barrel when what she needed was to see a stream.

That morning some new data had been squeezed into one of the few open spaces up there. Randall Feller's inquiry with Human Resources at Forenetics, LLC, indicated that Fred Lobbrecht had been hired there as an automotive safety assessor merely one week after the phantom car accident he had investigated on the Cold Spring Turnpike. His new job came with a 46 percent bump over his former pay as a New York state trooper.

Having absorbed that, Nikki closed her eyes just long enough to envision a complete erasure of the board living in her mind. She opened them and wandered the panorama before her without design or predetermined sequence, simply letting impressions come to her without chasing them. Instinct drew her back to the first entry, not because it was the starting point, but because Lon King's murder intersected with so much of what lay before her: the death of his patient, Lobbrecht; the single-shot MO the psychologist shared with two other victims who had also consulted with Forenetics; the drone that had apparently attacked them all except

Lobbrecht (an Odd Sock, or just an easier means utilized in the moment?) and had also targeted Wilton Backhouse.

In spite of herself, Heat started to fixate on Rook's duplicity in seeing her shrink without telling her. Nikki thought of batting that one away as being motivated purely by emotion, but stopped herself. In this meditative mode, any thought that drifted in might not be an accident. So she went back to it. There was, of course, that Lon King connection from Lobbrecht to Rook, and, by extension, the article Rook was researching on the cadre of forensic experts preparing to blow the whistle on the cover-up of an auto safety defect.

That nexus drew her gaze to the name Tangier Swift, the billionaire software magnate and target of the whistle-blowers, who was using his money and influence to quash all legal efforts to bring the alleged defect to light and so cowed the normally unassailable Forenetics consultants that their management had ordered all work to cease on the SwiftRageous investigation. Tangier Swift had a lot of skin in this game.

So did the whistle-blowers, who were so passionate, so outraged by the Forenetics shutdown, that they had formed a subcommittee—the Splinter Group, they had called themselves—to continue their research and build their case on their own, which was when Rook was brought into the picture.

And when whistle-blowers started dying.

The Forenetics dissidents had held a self-proclaimed Splinter Summit upstate to vote on whether to go all in on their explosive report. Heat scanned the board for the date and won a bet with herself. It was the weekend adjacent to Nathan Levy's accident on Cold Spring Turnpike. He was probably driving back to the city from Rhinebeck. Irony, she thought, a traffic death and a cover-up on the way home from a meeting to expose an auto safety cover-up. But Nikki was far from amused. A drunk driver had wasted an innocent life and a cop had pulled a rug over it for money.

"The timeline is your friend." That axiom, which Heat had drilled into her detectives over the years, had proved its worth again. Yet she had not yet established the links that transformed the churning water's surface into a graceful flow. Still unresolved were big pieces like Rook's kidnapping. Why had it happened, and who was Black Knight? Could he be the mystery voice in the parking garage? Tangier Swift? Even Congressman Duer? The fact that she was grasping at those straws only told her how far she was from seeing all the disparate events and players line themselves up in something that felt like an order. But at the heart of this a narrative was trying to emerge. It pointed to someone with enough at stake to kill in order to keep a secret. To her and everyone else on the squad, the answer was a no-brainer. But convictions didn't come without brains. Now Heat did smile. Because she just might have coined another freaking axiom.

Nikki burst through the door at a jog from her mandated health-and-safety inspection of the holding cells, then slowed to a speed-walk so she wouldn't be out of breath when she took the call. The switchboard had transferred it to the empty observation room in Interrogation One, and after a settling breath, Heat punched up the call. "Mr. Swift, this is a coincidence. I was just thinking about you."

"Well, I'm going to give you a helluva lot more to think about if you don't back off."

"Excuse me." She flipped the switch to a more sober tone. "You do realize I am a police officer and that sounded an awful lot like a threat."

He snorted. "Good, you're not as stupid as you seem. You sicced a fucking forensic accountant on me? What happened to our agreement?"

"You're going to have to refresh my memory, and I need to go on the record and inform you that I am going to begin recording this conversation."

"You are fucking toast."

She found the Record button on the wall phone and engaged it. A beep accompanied the flashing red mini-lamp, then there was a click. That was Tangier Swift hanging up.

"Aw, you scared him off?" said Rook. "Too bad. I wanted to get on the line and thank him for the swell barge ride."

Detective Feller, hearing the conversation, ambled over to Rook's desk. "Do you think it was a real threat? Like an actual death threat?"

"Mmm—no. It wasn't specific. Legally, he could defend it as just being a pissed-off dude expressing frustration," said Heat. "I didn't realize the forensic accountants had started work yet. A heads-up would have been nice."

Randall was a dog with a bone. "Screw *legally*. If he threatened you, we should do something about that. I dunno, maybe send Rook over to give him a Dutch rub, or something."

"Highly amusing, as always, Detective." Then Rook turned to Nikki. "Couldn't we at least use that to bring him in and . . ."

"And what?" she said. "Tangier Swift would just come sit here with his hot bench of attorneys and say nothing. It would feel good but only create friction."

"You do realize you are talking about two of my favorite things. Feeling good and friction."

"Outta here," said Feller, walking out with both hands raised. Ochoa, clearly on a mission, brushed by him on his way to Heat.

"OK, got something here on how Nathan Levy got to the ER, etcetera."

"You guys talk to your guy in Peekskill?" she asked.

"Dooley. I did. Raley's off on that special assignment you gave him."

"Yes, herding cats." Heat noted Rook's confusion. "I'll explain later."

"The flatbed driver says he hooked Levy up with a car service in Peekskill." Detective Ochoa held up his yellow lined pad for reference. "Triplex Limo."

Rook furrowed his brow. "There's a Triplex in Peekskill?"

Miguel chuckled. "I asked the same thing. It's Peekskill, Croton, and Haverstraw. I called the limo service and they checked the records. The driver took him to the ER and waited, then dropped him at an address in Astoria. I looked it up the old-fashioned way, in the reverse directory. It's a commercial space leased to Forenetics, LLC."

Rook got out his cell phone. "We should call Forenetics and see what it is."

Heat shook her head. "No, let's not light up the radar."

"Absolutely, let's *not* call Forenetics and see what it is," said Rook, pocketing his phone.

Ochoa asked, "Want me to go over there and check it out?"

"I need you here to hold the fort," said Heat. "I think I'll—"

"Shotgun," said Rook.

"I mean *we'll*—pay a visit to Queens."

On the drive over, Rook used the time to listen to himself spinning the various ins and outs of the case. He had stayed pretty much on the rails lately, not veering into his comfort zone of tinfoil-hat conspiracy theories. Nikki took it all in stride as his version of meditating at the Murder Board and, therefore, listened carefully to what he threw out there. "OK, so here's where I land. Hiding that fatal car accident is a perfect motive for Nathan Levy to kill Lobbrecht and Lon King in order to hush it up. With me so far?"

"So far. But let me riddle you this, Batman. Why go after Abigail Plunkitt and Wilton Backhouse?"

"All right," he said. "Fair enough. Because . . . Because maybe Fred Lobbrecht told them about the accident. Or else, maybe Levy confided it to his Splinter Summiteers, then regretted it after. That fits."

There was always a gridlock situation on the way out of Queensboro Plaza, but when the officer stationed there picked out Heat's car as undercover, she halted cross traffic, waving her through.

"Your theory fits," Heat said, giving a smile and a wave to the cop, "but it fits only up to a point. That only covers King and Lobbrecht. Who killed Nathan then? And why? And why is someone still trying to kill Wilton Backhouse?"

"I'll admit my theories are at the nascent stage, but getting there, wouldn't you say?"

"Further ahead than I am," she said. And wasn't so happy to admit that.

The address was off Northern Boulevard, about a mile from the bridge in a mixed neighborhood of row houses, auto-body repair shops, an ice cream factory, and the new nightclubs, steakhouses, and Starbucks franchises that were the area's hint of gentrification to come. Out of habit, Heat parked halfway down the block—close enough to get to the car in a hurry, far enough not to be made at the curb.

The street was quiet at that time of day. Soon the cafés and pizza joints would be pulling in lunch trade, but aside from an old man hunched over his walker, Heat and Rook had the sidewalk to themselves. The building was a beige one-story warehouse in the same basic size and configuration as the body shops and one-story warehouses they had passed on the way there. The front had a rolling steel garage door with the requisite amount of tagging. The main door turned out to be double dead-bolted and locked when Heat tried it. The chain-link fence on either side had no gate, and sharp razor wire was coiled along the top to further discourage would-be thieves. Heat pressed her face against the windows, but they had been painted over from the inside.

Rook took a step back from the building and shielded his eyes against the sun. "No sign. No phone number. No nothing."

"They've got security cams, though," she said, indicating the three lipsticks covering the building.

"Show-offs," said Rook. "How come they get security cams and the NYPD doesn't?"

Heat tried the bell and tried knocking again. They waited. Both pressed their ears to the door, but heard nothing. "Want me to bust a window?" he asked.

"Let's do something crazier. Let's get a search warrant."

They got back in the car and Heat phoned the District Attorney's office to request her paper. The assistant DA who took her call was a friendly, which was to say that Nikki wasn't going to get any obstruction from him, as she had with the administrative subpoena she wanted for Lon King's receptionist. After she hung up, she said, "All good. But it's going to take an hour by the time the judge signs and they can get it over here to us." They sat in silence for a moment.

"Wanna get some lunch?" she asked.

"Wanna make out?"

Nikki said, "Oh, yes, nothing would be better than getting all hot on a public street during a stakeout in broad daylight."

"Just asking."

"Just saying."

A few seconds passed, then he muttered, "So you wanna?"

Heat was laughing when the bullet ripped through her side window. The close-range report temporarily deafened her left ear. Fragments of glass pelted her cheek and shoulder. Rook cried out, "Oof!"

Heat could no longer see through the cascade of red pouring down over her eyes.

SEVENTEEN

D rone!" yelled Heat. "Down, down!"

"I see it. You OK?"

"I'm hit."

"Me too." Nikki swiped a wet smear of blood from her eyes and turned. Through the haze she saw the right shoulder of Rook's shirt blossoming crimson.

"Pressure," she said. "Do it."

He pushed a palm to his wound. "Your forehead . . ."

"Drone's on the move." Heat cranked the ignition. "Buckle up. Stay down." Then she mashed the gas pedal, sending her Taurus Police Interceptor tearing out into the street.

"How bad are you hurt?" Rook asked.

Nikki ignored him and squinted through the damp stickiness of her own blood, watching the cars, watching the peds, watching the drone—which was four car lengths ahead, humming away from her up the block. Rook scoped out the drone, then came back to her. "Are you seriously going to try to catch it?"

"How much do you know about these things? How fast can they go?"

"Let's see," he said. "Amateur UAVs? A horizontal

airspeed of thirty feet per second, or . . . let's call it twenty miles per hour."

"Then I am seriously going to try to catch it." She braked to quickly check the intersection side to side. The movement made her head ache and the skin above her brow line started to sting. She gunned the V8 and snatched up her two-way. "One Lincoln Forty, ten-thirteen. Request assistance on a ten-ten, shot fired. One-L-forty and passenger wounded. In pursuit of drone, repeat: drone. Caution, UAV is armed and dangerous."

The innately unfazed dispatcher came back, "Copy, One Lincoln Forty. State location."

"Astoria. Northbound Thirty-Seventh Street, crossing Thirty-sixth Avenue."

"Watch it, watch it," called Rook.

Heat swerved barely in time but missed the first in a caravan of halal food carts being pushed from a driveway into the street. "Thanks, got it." She lit up her flashing LEDs but decided against the siren in case the drone was wired for sound. There was a chance the operator hadn't realize she was crazy enough to pursue.

They caught a green light at 35th Ave., but Nikki brought her speed way down because a bus was unloading a group of middle schoolers on a field trip at the Museum of the Moving Image. "I got the kids, you stay with the drone," she said. Once clear, she squeezed by a double-parked oil truck, then accelerated up the block past a body-waxing studio, an awning manufacturer, and indoor batting cages.

"Uh-oh, getting some altitude," he reported. "Cutting a

left at this corner, I'll bet." He winced when Nikki gassed it to beat the red for her left turn.

"Sorry." She caught the rusty flavor of blood that had started to congeal on her lips and fought nausea. "You stop bleeding?"

"Some." He lifted his palm and amended that. "No."

The quadcopter had gained enough height to clear the two-story townhouse and descended again as it moved west after its turn. But then it goosed its speed and arced a sweeping left at 36th Street. "Don't turn left," he warned her.

"But that's where it went."

"You'll get dead-ended. Kaufman Studios just put up a permanent gate." Rook was right. The street was barricaded by a dark-blue fence. "I saw it when I did my guest spot on *Alpha House*." Heat watched the drone move south, having flown right over the barrier. "We tried," he said.

But Nikki wasn't giving up. She drove to the next corner and started to make a left. "You do know you're about to go the wrong way down a one-way street," said Rook.

"No, I'm not." Then she pulled the car into the driveway of the studio loading dock. "I'm going to drive down the sidewalk beside the one-way street." The entire block was taken up by the massive wall of a movie soundstage, which meant no doors, no shops, no foot traffic in and out. The concrete ahead was clear. Still, Heat drove slowly, just in case someone suddenly emerged from among the fleet of white production trucks lined up along the curb. When she reached the corner at the other end, they both craned their necks to the left.

"There!" He pointed, and she just caught a glimpse of the drone as it zipped down 36th Street, disappearing behind the far side of the Frank Sinatra School of the Arts.

She double-chirped her siren and drove off the curb with a hard thump that pained them both. She chirped it once again as she cut across lanes of traffic, then made a right down 36th, chasing the tiny dot at the end of the block. Heat's vision had fuzzed. She swiped at the blood, but it didn't help. "Lost it. What's it doing?"

"You all right?"

"What's it doing?"

"It's slowing down. And descending."

Nikki blinked rapidly to clear the blood coating her lashes. "Got it. Two o'clock, beside the parking structure." The thing had been easier to spot in the open sky. Now that it had decreased altitude, the speck became more challenging to track against the confusing background of buildings, windows, and signage.

"Still descending," he said. "Looks like it's going to land."

An ambulette shuttle full of seniors lurched out from the curb, and Nikki had to brake hard not to hit it. Rook moaned lowly and pursed his lips in pain at the sudden stop. Gray heads all in a row like a roll of postage stamps scowled out the van windows at them. Heat made a mirror check and shot around the front of the ambulette just in time to see the drone, now descended to street level, slowly drift inside the yawning back hatch of a small SUV, soundlessly, elegantly, as if in a scene from the future. The hatch automatically closed and the SUV drove on, turning the corner, heading west.

Heat palmed her mic. "Read me the plate, I can't see it."

"That's not your vision. It's got one of those tinted plastic covers."

She called in a description of the crossover and her twenty. They had just passed under the elevated tracks of the N and Q trains when Rook said, "Blinker."

"Good. Then he doesn't know he's being followed."

The SUV signaled a right, then eased down the sloping driveway of a brick duplex and pulled inside the open garage under the house.

There were no street spaces, so Heat double-parked. "Stay in the car," she said, and started up the sidewalk. Her legs felt weak from trauma and blood loss. She blinked to clear her vision and, when that didn't work, she wiped her eyes with her sleeve. The cloth came away wet with fresh blood, and her brow felt as if it were on fire. Without turning, she said, "Does 'Stay in the car' mean anything to you?"

"Pretty much no," said Rook, who was hurrying up behind her. "You should really catch on."

"Go back. You've been shot."

"So have you."

"Grazed."

"Let me look."

"Yeah, let's stop out here and do that." She increased her pace, drew her Sig, and stepped into the garage behind the driver's side of the vehicle. "NYPD, show me both hands— now!" After only a few seconds the door opened a fraction. "Hands!" Heat cupped her palm into a brace under the grip. Her weapon felt unusually heavy, and she had to press her elbows against her ribs to steady her shaking. "Now."

Both of the driver's hands emerged, empty, through the narrow opening at the top of the car door. "Good," she said. "Now keep them high like that and step out. Slowly. Nice and easy." A chill fluttered through Nikki and her shoulder bumped clumsily against the garage wall as she struggled with her equilibrium. She remained upright, though, and succeeded in stabilizing herself, but wished some backup would get there. Heat knew the undeniable symptoms of shock.

He did as he was told and squeezed slowly out the small space between the car and wall of the garage. And when he stood to his full six-two to face her with his hands raised, Timothy Maloney was actually smiling. It was the same grin she had seen during his interrogation and when he had peered through the restaurant window to taunt her.

Given Heat's condition and the vulnerable position she would put herself in if she tried to cuff him in that confined gap, she took a step back and indicated the wider space behind the rear bumper. "Come out here and go prone."

The ex-cop kept his hands up. He kept smiling, too. But he didn't move. "No," he said as pleasantly as if he'd been asked if he cared for any dessert. Nikki blinked and saw in Maloney's eyes a six-second Vine video of paranoid personality disorder symptoms: masking; dissociation; passive aggressiveness; and the one she preferred not to see acted out, chaos manufacture. Lon King's diagnosis had damned Maloney succinctly: high-functioning and dangerous.

Heat didn't back down, but demonstrated her control without directly challenging him, which might inflame the confrontation. "Come on, help me out here, Tim. You know how this goes."

He hesitated, but finally eased nearer, toward the back of the SUV, hands up. Then he stopped, and the snide grin returned. "This ain't going to happen, chief."

Behind Heat came the menacing *snick-snick* of a shotgun being pumped. Heat kept her pistol on Maloney but turned her head. Wilton Backhouse stood under the garage door with a Mossberg 20 leveled at her and Rook.

The sight of him wasn't such a huge surprise to Heat. Maybe Backhouse hadn't topped her list of possibles, but he'd been tugging at her sleeve to get on it. So watching the sole survivor of the whistle-blowers, armed and caught in the act, gave Nikki an odd sense of satisfaction, like filling the last matrix gap in Tetris. The only thing that would have made the situation better would be if she were holding the gun on him instead.

"Wilton," she said in the most calming voice she could muster. "This can end here."

Backhouse fired a blast into the ceiling. The sudden boom was deafening and made Heat and Rook jump. Maloney sprang forward through a shower of plaster and splinters and tried to snatch the gun out of Nikki's hand. She kept a grip and fought him for it, but the professor jacked another shotgun shell from the Speedfeed and aimed at Rook's chest. Heat froze. Maloney took her Sig from her. And the Beretta .25 from her ankle holster.

Backhouse pressed the button to close the garage door. As it lowered, Maloney scowled at him. "On my iPad screen you had a fucking gimme. How'd you miss the bitch?"

"I had her in the crosshairs until she started laughing and moved her head."

Rook turned to Nikki. "Remember that next time you tell me to stop clowning around."

She lowered her head gravely. "Next time . . ."

Their captors were still at it. "And don't give me shit," said Backhouse. "Some fucking cop. You got made."

"Who chases a drone?"

"And catches it," said Rook.

"Which means very soon there's going to be a police presence." Maloney turned to face Heat. "You called it in, didn't you? Of course you did. Procedure." He gestured to the floor. "All right, kiss cement, both of you."

"If it matters, I've already been shot once today," said Rook. Maloney's response came immediately and unexpectedly. He punched the wound in Rook's shoulder, bringing him down to one knee. Heat lunged at Maloney, who backhanded her injured brow with his gun hand, then straight-armed the 9mm in her face. She peered up from the ground at him through a curtain of fresh blood.

"Don't," said Backhouse. "Not here."

"Then we gotta go."

Backhouse snapped, "Will you wait? Jeez, give me a second." During a short pause to think, his eyes darted around, then he nodded to himself as if he had solved an equation. "Maybe this is a good thing. Get them up. We're going."

The ex-detective used Heat's bracelets and a pair of his own to handcuff her and Rook. Then he shoved them both in the backseat of her car. As Backhouse hopped in up front, Maloney elbowed out the remaining glass from the side window, punched the gas, and spun a hard U-turn, retracing the route they had taken to get there. Seconds after crossing under the elevated tracks, they passed a pair of blue-and-whites speeding the opposite way. Cocky, grandiose, or just a chaos creator, Maloney gave a cop-to-cop four-finger wave to the patrolmen going by. Nikki craned backward to put a desperate face in her rear window. The only response was from one of the unis, who returned Maloney's gesture, and why not? To anyone who didn't know otherwise, Heat's car looked like an undercover Police Interceptor with a detective at the wheel, transporting offenders in the rear. Prisoners in backseats always looked desperate. Some felt it more than others, thought Nikki.

"If you'll give me a chance to help you, I can make sure this goes a lot easier on you, especially if you stop now." Heat knew their situation was beyond grim, but the only hope she could see was to engage them on some human level, taking a page from the hostage handbook. Unfortunately, one of the men in the front seat had also read it.

" 'When engaging the hostage taker, speak calmly and do your best to establish rapport in a way that does not agitate the HT.' Pretty good, huh? Know what? I should be a cop." He cackled, loving his own joke.

"Can we just . . . you know, drive?" said Backhouse.

As they rode from Long Island City south into the back

streets of Greenpoint, Nikki switched her focus, trying to get a grasp on the pair's relationship, which seemed more pragmatic than truly friendly—as if Maloney was the professor's hired gun and accomplice, but it ended there. Part of her evolving strategy concerned finding some way to come between them in order to undermine their unity. Finding that wedge might save her life and Rook's. She also wanted to prove a hunch that had been simmering ever since she had interrogated Joseph Barsotti.

Rook seemed to be pondering the same question. "Question, Professor?" Backhouse didn't reply, so naturally Rook continued as if he had. "I'm playing my Six Degrees game back here, wondering how a police detective meets a forensic engineering consultant. And the Kevin Bacon I come up with is Fred Lobbrecht, am I right?" He got silence in return but kept on. "I mean, you knew Fred Lobbrecht professionally. But how would Detective Maloney meet him? You don't travel in the same social circles, I'm guessing. Unless . . ." Rook's experience had brought him to the same conclusion Heat was sniffing: that Wilton Backhouse had been the unidentified visitor in the psychologist's waiting room when Barsotti walked in on Maloney's tirade. And that was where the college professor had found his lethal TA.

Anger flared within Nikki. If she had gotten that damned administrative subpoena, she wouldn't be sitting there handcuffed and shot, a captive in the back of her own car right now. She pushed that thought aside and continued trying to engage her kidnappers. "Wilton, I'll bet Fred Lobbrecht had you come in to talk with his shrink, same as he did with Rook, am I right? You and Tim crossed paths in the waiting room. You saw opportunity to use him and struck up your little friendship."

Backhouse held his tongue. Maloney was another story. He flared. "Hey, I'm not being used." Then he calmed down a bit and chuckled. "I make friends very easily. I'm handsome enough, I'm strong enough, and darn it, people like me."

"Hey, Tim," said the professor. He shook his head to say, Cool it.

"So you guys met up that day and what, Wilton, you saw a prime candidate to help you deal with some problems?" asked Heat. "Like Lon King?"

"Lon King was a fucked-up individual," snapped the ex-cop.

Nikki kept her focus on Backhouse. "Because Lon King knew too much about something? Wilton, I can't hear you."

Maloney sighed. "I should have shot them back at the house."

"Drive," said Backhouse.

"But what did he know about? What did Fred Lobbrecht tell Lon King that meant they both had to die? And then the others. Abigail Plunkitt. Nathan Levy." She watched the pair up front exchange glances but hold their silence. "I have a theory," she said, "but I'd love to hear it from you."

"I have nothing to say."

"That's a switch for *you*, Backhouse." Rook leaned forward as best he could to peer around the headrest. "I thought you were the marquee headliner. The mouthpiece of the whistle-blowers. The next Assange or Snowden. That's how you told me you saw yourself."

"I never said that."

"Want me to get my notes? The address is in Tribeca. I'll direct you."

"He's right," said Heat. "You're quite the showman. Starting with that phony drone attack in Washington Square."

Rook agreed. "All staged to make us see you as a victim like all the others and deflect suspicion. Like the last faked attack in your office. The envelope, please."

"Hey, you swallowed it," said Backhouse.

Nikki shrugged. "At first."

"Bullshit."

"No bullshit. Know what always bugged me?" Nikki asked. "That drone only went after you while Rook was also a perfectly good target. I mean, if that attack was supposed to make me believe it was part of some plot to kill the exposé—literally—as the writer of the article, wasn't Rook as good a target as you?"

Rook frowned. "You never told me that."

"We had enough issues already."

Calls started coming on the scanner asking One Lincoln Forty to check in. Someone in the front seat switched the radio off. "That's not going to help," said Heat. "Maloney, you know what kind of radar is going to light up if someone does a cop. Why dig a deeper hole?"

"Not going to be a problem, trust me," he said with an unsettling degree of certainty.

The last red sliver of the sun disappeared over the New Jersey hills as they started across the Verrazano Narrows

Bridge. The pit in Heat's stomach deepened. Rook whispered, "We're going to Staten Island."

Nikki blurted, "I listed my apartment so we could live in yours."

He took in that news calmly and said, "That'll be nice."

If it hadn't been for the cuffs, she would have liked to hold his hand.

"We good?" asked Backhouse through his side window. They couldn't see Tim Maloney in the dark, but they could hear his shoes crunching gravel on the shoulder of the road as he walked back to the car.

The driver's door opened, and he got in. "It's all ours."

Backhouse was pulling on a pair of blue crime scene nitriles from Heat's glove compartment. "Took you long enough. Guard give you trouble?"

Maloney gave Backhouse a condescending look and closed his door. The interior went back to total darkness. "Took me a while to find the server box to disable the security cams. But we are done and done." He turned the ignition and the tires crackled on the siding. Nikki swiveled as far as she was able for a view out the back window, hoping for an approaching car. A police car would have been nice.

All Heat saw was blackness.

Of course, as an associate of Forenetics, LLC, Wilton Backhouse knew the security code to unlock the access door, but since his password was unique to him, rather than enter it on the keypad and leave a time stamp of his presence, he stepped over the unconscious security guard lying on the floor of the guardhouse and overrode the system from there.

They drove across the empty parking lot under the bleak orange light of the overhead lamps. Ground fog had begun to curl in off the surrounding marshes, and the enormous hangar ahead of them loomed like a castle jutting from a misty heath. Maloney parked the Taurus between the hangar wall and one of the eighteen-wheelers used to transport cars to and from the facility so it wouldn't be visible to the casual passerby on Gulf Avenue.

Backhouse got out first and jogged, cradling his shotgun, to the access door, which he opened with his gloved hand, and disappeared inside. Maloney got Rook out first, then Heat. Since their hands were manacled behind them, the big man showed no concern about controlling them. Heat tried to take advantage of their captors' separation to work on Maloney's head. "Backhouse is going to screw you over, you know that."

"Inside, let's go."

Heat complied, but moved slowly so she could grind on Maloney's weak spot, his clinical paranoia. "How do you deal with Backhouse? He doesn't respect you. I hear how he talks to you."

Rook was right there with her. "Yeah, I picked that up, too. Ordering you around. Telling you to wait. Telling you to hurry. Telling you to shut up and drive. Asking what took so long, like you're his butt boy."

"I'm not his butt boy."

"He treats you like a flunky."

"For sure. And you think he's going to take this fall?" said Rook. "Believe me, there will be a fall."

They were getting closer to the door, so Nikki piled on. "You'll be lucky to be alive to take a fall. You're a detective just like me, Tim. Use your training. Look at this guy's pattern. He kills his partners."

"She's right. You gotta know he's already thinking about how and when to do you."

"Turn it around while you have time. Preempt him." Nikki stopped walking and faced Maloney. "You have my word, I'll get you the best deal I can."

"And you'll live," said Rook.

"Problem out here?" They turned. Wilton Backhouse stood there, holding the door open. "This more than you can handle, bro?"

Nikki listened for a hitch. Maybe there was a moment of hesitation. But Maloney replied, "No, I got it," and jerked them forward.

Rook stepped into the enormous crash hall ahead of her and halted. Maloney gave him a shove but was savvy enough to respect Heat's combat training, and kept a firm grip on her arm. But when Rook moved and cleared her view, whatever strength Nikki had managed to hold on to following her day's violent ordeal instantly leached out of her. At the far end of the hangar a pool of light illuminated an American subcompact loaded on the launch catapult.

Its two front doors gaped open, waiting.

EIGHTEEN

n unspoken unison, Heat and Rook slowly pivoted their heads, tracing the route along the test runway to the other end of the crash hall a football field's length away, where the impact barrier—a monstrous concrete block reinforced with steel—sat waiting, immovable as Gibraltar. That wall of the former airplane hangar had been freshly painted over since their last visit nearly a week before. For anyone who had been there, no amount of white latex could erase the ghastly image of Fred Lobbrecht's blood-and-tissue splatter, least of all the pair slated to take the next ride.

Then, as only he could, Rook tried whatever it took to lighten Heat's burden. "Shotgun," he said.

Nikki choked back emotion, willing herself to command this moment. Weakness meant death; focus gave them a fighting chance. "Seriously?" she said, forcing herself to sound anything but fearful. She went for indignant. "You have to be kidding. How is this a good idea?"

"Not really sure how good it is," said Backhouse. "You caught me off balance when you showed up. I'm just making the most of this situation on the fly. I mean, this isn't some movie where the guy says, 'I've been expecting you, Mr. Bond . . .'"

"There's an understatement," said Rook.

Backhouse flared. "Hey, you can fuck yourself." Maloney threw an elbow into Rook's wound again. Heat fought her instinct to fight. Since she was handcuffed and unarmed, a head butt would only instigate something she couldn't finish. Rook gave her a sign that he was cool, even though his lips had gone white from biting back the pain.

Backhouse wasn't the only one grappling for a solution during freefall. Her bravado was only pissing everyone off at a time when she needed to keep them talking. As a cop who had experience in hostage negotiations, Heat knew that the longer this played out, the better the odds they had to survive it. So, Nikki shifted her approach, not merely stalling to prolong the agony, calmed the conversation, and tried to forge a sympathetic connection.

"Let's all take a step back and look at what's happening here, OK?" she began. "Wilton, I think we all feel like this is a knot we've got to untie, right? You said yourself that you're trying to ad-lib your way out. We all know you're a smart guy, but if you admitted it, I'm guessing every step you're taking feels like you're only pulling the knot tighter. Look around at this moment. Is this working for you?" She took it as a hopeful sign that he actually did survey the tableau. He scanned the two people before him, bound and bleeding, then his volatile accomplice, a problem to be dealt with later; then he looked down at the Mossberg shotgun in his gloved hands. He came back to stare at her, and she urged, "Come on, let's figure a way out of this. Let me help." Nikki saw in his eyes a hint of the weary dog-chasing-its-tail regret she had witnessed in so many perps caught in a situation gone south. They were a long way from done, but that small opening could be the first step to a resolution.

But then he shook the moment off. "There may not exactly be a proven metric for this but, no, I think this has a shot."

"Fuck yeah!" said Maloney.

All Nikki could say to herself was "Fuck."

"We'll have to see." Backhouse spread his arms wide to frame the vast crash hall. "I came up with doing this here for a couple of reasons. First was just panic, I'll admit that. I couldn't have bodies or residue of same at my rental in Queens. But this place . . ." He surveyed the space again, this time with too much attention on that car on the launch mechanism. "This could be a win-win."

"That, I'm not getting," said Heat.

"It won't be your problem. But since you wonder," he wiggled the fingers of his blue gloves. "I was never here tonight. I'm going to tie your crash to Tangier Swift."

Rook asked, "How?" Then he braced for another shoulder blow that didn't come.

"Not sure. For now, I'm thinking that drone back at my place is somehow going to turn up hidden on Swift's yacht. Or maybe in his car."

Maloney's face lit up. "I can make that happen." Nikki tried to mask her disdain for the ex-cop who could probably do a TED Talk on how to salt crime scenes with phony evidence.

"Seems viable," said the professor, more to himself than anyone else. "And if it doesn't nail Swift, I tried." He shrugged. "You improvise, you get solutions. It's the power of instinct."

Backhouse left them to wait in Maloney's charge while he dashed off to the control booth. From the sure moves he made up there, Heat could tell he had observed or even supervised test launches before. Certainly, at least one—Fred Lobbrecht's earlier in the week. Backhouse left the booth and knelt behind the car at a cream-colored steel patch bay that had an octopus of cables running from it, then down through holes in the floor, accessing the hydraulic propulsion system in the basement. After he had connected several leads and snapped four toggles in succession, he stood. The forensic engineer spoke matter-of-factly, but his voice echoed across the immaculate white floor of the hangar. "Locked and loaded," he said.

The muzzle of a gun, either her own 9mm or the Smith & Wesson M&P Compact .40 Heat saw in Timothy Maloney's shoulder rig, poked hard enough into her back to make a bruise. "You heard him. Let's get this done." Beside her, Rook stumbled forward from the rough shove he got as encouragement.

The twenty yards to the gold car gleaming under the industrial overheads felt like a gallows walk during which time had stilled. Even the reverberation of their footfalls in the cavernous hall seemed to be dampened, and all Nikki could hear was the liquid whoosh of her own blood rhythmically marking the cadence of her fear.

She tried to not let it freeze her thinking. Every second between then and launch needed to be a focused, primal hunt for opportunity. Worrying about Rook, wondering if it would hurt, or envisioning Lobbrecht's brain spatter would only distract her. Heat willed herself to be an animal. To be ruthless and survive.

"In," said Maloney. When Nikki stiffened her body to resist, making herself more difficult to move, Maloney swept a leg against the back of her knees and tripped her. She hit the deck hard, landing on her shoulder with the air knocked out of her. He holstered and yanked her up by the handcuffs, then manhandled her into the driver's seat, grunting a string of curses.

He shoved the door, and the slam thundered to the rafters. She massaged the skin where the metal edges of the handcuffs had cut at her wrists. The pain gave birth to a new tactic. Flailing, for sure, but she'd try anything. Her side window was down, and she said, "You *are* an idiot. No wonder you washed out."

"Hey, I'm not the one who's gonna be a bug on a windshield."

Heat had one last desperate idea and worked it. She licked away a clot of blood on her upper lip and said, "It's like I was telling you, he's setting you up. Jeez, Tim, you were a grade-three detective, and you can't see what he's done?"

"Tim, let it go," said Backhouse. "Load him, and let's do this."

It's in the job description of a paranoid person to be oversuspicious that someone is gaming him. Nikki exploited that—by gaming him. "Yeah, let it go."

Her dismissal troubled him.

"OK, what."

"Never mind." She gave him a wink. "You'll find out."

Heat had gotten into Maloney's head. His gaze darted to Backhouse, then to her.

"Want me to paint it for you?" she said.

Backhouse cleared his throat. "Now would be good."

Nikki inclined her head toward her arms secured behind her. "Were you wearing those gloves when you cuffed us? No. So when CSU works this scene, whose fingerprints and DNA are going to be on these? Yours. I told you he was setting you up."

"She's right," said Rook. "You don't think they're going to go all out for a dead captain?"

"We'll fish them out after," said Backhouse. "Let's move."

Nikki smelled an opening and continued to press. "There's a fun job. And what if you can't find them?"

"Or find all the pieces," added Rook for good measure. "All it's going to take is a partial, and they've got you."

Maloney turned to Backhouse. "I'm taking their cuffs off."

"Are you nuts? We should be out of here by now."

"See?" said Heat. "They're not his fingerprints."

"I'm not asking, I'm telling." Maloney handed Nikki's Sig Sauer to Backhouse. "Just keep it on her." Then he fished out his cuff key and opened Heat's door. She didn't wait for an invitation. Nikki twisted her back toward him, and he unlocked one cuff, then the other, and took them off. He stepped back quickly and slammed the door again. "Chill, Wilton. Under control."

He yanked Rook around to the other side. When Rook started to resist, Maloney jerked his wounded arm to bring him under control and stuffed him in the passenger seat. Rook presented his handcuffs, but Maloney's gloves were clumsy and he dropped the key on the floor. While he bent to retrieve it, Rook whispered to Nikki, "Smart move. What's your plan?"

"Hands free. Beyond that . . . ?" She shrugged.

Rook's eyes worked back and forth in urgent thought. Then he said, "Stand by."

The subcompact rocked to one side as Maloney put a knee on the threshold. "Hold still," he said. Rook's right shackle popped free, but instead of waiting for the left to be unlocked, he whipped that arm into the center of the car out of Maloney's reach. "Fucking asshole," he muttered. "Gimme that cuff." And he stretched across Rook to grab his arm.

Heat sprang at him with both hands. With one, she jerked his thumb back toward his wrist, and with the other, clawed for his shoulder holster. But it was wedged underneath his left arm, which was trapped between him and Rook's chest. Nikki pushed with all her might, trying to break his thumb. Maloney yowled in pain, but his nitrile glove kept slipping and she couldn't get enough purchase to match his strength. "Get his gun!" she shouted. "The holster!"

"I'm trying!" Rook's left arm was trapped under Maloney's body. Rook pushed against him to make a gap wide enough to reach the Smith & Wesson. The bullet wound in his right shoulder weakened his leverage, though, and when he did manage to pry open a space, Maloney forced himself back against Rook, closing it.

"Shoot her!" called Maloney. "Fucking shoot her!"

Backhouse fired. But in his frenzy, he fired wild. Nikki heard the 9mm slug sizzle past and slam into the dashboard in front of Rook. "Get closer, dickhead!"

Nikki caught movement to her right as Backhouse stepped up to the window to position himself for a point-blank shot. She let go of Maloney's thumb, unlatched the door, and shoved it into Backhouse. The Sig went off as it flew from his hands, landing with a clatter somewhere across the crash hall floor. Backhouse landed on the deck, too. She saw him looking over at his shotgun across the room and started out after him. But Maloney snagged her from behind and drew her in, trying to clamp a chokehold on her.

While she clawed at his forearm, trying to break the powerful lock he had on her, she watched Backhouse stumble to his feet. Satisfied that all three were fully engaged in the car, he bypassed his shotgun and darted out of sight in the direction of the control booth.

A klaxon sounded a triple alarm and the lights of the crash hall came up to full brightness. Backhouse had started the launch sequence.

Gasping, trying to butt Maloney with the back of her head and failing, Heat hollered, "Rook, get out! Get out now!"

"I can't, he's got me pinned!" Rook started punching Maloney's back, but with his weak wounded arm, he might as well have been pounding a bag of cement.

The prerecorded voice of a woman who sounded a lot like Siri echoed throughout the hangar. "Caution: Stand clear. Stay behind yellow lines. Commencing test launch sequence." Another sharp klaxon sounded, and the announcer continued, "Launching in thirty seconds."

Heat twisted, kicked, and struggled, but couldn't break the armlock around her neck. "Maloney," she gasped, "we need to get out."

His response was to drag her deeper into the car as he tried to crawl back out over Rook.

"Launching in twenty seconds," said the dispassionate voice.

Maloney's movement gave Rook an opening to move just a bit. Despite the searing pain in his shoulder, he worked his right hand down into his side coat pocket and fumbled with something inside.

"Launching in fifteen seconds."

"Rook, get yourself out! Please!"

"Launching in ten seconds."

Rook's hand came up from his pocket, clutching his Hemingway Montblanc in his fist—with the cap off—its radiant new nib exposed. He plunged the sharp point into Maloney's ear. Immediately, his entire body recoiled and he screamed in agony, pulling the hand that was applying pressure to the chokehold on Heat away to grab at the fountain pen embedded in his eardrum.

"Launching in five seconds."

The instant Maloney's grip slackened on Heat, she rolled out of the driver's side just as Rook rolled out the other door. Inside the car, blood pouring down the side of his face onto the seat, Maloney stared at her with the pleading eyes of the doomed. She didn't hesitate. Nikki reached out both hands. He took them and she pulled to drag him free.

"Launch."

A high-pitched whirr filled the room, then the catapult fired with a shrill hydraulic wail.

The car exploded off the catapult, zooming instantly to seventy-five miles per hour with Maloney stuck inside. His pathetic knowing stare on departure, as he left his empty blue gloves in her hands, would haunt Nikki's nightmares for the rest of her life.

She spared herself watching the impact. His screams followed by the thunderclap of the collision told her all she need to know.

Rook, ass planted on the deck, struggled to his feet. "You can't have too many of these," he said, and tossed her the Smith & Wesson .40 that he had stripped off Maloney during his bailout.

Nikki checked the chamber indicator, saw brass, and ran to the control booth. She braced flat to the wall outside the door and called for Backhouse. Then she saw that the Mossberg was gone. A door slam reverberated from the far end of the hangar.

She told Rook to call 911, scooped her Sig Sauer from the floor on her way past, then sprinted to the exit. Instead of stepping out, she kicked the door open. A blast from the shotgun peppered the steel where she would have been standing. She rolled out, prone, ready to fire before he could rack another shell, but all she heard was two feet pounding across asphalt into the night.

The exit Backhouse used was on the opposite side of the hangar from the door they had come in through, so Nikki's run took her around one corner, then another, before she got to the front of the building. From behind the parked eighteen-wheeler they had used for cover, she heard a car door slam, then saw headlights as Backhouse fired up the Police Interceptor.

Even riding an adrenaline rush, Heat knew her limits. In her weakened state from blood loss and the death struggle with Maloney, her legs had labored just to bring her this far around the building. Nikki calculated the distance to her Taurus and smelled a getaway. So, as the car backed out of its hiding place between the big rig and the wall, she didn't even try to go after it. She cut the shorter distance across the parking lot to get ahead of it.

If Maloney had been half the cop he thought himself to be, he would have backed into the space for a rapid nose-first exit. But he wasn't and he hadn't. Now, forced to inch out of the narrow slot in reverse, Backhouse lost time and Nikki bought precious seconds in her desperate race to head him off.

Once Backhouse got clear of the tractor-trailer, rubber squawked once on the damp blacktop as he slammed the car into drive with too many rpm's. Then he floored it, fishtailing from his standstill, tearing toward the gate. The V8's roar broke through the night fog like the cry of some beast from a Gothic horror film.

Lungs rasping, legs leaden, Heat poured on all she had, willing her knees to kick high, putting her oxygen debt out of her mind. She didn't want to lose speed by turning to look, but she could see from the flare of his headlights in her peripheral vision that Backhouse was gaining on her. Nikki stopped hearing her breath; stopped feeling like quitting;

stopped doing anything but becoming a machine herself.

When Heat got to the guardhouse, she was going so fast, she slammed against it. The car was now fifty yards away, and hauling. She drew a gulp of air and stepped out right into the driveway, her Sig Sauer in one hand, the Smith & Wesson in the other. She made out Backhouse, in silhouette from the orange fog illuminating the parking lot behind him. He stopped and tried to bring up the shotgun. But the length of the Mossberg prevented him from clearing the dashboard to point it at her. He dropped the gun, hit his brights, and punched it.

Heat aimed, took a steadying stance, and fired both pistols at once, spraying a hail of bullets into both front tires of the oncoming car. When they popped, the police-tuned suspension kept it from going out of control, but the Interceptor shimmied and Backhouse had to wrestle with the wheel. Nikki jumped aside as he veered weakly past her. She put another round in the closest rear tire, which put an end to his attempted getaway.

Nikki rushed to his side window with both guns on him before he could get any ideas about the Mossberg again. "Engine off! Hands on the wheel—now!" Backhouse complied, then looked up at her, defeated.

She pulled him out and deposited him facedown on the roadside. Heat pressed her Sig to the base of his skull and said, "Now who's the dummy?"

The first thing Rook saw was Nikki's face when he came out of sedation from his surgery at Bellevue that night. She gave his hand a squeeze. He smiled and said, "Diamondback."

"Hey, it's me. You're in Bellevue."

"Diamondback."

Heat's eyes went to the nurse taking his temperature. "You'd be surprised some of the things they say when they're out of it."

"I can hear you, and I'm not out of it." He squeezed Heat's hand in return. "I was dreaming about our honeymoon. We were at a dude ranch I heard about in Diamondback, Arizona. Nik, that would be so much fun."

"Keep dreaming. You want me to go on a honeymoon in a place named after a poisonous snake?"

"Not a selling point, perhaps. But maybe it's like Iceland. A lovely Nordic island so named to discourage Vikings from visiting and plundering."

"And he's back," said Heat.

"You did great, Mr. Rook." Nurse Seton finished taking his temp and updated his chart. "You were lucky. No blood vessels hit, no fragmentation or bone or nerve damage. The doctor extracted a .22 bullet that, fortunately, stopped close to the surface."

"That's because before it hit me, it deflected off a hard surface." He peered at Nikki and pointed at the gauze on her brow. "By the way, you've got a thing there."

She chuckled. "Yeah, his and hers scars. Oh, by the way, nice job with that Montblanc."

He couldn't disagree. "Hemingway would have been proud."

When the nurse left, Heat told him she was planning to

interrogate Backhouse first thing in the morning. "Looking like that? You should maybe wear a scarf or a veil or something."

"I'll see if I have anything that matches Neosporin. Meanwhile, you rest here. I'll fill you in after."

"Oh, no." He struggled to sit himself up higher. "You think I'm going to lie here and miss bringing the story home for my Pulitzer?"

"What was I thinking?" she said. "It's the bullet. It must have addled my brain."

At eight o'clock the next morning, Wilton Backhouse held the guest of honor seat in Interrogation One at the Twentieth Precinct. His attorney, a family friend who had more experience in patent law than criminal justice, sat at his side. Considering the multiple murders and the other serious charges he would be facing, Heat had a feeling he would be upgrading his lawyer very soon. For now, she was happy he'd brought in a dabbler from suburban White Plains.

"My client is invoking his right not to self-incriminate. Therefore, he will have nothing to say at this meeting," said Ethan Watts.

"Thank you, counselor. However"—Nikki indicated Rook beside her with his arm in a sling and her own bandaged forehead—"as may be evident to you, we've gone to a lot of effort to bring your client to this meeting, and a meeting we shall have."

She turned then to the client, who had exchanged his too-cool-for-engineering-school geekwear for inmate coveralls.

After a long silence, Heat began quietly and methodically. "Lon King. Fred Lobbrecht. Abigail Plunkitt. Nathan Levy. And now, Timothy Maloney." Nikki let that sit there. Backhouse shifted. He was having a hard time with eye contact. "We know you did it. What I'd like to hear from you—"

"My client is not admitting any responsibility for these unfortunate deaths."

"Don't make me laugh, counselor," Heat said, tweaking the lawyer. "Unfortunate deaths are what happen when *E. coli* gets into the spinach. We're talking homicide. Multiple homicides. And just so you know? I don't need him to admit responsibility. We have enough physical evidence to make the DA's case."

"Not to mention, our own experience as unfortunate victims," added Rook.

"So getting back to my meeting," Heat said. "I want to hear what your client has to say about why. Why did he need to kill these people?" She waited, knowing that the silence was a pose. Nikki had determined she was dealing with a highly egotistical type, probably a narcissist. The Julian Assange posters spoke volumes about his fantasies and self-image. She would lay it all out and see if that overwhelming jones for attention would get her what she needed.

"I have a theory, you know. Want to hear it? Why not, and you can tell me if I'm wrong." When Nikki had their curiosity sufficiently aroused, she resumed. "People kill for many reasons. Heat of passion—that's usually a one-off. Same with robbery, burglary . . . violent criminal stuff. Revenge, now that can be either a singleton or a multi. This doesn't smell like revenge. But. If you're stepping outside the world of serial killers or mass murderers, the motive my experience leads me to is . . ." Heat paused. Their heads flicked her way, which was just what she wanted—a sign of their chasing the bait.

"Let's do some show-and-tell," she said. "This is what I believe these murders were all about." Heat reached down and picked up a plain brown paper NYPD Forensics bag from the floor and set it on the table. "Want to know what's inside? I bet you do. First let's talk about some recent history. Around here we call that the Timeline.

"You've been working over the past year with your Forenetics consulting team to investigate the cause of an unaccountable spike in one specific type of traffic fatalities. You and your experts concluded that the cause of these deaths was a flaw in the SwiftRageous software for the stability-control system. Yet you ran into a stone wall when Tangier Swift and his battalion of lawyers shut you down. But your Splinter Group was so outraged and passionate that you met at a cabin in Rhinebeck one weekend, where you all committed to blow the whistle about the auto safety defect. Right so far?"

Backhouse just kept his eyes on the brown bag and said nothing.

"Continuing," she said, "you told me the meeting ended with a lot of alcohol. Well, late the same night your summit ended, there was a fatal crash on a country road between Rhinebeck and New York City. We've since learned that the car involved belonged to a member of your Splinter Group,

Nathan Levy. And that there was a bribery cover-up by another Forenetics associate, Fred Lobbrecht, who was then a state trooper. Levy left the accident scene to visit an ER in Cortlandt for a leg injury. We have his X-rays." Wilton Backhouse remained passive, but the narrative was animating his attorney, who had started jotting notes. "So much for hurting it in that fistfight you tried to sell me."

Nikki moved the brown bag an inch just to tease them. Then she said, "Let me bring this home. The why—the elusive why all the murders?—is right in here." Heat stood and reached inside the bag. She withdrew a black rectangle, about the size of a small computer keyboard, sealed in a clear plastic envelope. She set it on the table and watched Backhouse try to hide his discomfort. "As a forensics expert yourself, Wilton, you should really appreciate this." The lawyer cast a wary glance at his client, then both stared at the plastic Ziploc. "And I see you already do."

Heat slid the evidence bag closer to Backhouse. He averted his gaze like a dog confronted by the turd it has just left on the rug.

"We know Nathan Levy had bodywork done on his BMW. We know his tires popped and his rims got bent that night. We also know he damaged the door to his glove compartment." Nikki picked up the plastic bag. "This is that glove compartment door. It bothered us when we couldn't find it at first. The body shop didn't have it. Our crime scene professionals couldn't locate it at his home. It wasn't at his Forenetics office, either. Know where it finally turned up?" Heat set it back down, closer to Backhouse. "Of course you know. Because our detectives found it last night when they searched your apartment."

The sound of chains raking across plastic punctuated the silence as Backhouse stirred in his chair. His attorney's voice cracked as he said, "This is circumstantial."

"Yes," agreed Heat. "And the circumstances are that your client, after he induced Levy to flee his house, probably scaring him with news about Abigail Plunkitt's death, went there and stole this glove box cover. And why?" Nikki turned to Backhouse. "You want to say it, or shall I? . . . All right, I will." She pointed to the black cover inside the plastic. "The damage you see here is an exact match for Nathan Levy's leg injury." She took a printout of the X-rays out of her file and shoved them across the table. "Proving," she said, "that Nathan Levy was a *passenger* in that car that night. I know you lied. There was never any fistfight with Fred Lobbrecht. During the crash, Nathan's leg slammed into the glove box. Abigail Plunkitt was in the backseat. How do I know? Because she had to die, too. Because these people knew your dirty little secret, Wilton. That you were driving drunk. That you were at the wheel. That you killed that woman in the middle of the night on Cold Spring Turnpike."

Nikki let him marinate in that, then continued. "The question is, why kill them? When we get our court order this morning to pull your bank records, we're going to see that you already bought their silence, aren't we?" His lawyer rested a hand on Backhouse's arm as a signal not to answer that. "I am betting your first payoff was to Fred Lobbrecht. You knew him from CRU and your prior work with

Forenetics, so New York state trooper Lobbrecht was the one you called that night to come to Cold Spring Turnpike and clean up your mess. And for that, you paid off his mortgage and got him a big, fat job. Abigail Plunkitt quit working to save manatees. Thanks to your checkbook, no doubt. Same for Nathan Levy, who suddenly went from test driver to blues sax man.

"It was all going to be just fine, except for one thing." She gestured to the chair beside her. "Once this jackass, Jameson Rook, got an assignment to do a story on your auto safety whistle-blowing, everything changed. Because Jameson Rook doesn't fluff out press releases. Jameson Rook is your worst nightmare: a true investigative reporter. He started nosing around outside the tidy pages of your safety study, and you panicked. Especially when Fred Lobbrecht got pangs of conscience and engaged Lon King to broker his confession to Rook. And Lobbrecht almost talked. But you killed him first. Oh, but what about Lon King? Fred probably told his shrink, so King had to die, too. That left Plunkitt and Levy. In for a penny, in for a pound, right? But you had to divert suspicion. And how does a smart guy like you turn this into a win-win? You set up Tangier Swift to look like the man with the motive to eliminate all the whistle-blowers. What a great idea, too. Because ultimately, if all this had come out—your DWI and the woman you killed—not only would that have indicted you, it would also have undermined all your results. You were willing to sacrifice your entire team for the massive ego stroke of being able to take Tangier Swift down. Which is what you consider your life's work. Am I right, Wilton?"

Backhouse's chin dropped to his chest. Then he raised it so he could stare at her.

Heat pointed to the bandage on her forehead. "Bet you wish you hadn't missed me, huh?" Watts put a hand on his client. "Do not answer that. Do not say anything."

"Really? Because I'd like a statement." Nikki took the yellow lined pad she had brought in and slid it in front of Backhouse with a ballpoint. "If you cooperate, it's all going to go a lot easier for you."

The lawyer wagged his head no.

Heat tilted her head toward Rook. "Tell you what. Your version in your own words would make for a hell of an article."

"Oh, sure," said Rook sitting up straight. "I'll still do the piece on the safety defect. You care about that, I know. But imagine how many more people it would reach, I'm talking worldwide, if your story—this story—were part of it?"

Backhouse was teetering. His lawyer said, "Wilton—"

"Ethan, shut up, I'm trying to think. This is why Uncle Ray says you're an asshole." When the attorney slumped back with his arms crossed, Backhouse looked from the evidence bag to Nikki, then to Rook, clearly at the tipping point.

Rook, who had also seen the Assange poster in his office, said, "I think there's only one question to ask here, Wilton. WWJD?" As they all looked to him with puzzled faces, he finished with, "What Would Julian Do?"

Backhouse shoved the pad away. But then, just when it seemed he was finished, he said, "I'd rather just tell it. Do you still have your recorder?"

"Unless I dropped it in the car last night—just kidding."

Rook took his Sony digital out and turned it on so Wilton Backhouse could tell his whole story for the record.

Cop humor. There is nothing like it.

After Heat and Rook had wrapped the interrogation and entered the homicide bull pen for the first time that morning, every detective there was wearing a teeny Band-Aid on his or her forehead. Such is the wry coping mechanism of your police professional. Even after a beloved comrade's life-or-death ordeal—or, maybe, especially after one—sarcasm trumps sentimentality.

Heat played the game, showing her love by ignoring the display until they all just broke into laughter. So much better than people with guns, hugging.

A full recap wasn't necessary, since the squad had already witnessed the lengthy debriefing of Wilton Backhouse from Observation. In a rare display that could only be considered a mercy kiss for going the extra distance after his ordeal, the detectives gave props to Rook for his interview.

Holding up his end in the sardonic spirit of the day, Rook thanked them by saying, "You know, I'd like to think there's more at stake here than achieving justice. It's really about getting me that next Pulitzer."

"That would be a lot funnier if it weren't true," said Feller.

Raley asked, "Does this mean we owe Tangier Swift an apology?"

"Yeah, but instead of flowers, I'd like to send Mr. Swift a

dozen of these." Rook flashed the finger with the arm that wasn't in a sling. "And don't tell me this is my Area Fifty-one wacko speculation. Wilton Backhouse denied kidnapping me, and I believe him."

"Well, he sure doesn't have the infrastructure," said Ochoa. "Look who he settled for: Maloney."

Rook nodded. "But who does have it? Exactly. I don't have proof yet. Meanwhile, I'll just bide my time and enjoy my legally prescribed painkillers."

They took a short break. Those without wounds removed their bandages, coffeed up, and gathered around the Murder Board for that delicious moment when the scribbles up there started to make sense. Rhymer said, "Sorry, but I was driving back from Forensics and missed the first part of the confession. Did Backhouse say why the two different MOs? You know, the car crash for one and the drone for all the others?"

Heat nodded. "Actually, Opie, there were three MOs. They killed Lobbrecht first at the hangar on Staten Island because they knew he'd be there. Lon King was a different story. Remember Maloney had been stalking him and knew about his kayaking. They came up with the drone idea to get him, and that worked so well, they used it for Abigail Plunkitt, too. Then they experimented with a higher caliber on Nathan Levy and missed. So Backhouse did him face-to-face, knowing he'd duck away from a drone, but not from his friend. That's why Levy's window was rolled down and there was no lubricant on his pickup's door. Backhouse met him for a chat, and popped him close range, small caliber, just no quadcopter."

"Makes sense," said Detective Rhymer, "because Forensics

just found GSR on a shirt in Backhouse's laundry hamper."

Ochoa added that to the Murder Board. "One more nail."

"Which leads me to an imaginary fist bump to you and Detective Aguinaldo for working that apartment," continued Nikki. "Finding that piece of the glove compartment tipped the scale."

"Any sign of Lon King's missing patient files?" asked Rook.

"So far, MIA," said Feller. "Not at his apartment. Not at his office. Not at that Craigslist special in Astoria he rented under a fake name."

A familiar thorny knot tightened in Nikki's gut. It surfaced every time she thought about her intimate counseling sessions floating out there somewhere.

"Hey, I know where they are," said Detective Ochoa, trying to keep from grinning. "In the trunk of Captain Heat's car with that prisoner, what's his name, George Gallatin."

As the meeting broke up, she heard Feller say, "Poor dude's probably in New Mexico by now, looking out that back window, praying for a rest stop." Their laughter made Heat recall the old saying, "In all humor there is a grain of truth." Heat knew one thing for sure: Until she uncovered it, this case was far from closed.

After getting an update from Detective Raley on his special assignment, Nikki released her King of All Surveillance Media to continue his mission. Sean headed downtown to One Police Plaza; she went to the ladies' room to change her dressing.

Afterward, she went to Rook's desk in the bull pen to offer

made the fingerprints easier to pick out on the surface. "Humph," Rook said and set it back down. He closed his eyes, doing some inner-vision reenactment thing that involved humming. Then he broke into a grin. "Got it!" She regarded him skeptically. "No, really, I do."

The cyber attack was still impeding the department's databases, so Heat called Special Agent Jordan Delaney to run Rook's phone number for her. The FBI man was barely cordial but ultimately professional. In spite of his annoyance that she had poached his federal prisoner, who had then escaped, Delaney called Nikki back to report that the number she had given him did not exist.

"I highly doubt that," said Rook. "I've heard of numbers that are out of service. Or unlisted. But nonexistent? No way."

"Then why don't you call it and see who answers?" she said.

"Thank you, I will." He got out his cell phone but then changed his mind. "If my caller ID shows up, it'll be a tip-off. And suppose I use Gallatin's phone. If they pick up and hear me, then what?"

"Rook, you're talking yourself out of your own fix. What am I supposed to do here?"

He thought a short moment and said, "Indulge me?"

Heat listened to the groaning steel of the decrepit barge as it rocked at its mooring and smelled the musty decay wafting from somewhere in the dark recesses where she and Rook waited belowdecks. "We're going to get our wounds infected down here."

"We've only been here an hour, Nik. I spent two nights down here."

She corrected him. "Ninety-three minutes. We'll give this twenty-seven more, that's plenty indulgent."

"Deal," he said. "But I have faith."

"In a number the FBI says doesn't exist?"

"Then why does it say 'Delivered' under our balloon?"

Sending a text message from Gallatin's phone to the mystery number was the compromise she had reached with Rook. Although she wouldn't admit it out loud, Nikki did feel a bit of a thrill from his sense of adventure and out-of-the-box thinking. To tell him would only encourage more. Not so thrilling, in her view.

She held up Gallatin's burner again, which was powered up, but back in its plastic evidence bag. The screen did indicate delivery, right under their message, which was short and plenty concrete: "Urgent. Meet me at the barge. Hurry!"

Concerned about tying up resources on something so iffy, Heat decided she and Rook would wait in the barge hold alone. To be prudent, however, she had had Detective Feller follow them as backup, and he was parked a block away in the staging area they had used to rescue Rook just a few days before.

Nikki made another check of her Omega. Twenty-five minutes of dank eternity to go. Rook touched her shoulder. But she had already heard it—the scrape of a shoe topside.

She hand signaled him to move back out of the dull light that was filtering down through the overhead ventilation grate.

The next footfall was softer but closer, on the corrugated steps leading down from the hatch.

Heat stepped back into the shadows opposite Rook and eased her Sig out of its holster. She held it against her thigh, pointed at the floor. She counted five more footfalls on metal, and then whoever it was stopped, probably at the bottom of the stairs.

Then the footsteps resumed. Once again, a soft tread, but definitely drawing closer. Heat brought her gun up, then cupped and braced against a steel stanchion. A dark shape emerged from the blue shadows into the dusky light and stopped.

Yardley Bell had answered the text.

NINETEEN

I n the hollow silence that followed, broken only by another moan of steel plates chafing against the wharf, Heat studied Bell, keeping her gun sight on the secret agent's torso while she scanned for a weapon. As she did, Yardley fanned her arms out from her sides. At first Nikki thought it was a freak of timing, but when Yardley spread her fingers to show that her hands were empty, Heat knew it wasn't a coincidence at all. Yardley Bell did little by coincidence. This was pure situational aptitude.

"Jamie, Nikki, I know you're here."

While Heat processed how to play this, Rook emerged from his hiding place against the far bulkhead. He got just to the edge of the dim spill of overhead sunlight and stopped. "You? You're Black Knight?"

"Rook, step back," said Heat, holding position. "Yardley, keep them where I can see them, just like that."

Rook stayed where he was. Agent Bell did as she was instructed and even pivoted a few degrees in the direction of Nikki's voice, presenting her the widest possible target, in full compliance. "My piece is staying where it is," said Bell. That could be interpreted that two ways: either as a warning not to take it, or an assurance that she wouldn't bring it into play. Or both.

Heat read the moment and moved into view. She lowered her Sig Sauer but didn't holster it.

"When I got the text message, I thought about ignoring it." Yardley regarded her ex, who still hadn't absorbed the surprise. "Then I figured I owed it to you after all you've gone through . . . to let you know it's over. And that you're safe." The faraway sound of a motorcycle rumbling past on the street drew Bell's attention, and she turned her chin over one shoulder. "I shouldn't be here."

"Funny, I thought the same thing about four in the morning when I woke up with rats racing across my pant leg."

"None of that was my doing. I heard about the operation after the fact."

"If not you, then who did it?" asked Nikki. Now that Rook's text bait had panned out after all, she was determined to exploit the opportunity all the way to an arrest. If not of Yardley Bell, then someone.

"It's classified. I can tell you that there has been some internal strife at the agency, and—"

Heat jumped in, hoping solid pushes would get Bell to loosen up. "Which agency?"

"One I can't name. Or acknowledge. You know that."

"Not good enough. Kidnapping? I need more."

Rook recovered enough to get his head engaged and joined in. "If you weren't involved, why was Gallatin calling you?"

"He wasn't. I'm not Black Knight. Black Knight is neutralized."

"You killed him?"

"Please. We don't operate that way." For emphasis, she added, "We don't. He's been reassigned. He went rogue with an illegal op and paid for it."

"Was he the guy with the Okie accent?"

"I'm not able to say." Which was the same as a yes.

"And George Gallatin?"

"After Black Knight extracted him, he was also reassigned."

"He's my prisoner."

"Count your blessings," said Bell. She had a remoteness, a chilly aspect to her nature that probably helped her sleep at night. Heat wanted to bring her to human level.

"You don't need to tell me to feel blessed." She holstered her weapon. "I thought I'd lost him."

"I tried to spike this as soon as I learned about it, Nikki."

"You think that's good enough? Not for me. Not after all this. Not after what it did to him and to me."

Yardley spoke to Nikki pleadingly. "This is me making it right."

"This is you making it right for yourself." Nikki stepped closer. "People don't just 'go rogue' for laughs. Somebody sanctioned your man's operation. Who? Tangier Swift? Congressman Duer?"

"That is classified. National security."

"OK, fine," said Rook. "Off the record."

"Look, obviously I made a mistake in coming here."

"Seems like it," said Heat.

The air went out of the conversation. The three of them stood there in a triangle, each feeling equally unfulfilled:

Heat and Rook wanting hard answers, Yardley Bell wanting to be let off the hook emotionally.

"So." Rook gave his ex an appraising glance and softened. "You did all this—and put an end to the whatever operation, doing what you could to help me from the shadows."

"Yes!" Yardley's face brightened, and she took a half step to him. A bubble of jealousy surfaced in Nikki's gut. Irrational, she knew, but whatever connection these two still had, however distant, she wasn't eager to see it dramatized before her.

Rook said, "That is so . . ." He hesitated, searching for the word. Nikki thought he would say *thoughtful*, or *caring*, or maybe just *cool*. He surprised her—and Yardley. *"Bullshit."*

Bell's eyes, usually so fully under her control, widened. "Jamie? How can you say that to me?"

"Because it's true. You said you came here to make me feel safe. No, you're only here hoping to soothe your conscience, and know what? I'm not sure you even have access to it." In his agitation, he started to pace. "This is why we never made the long haul, you know that. The way you always keep a safe distance from anything. You held back from us, from your job—"

"Not this again."

"Yes this again, because you still haven't changed. Why? Because owning means risk."

Heat didn't know whether to enjoy this or not. His words had exposed an intimacy she might regret witnessing. Especially when he waved his free arm in her direction.

"Ask Nikki about risk. And I'm not talking about

courage. You have lots of that, Yards. I'm talking about the kind of risk where you go all in. No playing the margins or having, I dunno, an escape hatch of deniability." He paused and rubbed his upper arm through the sling. "Listen, I'm not trying to hurt you or work out our baggage. I just wish . . . I just wish you cared more. If not for yourself, for what the job really is. And I don't mean career. I mean why we really do what we do." He cast a look at Nikki before he continued. "I interviewed a dad who lost his wife and a four-year-old who thought he was going for a ride with his family to visit the grandparents. But their car had a freak rollover caused by a defect in the stability-control software. You can guess what happened to them. *They're* the job. At least for some of us."

Yardley swallowed loud enough for Nikki to hear it. "I can't go on the record. I'd lose my security clearance. Everything."

"I get it." He half smiled. "Anyway, thanks for telling me I'm safe. Look at us. We're all safe, right?"

Then Agent Bell said, "But I will speak off the record." As Heat and Rook traded surprised looks, she continued. "I've seen you do that before with unnamed sources. You'd protect me, right?"

"Uh, sure, absolutely." Then he added, "The unnamed thing only goes so far, but it's a start."

"Well, I can also give you names of people who will go on the record. There's plenty off pissed-off people at work who don't give a shit anymore."

"My favorite kind." Rook grinned.

"I'll be your whistle-blower."

"One of your specialties, as I recall." He chuckled, then stopped himself, suddenly mindful of Nikki's stare.

Heat got out her notebook. "Maybe we should start talking about why he was kidnapped."

"See?" said Rook. "She's all in."

Heat watched the sky empurple across the Hudson, just like the sunset she had glimpsed twenty-four hours prior from the Verrazano Narrows, except the bridge she was seeing it from now sat atop an NYPD Harbor Unit vessel. "There's your MD600," said the skipper, aiming the bill of his cap to ten o'clock so she could pick the chopper out amid the reflective glass of the West Side high-rises.

Nikki acknowledged him, then stepped out of the pilothouse to where Rook was riding the thirty-five-knot chop, bracing himself against a bulkhead. "So far, so good with Yardley. She said his Gulfstream filed a flight plan from DC to Teterboro, and now here he is."

"Yardley's solid, don't worry." As usual he was attuned to Nikki's feelings—this time, her anxiety about getting things right.

Together they watched the blinking lights of the helicopter descend gracefully onto the fantail of the *SwiftRageous*. A minute later the diesel twin tens of the Gladding-Hearn throttled back and the V-hull settled down into the river with a peaceful sigh.

While the captain angled the rescue recess toward the transom of the luxury yacht, Tangier Swift arrived and stood waiting to meet them personally, although not alone. His security crew flanked him. This time, however, instead of matching polo shirts, everyone, including Swift, wore serious suits from a day in the capital. "I saw your rooster tail from the six hundred," he said. "You might as well have sent up magnesium flares."

Heat said, "This isn't a tactical raid, Mr. Swift. But I'd like permission to board."

"No."

She held up a warrant. "I've got a golden ticket."

The billionaire nodded once. Three of his companions moved aft to accept the mooring lines from the Harbor officers. On the deck above Heat and Rook, a squad from the Hercules Unit appeared and lined up along the rail, a statement of power made with black helmets, heavy armor, and submachine guns cradled at rest. The bodyguards were cowed, and should have been.

"Not a tactical raid, huh?"

"Last time we talked you kinda threatened me."

"Heat, this is bullshit, and you know it."

"Maybe you should write your congressman," said Rook. "No wait. We can make that easier for you."

Tangier Swift's mouth actually gaped when Congressman Duer emerged from the bulkhead door and stood between Heat and Rook. "Hey, Kent," was all Swift could manage. None of this fit his algorithm.

"You going to invite me aboard, or not?"

While the *SwiftRageous* crew assisted the senior representative aboard, Swift approached Heat and stared at her bandage. "What happened to your face?"

"This?" she said. "It's my game face."

Nobody offered refreshments, nobody asked for any. There was no small talk, no compliments about the decor, no attempt to diffuse the tension as they took their places in the conference salon on the mezzanine. In deference to the congressman, Swift took a seat across from Heat and Rook and gestured for Duer to preside at the head of the long table. The old man ignored him and sat against the wall on the couch beside Detective Raley, whom Nikki had asked to come along. Although he took the backbench, the lawmaker kicked things off. "I have not been briefed by Captain Heat on the substance of this meeting, other than to be assured that it is of the utmost importance. That's good enough for me. I'm ready to listen."

"Thank you, Representative Duer." Even though Heat was there to confront Swift, the congressman played a key role in her strategy, and so she addressed herself as much to him as to the tycoon. "I can make this very brief. Mr. Swift has been a person of interest in a homicide investigation into several murders. The victims were whistle-blowers attempting to expose a fatal safety defect in one of his SwiftRageous software products. Today I have learned he was not responsible for those homicides."

"Then you did make this brief," said Swift, half rising in his chair.

His attempt at humor was met with silence. Nikki continued. "However, evidence exists proving that there is a safety defect in the auto software and that there has been an illegal cover-up by Tangier Swift and his company."

"You can't prove that."

"I don't have to." She touched Rook's knee with hers. "Others will. But this is about something else. Something of interest to you, sir." She turned to the congressman to make sure he was with her. Duer had stacked his wrists on the carved head of his cane and gave her a nod to proceed. "I have sources who tell me that, under your sponsorship, Mr. Swift has negotiated a contract with the Department of Defense to provide software allowing our military to hack enemy aircraft in flight."

Swift slammed his palm on the table. "That's not true. This is guesswork."

The congressman said, "As a ranking member of the Defense and National Security subcommittees, I can tell you, Captain, that if such a DOD program existed, it would be classified." A couched reply, for sure.

Tangier scoffed. "Sources. You have no sources."

"It's called SwiftJack," said Heat. "You don't have to respond, I can tell by your reactions that I'm right. And I don't have to tell you about the high stakes this creates for our national security. Which leads me to the kidnapping of Jameson Rook."

"Kent, come on. Murders I didn't end up doing, auto safety allegations, now kidnapping? I didn't kidnap anyone. She is going all over the map."

"Then let me give you a GPS. You had no part in the kidnapping—directly. That was carried out—illegally—by some US government black ops for the purpose of stopping Jameson Rook from continuing his investigation of you, Mr. Swift. And do you know why? Because they were investigating you."

That got Swift's attention. He turned to a member of his staff and signaled for water. While he took the bottle, Nikki swiveled her chair, directing herself to Duer. "Tangier Swift has been secretly double-dipping. While he has a deal with DOD, he has also been bidding out his SwiftJack software under different product names to foreign entities. A violation of federal law."

"And a patriotic no-no," said Rook.

"That's bull."

Congressman Duer's brow sagged. "What countries you talking about?"

"So far he has secretly been in contact with North Korea, China, Russia, and Syria."

"And you can confirm this?"

"More importantly, as committee chair with the power of subpoena, *you* can confirm it," said Heat. "But I can tell you that I have a contact in the Syrian government I spoke to this afternoon who has verified this for me personally." She let the old man absorb this with closed eyes and a wagging of his head. "And sir, since criminal behavior is generally not confined to one incident or area, I'd like to make you aware of one other critical breach. For that I have brought Detective Raley. Sean?"

Raley stood. "Short and sweet," he began. "The captain heard a report that this cyber attack we're going through was so hard to stop because the NYPD's MISD—that's the Management Information Systems Division, or our IT—relied on so many different applications from third-party developers. On the surface, it seemed like a bunch of programs that randomly wouldn't behave. One handled database communication, another controlled the intranet, you get the idea. With all these programs, fixing the damage caused by the cyber attack was like herding cats." He flashed a smile at Heat. "I'm sort of a techno geek, so Captain Heat sent me to MISD to investigate a hunch she had. Informally, of course. I learned that the applications causing all the trouble were written by about twenty different companies. They all seemed unconnected until I did some provenance tracking with some detectives in the Information Technology Bureau. It was all pretty well firewalled, but we finally broke through today and discovered that all the code for all the programs causing the blackout was written by secret subsidiaries or subcontractors funded by one company."

"Let me guess," said the congressman, staring balefully at Tangier Swift.

"That's correct. In short, this dude shut us down. Sir." Raley sat.

"That's bogus," said Swift. "Why would I want to hack New York City's IT? Makes no sense."

Heat wasn't so sure of that. "Really? It would make perfect sense if you were trying to curry favor with the Syrians. Like showing the cyber-jacking capabilities of your software by using it for their cause? Or to show Kim Jong Un what you could do? Or Putin? Or those Chinese gentlemen we ran into that you tried to pass off as industrialists looking to buy this yacht? And, if not that, then your cyber attack was targeted directly at NYPD. What better means to slow down my investigation, stalling my progress until all the whistle-blowers coming after you were dead?" She turned from Swift to the congressman. "Or it could be both. Kind of synergistic. But the thing is, now that we know it was him, the reasons are academic."

"More academic than you know," said Duer. "My buddies at the Department of State are brokering a deal on this Mehmoud character as we speak. That kid's going to be on a plane back to the desert by the weekend." The congressman then rotated his hooded gaze to Tangier Swift, who continued to play the role of the victim.

"You're smart enough to know, Kent, this is a total railroad job. Nothing here can be proved."

"You'd better hope not. Because I'm going to dig until all the dirt is out of the hole. Starting tomorrow when I call closed-door hearings with the Pentagon and Intelligence Services." Kent Duer got to his feet. The hero who had earned a Purple Heart leaned on his cane. "I'm all for profit. I'm more about giving this nation the best defense in the world. I think you can forget about the DOD program."

"I'm innocent. I have a contract."

The congressman nodded as he made a quiet decision. "I think I just canceled it."

When Duer left, Heat got out her cuffs and rounded the table toward Swift. Two of his bodyguards took a step as if to block her. Raley pulled back his coat to show tin and his .357. They stopped.

"Tangier Swift, I am placing you under arrest for fraud, conspiracy, sabotage, and terror activity. Plus I am sure there will be numerous federal charges coming that will help your lawyers afford a boat like this of their own." She cuffed him and added, "Meanwhile, you can have a nice ride on mine."

Nikki indulged herself by sleeping in the next morning—though indulgence for her meant one extra hour and getting up at a slovenly six-thirty. Rook had been tossing most of the night with shoulder pain and bagged the notion of sleep altogether at about 4:00 A.M. to get up and keep pushing words forward in his article.

"Is making coffee going to bother you?" she asked after they kissed at the counter where he had set up shop.

"Only if you don't give me any." He finished the sentence he was typing and said, "BTW. Saw it online. Hack attack's over."

"Yeah, I got my first clue when my BlackBerry was vibrating across the nightstand, and I had a gazillion e-mails and memos."

"Most of which you haven't needed in a week, and bet you don't need now."

"True. I won't call it preferable," she said, pouring water from the Brita into the kettle. "But it does make you wonder how much tech we need."

"Personally, there's a certain drone I could have done without."

"With you there." She scrolled through her messages. "Surprise, surprise, an email from Zachary Hamner."

"I picture that guy wearing an opera cape and sleeping in a coffin. And rising each day to breakfast on the hearts of young idealists who never heard his wings flapping."

"Not so fast, babe. Get this." Nikki then read the message aloud for him. "'Captain Heat, it is my pleasure to relay congratulations from the chief of detectives on resolving your homicides. Your role in ending the cyber attack is also greatly appreciated and duly noted up the chain.'" She laughed as she read the rest. "'Nonetheless your less-than-stellar performance as a precinct commander will be subject of an in-service review by your district supervisor. Also be mindful your CompStat numbers will still be expected next week along with your required presence at the One PP meeting. Warmly, Z.'" Heat laughed again. "'Warmly?'"

"Must have just eaten a freshly beating heart. Bet he munches them like apples."

"Here's one from Special Agent Delaney. 'Your FBI thanks you for TS. Almost makes up for losing GG.'"

Rook closed the lid of his laptop. "Want to know the worst part of busting Tangier Swift? Brace yourself for the onslaught of tabloid headlines: 'Swift Justice. That's SwiftRageous!' Or when they show him in his orange jumpsuit, 'Tailored Swift.'"

"*Confessions of a Blown Whistle* is starting to sound better and better."

"I'll stop."

"Do."

Heat drove Rook to his doc's for a check of his bullet wound. While they were there, he gave a twofer, re-dressing

Nikki's forehead with a smaller bandage and pronouncing her stitch work pristine. If she slathered on the SPF, she might get away with minimal evidence of the scar.

"Good," said Rook, "because we're getting hitched, and when I lift that veil, I don't want to be looking at Freddy Krueger." When Heat and the doctor gawked at him, he said, "I, um, should probably cut back on the painkillers."

The squad applauded when they came into the homicide bull pen. But each did it by clapping one hand on a thigh because they all had their other arms in slings. "I told myself I wouldn't cry," said Rook. "And I won't."

Ochoa took his sling off. "Breaking news."

Heat said, "I know. Cyber attack's over. Thank your partner."

"Yeah, that, too. But I'm talking about something bizarre. Ready?" He inclined his head toward Raley, who took the handoff. They were just like the old Roach again.

"Lon King's files turned up."

Nikki felt a witch's finger scratch her gut again. "Where?"

"At Wilton Backhouse's apartment. Forensics has them."

She turned to Rhymer and Aguinaldo. "I thought you searched there."

"We did," said Inez. "They just showed up. A bunch of banker's boxes on his kitchen table."

"Strange," said Rook. "Almost covert."

"Yeah," Heat said. And excused herself to go to her office.

***

The Forensics detective she spoke with confirmed the files were there, and that they all had remained in alphabetical order, although there was no way of knowing who had had them or how they got back. There was no labeling, and they were trying to lift prints off the boxes, but so far there were none. Whoever had handled them wore gloves.

Nikki wasn't certain which pained her more: to think that the written record of her most intimate thoughts and private confessions had been unaccounted for or that her file had been found and was now part of the investigative process, potentially available to be scrutinized by colleagues and detractors. She didn't even want to imagine what Internal Affairs would do with it. Things had been said that she had only said because she had trusted them to be confidential. Forever.

She hadn't come to that trust easily. But now she felt naive and stupid. And frankly, scared.

Nikki closed her door and asked if he would look to see if there was a file there under the name Heat. If it registered with the detective at all, he was too discreet to comment. She listened to the lid come off some boxes, heard tabs being riffled as he searched.

Lon King, PhD
Counseling Transcript
Session of Mar. 29/13 with Heat, N., Det. Grade-1, NYPD

LK: I'm surprised you came back. But glad.
NH: I told you I would.

LK: You keep your commitments, I do know that. But you became so agitated during our last session when we got to the subject of Rook. And your engagement.

NH: And I told you I was committed.

LK: There's that word again. But it's not like keeping an appointment, is it, Nikki? . . . Marriage.

NH: [Long pause] I love him.

LK: But?

NH: No but. [Longer pause] I think this should be our last session.

LK: That's your choice, of course. But may I ask, is it because you have gotten what you needed here, or is this now taking you somewhere too painful to confront?

[Very long pause. NH stoic. Dabs eyes with tissue]

LK: Is it helpful if I speak? Good. It's very important to know that it's OK to have our feelings. Even ones we are not happy to have. So it leads me to ask, what is this feeling you're having that you're not happy to have?

NH: [Pause] I don't know if I can say it.

LK: You know your are safe here, Nikki. Whatever you say here stays just between us. So. What are you feeling that is so troubling?

NH: That . . . [Long pause] I'm not sure I should marry Rook. [Pause for tears]

NH: It's not that I don't love him. I do. Completely.

LK: Completely?

NH: I just have so much in me that is . . . I had some time

since our last session to think about why I've dug in
so hard about keeping my own apartment. That's not
really about a connection to my mom.

LK: You can say it.

NH: I can't let go of my independence.

LK: I know that's not just a word to you, Nikki. Your
independence is what got you through it all, isn't it?
It's where you drew your strength. From yourself.

[NH nods]

LK: But fear of losing independence. That isn't really a
revelation. What if you did lose it?

NH: Let's not.

LK: What are you afraid of?

NH: Why are you pushing me?

LK: I am driving you, Nikki. To go deeper. What are you
afraid of? Just say it.

NH: I . . . I am afraid to be alone.

LK: Interesting. You want your independence because
you fear being alone.

NH: Is that nuts?

LK: No. You have had to cope with so much loss. Your
independence is your cocoon. It lets you be alone, but
on your terms. It explains your sex-only relationship
with the Navy SEAL before you met Rook. Sounding
right?

[NH nods]

LK: I'd ask you to examine whether independence is a
life goal, or a perception. As you've told me, Rook is
quite independent himself, and he honors your

independence. That's what works—so you've said.

NH: I feel like, if I marry him, it's the first step toward losing him.

LK: And if you don't, you lose him anyway, but on your terms.

[NH pauses, takes more tissues]

NH: You wanted a feeling I was unhappy to have. There it is.

LK: What would it take to change it?

NH: I don't know. It would have to be big.

The phone scraped across the tabletop as the Forensics detective picked it back up. "No Heat," he said. "And I checked the whole box, in case it got misfiled or shuffled. Want me to keep an eye out for it?"

She told him she'd like that and hung up, then had to sit down, just to collect herself.

Her feet kicked into something under her desk. She tilted her head sideways and saw a gift box wrapped in wedding paper. Nikki set the box on her desktop. It had no note. She used her scissors to snip the ribbon and carefully slit the decorative paper to touch as little of it as possible. She removed the wrap and saw a gift box like you'd find at any Hallmark. She hesitated, then lifted off the top.

Inside was a manila file folder, the kind you'd see at a doctor's office. The tab read: "Heat, N., Det. Grade-1, NYPD." Taking it by one edge, she opened the file.

It was empty. But there was something.

She took out the manila folder. Beneath it, the box was filled with bits of paper that had been run through a microshredder. She scooped some of it up in her palm and couldn't read any of what was on it.

But she knew what it was.

An ecru Crane's envelope was nested inside the confetti. No writing on it, and it wasn't sealed. Nikki slipped the card from the lined envelope and, when she read it, the warmth of another's grace filled her, and she smiled.

Heat carefully rested the note inside the box on top of her shredded files, face up, so she could appreciate once more the woman's neat handwriting and the message that contained only two words.

"All in."

TWENTY

On the dazzling August morning of Nikki Heat's wedding day, she stepped before the full-length mirror in her dress fashioned of silk taffeta with a sheath of silver bullion lace and wished her mother could be there to see her. She kissed her fingertips and touched them to the heirloom wedding ring she wore on a thin chain around her neck and knew that her mother actually was there, and that in a way she always would be.

Lauren Parry, her maid of honor, and Margaret Rook gasped at her beauty, declared her stunning, fussed with her hair, which was up, accentuating her elegant ballet dancer's neck, and assured her that the scar did not show at all. Time heals, and four months had done Nature's work. Nonetheless, she asked Lauren to brush on a bit more powder. Just in case.

Heat's only worry was Rook. He had been in Los Angeles pitching the book he had sold based on his magazine exposé—*For Whom the Whistle Blows*—to movie studios, and was supposed to have returned the day before. But some welcome thunderstorms had rolled through, breaking New York's heat wave, but also causing the cancellation of his flight. His plane had finally arrived that morning at JFK, and the Hitch! he had hitched to the Hamptons had caught fire in

Shinnecock Hills. Detectives Rhymer and Feller had sped off an hour before using sirens and a gumball to retrieve him, but there was no sign of the groom yet.

Nikki parted the drapes on the beach side of the suite to make sure everything was ready. The day was simply spectacular. That storm had broken the oppressive humidity, and Saturday in Bridgehampton felt more like May than August. The guests seemed relaxed enough, most of them already seated in the rows of white folding chairs facing the gazebo where the lawn met the white sand and the blue Atlantic beyond.

Her dad stood off to the side with the woman who had moved in with him in June. Jeff Heat had known Linda from his days as a student at GW, and they had reconnected through a social medium: AA. It warmed Nikki to see that her father had found love again. Ironically, someone new had made him the man he once was.

Heat heard laughter and leaned forward to see Raley and Ochoa cracking each other up in their front-row seats. Her road to taking command had not been smooth and, in hindsight, she should have listened to Rook on her first day when he highlighted the perils of being a leader who couldn't pull the trigger. Naming Sean and Miguel interim squad leaders not only made her seem indecisive, the uncertain nature of the promotion had pitted her two best detectives—not to mention bulletproof partners—against each other in unhealthy competition. She had admitted her error; they had admitted theirs, and their raucous Roach laughter and—was that them sharing hits from a flask?—proved just how bulletproof they were.

Rook texted that he was "ninety seconds from bliss," and she could hear the rumble of Feller's V8 nearing the driveway of the inn. She laughed, imagining the indignity of a certain investigative journalist trying to change into a tuxedo in the backseat of an undercover police car as it negotiated all those turns from the highway down to Mecox Bay. Then the flutter of the largest butterfly she had ever felt took her by surprise, and she had to steady herself on the windowsill. She paused until it passed.

Then hoped to hell it would return to stay.

It did return mere minutes later, giving wings to Nikki's heart when she saw her husband-to-be in his bespoke tux, standing up taller at the sight of her as he waited, all smiles, surrounded by flowers in the gazebo. Her father escorted her up the aisle to an aria from one of Bach's wedding cantatas played by a chamber ensemble from Juilliard and sung angelically by none other than Rook's mom, Broadway's Grande Dame.

All eyes were upon Nikki as she proceeded slowly up the white linen runner that had been unfurled on the lush grass, but their joyful faces all simply blurred out of focus. Heat could only see Rook. And the smile she wanted to see for all time.

She arrived beside Judge Horace Simpson, their longtime poker buddy, and waited as the cantata came to an end. Rook whispered, "You look absolutely lovely."

"And you, ruggedly handsome."

He turned to the judge. "I knew I was marrying the right

person." And Nikki nodded with a grin as lustrous as the sea behind them.

They had written their own vows and, in a leap of faith, had not shared them with each other. After Judge Simpson had performed his opening remarks and the guests were all settled, Rook took Nikki's hands and spoke his promise.

"I fell in love with you the day we met. I believe your first words to me were something like, 'Stay in the car, or I swear I'll shoot you.'"

While the guests all laughed, Nikki turned to them and said, "It's true."

"I have to cop to being a writer instead of a cop. But instead of thoroughly dismissing me as the pest I probably was—and/or shooting me—you performed a miracle in my life, Nikki, by doing the best thing anyone has ever done for me. You trusted me. Simply, completely, and unconditionally. Except for my occasional conspiracy theories, many of which, may I say, have been borne out.

"What happened when *you* and *I* started to become *us* was the next miracle. I began to live a dream because you enhance everything. Even a New York skyline. With you I saw for the first time how the windows of the Carlyle gleam like orange jewels at sunset. You taught me that if I close my eyes on the Highline, it smells like a poppy field in Tuscany. I'll never forget how we went for an early-spring run once, and it suddenly started snowing big fat flakes, turning Central Park into our own private snow globe. And then, when I whispered 'Rosebud,' you got it—you really got it! The world with you is exciting, whether it's a Bowery sidewalk or the Île de la Cité. I can't wait to see what magic you work on Iceland when we get to Reykjavík tomorrow." Rook paused while quizzical murmurs of "Reykjavík?" spread across the lawn.

"We have so much in common. We like the same wines, we've read the same books, and now, we share the same home. We've even shared a bullet. How many newlyweds can say that?" He tugged at her hands and felt compelled to kiss her but waited. That would come.

"I owe a lot to Ernest Hemingway." He addressed the guests and said, "Don't ask, long story." Then he gazed at his bride. "Hemingway once said, 'The best way to find out if you can trust somebody is to trust them.' I'm no Hemingway, but I would add, 'And the best way to tell if you love somebody, is to have it be Nikki Heat.'" He unexpectedly choked up, then proceeded.

"And now I, Jameson Rook, promise my eternal love to you, Nikki Heat. Simply, completely, and unconditionally. Until death do us part."

They mouthed a silent *I love you* to each other, and Nikki took her turn.

"We met through our work and ended up partners in crime. And now, here we are, about to become partners in life. Yes, we did share a bullet, but we do share much more. Like a belief in goodness, in people, in laughter, in friendship, but most of all, in each other. What we didn't already share when we met, I have learned from you. You have shown me that things are never as far as you thought, nor as impossible as they seem. And that fools drive, lovers enjoy the ride.

"Our ride has been unconventional to say the least. Just surviving to get to this moment was a minor miracle. But just when I thought I couldn't get any closer to you, or feel more certain of our marriage, that experience created a bond nothing will ever break.

"I, Nikki Heat, stand before you and everyone I care about . . ." She paused and swallowed hard. He gave her a nod of encouragement, and she continued. "And one who could not be here . . . to promise that I will always love you, Jameson Rook. I will always be there for you. I will be your friend, and, yes, your partner in crime forever. As every moment from this day forth becomes the time of our lives."

Rook beamed as he slipped the wedding band on her finger. Nikki's radiant eyes barely left his as she put the ring on him.

The judge said, "By the power vested in me by the State of New York, I now pronounce you husband and wife." He didn't have to tell them to kiss.

Heat and Rook had already found each other.

ACKNOWLEDGMENTS

t's 2:00 A.M., and here I sit, too pumped to sleep, still buoyant from receiving that Career Achievement Award at tonight's big Poe's Pen ceremony and, frankly, unable to wake her up. Oh, well. Picture, dear reader, my bespoke tux jacket on the floor, bow tie undone, and a rocks glass of the Irish at hand with no cubes to spoil the amber magic. Yes, it was all very heady tonight. The Poe's Pen statuette, the gracious words from the award presenter, the great Michael Connelly, the bloodred carpet . . . But, in truth, it was the faces—the gathering of all those who are so close and so dear to me around that table of honor as I looked out from the podium—that meant the most, the chance to toast those who made it all possible.

So while I'm in a toasting mood (and who knows, afterward, in the mood for dancing the Time Warp), let me lift an aged spirit to all those who once again proved that these puppies don't write themselves. It all begins and, hopefully, never ends with Kate Beckett, my inspiration, my teacher, my lover, my bestest friend . . . for the time of our life. The crew at the Twelfth Precinct rocks it, and is my rock. Javier Esposito and Kevin Ryan, my only regret is that I could never coin a portmanteau for you. Espry? Javin? How about "buds"? Victoria Gates continues to let me run rampant, and for that I am grateful, as ever.

An autopsy, truth be told, is never a party you want to be invited to, but Dr. Lanie Parish down at the Office of Chief Medical Examiner makes that basement room as close to upbeat as it can be without, well, waking the dead.

My mother, Martha, is equal parts consternation and inspiration and neither of us would have it any other way. My daughter, Alexis, continues to outshine her ol' dad at every turn. She needs to knock that off. Smarty! (Next book, I'm having her write this section!)

Pardon me while I clang a spoon on my glass in celebration of the amazing Nathan, Stana, Seamus, Jon, Molly, Susan, Tamala, and Penny.

The folks in the Clinton Building at Raleigh Studios also get a smart *salut!* Hey, it just occurred to me, I could turn this toast into a swell drinking game.

Terri Edda Miller, you intoxicate me simply by being near. Hand in hand, arm in arm, onward—together. Always.

To you, Jennifer Allen. My eyes mist over, and I think of Hemingway, who said, "It is the journey that matters, in the end." Our lovely ride continues with all commas in place and accounted for.

Thanks to Laura Hopper, Executive Editor at Disney Publishing Worldwide, Kingswell, and to Lisa Schomas and her terrific support team at ABC for success built on amazing cooperation and forethought.

My agent, Sloan Harris at ICM Partners, has always made sure my glass is half full, and I am grateful for his belief in me from the start.

Will Balliett, Gretchen Young, and Elisabeth Dyssegaard also deserve a clink and a sip for this little experiment that could.

Ellen Borakove continues to provide ace technical assistance for all things OCME. Additionally, I got amazing help from Monica Smiddy, M.D., forensic pathologist, New York City.

Shamus Smith, NYPD, not only provided a trove of background and technical assistance, but come on—a cop with a name like Shamus helping with a detective story? How could I go wrong?

Thanks to Jacqui Rivera for the introduction to Shamus, and to Joe Murphy, the pride of Melbourne, for logistical and research assistance. And, year after year—ever astute, ever faithful, ever enterprising—Cooper McMains, thank you for your cherished assistance.

If ever I thought someone was invaluable to a project it would certainly be David Liske, CEO, CPE, ACTAR, and a Principal Associate with LISKE Consulting Group Forensic Professionals. David most generously gave me hours of his time and whole sections of his brain as I researched this book. Whatever I got right about vehicle crash forensics and reconstruction, credit David. Whatever I got wrong, that would be on me.

Also, I got lots and lots of help from the New York Public Library, so special shout-outs (*Ssssssh!*) go to Research Community Manager Carolyn Broomhead, PhD, and Reference Librarian Jay Barksdale for research assistance, as well as the writing space accommodation in room 228E,

"The last quiet place on earth."

John Parry once again came through with perfect Upstate recon, including actual GPS location scouting for the Triplex.

Alton Brown, no cutthroat he, not only came up with the Jameson punch recipe, but sweated the detail of finding one that could be served chilled for a summer wedding, not the traditional warm one.

My friend Jill Krementz would have indeed shot Pulitzer-quality wedding photos, and I thank her for that. And a fist bump to my pal Ken Levine, who always reminds me at the start of each book that a murder might not be a bad idea.

And now, I'll refill the glass for this one, because it's a huge thank-you: Andrew Marlowe, you took a castle and made it Camelot. 'Nuff said? Never enough. Consider me an author whose best words would only be inadequate.

And, Tom, what can I say . . . ? Except that I'm still living up to that *nom de plume* award. Maybe not as cool as getting one from Michael Connelly, but I guess it was a start.

RC

May 12, 2015, 2:34 A.M.

New York City

RICHARD CASTLE is the author of numerous bestsellers, including the critically acclaimed Derrick Storm series. His first novel, *In a Hail of Bullets,* published while he was still in college, received the Nom DePlume Society's prestigious Tom Straw Award for Mystery Literature. Castle currently lives in Manhattan with his daughter and mother, both of whom infuse his life with humor and inspiration.

ALSO AVAILABLE FROM TITAN BOOKS

#1 *New York Times* bestselling author

RICHARD CASTLE

HEAT WAVE
NAKED HEAT
HEAT RISES
FROZEN HEAT
DEADLY HEAT
RAGING HEAT

STORM FRONT
WILD STORM
ULTIMATE STORM
A BREWING STORM (EBOOK)
A RAGING STORM (EBOOK)
A BLOODY STORM (EBOOK)

WWW.TITANBOOKS.COM